TROUBLESHOOTER

ALSO BY GREGG HURWITZ

The Tower

Minutes to Burn

Do No Harm

The Kill Clause

The Program

TROUBLE
SHOOTER

GREGG HURWITZ

𝓌𝓂
WILLIAM MORROW
An Imprint of HarperCollins*Publishers*

This book is a work of fiction. Characters, incidents, and dialogue are drawn from the author's imagination and are not to be construed as real. Any resemblance to actual events or persons, living or dead, is entirely coincidental.

HarperCollins books may be purchased for educational, business, or sales promotional use. For information please write: Special Markets Department, HarperCollins Publishers, 10 East 53rd Street, New York, NY 10022.

FIRST EDITION

Designed by Renato Stanisic

Printed on acid-free paper

Library of Congress Cataloging-in-Publication Data

Hurwitz, Gregg Andrew.
    Troubleshooter: a novel / Gregg Hurwitz.—1st ed.
        p.   cm.
    ISBN 0-06-073141-9 (hardcover : alk. paper)
    1. Rackley, Tim (Fictitious character)—Fiction.   I. Title.

PS3558.U695T76   2005
813'.54—dc22   2004059650

05   06   07   08   09   WBC/RRD   10   9   8   7   6   5   4   3   2   1

For Jordan Peterson

Professor, psychologist, author, scholar, businessman, composer, art collector, mentor, and sometimes minister. Who has the mind of an explorer, the soul of a poet, and—most important—the heart of an outlaw biker.

1

Den Laurey strained against the cuffs so his shoulders bulged under his jailhouse blues, sending ripples through the FTW tattooed above his collarbone. An amused smile, all gums at the corners, rode high on his face. In an additional security measure, the chain of his leg restraint had been knotted, narrowing the space between his ankles. Kaner sat beside him on the transport's bench seat, stooped so his head wouldn't strike the roof during freeway turbulence. Because he was too broad for his wrists to meet behind his back, Kaner's arms were secured with two sets of handcuffs linked together. A onetime sparring partner to Tyson—in prison—he'd snapped more than one set of cuff chains, so a second pair of restraints secured him at the forearms. Beneath a wild man's spray of black hair, a 22 tat on the back of his neck advertised his previous stint in the pen. Kaner had a broad, coarse face and prominent earlobes, fleshy tags that lay dimpled against his skull.

Den, president of the Laughing Sinners nomad chapter, and Kaner, the biker gang's national enforcer, were being driven under heavy guard directly from sentencing to San Bernardino County Jail, where they'd await Con Air transport to a federal penitentiary. They'd been convicted of the torture-killing of three members of the Cholos, in retaliation for the shooting of a Sinner. Den, renowned for his knife skills, had severed the victims' heads with surgical precision and set them in their laps. For good measure he'd removed their hearts and left them on the Cholos' clubhouse doorstep. The gesture marked another leap in the escalation between the Sinners and Cholos, a broad-ranging turf war for control over key arteries of Southern California's drug-trafficking network.

Deputy U.S. Marshal Hank Mancone, a fixture behind the wheel of the transport van, was the only nonprisoner in the three-vehicle convoy not a member of the Service's Arrest Response Team. Frankie Palton in the passenger's seat, the four deputy marshals in the armored Suburban behind them, and the two in the advance vehicle five miles up the road were all part of the district's ART squad, called in for tactical strikes and high-risk transports. Mancone was a deputy as well, but given his retirement age and contentment in grousing about his narrow bailiwick, he had little interest in the ARTists aside from giving them the occasional lift.

Palton pivoted in his seat, meeting Den's shit-eating grin through the steel security screen. "Nice tats."

"You can take our clothes, but you can't take our colors."

"What's 'FTW' stand for?"

"Fuck the World."

"We keep having these Hallmark moments, I might get dewy-eyed."

The radio crackled in from the chase car. Jim Denley—Palton's partner: "Eyes up on your right. We got some more bikers coming on."

Palton looked in the sideview. Two bikers rattled past, double-packing, their mamas reclining against sissy bars and offering the deputies languorous waves. Another three bikers zipped by on the right, flying colors, filthy club logos flapping on the backs of their leather jackets.

Mancone's grip on the steering wheel eased once the whine of the Harleys faded. "What's with all the bikers?"

"Relax, lawman," Den said. "It's the season. You got your Love Ride in Glendale, the Long Beach Swap, San Dog Run, Left Coast Rally in Truckee, Big Bear Ride, Mid-State Holiday Hog Run in Paso Robles, Squaw Rock Run, Desert Whirlybird Meet." His smirk bounced into sight in the rearview mirror. "All the wannabes on the move."

Kaner's three-pack-a-day voice emerged from the tangle of hair down over his face. "I'll still take it over you citizens driving around in your cages."

"Hear that, Mancone?" Palton said. "We got nothing to worry about. Just wannabes. And to think I was carrying this gun for no good reason."

Den said, "You want to get your shorts twisted over some weekend warriors, be my guest."

From the chase car: "Shit. Greaseball alert number two."

Two streams of bikers throttled by on either side of the van, their top rockers—the strips of stitched leather cresting the jackets' logos—announcing them as Cholos. Their bottom rockers showed their mother-chapter affiliation: PALMDALE. A few minutes later, a beefy biker rolled past and did a double take at the prisoners. When he lingered to gloat and flip them a middle finger, Palton raised the stock of his MP5 into view. The Cholo opened the throttle, ponytail flicking, and his bottom rocker came visible: NOMAD.

Den laughed, scratching his cheek with a swipe of his shoulder. "Good ol' Meat Marquez. Now that his nomad buddies met their untimely demise, poor spic's gotta ride all by his lonesome."

They came around a bend in the 10 and were greeted by hundreds of brake lights. As Mancone cursed and slowed to a crawl, Palton got the advance car on the air. "What's with the traffic?"

"What traffic? We sailed through."

"Accident?"

"Probably, but stay alert. We'll exit and wait."

Once traffic ground to a standstill, a biker wearing a duster pulled a few lengths ahead of them, stopping where the space between idling cars narrowed. He was low in the seat, pint-size but exuding attitude. He turned and looked back, the van reflected in the silver blade of the helmet's faceplate. The distinctive Indian logo identified the motorcycle frame's maker, but the rest of the sleek bike seemed to be custom-built. It sported a leather saddlebag on the left side, but its mate was missing on the right. The biker revved the engine, giving voice to 1,200 cubic centimeters of rage.

Jim's voice came through the radio again, and Palton replied, "Yeah, we got him. Looks to be unaffiliated—he's not flying colors."

A Harley white-lined through the traffic jam, easing up past the right side of the Suburban and van. The helmeted rider paused a few feet back from the other biker, across the lane, idling.

Hands tensing around his weapon, Palton checked the side mirror. Jim had the stock of his MP5 against his shoulder, ready to be raised. Something was lying on the ground under the Suburban at the front left tire. Palton clicked the rearview controls, centering the object in the mirror.

A leather saddlebag.

Palton's eyes lifted, noting the bare right side of the Indian bike ahead. He raised his gun, spinning around. Den and Kaner were lying on the floor, braced against the seats, covering their heads. Palton grabbed for the radio. "Shit, get off the—"

The biker on the Harley raised a lighter-size initiator. His gloved hand tensed.

A low-register boom. The Suburban rose up on the fireball eruption, crashing on its side. The surrounding cars slid a few feet from the blast, doors caving in, windows shattering.

The transport van skidded forward on its front tires, its ass end lifted by the explosion under the trailing vehicle. It smashed the car in front and slammed down directly beside the Harley. Seat belts gut-checked Palton and Mancone, their weapons banging against the dash. The Indian's kickstand was down; the small biker sat backward on the seat, sighting with the AR-15 he'd produced from beneath his duster.

The two deputies raised their heads as the first volley of bullets punched into the window, degrading the armored glass. The inside layer fragged out, glass embedding in their faces. When the windshield gave, their bodies jiggled like marionettes.

The man on the Harley had dismounted and was firing into the van's side lock. When the door slid open, he threw down his gun and caught the bolt cutters his partner tossed him. Rolling to the edge of the van, Den offered up his arms, then his legs, the steel jaws of the cutters making short work of the connecting chains. He bounced out of the van and hopped onto the empty Harley, cuffs rattling like jewelry around his wrists and ankles, chains dangling. A jagged edge by the door lock caught Kaner's prison jumpsuit as he stood, ripping it from collar to tail. Kaner hopped on behind Den, their rescuer leapt on the back of the Indian, and the two bikes took off in opposite directions, splitting lanes.

The four deputies in the keeled-over Suburban strained against their seat belts, coughing out glass and bleeding from the ears. One set of motorcycle wheels zipped past, heading the wrong way. Innumerable car alarms bleated; someone's cry of anguish expired in a gurgle.

The wind picked up the severed chains dangling from Den's and Kaner's shackles, drawing them horizontal. Kaner's torn shirt flapped open, showing off his backpack, the club logo rendered on his flesh in orange and black. They sped off, the flaming skull screaming back from the receding bike at the dead and wounded.

2

Silver rattled on china as white-gloved waiters cleared the remains of the five-hundred-dollar-a-plate luncheon. Marshal Tannino stood milling with other Angeleno political luminaries, looking mildly out of place with his coiffed salt-and-pepper hair and his department-store suit. He tugged at his too-short shirtsleeves to bring his gold-star links into view and squinted up at the chardonnay-haired woman holding a glass of white wine.

"If we really are serious about committing resources—"

Across the vast ballroom of the Beverly Hills Hotel, someone's beeper chirped—a cutesy electronic rendition of "Jingle Bells."

"—to fully secure the courts, we need to—"

Another pager added a discordant melody, and then a multitude chimed in. Tannino glanced down, frowning at his own beeper. "Excuse me, Your Honor."

State assemblymen and deputies alike scurried to the ballroom's exits, checking the reception levels on their cell phones. Tannino was halfway to the lobby when the city attorney approached, holding out a Nextel. "It's the mayor."

Tannino snapped the phone to his ear, still moving. "Yes, sir. Uh-huh. Uh-huh." His face tightened. As he continued to listen, he fished his cell phone from his pocket and, holding it down at his waist, speed-dialed. "Right away, sir."

He handed back the Nextel and pressed his own phone to his ear. "Get Rackley."

3

Tim jogged down the Federal Courthouse corridor, pulling off his blazer and cuffing his sleeves. Tannino had called him with the news—an emergency of sufficient magnitude to yank Tim from mind-numbing court duty, where he'd been suffering through day three of jury selection for a tax-evasion case. He'd been offered a road back into the Service—but only so far back in—as a reward for a stellar freelance investigation he'd conducted on a mind-control cult in the spring. Court duty was a penance of sorts, one he'd gladly been paying. But this afternoon he felt no happiness at receiving the long-awaited summons back to the Warrant Squad's Escape Team—two deputies dead, four injured, and Den Laurey and Lance Kaner out cruising California Central District's asphalt.

The marshal's assistant glanced up from a bank of blinking phone lights and nodded him in. Despite his stern posture, Tannino still looked short behind his great oak desk. He eyed the hole shot through a warped piece of metal—just minutes earlier a badge. A distinguished man with an age-softened linebacker's build half sat on the arm of the opposing chair, hands laced over a knee. A razor-straight crew cut completed his square face.

"Rackley, you know the mayor?"

"Of course. How are you, Your Honor?" Tim regarded the mayor's expression. "Right."

They shook hands all around, then took seats on the couch and surrounding chairs. Tim's right knee popped when he sat—it still gave him trouble from time to time, though the scar on his chin had resolved nicely. Souvenirs from the investigation eight months prior. He adjusted his old-school Smith & Wesson wheel gun in its hip holster; checking the revolver was second nature. He'd never made the jump to an auto and probably never would.

"How are the boys?"

"Everyone's holding. Jim seems to have lost hearing in one ear, but the docs say it ought to be temporary. We're arranging Frankie's service for tomorrow. And Hank's." Tannino tugged at his face, which had gone gray, and his eyes pulled to the bent star on his desk. "I just got off with Janice, convinced her we need to go closed-casket. Bastards put a lot of holes in the bodies."

"Let's get down to business." Mayor Strauss, like Tim, was a former Army Ranger. In his brief time in office, he'd developed a reputation for being a man long on efficacy but short on tact. "You'll be the deputy in charge of the task force."

Before Tim could register his surprise, Tannino said, "Obviously we've designated Den and Kaner as Top Fifteens. We already put out a news release, and a BOLO's gone out to other agencies."

"We're gonna need our locals," Tim said. "Bikers spread out."

"We're getting a command post up and running. As I'm sure you're aware, Jowalski's partnered with Guerrera now. You and Guerrera work together?"

"Very well."

"You'll be a threesome in the field."

"Tip hotline?"

Tannino nodded. "We beefed up the comm center to handle incoming."

"I'll announce the number during the press conference I called for"—Strauss checked his watch—"about fifty-two minutes from now. We'll also use the occasion to get the mug shots out there. Gives us a jump on the morning papers."

"Any leads?"

"At this point we've got shit," Tannino said. "The copters had to come from Piper Tech, took seventeen minutes to get on scene. The crew was smart, hit the van between two close exits—a lot of exchanges and intersections in the area, not to mention the fact that there are bikers all over the roads this month."

"Whose handle?"

"Ours. But it's a mess. Since it was on a highway, we had to back off the Chippies. Sheriff's will pick up the murder—Walnut/Diamond Bar Station, though I'm sure they'll roll someone from Homicide Bureau. Oh—and we have the pleasure of an FBI tagalong on the task force. I fought off a joint operation, but their agent sits in. It came from up top."

"I understand you've worked bikers before," Strauss said.

"Some. Not much. I know the Sinners, but so does anyone with a badge in L.A."

"Give me the CliffsNotes."

"The mother chapter's in Fillmore. I live just south in Moorpark. We get them through town now and then, pissing off all the off-duties—Moorpark, right? The only thing sacred to a Sinner is his bond to the club. Don't expect honor among thieves—they're famous for double crosses, drug burns, cop killings. They've been deep into the meth racket for years—last intel briefing we were told they've done twenty mil on the western seaboard in drugs and weapons smuggling. And they're in an expansion, muscling in on the Cholos for who's gonna move quantity in and around L.A. Other gangs they've just absorbed, but their hating Mexicans is a big part of the Sinners' appeal to the national membership. The Cholos have a more diversified portfolio of controlled substances, but the Sinners want to take the meth away from them completely—get a monopoly. They've almost got it with operations in Nevada, Arizona, New Mexico, West Texas, maybe Oregon. As far as one-percenters go, they rule the seaboard and the Southwest."

"One-percenters?"

Tannino stepped in, "The American Motorcycle Association issued a statement after the Hollister incident—you know, Brando?—that ninety-nine percent of bikers are law-abiding citizens. The outlaws embraced the one-percent tag."

"So it's a badge of sorts."

"Would you rather be a loser or an outlaw?" Tim asked.

"Neither. But point taken." The mayor shot a sigh. "What other rackets are they into?"

"They're strong on handguns, assault weapons, and low-end prostitution. Call girls they leave to the mob, along with gambling and hijacked electronics. They're smart that way—they mind the terrain, dominate their sectors."

"They're a business," Strauss declared.

"More like a conglomerate."

Tannino focused his dark brown eyes on Tim. "What's your gut?"

"Having looked at no evidence?" Tim asked.

The marshal waved his hand impatiently.

"Normally bikers take their medicine and do their time. They don't want to stir trouble for the whole organization, so they go down nice and quiet. A decision like this had to come from above. Something big's in the works for the club to take a risk like this. And Kaner and Laurey are key elements of it."

"Like what?"

"That's what we have to figure out. But whatever it is, it requires their chief nomads back in action."

"Who do you think worked the break?"

"The other Sinner nomads already top your suspect list. They're the hit men and muscle, the guys with the know-how and the balls to pull off something like this. Guerrera came up in that scene. I'm sure he and Bear are working up the names as we speak."

"What are the nomads?" Strauss asked.

"They're a chapter not based at a location. Always on the move. No home turf. When a club member becomes a fugitive, they'll send him to the nomads—it keeps him from the law and insulates the other chapters from investigation. The different chapters help hide the nomads as they move around the country."

"An Underground Railroad for shitheels," Strauss observed.

"Right. And in exchange the nomads do the dirty work for the national club, since they're already wanted." Tim turned to Tannino. "One thing should be clear: Guys like this, they rarely come in alive."

Tannino's weariness showed in his face, the kind of tired that anger wore down to. "Fine by me."

"They're white guys, right?" Strauss asked. "The Laughing Sinners?"

"Yes."

"Good. The press can't play the race card. That'll make it easier to sell the body bags." Strauss observed Tim, his face holding a hint of curiosity. "You do know why you got called in for this case, Deputy Rackley?"

"I have an idea."

"That freelance work you did a while back. Infiltrating and dismantling that crew of vigilantes." Though Strauss offered the for-public-consumption version, the gleam in his eyes showed he knew better. "We have a name for you around City Hall." Strauss drew out the pause, his expression an odd hybrid of respect and disdain. " 'Troubleshooter.' So this case? As we'd say in the Rangers, it's a free-fire zone."

Tim met Strauss's eyes. "I'm gonna bring them in alive if I can."

"And if you can't?"

Tim studied the mayor, then Frank Palton's twisted badge on the desk. "Then I won't."

4

The right side of the six-foot-by-four-foot face was a mass of bubbled scar tissue. Were it not for the mug shot thrown from the computer projector onto the far wall, the command post would have been pitch black. Staring out from the nomad's right eye socket was the flaming skull, etched onto an otherwise realistic glass eye.

Bear Jowalski walked in front of the image, his enormous frame cutting a black outline from the stream of light. His somber tone matched the mood in the room. "Gents, Goat Purdue. He went over the high side in '02, left half his face on the asphalt in Malibu."

Ordinarily Goat's appearance would have elicited a volley of off-color commentary, but there were no chuckles or wisecracks today. The deputies functioned through a post-disaster haze; Tim hadn't felt morale this grim since reporting to duty as a Ranger platoon sergeant in the wake of 9/11. In Frank Palton's usual place beside Jim Denley sat an FBI special agent, Jeff Malane—a slender man with fine hair and sad, intelligent eyes.

Bear bent over the laptop, and a new photo flashed up on the wall. A surveillance shot, taken from some distance, showed a biker with pencil-thin strips of facial hair—a stenciled beard. He couldn't have been taller than five-four. His barrel chest seemed transplanted from a larger torso.

"His tag is Chief," Bear continued. "He earned the nickname be-cause he rides an Indian instead of a Harley."

Guerrera ran a hand through his gelled hair. "Chief's the Sinners' intel officer. He keeps the files on the rival clubs, law enforcement, you name it."

"An Indian," Tim said. "Sounds like our lead biker on the bust, right Jim? Jim?"

Denley rustled in his chair. "Yup?"

"You said the short guy rode an Indian?"

"An Indian, uh-huh."

"He the one who sliced up that club mama a few years back?" Thomas's voice called out from the dark.

"No, that was our good friend Den Laurey," Bear said. "He's the knife man. Legend has it he cut one of the club mamas from her hips to her ankles, like a pair of chaps."

"But it was *Kaner* who nailed his old lady to a tree a few years back?"

"Through the hand, that's right, out near Devil's Bowl." Guerrera's accent turned *that's right* into *thass ride*. "When CHiPs found her a day and a half later, home girl didn't want any help. Said her man told her to wait there."

"Quality girl."

"Den and Kaner are the most vicious of the nomads," Guerrera said. "Which is no small claim."

A click brought the next photo up on the wall. A leering mug shot, the wide face peering out from beneath a mop of white-yellow curls. Faint, nearly invisible eyebrows.

"Tom Johannsson, aka Tom-Tom. An explosives specialist. And a nomad."

No neck was in evidence; Tom-Tom's head was set directly on his shoulders.

"I saw some white hair peeking out from beneath the helmet on the Harley man." Jim's voice, flavored with a strong Brooklyn accent, was always slightly hoarse and strained, as if he were yelling.

"Does he have the skills to have designed the boom ball that flipped the Suburban?" Tim asked.

"Oh, yeah," Guerrera said. "Word is Tom-Tom came up in the

Michigan Blood Patriots. Those boys could teach the ragheads a thing or two about improvised explosives."

Freed opened the blinds, revealing the modest view from Roybal's third floor, and everyone blinked against the light.

"We know of any other Sinner nomads?" Haines asked.

"Nigger Steve, but he was shot off his bike three days ago," Guerrera said.

"A black guy?" Thomas asked with surprise.

"No," Guerrera said. "Just tan."

"And dead," Bear added.

Guerrera said, "He's the first Sinner nomad to be killed by another club. The Cholos took advantage of Den and Kaner's lockup to take him out."

Thomas again: "You think that's why the Sinners busted them out?"

"That's my guess," Bear said. "Protection and—coming soon to theaters everywhere—retaliation."

"You know how Sinners avenge the killing of one of their own? They take out five." Tim set down his pen, noticing he'd chewed the cap flat. "We're gonna see more blood."

"Yeah." Miller's face was tense with anger. "Theirs."

"Thomas and Freed, establish contact with the Cholos," Tim said. "See if you can get in with their boss man in the mother chapter, the dude with the headdress—what's his name?"

"El Viejo," Guerrera said.

"It's probably an exercise in futility, but if that's where Den and Kaner are headed, we'd be remiss not to touch base and see if we can post a few men around the clubhouse."

"No way, Rack," Guerrera said. "They'll never go for it. Bikers handle biker problems, *sabes*? Plus, the Cholos are all over the roads—we couldn't run surveillance on them even if they wanted us to."

Freed shrugged, the creases vanishing from his Versace suit. Growing up in a family business—money from which supplemented his GS-12 paycheck—had taught him great respect for particulars. "We'll get on it. Can't hurt."

Thomas gestured at the now blank wall. "So you have those three beauty queens pegged as the break team?"

"Looks like it," Bear said. "They're the remaining nomads—it *is* their job. Plus, we've gotten back corroborative buzz from our CIs, for what that's worth."

A number of the Service's confidential informants had biker ties, though their veracity was open to question.

"We have last-knowns on any of the nomads?" Tim asked.

"They've been in the wind forever."

Jim was picking his ear, his eyes glassy. "Cynthia just had her sweet sixteen." He was talking too loud. Everyone tried not to look at him.

"You all right, Jim?" Tim asked.

Jim stared down at the tabletop. "Frankie's daughter." Of the four deputies injured in the escape, he was the only one who'd already returned to duty; he'd checked out of the hospital and come straight back to the office. He'd trashed his jacket, but his shirt was still marked with blood—thin lacings at the collar like ink. Palton had been his partner nearly eight years. Jim, the point man for lifting spirits on the Warrant Squad and ART, hadn't shown a glimmer of his irreverent humor.

"We'll get 'em," Bear said lamely. He mustered a smile and aimed it awkwardly at Jim, a small generosity that reminded Tim why Bear was the first person he and Dray called when they had good news or bad. And they'd had plenty of both in the past few years of their marriage.

Tim flipped through the file before him, refocusing. "Any angle into the mother chapter?"

"The Feebs—er, the *Bureau*—tried to nail Uncle Pete when Den and Kaner went down," Bear said. "They rousted him under Continuing Criminal Enterprise but got nowhere. You remember the subpoenaed-credit-card-records debacle?"

Tim and Dray—like most everyone else in the state—had followed the case closely. When on the stand, Uncle Pete, the droll three-hundred-pound Sinner national president, had made mincemeat out of the prosecutors over some innocuous credit-card charges they'd interpreted loosely to make their case. They'd had no better luck trying to untangle the knots in his drug-distribution network and his money-laundering operation.

Malane had sat quietly through the first part of the intel dump with an expression of reserved superiority that Tim had learned was the prevailing attribute of an FBI agent. Malane cleared his throat and spoke, not lifting his eyes from the Cross pen that he tapped on the blank pad before him. "Uncle Pete is careful to keep the mother chapter free and clear of anything incriminating."

"Why'd you hit dead ends on the drug charges?" Tim asked.

"Same reason we always run into trouble with bikers—their drug network is self-contained and resilient. They *are* the distribution network, so they control the scene from the stash houses to the wholesalers to the street-level pushers. They're set up in the liquor stores, the mom-and-pops, the gas stations, doing little hand-to-hand deals that collectively move big product. They have a lot of free labor, in their women and their pledges. The threads of the operation are buried. You make a bust, that's all you got. One bust. Minimal product. Plus, they've got a reliable and internal pipeline for flowing drugs to other chapters and cities—themselves. During run season especially, forget it. You got hundreds of bikers on the roads, you're not gonna get cleared to implement cavity searches to suss out the few mules." Malane's face had contracted as if he'd tasted something sour. He was angry, but also humbled; he and his agency had been well and publicly spanked.

"Why don't we haul Uncle Pete in for a close look?" Tim asked.

"He's got that hotshot TV lawyer," Bear said. "Dana Lake."

"I would advise," Malane said, "treading lightly on that front."

Tim leaned forward, rubbing his temples, mulling over what little evidence they'd managed to acquire. The break itself had left few clues. The precision of the strike indicated that the route survey run by the transport team Monday—the day after Nigger Steve's murder—had been carefully surveilled. The operation itself had been impeccably planned and executed. Minutes behind the advance car, the driver of a venerable yellow Volvo had locked up the brakes on the 10, slant-parking across two lanes and leaving a smoke grenade in the backseat. Wearing a helmet, the person had fled on foot, vaulting over the freeway barriers, hopping onto a waiting Harley, and racing off. The car left behind to block traffic had as yet yielded no leads.

The sheriff's lab had already determined that the saddlebag explosive was an ANFO special, initiated by a dynamic detonator. Ammonium nitrate fuel-oil bombs, composed of ingredients obtained at any hardware store or construction site, are easily home-cooked, leaving a generic forensic signature and no Taggants microtraces to be run through the system.

The break team had used high-grade weapons: AR-15s were a step up from the Uzi-style MAC-10 blow-back grease guns wielded by less sophisticated offenders. Civilian versions of M16s, the AR-15s had been converted to full-auto machine guns. The process takes all of twenty minutes with a seven-piece mail-order conversion kit; a basic home workshop stocks the tools to machine out an AR-15's lower receiver and make room for a drop-in autosear. The best investigative bet would be tracking the rounds, but even armor-piercing ammo could be bought for cash at gun shows these days. The armor on the Dodge transport van, like all bullet-resistant protection, was designed only to buy a little time. For all his experience, Hank Mancone hadn't gotten off the X when the bullets started pounding, and that had cost him and Palton their lives.

Tim stood and walked to the head of the table, the others regarding him with anticipation. "Listen, we got our cages rattled pretty good. Frankie was a close friend to everybody here. I didn't know Hank as well, but whenever one of ours goes down, we all feel it."

Malane was wearing a bored expression, and Tim hated him for it.

"But being hotheaded isn't going to get us the perpetrators. Sheriff's is working Frankie and Hank's murders, so that frees us to focus on what we do best—catch fugitives. *That's* how we'll honor the dead. Work your CIs. Former cellmates, known associates, hangouts—you know the drill. Talk to gas-station attendants along biker routes, let them know there's a reward. Get the word out to motor shops, wrecking yards, swap meets. Let's ask our locals to red-flag bike thefts in case they're stealing new rides to throw us off the trail."

"But don't bother with Jap Scrap," Guerrera said. "Or chasing VIN numbers on frames. Outlaws grind and restamp. That's the problem with choppers—they're almost impossible to trace. Every part can come from a different bike."

"Can you narrow it down more on the bikes?" Freed asked. "What we're tracing and what we should keep an eye out for when we're in the field?"

Guerrera frowned thoughtfully. He had the face of a teenager, still not hardened out despite the stubble on his cheeks. His long eyelashes and full lips looked more Italian than what people might think of as Cuban, but he was Little Havana through and through. "Outlaw bikes are lean and mean. It's a rough ride, beats your insides. Full-dressers come off an assembly line at seven hundred pounds, but outlaws'll strip 'em down to four—that's called a cutaway. Maybe they steal a garbage wagon from a weekend warrior. If they don't part it out, they'll dump the saddlebags, the fairing, the extra chrome, the springs on the forks, the rear shocks, the fender. They'll re-form the seats, downsize the headlights, install dual carburetors.

"Most outlaws'll swap out the thick stock tanks because they cover the top of the motor and hide the horses, but Sinners, especially nomads, leave them on in case they need more gas for cop chases. That's why they prefer swing-arm handlebars to ape hangers, too—easier to navigate on the run. They'll pull every trick in the book to make their bikes faster—cut down the flywheels on the left side for faster acceleration, throw in suicide clutches, and power-jump with hot cams, fat valves, and increased bore and stroke. You won't find Sinner nomads doing dumb shit like going sky-high on the front tire. They're more pragmatic that way—they'll sacrifice looks for speed. They have to outrun Johnny Law, and they're not gonna get tangled up because they raked out the front wheel four feet. That's something to remember with the Sinners—despite the noise, they're outlaws first, bikers second."

"We need to find every point of leverage," Tim said. "I want to know if any of these mutts ever skipped on a bail bondsman. I want you talking to members in jail—isn't their former secretary doing a dime up at the 'Q'?"

"Yeah, but these boys don't roll over," Guerrera said. "Not even in the clink."

"So? We just let him pump iron and watch *The Bachelor* all day? I want him interviewed. Haines?"

"Got it."

"Zimmer, you'll liaise with Homicide on the murders. Thomas—what do we have on active Sinner investigations?"

"Where do you want me to start? An old broad in a Mary Kay pink Caddy hit and killed a Sinner out on PCH last year. She was murdered in her Pasadena home two days later. A hitchhiker got turned out in August—gang-raped and kept with the club for three months. She won't press charges. Supposedly the Sinners keep files on family members for shit like that. They know where your niece goes to elementary school—you want to squeal, you got a hefty decision on your hands. A floater washed up—"

"Get all the case files, see if you spot any inroads. How's the intel on members of the mother chapter?"

"Surprisingly bad," Bear said. "The clubhouse is sealed off, helmet laws ensure we can't tell them apart on the road, and distinguishing marks don't help for shit when they've *all* got them. Believe it or not, the nomads are easier to ID because they're all fugitives."

"Sheriff's Station in Fillmore has been sitting on the clubhouse since right after the break. Jim—take Maybeck and get up there. . . ." Tim noticed that everyone was staring at Jim. Another drop of blood fell from Jim's ear, tapping the paper in front of him. "Jim. Jim . . . you have . . ."

"Oh." Jim cupped his hand, catching the trickle. He looked at his stained hand blankly. "Sorry, guys."

"Why don't you step out, go down to the nurses' station."

"Right. Okay."

The door closed behind him. Tim took a moment to recapture his thoughts, the pause stretching out uncomfortably. Thomas exhaled hard, puffing his cheeks. Bear slid his jaw to one side, cracking it.

"Okay, Maybeck, go check in with the deputies keeping an eye on the clubhouse. Tell them to keep the Sinners tangled up in penny-ante nonsense—muffler violations, high handlebars, helmet infractions. Have them put another set of locals a few miles down the road to write them up for the same stuff. That'll help us match faces to names and give us good records on who's moving in and around the clubhouse and on what bikes. What are the odds on sliding someone in undercover?"

"Nil," Malane said quickly.

Guerrera, loath to agree with a Feeb, nodded reluctantly. "It's almost impossible. You gotta snuff someone to get in these days, just to prove you're not law enforcement. Then you have to get through the initiation ceremony. Nasty, nasty shit."

"Okay, forget it. But let's red-flag the leads near the mother chapter—the safe houses double as crash pads, so they usually aren't far away." Tim turned to Malane. "We're gonna need the files you used during the trial, everything from the murders to the CCE."

"I'll see what I can do."

"Do better than that."

Malane folded his hands across his belly, a gesture that might have looked assured on a broader man. "I'll tell you right now, everything's registered in the names of their women—real estate, portfolios, the whole mother lode. That's how they do it. Since a lot of them are felons and can't pack, they even have their women carry their guns for them."

"Let's use that, then," Tim said. "The women might be our route in. I want to know who they are and who they're paired with. Guerrera, how's it work?"

"The Sinners use different terms for their broads than the other biker gangs—part of their new-breed image. 'Mamas' are called 'slags,' 'old ladies' are 'deeds.' Slags are club property, tagalong *putas*. Any of the boys can dip into one whenever they want, trade her to another club for bike parts, whatever. Now and then the club'll kidnap a girl or 're-cruit' her from a battered-women's shelter and turn her out. A deed belongs to one dude, and no one messes with that, you know."

Tim asked, "One deed for each biker?"

"Except Uncle Pete, who keeps a handful. Property jackets ain't enough for him—all his old ladies give up a little finger. That's the cost to sled with *papi chulo*."

"Okay," Tim said. "It all starts with intel. We need better information. Let's go get it."

One of the court security officers leaned into the room. "A Cholo just got shot off his bike in Piru."

Bear cocked back in his chair, catching Tim's eye. "Game season open."

5

Bear drove his beater of a Dodge Ram, Tim riding shotgun and Guerrera sandwiched between them on the bench seat. They wound over Grimes Canyon Road from Moorpark to Fillmore. When they passed the dirt turnoff to the garage shack where Tim had first confronted Ginny's killer, he felt his stomach tighten as it always did. He'd eradicated many of his painful reactions—to little girls' laughter, the smell of Jolly Ranchers, hacksaws—but the familiar dirt road still got to him. Distracted with a phone call, Guerrera didn't take note of Tim's discomfort, but Bear, familiar with the secret history, glanced over, gauging Tim's temperature.

The fall blazes hadn't left much in their aftermath—scorched hills, ash-streaked foundations, beavertail cactus cooked to a pale yellow and collapsed in limp piles. The few trees that had magically avoided incineration thrust up from the blackened ground like charred skeletons. The late-afternoon sun was low to the horizon, lending a cinematographer's cast to the bleak landscape.

Earlier Tim had dispatched Haines and Zimmer to check out the Piru shooting so he could review the admittedly slight case information at hand and get the command-post structure up and running—bureaucratic responsibilities he was only too glad to assume with his new role. His afternoon meeting at L.A. County Sheriff's Headquarters in Monterey Park had gone well, as he'd anticipated—the two agencies had a history of working closely, and both accorded the unfolding case top priority. A mutual aid agreement between departments pulled in Ventura Sheriff's, Dray's agency, seamlessly. Already the techies had put together a database to record the intel Tim had requested on biker stops—it could be accessed and updated online from the various stations. Before Tim had left the meeting, names and descriptions of the Sinner mother-chapter members were already trickling in. The Ventura deputies, familiar with individual Sinners from drug-related arrests within their jurisdiction, seemed to be leading the charge.

Guerrera flipped his phone shut. "So Haines confirms that there were no witnesses to the Piru shooting. Our boy Chooch Millan was gunned down on a quiet road at the city outskirts. They stripped his originals, left *muchacho* in an undershirt."

"Why take the jacket?" Bear asked.

"An outlaw's originals are his ultimate symbol of pride—more than his bike, even. Once they're awarded, they're never washed."

"Never?"

"Not even after initiation ceremonies where the jackets—and their proud new wearers—get baptized by oil, piss, and shit. The hard-core dudes even leave their jackets under their bikes at night to collect crankcase drippings. Yeah, it's *sacrilege* to wash the originals. Punishable by death, even."

Knowing that Bear's fascination with the lurid would likely lead to a conversational detour, Tim steered Guerrera back on track. "What else did Haines get?"

"Looks to be an AR-15, same they used in the break. Sheriff's devoted a lot of units to the area, but nothing doing. Bikers are too fast. Those boys were long gone before Sheriff's even got the call."

Bear gestured ahead, to where the road wound down through the hills. "Piru's less than ten miles from the Sinner clubhouse."

The truck veered close to the high-rising canyon wall, and Tim could see where people had etched graffiti into the rock. SEAN + SUZIE. MICKEY P IS NO STRANGER TO THE HOG. SINNER TERRITORY: GUARD YER WOMEN. "Chooch Millan," Tim said. "He an officer?"

"Not according to Haines."

"Nomad?"

Guerrera shook his head. "No one important. Just a regular Cholo. What's up?"

"It seems odd. The Sinners risked a high-profile break. If the motive was revenge for Nigger Steve—the *first* Sinner nomad to be killed—why wouldn't they waste someone higher up the food chain? Or pull off something bigger in scope? Shooting a regular member on a deserted road? That's chickenshit. It doesn't add up."

"Maybe they just wanted to punch someone's clock," Bear said. "Get the ball rolling."

"I'm with Rack," Guerrera said. "It's not how these guys think. They usually want to go *bigger*, you know? Their egos are built for escalation."

"How do you know so much about all this shit?" Bear asked.

Guerrera shrugged. "I grew up in a crap town outside Miami. Me and my brothers rode with a junior club out there, the Vatos. That's all there *was* to do. Tool your sled and follow the asphalt. So we did. The motherfuckers graduated to the Cholos."

"And you?" Tim asked.

"I bailed out. Went to the Corps."

A half-burned tree barely maintained its clutch on a ridge, and all three took a moment to admire its tenacity.

"I hate those guys. Ate up my barrio. Left a lot of *mis hermanos* horizontal."

"Your actual brothers?"

"Nah. We all got out. *Mamá*'s too tough to put up with that shit."

They were in the Fillmore flats now, weaving through a gone-to-hell neighborhood. Guerrera took in a Confederate flag waving atop a lawn-stranded car up on blocks. "We don't need backup, huh?" He tried to strike a casual tone but fell short of the mark.

"The nomads aren't dumb enough to be there," Tim said. "We have to draw them out. And we have a better shot at watching them if they're trying to watch us."

"Or trying to kill us," Bear offered.

"That, too."

Bear idled up to the curb, parking behind an endless row of Harleys. Set back behind a jagged fence loomed a sprawling, dilapidated house. At one point it had been farm style, but it was burdened with so many build-ons and repairs that it had surrendered any show of unity. Bike parts littered the front yard, half buried in dirt where a lawn had expired. The Sinners had enough money hidden in various accounts to tear the place down and erect a castle, but the road-grit theme seemed more suitable. Sandbags were piled thigh-high around the walls, and chicken wire guarded the already barred windows from grenade lobs.

Guerrera dabbed the sweat off his forehead. He checked the clip in his Glock and reholstered it. His hands were trembling, ever so slightly. "You should see the shit they've done to *hispanos*."

"It's okay," Tim said. "We'll take lead."

"I'm not worried about it, I'm just saying I hate these guys."

They climbed out. Immediately floodlights clicked on, and two junkyard mutts with pit bull–square heads hurled themselves against the chain-link, snarling. A security camera pivoted atop a post, facing them like the head of a robot. Tim pulled out his badge and creds and held them up to the lens.

A moment later a hulking guy with an ace of diamonds tattooed on his shaved skull stepped onto the porch and whistled off the dogs. Tim matched him with a description from the Sheriff's incipient database—Diamond Dog Phillips.

"You got a warrant?"

"We're not here to bust your balls," Tim said. "Just want to introduce ourselves to Uncle Pete."

"We could go get one. . . ." Bear offered helpfully, angling his wide frame back toward his truck.

Diamond Dog scowled and retreated back into the house. They waited patiently. He reappeared five minutes later, strode down the walk, and opened the myriad locks on the gate. They followed him inside, stepping into a dark, cavernous living room.

A few members milled around with slags tarted up in holiday-red-and-green spandex midriffs and microminis. A bank of closed-circuit telemonitors showed off exterior views of the clubhouse. In the background over the pinball machine's annoying leitmotif, Bearcat scanners chirped, monitoring police frequencies. Steel armor and cinder blocks rimmed the walls from the floor to the bottoms of the windows. A few gunports had been cut on either side of the front door, which had been transplanted from a Mosler walk-in safe. A hint of rot informed the humid air, maybe the smell of soiled leather. Still, the house was in its way another example of high-end L.A. real estate. The decorating budget had just been dispensed according to biker taste and priorities.

"Sit on the couch," Diamond Dog said.

A slag paraded past, swaying her hips, flame tattoos coming up from the waistband of her jeans as if announcing vigorous VD. The front of her shirt proclaimed I'M THE BITCH WHO FELL OFF THE BIKE. Slung in one arm was a baby with a chain tattooed around its neck. Bear and Guerrera sat, but Tim got caught staring.

"Relax, Heat. It's henna."

"That's *Federal* Heat to you."

Diamond Dog stood over them, arms crossed, two other club members behind him in a V formation as if posing for a Tarantino one-sheet. One wore shades despite the dim light, the other an unbuttoned biker vest with no undershirt, a toe tag dangling from his pierced nipple. The guy in shades turned around to catch an airborne can of beer. The back of his T-shirt declared, IF YOU CAN READ THIS, THE BITCH FELL OFF MY BIKE.

"Oh," Bear said. "I get it now."

A coffin in front of the couch served as a coffee table. To the left, a bike painted with distinctive skull patterns dripped oil onto the worn carpet. A lollipop dental mirror poked out from the handlebars as the rearview—letter-of-the-law compliance.

Guerrera gestured at the bike. "Beautiful spray job."

Diamond Dog scratched his crotch, disrupting the tough-guy aesthetics. "That's Danny the Wand's work, *hijo.* Twelve coats of paint on the gas tank alone. You don't even deserve to look at it."

"Danny the Wand?" Bear said. "The guy's a John Holmes or something?"

Diamond Dog laughed with his cohorts, showing off a missing front tooth. "Yeah, that's it. Danny's big dick."

A few Sinners gathered in the doorway to the accompanying room. Prosthetic limbs, do-rags, missing earlobes—they looked like a gathering of well-fed carnies. "Hey, Annie." An older biker curled his finger at her. The end of a bare mattress was barely in view beyond the doorjamb.

As Annie handed off the baby, Tim noticed shiny scars running down her legs like seams. Den's sartorial experiment?

She headed into the other room. Noting Bear's expression of

disgust, Diamond Dog smirked and tilted his head at Annie. "You want a piece?"

"I wouldn't fuck her with your dick and him pushing."

"I ain't screwin' no cop," Annie called back over her shoulder.

"Right," Bear said. "Wouldn't want to lower your standards."

She disappeared into the fold of men. The older guy grasped her shoulders, and they stepped back onto the mattress, disappearing from view. The others waited, thumbing their belt loops and grinning.

"Why don't you lend a hand?" Bear said, gesturing to the other room. "I think they need someone to run anchor."

One of the other bikers laughed. "Dog picked himself up a good case of the Mexican crabs."

The skin on Guerrera's face was taut. "They're different across the border?"

"Yeah." He launched into a not-bad accent. "They doan gah no car insurance."

Laughter and high fives.

Guerrera said, "Now I get why you're missing that front tooth."

The sounds from the other room grew louder. Someone called, "Hey, Toe-Tag. Whelp. You waiting for a written invite?"

"Cool names," Bear said. "You guys have a tree fort out back, too?"

The two shuffled off to take their place in the train, clearing Tim's view of the far wall, where leather jackets were strung like game fish, crude placards affixed to them. Most of them featured Cholo originals, stripped from ass-kicked members. Outlaws who lost their colors—but survived—had to reclaim them to return to their clubs or, in some cases, to keep their lives; the bold display was a virtual advertisement to their rivals for a clubhouse raid. Tim thought of Chooch Millan's jacket, stripped from his dead body only hours ago, and figured that the Sinners destroyed stolen colors that doubled as evidence. Only two Sinner originals were in the mix, Nigger Steve's barely visible through the gloom.

Tim pointed to the other jacket featuring the Sinner flaming skull. "Did Lash get killed, too?"

"Nah, good ol' Lash couldn't behave himself. He had his patch taken back."

Tim looked over, catching Bear's eye. A guy who got kicked out of the club was a guy who might talk.

"For what?"

"Nosy fucker, aren't you?"

Bear put his feet up on the coffin, and Diamond Dog shoved them off with a boot. "Don't you got no respect?"

Bear drew himself to his full height, a head above Diamond Dog. Whelp jogged over, and a moment later Toe-Tag followed, buttoning his pants. Guerrera stood quickly, then Tim, and then eight or ten out-laws pulled behind the other bikers as if magnetically. Annie was in the doorway, cloaking her body with a jacket, breathing hard.

Bear's eyes stayed locked on Diamond Dog's as if the others didn't exist.

A knocking of boots on stairs, and then a woman with feathered brown hair and a leather jacket appeared. "Uncle Pete'll see you now."

The bikers' posture loosened a bit, and Tim, Bear, and Guerrera backed away from the standoff. They followed the woman, her PROP-ERTY OF UNCLE bottom rocker tilting back and forth as she made her way upstairs. The pinkie on her left hand was missing.

They threaded their way through dark halls on the second floor. A teenage girl popped into view, startling Tim. Her head was down, her arms tightly crossed above her breasts to hold together a ripped shirt. She flashed past, almost colliding with their nine-fingered escort, mumbling to herself. Her tangled blond hair clung to her moist cheeks, and one eye was swollen.

The woman in the leather jacket pointed at the double doors through which the crying girl had emerged. "In there."

The three men stepped through the door into a large room—the original master suite?—where an enormous figure sat on a bowed king-size bed. A standard poodle lying at the foot of the mattress bared his teeth silently at them, black skin showing beneath the white hair where it was shaved close. The windows were shuttered; it took a moment for Tim's vision to adjust.

Uncle Pete held a spotted rag poised over his flabby arm. He re-turned to dabbing blood from a meaty biceps, applying himself to the undertaking with the silent contentment of a retired general painting model tanks. Three deep streaks, the kind left by fingernails. A hank of long blond hair lay on the carpet at his feet. The sheets were mussed.

"Frisky cunt. I like 'em that way." Uncle Pete folded the rag and reapplied it, his flat eyes never leaving his task. A rubber-banded thatch of beard poked out from his chin like a stiff rope. "You the ones behind all the sudden interest from the heat? We're catching a lot of static on the streets."

"Yup," Tim said. "That'd be us."

Uncle Pete shook his head. "Some mornings, it just ain't worth chewin' through the four-point restraints." He raised his head, and his eyes sharpened. "Get that Mexican outta here."

Guerrera's voice came out a little tighter than usual. "I'm Cuban."

"Oh. Well, then . . ." Pete laughed, his chest rippling beneath the undershirt. "Don't want no spics of *any* kind in here. Just born-and-bred Americans."

"Okay, Pocahontas."

Uncle Pete stared at Tim, figuring him for the front man. "Get that spic out of here or no conversation."

Guerrera started for the biker, sharply, but Tim stepped in front of him, cutting off his advance while keeping his eyes on Pete. Guerrera stayed pressed against Tim's back but didn't move to brush past him.

Pete seemed invigorated by Guerrera's reaction. "Get the spic out of my clubhouse."

"You want him out, you get him out," Tim said. Bear ostentatiously took up position beside Guerrera.

Uncle Pete squinted through the dim light, no doubt debating an escalation, but then he smiled. "I recognize you. Vigilante guy, right? You're the one who croaked all those motherfuckers back when. You need a nickname."

"Use my real name, thanks."

"Sorry, pal, *everyone* gets a nickname." Uncle Pete rolled his head back on his neck, appraising Tim. The rag disappeared in the swirled sheets, Pete's thick hand in the pouf of hair at the dog's hindquarters. "I'm gonna call you Troubleshooter."

"Original," Bear said. "You might want to take out a trademark."

"Right. I thought I heard it somewhere. Fox News, maybe."

"You know why we're here?" Tim asked.

"Does a crack baby shake?"

"Den's your go-to guy, your hard charger. He and Kaner don't get sprung without word from the top."

"Den don't take no orders. And there is no top. Us Sinners, we're grass-roots all the way."

"What do you need him out for?"

"I don't have to talk to you."

"What am I gonna say?"

"Huh?"

"You're a bright guy, Uncle Pete. What am I gonna say?"

The furrow between Pete's eyebrows disappeared. He didn't smile, but his expression held amusement, almost delight. "You'll get a warrant and you'll make my life hell."

"Right. So."

Uncle Pete lifted his obese frame from the mattress; even Bear looked narrow by comparison. Pete rooted in a drawer, pulled out a digital recorder, and set it on top of the bureau beside a Z-shaped piece of metal. The bed groaned under his weight when he settled back onto it. He lit up a cigarette, inhaled with obvious satisfaction, and beckoned for the next question.

"Where are they?"

"I have no idea. That's why they're nomads, ya see. *No-mads*. Look it up."

"How about Goat, Tom-Tom, and Chief? We want to chat with them, too. Know where *they* are?"

"Sure. Follow the asphalt to the PCH turn by Point Dume. The twenty-foot skid mark? That's Goat's face." Pete's booming laugh ended in a coughing fit. "You're welcome to see if it'll talk back." He tugged at his protuberance of a beard, his smile fading. "You citizens don't got no sense of humor. That's what I hate about you. You and the whole citizens' world. I am so far lost from what this fuckin' nation represents. I read the papers, watch the TV. It disgusts me. It don't reflect me. So I say, fuck it. I won't reflect *it*." He was winding up, a man used to being listened to. "This country's all about what you *can't* do. Can't speed, can't buy a whore, can't smoke a joint. We can't even ride our hogs without helmets now. We got a funeral tomorrow for Nigger Steve—we can't see him off like warriors."

"Warriors don't wear helmets?"

"Not our brand."

"Most real warriors understand that their head's worth more than their hairdo."

"Think of it as a show of respect for the fallen."

"We've got a couple of funerals of our own tomorrow." Tim

bobbed his head, wearing an appropriately thoughtful expression. "I'll tell you what—I'll let you guys do your funeral run without helmets."

"I want it in writing. I don't want a boatload of bullshit when we pull out of here."

"I'll get you a municipal permission."

Bear shot Tim an unveiled look of angry incredulity.

"Yeah, well, I'll believe it when I see it." Uncle Pete studied Tim, then Bear's quite genuine reaction, and the distrust faded gradually from his face. "Maybe you got some class after all, Trouble. We're not bad guys. We're just tired of all the bullshit. We never get anything but the rules—nothin' like a little raping and pillaging to stir things up."

Still burned by Tim's concession, Bear said, "Like the hitchhiker you gang-raped through August? And September? And October?"

"Shit fool, that ain't gang rape. That's training. The boys downstairs are havin' a group splash with Wristwatch Annie. You don't hear *her* complaining."

"That's because her mouth's full," Tim said.

Uncle Pete laughed. "See, there it is. A little humor never hurt no one. Plus, if we gang-raped that broad, where's the charges? Well? Shit, we did her a favor. Opened her up some. Know what I think? I think you citizens are jealous. Drivin' around in your cages, you never get the gurgle in your groin, the wind off your face. And you cops? Shit, you get paid to watch us have fun. I got my slags here all day long. And when I get home, I still knock a few out with my main deed."

"Christ," Bear said. "Don't you have a TV?"

Uncle Pete cocked his head, deciding whether to laugh. "We have our own world, we make our own rules, and we live and die by them. Just like you. Except you live and die by other people's rules."

"And your rules involve pissing on each other's jackets and collecting wing patches for going down on dead women," Bear said. "Where do I sign up?"

"Yeah, we do that shit now and then, just to freak the citizens. P fuckin' R. Don't underestimate the power of intimidation." Pete ruffled the poodle's topknot. "But we stopped making pledges get fucked by Hound Dog here, though."

"Well, that's an institutional advance," Tim said.

"We make the pledges do *useful* shit now."

Tim thought of Guerrera's claim that Sinners had to kill someone to join the club and wondered if that was the "useful shit" Uncle Pete was referring to.

"The name of the game now is *class*. I got a house on the hill. I only bike on runs and funerals anymore. Got me a blue onyx pearl Lexus coupe with cruise control, Paris rims, ivory interior—hell, it's even got a sat-nav system. Thing practically drives *for* me. We don't hang up in the small time. Fuck the white-power shit. We're color-blind. All we see is green." He offered Guerrera an accommodating grin. "That's how we cut in on the other outlaw gangs. We're younger and meaner. We don't believe in shit but the backs of our jackets and cold, hard cash."

"That how you cut in on the Cholos?"

"The Cholos, shit, they're not a blip on our radar. Those mother-fuckers are all show and no go."

"Chooch Millan, too? I heard he's no show *and* no go now."

The poodle came up on all fours, and Uncle Pete scratched his belly until he hunched and phantom-scratched with a hind leg. "We're done now. You want more, you go get that warrant and I call my lawyer and we do the dance."

Tim walked over and turned off the digital recorder on the bureau. He picked up the Z-shaped piece of metal and approached Uncle Pete. Bear and Guerrera looked tense, unsure. The poodle bared its teeth at Tim, but—standard or not—it was still a poodle.

"We both know that the weapon used on the prison break and to kill Chooch Millan was an AR-15. We both know that *this*"—Tim flipped the piece of metal and caught it—"is an illegal drop-in autosear that converts the gun to full auto. We also know that our lab can't link this sear to those bullets. Probably wasn't even this sear that was used. But we could haul you in, give you major *static*, as you say." Tim leaned closer. "You spew your own brand of propaganda, but to us you're an ordinary murderer. I'm not interested in a two-bits weapon charge. I want your ass."

He pressed the autosear into Uncle Pete's fleshy chest and let it fall into his lap.

Uncle Pete returned Tim's glare, but then a smile crept across his wide face, making his rope beard bob. He started clapping. "Good stuff, Trouble. I like your delivery."

Tim headed out, with Guerrera after and Bear bringing up the rear.

Uncle Pete called after them, "I'm gonna hold you to that no-helmet deal for the funeral ride. I got your word?"

"You have my word."

"All right, Trouble. Get it to my lawyer by the A.M. We're riding at noon."

The woman awaited them in the hall and led them downstairs. Tim peeled off at the front door despite her protests. A few of the bikers muscled up to him, but he ignored them, finding the girl with the swollen eye on the couch. A tattoo on her skinny arm read SINNER PROPERTY. NO TRESPASSING. She, too, had four fingers on the left hand, the knuckle wound still bearing stitches.

"How old are you?"

"Nineteen."

"You all right?"

"I'm fine, Heat. Get the fuck out of my face."

"Okay." Tim rose from his crouch. "Best of luck with your budding romance."

He joined Bear and Guerrera at the door, and they stepped out, blinking into the light.

6

Dray was stretched out on the couch when Tim finally got home, her special-order sheriff's-deputy pants unbuttoned around the eight-months heft in her belly. She looked up when he came in through the kitchen, and her cheeks were wet. He dumped his files on the table and stepped over the couch back, sitting high so he could cradle her.

"Goddamnit, I liked Frankie. How's Janice holding up?"

"Jim said not good."

"These are the risks we take." She was trying to firm up her face, play it tough as she'd learned from four older brothers and eight years as the sole female sheriff's deputy at the Moorpark Station, but her lips kept trembling, and her voice, when she spoke again, came out hoarse. "I want to blame *him*. I want to know Frankie made a mistake. That he did the wrong thing. That it's not that easy for our chips to get cashed in. I keep picturing Janice getting that phone call. . . ."

She rested her head on his thigh, and he stroked her hair for a few minutes. Melissa Yueh, KCOM's ever-animated star anchor, proceeded with muted vigor, images and rolling tickers providing largely inaccurate tidbits about the prison break. As usual, Tim and Dray had spoken a few times throughout the day, so she knew the real version.

Dray thumbed down her zipper with a groan and slid a hand over the bulge, Al Bundy style. Her muscular frame accommodated the baby well. She carried the weight mostly in her midsection, though in the past month her toned arms and legs had swollen and softened, which Tim remembered from the last go-around and adored. Dray hated it.

"You ate?" he asked.

"In excess. You?"

"Not since breakfast."

He noticed her scowling and followed her gaze to the TV. Dana Lake, a component of that bizarre Los Angeles order of substars—the celebrity attorneys—sat in a swivel chair, fielding questions from Yueh about her two escaped clients. Dana was in the press constantly, representing everyone from the Westwood Rapist to an al-Jihad shoe bomber taken down at LAX. With her porcelain skin, precise features, and rich chestnut hair, she was stunning. She should have been beautiful, too, but she lost something in the summing of her parts. Despite her overwhelmingly apparent femininity, something about her was off-putting. Too hard a jawline, perhaps, or too severe a set to her mouth. Her face was like a beautiful mask, hardened from shaping itself pleasingly against its will. She rested her forearms on the news desk, squaring her shoulders and showing off the lines of her impeccably tailored suit.

"I hate this broad," Dray said. "She's been making the rounds all night. Larry King introduced her as 'the flashy female lawyer who never wears the same suit twice.' As if that's something admirable. Besides, what does she do with the suits when she's done? Is there some exchange program for anorexics?"

"She donates them to the needy."

Dray snickered, still wiping her cheeks. "Yeah. I'm sure the homeless are using her DKNY silk to stave off the holiday chill." She glanced at the field files piled up on the kitchen table, then thumbed Tim's Marshals star dangling from the leather tag at his belt. "Of course, *now* they want you back on the Warrant Squad."

"I'm the Troubleshooter."

"Oh, yeah, I forgot." She shoved her short blond hair up off her flushed face and fanned her olive deputy shirt. "I'm hot all day. I sweat like a pig in the vest. I feel like I'm melting. Except when I'm cold. Then I'm freezing."

"Maybe you should start your leave now."

"And miss all the fun of rousting biker assholes? Me and Mac pulled over three today. Yeah, wipe that surprised expression off your face. While we can't all stroll into the lion's den like a certain big shot, we're doing our part, even out here in bumfuck Moorpark. Captain said the database is coming along nicely?"

"That it is." He slid down next to her. She raised her boot, and he tugged it off and rubbed her foot. She groaned with delight, arched her back like a cat. "My visit with Uncle Pete actually gave me some good ideas," he said. "I decided I want you to start wearing a property jacket. And I want a tattoo. Right . . . *here*. 'Property of Tim Rackley.' "

"Then you'll let me sled with you?"

"Then I'll let you sled with me."

"Bring on the ink, Big Daddy." His Nextel chirped—radio freq this time—and Dray laughed. "Here we go. Don't mind me. I'll just be here on the couch, sweaty and knocked up."

Tim flipped the phone open, heading back to the kitchen, and keyed "talk."

"Rack, it's Freed."

"How'd it go with the Cholos?"

"How's, *'Chíngate, pinche cabrón'* sound? I'm not really sure how to interpret that."

"Well, we figured, right?"

"I couldn't even get in to see El Viejo—they keep the boss man pretty well shielded. I sat a local unit on the clubhouse. We can't do much more than that. The Cholos buzz out of there like gnats. If the Sinners want to pick 'em off, they'll find a way."

"What are you doing now?"

"After this day? I'm gonna head home and see my kid."

"Don't blame you."

Tim clicked off and dialed the command post.

Haines said, "I told you already, we'll call if anything breaks."

"*Anything*. My phone is on."

"So you mentioned."

Tim pored over the files as Dray focused on the TV, making occasional wordless exclamations—disgust, contempt, derision. The only thing Dray liked more than watching the news was reviling it.

He spread out the photos, marveling at Goat's face, Kaner's breadth, Den's dark, baleful eyes. He scanned over the crime-scene report, feeling the cold weight of the scientific phrasing. His eyes stuck on the name of his friend.

Six apparent entrance shots to Deputy Frank Palton's torso, two to the head. Skull fragments and soft tissue noted in the mesh and the back of the van.

He flashed on his first day back on the job after Ginny's death, Frankie doing his shtick with Jim, joking about the "Commie Sutra" book his wife had foisted on him. Tim remembered it vividly because it had been his first single moment of levity in three days, the earliest glimmer of a possibility that the world might still be inhabitable. When Tim had gone missing, Palton had been the one to find the blood at the pickup near the cult ranch. Tim pictured the annoyingly endearing batches of photos Frankie used to e-mail out every few months—updates on his daughters' swim-club awards, theme birthday parties, Halloween costumes.

Dray looked over, psychically attuned to Tim's shifts in mood from ten years of marriage. She met his eyes, her face soft with empathy.

"Two kids left behind," Tim heard himself say, as if he and Dray weren't aware of this already.

"Not over there," Dray said gently. "Talk about Frankie's two kids with me over here on the couch. Not when you're a deputy over files." She watched him, the yellow light of a Claritin commercial shining through her translucent, ice green eyes. "Only let it be personal when you're off duty. Otherwise just get it done. That's how you'll honor Frankie's memory. And Hank Mancone's. And Fernando Perez's."

"Who?"

"The illegal guy killed one car over in the blast. Which is my point. If that guy doesn't matter, no one matters. Everyone counts. And everyone counts the same. Getting personal is like putting on blinders. It blocks you from weighing deaths equally, which blocks you from weighing *clues* equally."

"You're implying I've been hotheaded in the past?"

She laughed. "Never. I'm saying your friend just died. Take a time-out when you need it. Besides, haven't you seen enough of Goat Purdue's fetching smile for one day?"

Tim looked down at the files and pictures spread across the table, let out a breath, and pulled back his shoulders, which he realized had been cramping his chest for the past hour. "What am I supposed to do?"

"You're supposed to feed me." A long pause as they studied each other across the room, both on the verge of a smile. "And yourself."

He got up and looked inside the refrigerator. Save jars of condiments, a browning apple, and the residual legs of a chocolate Santa Claus, it was empty. "I thought you were waiting to eat Santa until Christmas."

"That's four days away."

"I'm gonna have to start hiding food around here."

"There are some sunflower seeds in the cupboard."

"I was hoping for something heartier."

"You," Dray said, "are a Black Hole of Need."

He closed the refrigerator door.

"And while you're out," Dray continued, "can you bring me Strawberry Crush? In the bottles? And Lunchables?"

"Lunchables?"

"Yeah. The turkey ones."

"Right."

He took his newly purchased used Explorer to Albertsons and shoved a cart up and down the aisles, checking his phone—still nothing—and stocking up on everything he could remember Dray eating in the past eight months. No small feat. When he came home, the living room was empty, but he could hear the television going in the bedroom. He peeled off the Lunchables lid, popped open a Crush, and arranged the meal on a silver tray they'd received as a wedding gift from someone they no longer recalled. Across the folded napkin, he laid a clipped grocery-store-diminished Siberian iris—Dray's favorite flower, one of the few girlie indulgences she permitted herself.

She was lying flat as a cadaver on the bed, her tummy sprouting between her boxers and her shoved-back academy T-shirt. Her head rolled to take him in, and then a spontaneous smile reshaped her face and he thought of the first time he saw her smile, in the parking lot at a fire-department fund-raiser. "Timothy Rackley."

He lowered the tray to the mattress and kissed her sweaty bangs. She regarded the food and—through a grin—issued her trademark grimace. "That looks *disgusting*. Turkey on crackers and strawberry soda? Whose idea *was* that anyways?"

He handed her the iris, slid the tray onto his lap, and began his dinner.

7

The five men walked a slow turn around the broken figure on the chair. Duct tape bound the man to the chair arms from wrists to elbows; both his arms had left their sockets. His features were no longer discernible. He coughed out a mouthful of blood; it ran from his cheek to the thin carpet. His matted ponytail hung stiffly.

The room, a garage conversion with milky plastic windows set high in the still-functional roll-up door, smelled of oil from the Harley and from the greasy tools occupying the brief run of kitchen counter. A vise protruded from a wobbly table littered with engine parts, spare wheels, and blackened wrenches. The cot against the far wall and a scattering of dirty plates and cups were the sole signs of habitation.

Den halted, and the others stopped their pacing, waiting for his next move. They looked unnatural off their bikes, eroded into slouches acquired from too many hours leaning on handlebars.

"Tell me," Den said. "I know you planned it out by now."

The man was weeping quietly, a hiss that turned to a gurgle somewhere around the mouth. "I haven't. I swear, *ese*."

Den looked at Kaner. "Put out the cigarette. Warm-up's over."

Kaner ground the butt against his front tooth, popped it in his mouth, savored a few chews, and swallowed.

"Still never met a nicotine junkie like you." Goat tapped his glass eye with a long fingernail, a gross-out stunt that had developed into a nervous tic. "Chasing the cancer like a piece-a ass. What you gonna do when you catch it?"

Kaner's words came in a deep rasp: "Smoke through the hole in my throat."

He tugged off his shirt, revealing an enormous pectoral tattoo—a revolver aimed straight on, with six Sinner skulls staring out of the holes in the wheel. The dim light—morning's first gray glow—turned his flesh pale and moldy. He found a fresh T-shirt in a cabinet and tossed it to Den. Den slid his bowie knife from his shoulder holster. Its genuine-ivory handle shimmered. On the butt, tiny inset rubies formed a flaming skull. He'd paid over a grand to a Kenyan poacher for the section of tusk, or so the story went. Den slit both sleeve cuffs and threw the shirt back to Kaner. The fabric still stretched at Kaner's biceps when he pulled the shirt on.

Tom-Tom laughed. He was bouncing in his boots, white hair flapping, fingers going at his sides as if he were hopped up on meth, though he required none. "Lookadit. His shirt. Doanfitchasogood." His voice sounded funny, altered through an oft-broken nose.

Kaner said, "Why should I stain mine?"

The man in the chair emitted a faint cry.

Goat laughed. "You sound like Chief. Next you'll have your bitches polishing your boots."

Chief stared ahead, unamused and silent, his thin lines of beard fastidiously sculpted.

As Kaner drifted behind the man, Den drew forward into a square of foggy light thrown through one of the tiny windows. The man tried to recoil in his chair, pulling his head back and to one side, muttering a prayer in Spanish.

Den's surprisingly handsome face tensed. "I won't ask again."

"Por favor . . . por favor . . ."

Den nodded at Kaner, who palmed the man's skull, his other hand locking beneath his chin, and ripped him and the chair backward. Kaner dragged him, shrieking, toward the kitchen area.

Den got there before they did and spun the arm of the vise. A metallic whir as the jaws spread. At the sound the man found a hidden reserve of strength, bucking against Kaner's hold. Goat and Tom-Tom stepped in, and then Kaner gripped the man's blood-slick ponytail, forcing his head back. The man grunted and strained forward against his hair, face reddening, veins standing up in his neck. At a snail's pace, both hands tightening around the ponytail, Kaner fought the head between the open jaws. Den knocked the handle with the side of a hand, and the device clenched.

A piercing scream that faded to whispered babbling.

Chief watched impassively from across the garage, looking mildly bored. He had not moved.

Den appraised the tools on the counter, picking up a pair of needle-nose pliers. He looked down at the trapped head.

The pliers rose into the man's view. "I tell you. I tell you *todo*."

"I know." Den bent sympathetically over the upturned face. "But I'm gonna work for a while first."

8

The air-conditioned elevator filled with the Muzak stylings of "Arthur's Theme." Bear hummed along at the chorus, then rustled under Tim's and Guerrera's looks.

"What? I was clearing my throat."

The elevator stopped, and they stepped out into a marble foyer that led to glass doors with deco etching. Bear, who'd made short and noisy work of an eye-opener Super Big Gulp on the way over, ducked into a bathroom.

The foyer window looked down four stories onto South Rodeo Drive. Tim and Guerrera stood shoulder to shoulder and watched Jags and Hummers flash back the morning light.

Guerrera brought his knuckle to his jawbone, a nervous tap. "Listen, I'm sorry I lost my cool at the clubhouse yesterday."

"You let Pete get to you a little, that's all."

"Never seen *you* get rattled like that."

Tim laughed. "You don't read the papers."

"You know what I mean. You're level, even when you're not."

"They say racist shit to get a rise out of you. Don't give it to them. Detach."

Bear stepped out from the bathroom, readjusting the star on his belt, and by tacit understanding, Tim and Guerrera let the exchange end. The three headed to reception and flashed creds. After a fifteen-minute wait, during which they were forced to endure the receptionist's too-loud phone recollections of a recent shopping expedition, they were escorted past a secretary and a dressed-for-success paralegal to the Inner Office.

Dana Lake stood with her back to them, silhouetted against a sun-bleached pane of glass. A cordless headset slightly crimped her hair. "If you won't offer us anything better than that, I'll wait until five minutes before trial to plead him out. I'll make you spend *six months* building a case you won't even try. Yeah? Then don't waste our time with bullshit offers."

She pulled off the headset, shook out her hair, and pivoted to face them. "Don't fuck with my client. You want to talk to him, you bring a warrant or you phone me."

"Uncle Pete and I reached our own arrangement," Tim said.

She tossed the headset onto her meticulously ordered desk. "Credentials."

They handed them to her, and she wrote down their names and badge numbers on a yellow legal pad. A framed lithograph of the Laughing Sinner logo commanded the wall behind her desk. *"To DL—a friend to bikers, my kind of tough broad."* Danny the Wand's flourish of a signature was Sharpied beneath the dedication.

Dana stared at Tim's creds for an extra beat. "I hope you don't think you can get away with your celebrated stunts with my clients, Deputy Rackley. I'll have your ass in a sling."

"Ms. Lake, my ass *lives* in a sling."

"So. You've sicced the heat on the entire Laughing Sinners organization. Incisive investigative strategy. Was the Marshals Service the brain trust behind color-coding Arab travelers after 9/11?"

"You rep all the Sinners?"

"I do."

"How's that arranged?"

"Not that it's any of your business, but I'm on retainer to the club."

Bear said, "Lucrative, I'd imagine."

Her gaze dropped to his feet. "I don't buy my shoes at Payless."

"You know where that money comes from?"

"And your paychecks come from an Enron-funded junta government that supports tyrannical monarchies and wages illegal war in violation of international law and against UN votes. Looks like you've got the moral upper hand on a sleazy gal like me. Let's get to business. I bill six-fifty an hour. This diverting badinage with the constabulary has already cost me"—a glance to her Baume & Mercier—"a hundred and twenty-five dollars."

"I'm sure Uncle Pete'll pick up the tab," Bear said.

"Good idea. I'll inform Billing."

Tim produced the municipal permission allowing the Sinners to ride without helmets in that morning's funeral procession. She lowered her head into a pair of frameless half-glasses and perused it. She finished, and her glasses took flight, landing softly on the legal pad on her desk. "What's your angle?"

"Goodness of my heart. I was told to smooth things over so our fine city's middle-class churchgoers can sleep soundly in their beds."

She refolded the permission. "I'll drag you through the press if we take you at your word and you use it to roust my clients." She seemed to speak without breathing, a rapid-fire assault perfected by years of courtroom performance. "It's preposterous that riding bareheaded even *has* to be granted as a favor. We've been petitioning against the helmet laws for years. So much for Patrick Henry—you won't let people risk their own skulls."

Guerrera said, "Helmet laws save—"

"Great. A bean counter. Accounting can't justify everything. What you forget is, *your* numbers erode *our* freedoms. What's the deaths-per-year cutoff to make something illegal these days? What's next? Diet legislation to cut heart-disease stats? Burgers? French fries? Supersize it and ride the pine in county for the night. What do you say, boys?"

"We refer to them as freedom fries now, ma'am."

Tim said, "If any of the nomads contact you, we want to know."

"Of course. Insert yourselves into every aspect of everything regardless of your understanding or the casualty rate."

"I'm not sure I'm catching your drift."

"Bikers are true patriots. As American as laissez-faire economics. They administer their own justice. Surely you can relate to that, miraculously reinstated Deputy Rackley." She seemed disappointed by Tim's nonreaction, not that it slowed her down. "During the grudge match between the Sinners and Cholos, neither club complained to the police *or* requested protection. You should have let them be."

"To kill each other?"

"Beats killing federal officers and innocent bystanders. Which is what happened when you imposed your laws on them. Laws and bikers are like sodium and nitric acid. You're the geniuses playing chemist."

"*Some*one drank the Kool-Aid," Bear muttered.

"You're right. All three of you have stained chins. Aren't you sick of being told what to do? The corporations pay the lobbyists, the laws get passed, and you enforce them. Tax laws. Drug laws. Patriot Act II, the Sequel. Your boss tells you to come sniff around here, and you prick up your little ears and obey."

"I hadn't realized my ears were pricked," Tim said.

"And my ears just stick out that way naturally," Bear added.

"So by way of protest," Guerrera chimed in, "you take the side of gang-rapists and cop killers."

"Don't you read the papers, Deputy? This country is rotting from the top down. There *are* no sides anymore."

Tim said, "There are *always* sides."

"Not for me."

"I bet that makes it easier to sleep at night."

"Don't play that card with me. I like my Jaguar. I like flying a chartered jet. I like billing six-fifty an hour. And I have no problems sleeping at night. You walk in here, your shoulders squared with all that unequivocal midwestern confidence that comes with thinking you're moral—"

"I grew up in Pasadena."

"Same difference."

"Not to me. I would have preferred the Midwest." Tim nodded at Bear and Guerrera, and they headed out. He paused at the door. "We'll be seeing you soon."

Her cheeks were still flushed from her tirade. "How's that?"

"I'm planning to spend more quality time with your clients."

9

Twenty motor units led the official funeral cortege, an ironic biker send-off, followed by fifty black-and-whites. Behind the caissons bearing the caskets and two riderless horses with reversed stirrups—a tradition holding on from Saxon days—came another police phalanx, trailed by a solemn convoy of unmarked cars. The procession slowed around Chinatown to accommodate a pipe-and-drum band. Local-affiliate TV crews formed up with crowds along the downtown streets, grabbing highlights for the six o'clock news. Evincing terrorist-age sensitivity, people waved flags, prayed silently, pressed their hands to their chests. Uniformed peace officers wore black ribbons across their badges. Grief was rampant but, no less, fear.

As the draped caskets rolled past, spectators gave in to emotion. The martial choreography was, after all, largely for them—the citizens on hand and the multitudes tuned in from home. The void opened up by the slaying of an officer could be compensated for only by symbolism, an overwhelming show of force and tradition to reassure citizens that they weren't under attack, that the bedrock wasn't fractured, that the moorings still held.

The procession filtered through surface streets and access roads, skirting the freeways with as much dignity as it could, to arrive at Forest Lawn.

U ncle Pete straddled the yellow dotted line that ran past the club-house, his legs like pillars. The sun glinted off the exaggerated blade of Den's bowie knife, lent to him with considerable pomp and circumstance for the occasion. Before him the bikers, in a half-mile formation, throttled and lurched on their marks like angry steeds. Sinners had descended from all the satellite chapters, their bottom rockers a sampling of West Coast and Southwest geography.

Behind the vanguard of Sinner officers' bikes, a flatbed funeral trailer hitched to a Harley Road King interrupted the two-by-two configuration. Every inch of the exposed glossy coffin bore club imagery— licks of fire, clusters of skulls, Nigger Steve's likeness astride a dragon. Vans bookended the bikes, war wagons piloted by deeds and holding ordnance in case of attack. Another defensive weapon, Dana Lake, was suited up on the back of Diamond Dog's bike, looking for once out of place, about as hip as Dukakis in the tank.

Uncle Pete raised both hands over his head and jabbed the tip of the bowie blade into his thumb. He extended his arm, working the thumb below the cut. A bead of blood formed, then dropped.

"May this be the only Sinner blood spilled on asphalt this year!" Uncle Pete roared.

The bikers exploded into whoops and applause. Pete saddled up, hammering his heel down on the kick start. The column of motorcycles moved as one, filling the air with the grease-spatter thunder of engines venting.

M otorcycles flowed down from the San Gabriels' summit as if poured from the horizon. The Cholos rode erect, knights at attention, floating like a mirage over Palmdale tarmac. They traveled slow, the heavy bikes purring calmly beneath them. A coffin was linked sidecar style between two bikes, a cross spray-painted above the name— CHOOCH MILLAN. El Viejo led the pack, his worn-leather face braving the wind, the feathers of his headdress rippling. Carefully cultivated legend had it that he was half Navajo, half Mexican, descended from the Aztecs. Most of the Cholos wore helmets, but a few, like El Viejo, refused, flouting the law to enhance funeral dignity.

Cholo war wagons held lead and rear positions, keeping a respectful distance from the bikes. The convoy turned onto a two-lane highway, following the predetermined route to the Catholic graveyard.

A bagpiper led the procession through Forest Lawn to the first dug grave, the inner circle shuffling along, press and spectators keeping their distance. Palton's girlfriend showed up and lingered red-faced in the back until Jim went over and unceremoniously suggested she grieve elsewhere. Four helicopters did a flyover, one peeling off in missing-man formation just above the neatly dug rectangle. As a bugler played taps, the honor guard stood at attention, white parade ascots dotting their open collars. After they performed the flag fold, Marshal Tannino stepped in, awarding the firm triangle of nylon to a stoically postured Janice Palton. One of the Palton girls collapsed, and every deputy in the vicinity, glad for an opportunity to be useful, surged toward her.

The nonuniformed onlookers dispersed, catharsis complete. The cops and deputies remained, trying for impassivity though a few trickles glittered on motionless cheeks. After the brass's obligatory remarks about sacrifice and unwavering resolve, Jim took the podium. He still hadn't recovered hearing in his right ear; he spoke with his head inadvertently tilted.

"I never understood what 'human resources' meant. I thought it was more of that corporatespeak I hate. *'Human resources.'* I mean, what the hell?"

Some nervous shifting in the crowd.

"But now I think I get it. You know how long it takes to make a deputy of Frankie's caliber? An all-state fullback in high school. A B.A. in criminal justice from City. He went through the academy first, you know, before FLETC. Two years as a patrolman, two more as a D-1. Then the Service. SWAT school. Surveillance school. Gang training. Six-month stint with DEA."

Janice was crying for the first time.

"You think that matters to some prick biker with an AR-15?"

The front rows bristled. Miller started toward the podium but caught himself.

"I been thinking a lot lately about how easy it is to destroy. To ruin.

It took us how many years to learn to fly? Building airplanes, I mean. And the Towers. The engineering and architecture that went into them. The materials. Scaffolding. Man-hours. A whole civilization building on itself, decade after decade, and what?" Jim's cheeks glistened, but his voice stayed steady, gathering rage. Miller was at his elbow now, contemplating a tactful break-in. "A bunch of jackasses with box cutters can take down the whole enterprise. That's the thing with it. It's so goddamned easy. And what do *we* do? We make pledges. Like we did today. Law and order. Righteousness. Justice." A noise of disgust escaped between his teeth. "Even if we *do* nail the guys who killed Frankie . . ." He caught himself, nodded at Tannino's wife. "Sorry. I'm sorry."

Miller slipped an arm around Jim's shoulders and, smiling at the crowd, directed him away. Jim leaned back toward the mike. "We won't replace you, Frankie. We can't."

The crowd took a moment to resettle. Janice caught Jim stepping off the dais and hugged him, crying into his shoulder. As the coffin began its descent into the grave, a seven-man detail fired a rifle salute, three volleys that rolled back off the foothills.

Tannino rang the brass bell, sending Frank Palton off duty for the last time.

Y ou got 'em yet?" Guerrera's voice crackled through the Nextel. Tim pressed his binoculars to the tinted glass and refocused at the top of the opposing hill. Beside him in the Chevy cargo van, Roger Frisk and another Electronic Surveillance Unit inspector resumed their discussion about virtual dragon building. "Nope. Nothing."

Tim, Bear, and Guerrera were positioned around the cemetery, each with a pair of ESU geeks. It would have been too obvious if they'd tailed the biker procession from the clubhouse. The Sinners' highly secretive route, designed to throw off both law enforcement and revenge-seeking rivals, had most likely been charted out yesterday. Rather than burning resources playing clairvoyant, Tim had decided to pitch camp at the finish line.

The ground vibrated, ever so slightly, and the ESU inspectors finally shut up and grabbed their long-range lenses. The sound rose to a rumble, then a roar, as a landslide of metal overtook the road.

Tim had to raise his voice, even at this distance, to be heard. "Cue the locals. Remember, they've got to sell it."

A sheriff's car pulled forward, blocking the street to halt the procession, and the two brave souls emerged. Already Dana Lake was off the bike, unfolding the municipal permission. The notion of her accompanying the mourners to protect their right to bare heads—all the while earning her hourly—brought a grin to Tim's lips.

An animated discussion ensued, the lead deputy glancing from the paper to the bikers, who looked on with menacing impatience. Tim hoped that Guerrera's team, holed up in the warehouse beside them, was getting all the shots they needed; capturing the Sinners in formation without helmets would provide a wealth of information on the club's pecking order.

Tim keyed the radio. "Who's the guy front right, next to Uncle Pete?"

Guerrera's whispered voice: "We'll match face to name later, but that's the road-captain position."

"What, in case Uncle Pete gets lost?"

"You guessed it. He's got a notoriously bad sense of direction. He once steered an entire run one state wide of the mark, went to the Black Hills by way of Montana."

Bear chimed in on the primary channel, "Never said you needed brains for the gig."

"No," Tim said. "But he's got 'em."

Finally the sheriff's deputy held up his hands in concession, and he and his partner climbed back into their car and took off. The Sinners continued down the hill and slant-parked, one after another. Within seconds both sides of the road below were filled.

"Okay," Tim said. "This is our best shot to capture their faces. Get as many close-ups as you can. Focus on mother chapter members and deeds. With the women make sure you get their property jackets, too."

As several Sinners hoisted the coffin and marched it into the grassy flats, the van filled with the click of high-tech cameras and the hum of autoadjusting lenses. No cemetery workers were on hand; no one threw dirt on a Sinner but a Sinner.

Toe-Tag, Whelp, and Diamond Dog stayed together, keeping close proximity to Uncle Pete, who seemed to be relishing his master-of-ceremonies role. A skinny biker with an eye patch hung at Pete's side,

his posture indicating more-than-usual obeisance. Rather than originals, he wore an armband, Third Reich style, exhibiting the Sinners
logo. A stone glinted on his pinkie ring. A woman with a masculine build
stayed on his arm, seeming to negotiate his brief introductions to
satellite-chapter members.

Tim clicked on again: "What's with Himmler at your nine o'clock?"

"The armband shows he's a striker," Guerrera said. "Means he's
graduated from being a prospect, but he's not an official Sinner yet."

Bear's voice: "How'd he graduate?"

"He rolled bones."

"You gotta kill someone?"

"From their preselected list of club enemies. Proves you're not a
cop."

"Yeah," Bear said. "That'd pretty much do it."

Tim caught a glimpse of an attractive brunette swaggering through
the crowd. A few of the Sinners cleared out of her way, their deference
drawing Tim's attention. Trying to keep her in sight, he came up off the
stool until his head pressed against the roof of the van. Her bottom
rocker—PROPERTY OF DEN—flashed into view before she disappeared
behind a stand of trees.

He keyed the radio. "Bear. You spot Den's deed? Far side of the
trees?"

"We have a worse angle than you. How 'bout you, Guerrera?"

"We lost our view to a moving van."

Tim grabbed a camera and slid out of the vehicle, easing the door
closed. He jogged in a crouch a few feet along the wrought-iron fence
and fell to a flat-bellied sniper's position. The brunette stepped back
into the scope of his lens and he fired off a series of shots. The whir of
his advancing film seemed to echo back at him. He pivoted with the
camera, tracking the sound.

A short biker sat on an Indian about twenty yards upslope, a camera
raised to his helmet. For a frozen instant, he and Tim regarded each
other through their lenses. The biker flipped down his wind visor and
took off up a cross street. Tim was on his feet, sprinting for the van, the
information coalescing—Chief, the Sinners' intel officer, taking pictures of Tim taking pictures.

Tim leapt into the driver's seat and peeled away from the curb, the
ESU guys going ass-up in the back. Barking for backup into the radio,

he careened around the turn in time to see the bike cut down another
street ahead. By the time the cul-de-sac flew into view, Chief was heading back directly at them, a game of chicken he was sure to lose. About
twenty yards from a collision, he turned sharply, motoring up a walkway
toward a house. He hopped the three steps onto the wide porch, a fu-
sion of man and machine, and screeched left, leaving a wake of fire.
The bike took flight off the porch and landed in a flower bed, throwing
off a shower of dirt and petals. Chief reared up, his front wheel smash-
ing down a rickety gate, and disappeared into the backyard.

Tim skidded to a halt, Frisk rolling to strike the cushioned front
seats, and reversed hard. He raced around the block in time to see the
bike drop down a sloped median—a ten-foot fall ending in concrete—
and race off, heading the wrong way, cars and trucks honking and veer-
ing as Chief split the road down the middle.

A glance in the other direction showed Bear's van and Guerrera's
G-ride boxed in by a cluster of strategically repositioned Harleys.

Suffused with frustration and no small measure of admiration, Tim
had no choice but to turn and watch Chief disappear.

The Cholos rolled along, a river of flying colors. Aside from the war
wagon twenty yards ahead, El Viejo led alone—no road captain to
detract from his eminence. His face and bearing were classics, torn
from pulp-western covers and second-rate cowboy etchings that tour-
group participants hung in bathrooms. The narrow highway stretched
flat and unforgiving through Antelope Valley, where the high Mojave
grudgingly gives way to dusty civilization. The occasional car flashed
by on the sole opposite lane, an anxious pale face or two pressed to a
window.

The ride was windless and serene. Just the purr of the bikes, the
flutter of synthetic rubber over blacktop, the whistle of air through helmets.

The front and rear war wagons exploded simultaneously, lifting off
the ground and sending out a burst of heat and orange flame.

The Cholos went down in waves, only those in the middle of the
convoy managing to stay upright. The trapped bikers wheeled and
revved, wild horses corralled.

Two Harleys peeled out from behind an embankment shoring up a hillside ahead, Den and Kaner in the driver positions. Goat and Tom-Tom rode sidesaddle behind them, AR-15s at low-ready. They shot through the orb of fire engulfing the front war wagon, racing along the side of the convoy, AR-15s blazing. The Cholos absorbed the fusillade in tangles of metal and flesh, engines revving, tires biting through cloth and skin.

The Sinners screeched to a halt at the end of the run, guns smoking. The procession had been decimated. A few weak groans and coughs. Limbs rustling among the bodies and machinery. The smell of burned flesh.

The four Sinners dismounted, pulling handguns from their waistbands. They walked calmly among the fallen, kids at a tidal pool, shooting the wounded in the head.

In the front El Viejo lay broken-limbed ten yards from his steaming bike, an ideal chalk-outline model. His headdress lay behind him, ablaze. The heat from the fiery van had baked his rich bronze skin auburn. His cheek was stuck to the asphalt.

Den strolled over and stared down at him, blotting out the midday sun. "Look at me."

With great effort El Viejo pulled his cheek free of the road. He met Den's eyes defiantly, his wrinkled face hardened into a grimace.

A single report.

Goat pulled a bike over, and Den slung himself onto the back. As they took off after Kaner and Tom-Tom, the heat ate deeper into the war wagons, setting off a crackling of ammo.

10

Tim crouched among the bodies, some charred from the bonfire blazes, taking in the quarter-mile death scene. The smoldering shells of the war wagons remained, exhaling black smoke. An up-ended bike framed his view, its tire spinning lazily like a pinwheel in a faint breeze. Tim closed his eyes, trying to drown out the pervasive buzz of black flies, and images pressed in on him with the smell—Black-hawks circling, desert sand swirling, dossiers smudged with camo-face-paint thumb marks. His combat memories underscored what he'd already gathered: This wasn't macho bikers squaring off over wayward glances at club mamas but a tactical hit, expertly planned and executed.

A sheriff's deputy chuckled and pointed to the quarter-size holes that the cooked ammo had punched in the war wagon's metal. "Looks like they got their twenty-one-gun salute."

Tim said, "This is funny to you?"

"They cut irony outta the federal budget, too?" The guy casually went back to scribbling in the crime-scene attendance log.

Tim rose and walked over to a cluster of criminalists by the CSI van. Before the hit TV show, they'd called the division Crime Lab, but a number-one ratings winner can be a strong impetus for change. Guerrera stood a few feet off from the group, finger in his ear, phone pressed to his head. He gave Tim a quick nod.

Aaronson was squinting at a slug he held up before his face on tweezers. He was a slight man, prone to wearing crisply ironed, tissue-thin button-ups that showed off the lines of his undershirt. His crime-scene reports were filled out in a hand that looked like typewriting.

"Explosives look to match?" Tim asked.

"Those used on the transport convoy? Oh, yeah."

"AR-15s again?"

"Yup. They don't call 'em street sweepers for nothing."

Bear jogged over, high-stepping through the wreckage, and beckoned Tim and Guerrera. By the time they reached him, he was holding a handkerchief against his mouth and nose.

"So get this. I found out where Uncle Pete was after the funeral." Bear undercut his dramatic pause with a sneeze. "In church. He and the whole chapter rolled into First Baptist, scared the hell out of all the blue-hairs. Not the pastor, though. He thought he made the score of a lifetime."

"The times line up?" Tim asked.

"Perfectly. Before that the entire mother chapter was mourning peacefully under our surveillance. No way they had time in between to get out here. It was a nomad job, all right."

"They got solid intel for this. They knew the route, which vehicles to rig."

"Maybe they had someone on the inside."

"With this rivalry? Doubt it."

"They could've put the squeeze on one of the Cholos."

"Can't interrogate them now." Tim surveyed the steaming land-scape, the wooden box of the coffin resting untarnished amid the de-struction. A mournful club mama sitting out the ride with a broken leg had turned over the restricted Cholo mother chapter's roster; a prelim-inary check matched a body to every name.

"*That's* why they shot Chooch Millan," Guerrera said suddenly. He looked at them expectantly, then seemed to realize they were waiting for him to connect the dots. "What's the only thing that gets a whole club together in one place?"

Tim bobbed his head—of course. "A funeral ride."

"Right. Shoot someone in the rank and file, within a few days you'll have the entire club assembled right before your sights."

Bear surveyed the scene with watering eyes. "Hell of a revenge for Nigger Steve."

"This isn't revenge," Tim said. "This is extermination." He took in the baked tableau. "They're paving the way to something bigger."

Bear made a muffled noise in his throat, and Tim started back to his car. Before driving off, he sat for a few minutes, staring at the wheel. He headed toward downtown in silence, stopping off at Forest Lawn.

His phone chirped as he climbed out of the car.

"Hey, babe. Jesus, huh?"

"Yeah."

He heard Mac shout something in the background, and then Dray said, "Shoot, I have to peel out. You think you'll be home?"

He chuckled.

"Right. Okay, the captain needs someone to pick up a few overtime parole hours—this case is stretching us thin on man-hours, too. I'll take 'em if it'll be a late one for you."

"It will."

"See you whenever. If it's before dawn, bring Yakitoriya."

"Yakitoriya?"

"Don't ask. I'm craving chicken neck." More distant voices. "Okay. Gotta run. Be safe."

Tim folded the phone and got out, strolling among the gravestones. It wasn't hard to locate Palton's fresh carpet of sod. A blanket of lilies cascaded over a table laden with candles and bouquets. Frankie's decade-old credential photo from the Federal Law Enforcement Training Center had been blown up and placed in a gold frame, like a signed former-celebrity eight-by-ten at a dry cleaner. His pose, stalwart and uptight, didn't reflect his humor. He wore a suit and no smile, twenty-four years of tough with a shaving nick at his Adam's apple. He and Janice, high-school sweethearts, would have been six years into their marriage when the photo was taken. And now he lay six feet under, collateral damage in a biker gang war.

Tim's mind pulled to the civilian killed in the explosion, the illegal guy in the Pontiac, but he couldn't produce a name. He thought about Dray's cautionary words as he'd sat perusing the field files at the kitchen table. Though he was three years older than his wife, she still had him hands down on wisdom.

He walked up and down the rows of graves, looking for Hank Mancone's plot. Hank was old, divorced, no kids, on the eve of retirement
for five years now. Tim's impressions of Mancone were culled strictly
from elevator nods and hallway passings, and he recalled only that the
deputy was cranky, pouch-faced, and smelled of stale coffee. In the
post-break hysteria, Hank hadn't played as well to the news cameras and
weepy public; he was Shoshana Johnson to Palton's Jessica Lynch. Staring at the rows of gray headstones, searching for a cushion of color like
that surrounding Frankie's grave, Tim flashed on the photos of Hank's
corpse seat-belted into the transport van. Was the crime against Frankie
any worse? Did the pretty wife, the two kids, the square jaw, the spe-
cialized credentials make it any more a tragedy?

Tim stepped between two high headstones, coming upon an older
woman on her knees. A few bouquets dotted the fresh-turned soil. Tim
followed her gaze to the chiseled name.

"I'm one of Hank's colleagues," he said gently. "Are you his ex-
wife?"

"His sister." She raised her eyes. They were tired and sad, though
Tim would have bet they looked that way outside of cemeteries as well
as in. "Were you a friend?"

"A colleague," he repeated. "I'm sorry. I didn't know him well."

"Nobody did."

Tim let that one expire in the graveyard silence.

"Hank was supposed to retire last year. And the year before that.
Just wouldn't. He always said he had nothing else to do." She wiped her
nose. "You reap what you sow, I guess. You stay closed off, you get less
flowers at your grave. And you know what? Hank wouldn't have minded
that one bit. He wouldn't have complained. He just wanted to drive his
van and be around."

Tim felt an urge to give her something, to share with her his own
loss, but he recognized the impulse as self-serving. His cell phone vibrated at his belt. "I'm sorry." He started to add something in closing,
but she waved him off. Her voice was more regretful than sad. "I know.
I know. Me, too."

When Tim reached the edge of the cemetery, Bear still rattling off
updates in his ear, he looked back. Mancone's nameless sister was in the
same position on her knees before the gravestone, hands folded calmly
in her lap.

11

Photos of Sinners and deeds, taken at the afternoon funeral, already plastered the command post's walls. Every few minutes a deputy would get up from a computer monitor and tack another paper name tag beneath a picture. Everyone worked diligently except for Jeff Malane, who stood in the corner speaking furtively into his cell phone as if conferring with a bookie.

The clear shots Tim had captured of Den's deed were clustered on the bulletin board at the head of the table. From his fleeting glimpses at the cemetery, Tim hadn't recognized how beautiful she was. Lush brown hair, center-parted and flipped back from a face that was paradoxically tough and delicate. Angry cheekbones, pulled even higher by a squint. An elegant bridge of a nose that banked into a surprising pug. Shiny irises, almost cobalt. She could've been the eye candy in a rock-ballad video.

Most of the other deeds and all the slags had been identified already and matched to addresses and jobs. Wristwatch Annie's given name was Tracy White. She'd been busted a few times on prostitution beefs, free-lancing for Sinner-owned massage parlors, but she'd graduated to club-house den mother. Some rumors had her as a pro on the side, but by most accounts she was merely a slut.

The striker and his mystery date remained unidentified. Guerrera hung enlarged details from his photos—armband and pinkie ring—beside his full depiction.

Tim finished scanning the updates and stood. "Gimme your attention for a minute here." The tapping on keyboards stopped. Phone receivers pressed against chests. "Sheriff's has the case, but that doesn't mean that the Palmdale massacre isn't our responsibility. Thirty-seven men were murdered." He didn't like the set of some of the faces looking back at him. "I don't care if they *were* one-percenters. They were murdered, and they were murdered by fugitives. And that means it happened on our watch. So I don't care if the victims are outlaw bikers or a slaughtered convent of nuns"—at this, Guerrera stiffened—"we do our jobs here, and we do them well." Tim pointed at the photos. "Let's carve up the names, shake some cages, and see what falls out."

His colleagues rustled back to work, the command post cranking into motion like an elaborate windup toy. Tim huddled with Guerrera and Bear at the end of the conference table.

"Media attention's through the roof," Bear said. "This is the second-biggest mass murder in California history."

"What's number one?"

"Jedediah Lane's attack on the Census Bureau. Heard of it?"

"Vague recollection." Tim blew out a breath. "We've got a major gang-war blowout. That, the public will see, hear, and feel. Tannino and the mayor are in press-conference hell right now. We've gotta stay focused on the case, keep fielding the grounders." He turned to Guerrera. "You find anything on Lash yet?"

"The Sinner who got his colors taken back?" Guerrera waited on Tim's nod. "We put it out on the street, but nothing so far."

"I want you to run Danny the Wand through the moniker database, too. The guy's clearly got close ties to the club."

Bear, contending with a burrito leak, took a moment to respond. "Already did. Got nothing. Thomas and Freed are working it, checking out bike paint stores, all that shit."

Tim turned to Guerrera. "Can we expect big-league retaliation from the Cholos?"

"This afternoon seems like the club's final coffin nail. Palmdale was the mother chapter, by far the biggest. Cholo ranks are already thinned from the war. I'd be surprised if they muster any real retaliation. The Sinners are too powerful. Especially now."

"What's the motive to wipe out an entire club?"

"*Odio.*"

"Just hate?"

"There's no 'just' about hate, *socio*. Not among bikers."

Tim was about to express his skepticism when Thomas racked a phone and hopped up from his computer. "Our mystery deed just rang the cherries over at the Fillmore Station. Babe Donovan." He spun the monitor to show off the JPEG of her mug shot. "She got popped for possession six months ago, squirmed off with a little help from Dana Lake. And—get *this*—she works for the DMV."

"ID heaven," Freed said.

Tim felt a rush of adrenaline, and he slowed himself down, thinking out the steps. "We'll get a warrant cleared, have ESU track her user name through the DMV system whenever she logs on. If she makes any fraudulent licenses, we let 'em walk. We'll catch up to our guys in a hurry if we know what fake names they're using."

"If she was gonna generate false IDs, she would've done it by now," Thomas said. "She's been there three months. I doubt she'd be dumb enough to wait until *after* the break to make a move."

Tim shot a look at Frisk. His favored ESU inspector angled back a thin scowl; he still hadn't forgiven Tim for the gymnastic ride in the back of the van during the chase. "Roger?"

"DMV's a mess. We can probably regulate her from here on out, but it's doubtful we'd be able to get clear records on her prior activity. The technology over there is archaic, plus retardation is a job requirement. Ever wonder why it takes six months to process a license?"

A court security officer stuck his head around the partition that separated the phone banks. "Rack? Uncle Pete on line four."

The command post fell silent.

"Okay, send it in here." Tim waited for the phone in front of him to blink, and he took a deep breath, hit the speaker button. "Yeah?"

"Howdy-do, Trouble. Nice move on the munici*pal* permission. Getting our helmets off so you could snap pictures." Pete tut-tutted a bit. "I got some moves up my sleeve, too."

"So we saw."

"You're a tricky dog, Trouble. I'm gonna keep an eye on you."

"Right back at you, big guy."

"Here I thought you came by the clubhouse just to give me a little static. But you had this whole other plan working all the while. Imagine that. Hmm, hey—too bad about them Cholos. El Viejo got hisself *el muerto*, huh?"

His gravelly laughter cut off abruptly when he hung up the phone.

12

Each deputy took six names and a loaded gun. The task force had managed to tie most of the mother-chapter Sinners and deeds to a place of employment or a gas or phone bill. The key was closing in on the nomads' likely hideouts—garages, safe houses, family members' spare couches, utility sheds at Sinner-affiliated businesses.

Tim's first stop was at a renovated apartment complex in Fillmore. He circled the surrounding blocks in the government-owned Buick Regal, looking for parked choppers and finding none. The apartment was at the interior of the well-lit complex—too bright and tough on the getaway to make an ideal hiding place. A peek through various windows confirmed that both bedrooms and bathroom were empty. In the living room, a young woman—the roommate?—sat sullenly on a poufy couch, watching a *CHiPs* rerun and plucking at the hem of a flannel bathrobe. The carpet was strewn with clothes.

Tim knocked, standing on the knob side until the door opened.

"Hi. Tom Altman, building code inspector. I'm investigating some lease irregularities. You are . . . ?"

The girl looked unimpressed with Tim's badge and air of urgency. "Sonia Lawrence."

He furrowed his brow. "I thought this apartment was leased to a Babe Donovan?"

"Yeah, I sublet a room from her."

"Is she home?"

"She's never around. She just leaves her crap here. It's *everywhere.* Look at this. Drives me nuts."

"She *does* live here?"

Sonia coughed out a laugh, making her bangs jump. "*You* can try and keep tabs on Babe Donovan. I gave up that gig a long time ago."

"When's the last time you saw her?"

"You just missed her. She dropped by to pick something up. There some problem with the place?"

"No. She just didn't return some paperwork we requested, and I wanted her John Hancock. Do you know where she went? The deadline for the documents is tomorrow. I really don't want to have to designate the place as unsafe for habitation."

The roommate looked anxious. "She asked if I wanted to go over to the Rock Store. You know, that biker hangout up in the Malibu hills? She took me once. I don't get the deal with that place."

"You said she dropped by to pick something up?"

"Yeah. A big envelope."

Containing falsified IDs from the DMV? If Babe *had* managed to mole out IDs, there was at least faint hope she hadn't gotten them to Den yet. He and Kaner had just broken out yesterday.

"Maybe that was the paperwork I need. She take it with her?"

"Uh-huh."

"Any writing on it?"

"I didn't *read* the envelope."

"She say she was coming back tonight?"

"Doubtful. I probably won't see her for another couple weeks. That's how she is."

"Thanks for your time."

"Wait. If you don't catch up to her, then what? You're not gonna kick us out, are you?"

"Hope not. I'll see if I can have the building owner's lawyer sign off on the forms first thing tomorrow. I was trying to save myself from having to deal with lawyers."

"You catch up to her, remind her to leave rent money for next month."

"I'll be sure to."

A few Hells Angels sporting mad-dog goatees and trademark winged death's head originals swigged beer and smoked joints on the picnic table in front of the Rock Store. The hundred or so weekend warriors on hand kept a respectful distance. The out-of-the-way Malibu haunt, touted on T-shirts and beer cozies as "America's #1 Pit Stop," drew a bizarre amalgam of customers—leather-jacket losers, bad-boy movie actors, stockbrokers on crotch rockets. A biker paraphernalia shop made up the front of the stone-composite building; the structure rambled upslope, transforming into a burger-and-beer shack that overlooked a cracked patio. Most of the bikers congregated on the throw of concrete alongside the shack or by the spotted oak that fronted the adjoining building, the pit stop's greasy-spoon diner.

Tim worked his way through the crowd and completed a circuit of the raised patio, doing his best to dodge white plastic lawn furniture and body odor. He spotted Babe sitting on the railing sipping at a Bud bottle, her eyes on the dark canyon road that twisted past the storefront. Solo headlights floated in from the surrounding nothingness, joining the neon glow. Bikers docked, drank their fill, and shoved off drunkenly, braving the tortuous landscape. A few guys in wheelchairs banged off hips and tables. Babe drew more than her fair share of looks, but men aborted their approaches when they spotted her colors.

Tim grabbed a beer and leaned against the forked tree that interrupted the narrow front lot. At his back, tear-tab flyers fluttered from the bark—discount oil coolers, cheap chrome finishes, contingent-fee paralegal services. The post gave him a good vantage on Babe. Her continued focus on incoming traffic heartened him. Trouble was en route. He leaned back against the tree to feel the reassuring press of his .357 at his right kidney. An hour and a half passed tediously and without consequence.

A guy with a weirdly full build lumbered toward him, threw a leg over a Roadster, and dug into a gut bomb of a burger, grease running down his wrist until he licked it off. Tim observed him, noting the tan knuckle spots from the gloves, the strip of worn leather on his left boot where he shifted.

The biker shot Tim a grin full of crooked teeth. "Wanna take a ride?"

It took Tim a moment to piece together the surprisingly high voice, the full hips, the massy chest. "Oh, no thanks. I'm waiting on some-one."

"Too bad." She had piercing green eyes and a thin nose, like a really pretty boy. "You don't come here much, huh?"

"Is it that obvious?"

"You're cute, that's all. I could spread you on a cracker."

He laughed. "I'm an impostor. I bought my way into the club. New Harley, can't ride it for shit. Thought I'd come down here and look at people who could."

Up on the patio, a couple blocked Babe's view, so she scooted down the railing to keep the road in sight. She grabbed someone by the sleeve and asked him something. The guy held out his watch, and she nodded her thanks. Tim was beginning to share her exasperation at waiting.

"Takes all kinds, the Rock Store does."

"A lot of one-percenters hang out here?"

"Nah, don't worry. Bikers here are mostly unaffiliated." She nodded at the crew toking up on the picnic table. "HA shows up now and again, but just to model the originals, make fun of the wannabes." She winked. "That'd be me and you and everyone else here."

"Cholos ever blow through here?"

"Not likely. Sinners do, whenever the heat's high. The heat don't think to look here because it ain't supposed to be an outlaw joint." On her toes, she backed up her Harley, careful to dodge the adjacent bikes. She screwed on her helmet, nodded at him, and took off into the dark of the canyon.

When Tim looked back up at the patio, Babe had a cell phone pressed to her face. She nodded a few times, then disappeared in the crowd. Tim came off his lean against the tree and picked her up de-scending the stairs. She walked with a slight limp, a new injury judging by her gingerly gait. Maybe she'd been the one to leap the Jersey barri-ers after leaving a smoking car blocking traffic on the 10, and maybe she'd twisted an ankle doing it. Tim heard Dray's voice, as he often did, playing devil's advocate: *Or maybe she hurt it stepping out of the tub.*

The Hells Angels noted Babe's property jacket and bumped fists with her as she passed. She walked directly at Tim. Nervous that he'd been made, he took a pull from the bottle to hide his face. She passed so close he could smell her shampoo—something lean and foresty—and then she mounted the Harley right next to him. Starting down the road for his car, he heard her kick-start her engine behind him. He was at the wheel when she drove past, but he waited for her brake light to disappear around the sharp bend before starting the tail. He followed her through a tangle of canyon roads, keeping that same distance.

At a wide bend, she slowed, and her free hand went inside her jacket. A manila envelope took flight, landing at the feet of a biker parked on the dirt apron. The biker crouched and flipped up his wind visor to peruse the envelope's contents.

Tim rolled through the turn, and his headlights swept across Den Laurey's face.

13

Tim hit the brakes, and for an instant the two men regarded each other through the windshield. The split second of shock passed, and then Tim's gun was out, the PA at his lips. Den hopped onto his bike, which faced the Buick.

"*Get off that bike now!*"

Den spun the Harley in a half circle, throwing up a sheet of dust. Breaking Service policy, Tim fired a warning shot out the open window. Den revved the engine but didn't take off. Finally he turned, the insect bulge of his helmet fixed on the gun pointed at his shoulders.

"*Turn off your motor. Throw your keys to your right. No—do* not *put down your kickstand!*"

Den remained on his tiptoes, forced to balance the weighty bike.

Tim alternated the PA with the push-to-talk mike of the dashboard Motorola. "Request immediate backup following high-risk motorcycle stop on Den Laurey."

The CSO responded from the comm center downtown, his voice ratcheting high with excitement. "Where are you?"

Tim paused, frustrated with himself. "The Malibu hills. I'm not sure exactly where—check my location with OnStar. Do we have any units available in Malibu or Simi?"

"Hang on, lemme see who's on the air."

Den bristled restlessly. Tim got back on the PA. *"Take off your helmet. Throw it to the right. Now!"* The helmet bounced once and rolled a few feet down the slope.

The CSO came back in his ear: "It's a twenty-minute ETA."

"Then contact the watch commander at the Malibu/Lost Hills Sheriff's Station, give him my bearings, tell him to get a few units up here ASAP. This won't wait."

"Ten-four."

Tim eased out of the car and stood, both hands on the .357, his wrists resting on the V created by the open door. A faint breeze blew musky canyon smells across his face—sage, eucalyptus, dirt, and leaves commingled in a marijuana-like sweetness. Despite the December night, his neck tingled with sweat. Due to the sudden nature of the encounter, Tim hadn't been able to locate the stop to his advantage. The curve left blind road in front of and behind them. At the edge of his vision ahead, the narrow road split three ways. Through traffic would be disruptive— and provide Den opportunities.

A knucklehead engine powered Den's Harley cutaway, the row of bulky nuts on the right side sticking up like an iron fist. The front wheel was barely raked out, maybe a few degrees, flame-decorated extensions lengthening the front fork.

Holding a shooting stance, Tim slowly approached. Den shifted slightly, his right leg tensing to take more of the bike's weight. Tim froze, a red flag rising. His eyes picked over Den's back and the motionless bike.

Crosshairs had been etched on the left rearview mirror. The left grip, pointing back at Tim, terminated in a hole, the bore of a jerry-rigged shotgun hidden in the handlebar.

Tim shuffled quickly to the side, out of the scatter radius, holding the gun on Den's head.

"Put down your kickstand. *Put it down!* Dismount on your right. On your *right.*"

Den had to turn unnaturally to dismount on the wrong side, presenting Tim with a full view of his body and hands. His road-filthy jacket didn't feature the more visible rockers and flaming skull on the back, but the front bore his markings, safe from the view of drivers. A scattering of upside-down cop patches for the officers the nomads had killed. The ubiquitous 1% triangle. A rectangular in-memory-of patch,

NIGGER STEVE written in block letters. Tim felt his stomach tighten when he took in the two upside-down U.S. Marshals Service patches, not yet dulled by road wear.

Den's face, bearing a few days' stubble, remained relaxed. He offered a disarming smile. "This ain't gonna end well for you."

The sight of the patches had put a charge into Tim; he did a poor job keeping the anger from his voice. "Turn around. On your knees. Lace your hands behind your head. Good boy, you know the drill." He eased forward, holding his .357 steady, his other hand going to the cuffs at his belt.

Den's shoulders started shaking, and then Tim heard a low, ticking chuckle.

The crackle of a Harley engine disrupted the night. Then another. Within seconds two Harleys materialized, skidding up on the dirt plateau to flank Den protectively. The helmeted drivers, like Den, wore plain leathers in place of their originals. The larger of the two—Kaner—showed off arms covered with ink, the Illustrated Man on growth hormones. Double-looped around his neck hung an impeccably cleaned motorcycle drive chain. Its silver links, unblackened by grease, were surprisingly elegant. Whereas Den radiated quiet menace, Kaner was all brute force—head-on posture, wide fighter's stance, chin pulled back over blocklike shoulders as if he'd just reared up to his nearly seven feet.

A spill of white hair collected at his partner's collar beneath the helmet—Tom-Tom the towhead.

They were too close, almost right on top of Tim. His voice came out hoarse. "*Hands up! Hands up!*"

His eyes flicked to Den's discarded helmet, the tentacle of a wire mike floating below the visor to provide hands-free radio communication with the other bikers. The nomads were traveling close for protection but riding separate to stay inconspicuous.

The night chill filled Tim's nostrils, his lungs. Keeping his gun level at Den's head, he began a cautious retreat to his car—the distance would give him a better shot at holding all three in his scope. When the other bikers moved, Tim jerked the gun to cover them, and they held up their hands casually, as if amused.

"Lugathat," Tom-Tom said. "Guess he's got the sitwayshun under control."

The sound of two more bikes approaching, this time from behind Tim, sped his pace. He ducked behind his open door, reaching for the mike of his radio as the bikes swept past. They stopped about ten yards back from the others, where Tim couldn't effectively cover them. Another Harley and an Indian. Chief's helmet tilted in mock greeting. The bikers turned off their engines, one after another, until the night held only a dizzying silence and a few crickets scratching their legs disharmoniously. Four helmeted heads pointed at Tim intently, the alien, eyeless stares of the dark wind visors projecting threat.

Tim heard his breath as an echo in his chest, his gun flashing left and right as he tried to keep everyone pinned down. When he spoke into the radio, he could hear the slight tremor in his voice. "I have all the Sinner nomads here. Repeat: *all* the Sinner nomads. I'm outnumbered and need backup *immediately*."

Den lowered his hands and rose from his knees, keeping his back to Tim. His breath fogged over his shoulder. He turned slowly, his profile cut cleanly from the glow of Kaner's headlight.

"Sheriff's gave me a ten-minute ETA." The CSO sounded a touch panicked himself. "That's the quickest we got, Rack. Want me to stay on with you?"

Tim released the mike, the coiled cord sucking it back across the seat.

He sighted on Den's critical mass, but the others in his periphery were moving, and there was nothing he could do about it.

Kaner tugged the drive chain from his neck and wrapped it once around his forearm like a flexible bludgeon. Tom-Tom pulled the sissy bar free from his bike, its filed points rising into view, and wielded it like a double lance. The red road flare latched to Chief's frame transformed into a pipe shotgun in his hands. Goat slid off his bike, twisting his gas cap to reveal the hunting knife welded to the inside. Tim swung his gun over to Chief, who had the only firearm, but then a handgun appeared at Den's side, pressed to his thigh.

Tim lowered himself against the hinge of the open door, presenting as small a target as possible. Figuring he'd die either way in an exchange of shots, he aimed his .357 at Den. If lead started flying, he'd rather take out the head man before going down. Imminent death registered as a throbbing at his temples and wrists. He felt his desire to pull the trigger as a craving, maddeningly reined in by thoughts of his family and the loathsome necessity of thinking tactically in a blood standoff.

They squared off, no one eager to start the fireworks.

Then the Sinners pulled back to their bikes, Chief and Den keeping their weapons aimed at Tim's head. As desperately as Tim wanted the takedowns, he weighed the situation. There was no imminent threat to a civilian. If the nomads continued their ordered retreat, his life wasn't at risk. If he initiated a gunfight, he'd be able to take out one nomad at most, and at high cost.

Rather than search for his keys, Den threw a switch on his bike, bypassing the ignition—another design trick to catch law enforcement off guard. The bikes fired up, one after another, and they were off in a cloud of smoke. They spread at the fork like a squadron breaking formation and faded into the darkness, dispersing through the hillside.

Tim took off after the last bike, getting back on the radio. "I lost them. Alert every agency. Send manpower. Redirect the units that are en route. These canyons are a sieve—let's do our best to seal them off. And get the Chippies out all over the surrounding highways in case they make it out." He rattled off Den's license-plate number and spit a gob of cottoned saliva out the window. "He's without a helmet, but the others have them on. They're wearing plain black leathers, riding chopped hogs—four Harleys and an Indian. They're traveling alone but staying in the same vicinity. They're armed and dangerous. They have weapons in their possession and built in to their bikes. Do not approach them on their bikes. And do not approach without backup."

Only when he clicked off did he note his heart double-thumping with adrenaline. He tried to slow his breathing, but every few minutes a motorcycle whined past, heading for the Rock Store, quickening his pulse. He fought the convoluted landscape, chased down a few bikers for a closer look, returned to search the dirt apron, all the while updates pouring in on federal and local frequencies. Nothing and more nothing.

When he glanced at the clock, forty-five minutes had passed. By now the nomads could've wound their way free of the canyons or holed up in a safe house within the maze of roads. The night air smelled of brush and distant smoke. The Buick pushed an orb of light before it, seeming to generate the road it was driving on. The canyons grew quiet, but Tim continued to navigate, his nerves frayed, the radio abuzz, his apprehension growing.

Near the hour mark, a shaken sheriff's dispatcher radioed in to advise that a pregnant deputy in Moorpark had been shot point-blank in the chest.

14

He didn't remember turning the car around or the drive to the hospital. He didn't remember parking or the walk across the ambulance bay. His first flash of cognizance came when Bear appeared in the emergency-room lobby, running toward him, gear jangling on his belt.

Bear halted, winded; his voice was high. "She called in a high-risk stop."

Tim felt his veins go to ice. "Who?" he asked, though he already knew.

"Den Laurey."

Tim's vision narrowed again. When he came out of it, a doctor was midsentence with Bear, thin hand on his chest to stop his advance through the swinging doors. A nurse at Tim's side was trying to comfort him with facts, but he couldn't quite keep up with the words. "—medevacked her. We're the closest trauma center with a helipad—"

He looked around blankly. "Where are we?"

The nurse's face registered concern. "UCLA Medical Center."

Bear lifted the doctor by both shoulders, moved him out of his way, and set him back down. The security guard took one look at Bear and stayed in his seat but kept his hand on the phone. Tim followed Bear through the doors, down the sterile corridor.

Bear froze up ahead, peering through the windowed doors to Procedure Room Two. Filled with dread, Tim drew to his side and looked through the glass.

Surrounded by nurses and doctors, Dray lay naked, her pallid skin smeared with blood. The blue tint of the fluorescents and her position—supine, elevated, focal—gave the scene a religious aspect. A fat needle stuck out an inch below her left clavicle, and a web of blackening blood glittered on her side. Her brilliant green eyes were cloudy, or maybe it was just the lighting.

Tim heard the shuffle of boots walking in unison—the approach of the guards—but he couldn't tear his eyes off his wife. One of the doctors glanced up, then stepped away, moving toward them. He shot his gloves on the way through the doors and stepped between Bear and the guards. "I got it fellows." When he pulled down his mask, Tim recognized him as the doctor who'd treated him last year. As the guards backed off, the doctor shot Bear a stern look. "Behave yourself and you can stay back here. *Don't* go in that room."

He took Tim's arm and drew him into an empty exam room. He started with details and hard facts—a good read on what Tim required right now.

"She took a blast from a twelve-gauge, double-aught buck. The vest absorbed the brunt of it, but a pellet got through the armhole, penetrated beneath her breast at the fourth intercostal. It pierced the pleura, the sac surrounding the lung, and caused the lung to collapse." He moistened his lips. "When the paramedic got to her, she wasn't breathing. Unresponsive, no pulse, blood pressure was at fifty. He bagged her and did a needle decompression in the field, but she'd been down for a while. She didn't have oxygen to her brain for seven, maybe eight minutes. There might be brain insult."

Tim took it standing. The doctor gave him a moment to digest this, waiting for his eyes to pull back into focus.

"She may have had some hypoxic injury while she was down. The CAT looks okay, but it's a wait-and-see."

"She stable?"

"She is now. We put in a chest tube. And she started breathing on her own—clear airway, good breath sounds. But the chest tube put out some blood, and she's not waking up. Because she's pregnant, she has a lower resting blood pressure to begin with. . . ." He wiped his forehead with the abbreviated sleeve of his scrub top. "We did an ultrasound, and the baby's heartbeat is regular. We want to keep the baby inside her, but we need to know. . . . If an operation is required and we think we might lose your wife on the table, do you want us to perform an emergency C-section or devote our full resources to your wife first?"

Tim tried to think of what Dray would want but heard himself say, "Devote your full resources to my wife." He put his hand on the exam table just to make sure he had hold of something solid and unyielding. "If you lose her, can you still . . . ?"

"Perform a postmortem C-section? Yes. But let's hope we don't wind up there." The doctor rested a hand on Tim's shoulder. "I heard about what happened. Your stopping the bikers."

"They put it out over the PA?"

"The deputies were talking." He regarded Tim heavily. "You can play the guilt game—" He opened his mouth, closed it, wiped his lips with his hand though there was nothing to wipe. "I lost my first wife. You can play that game until you've got nothing left to play with." When Tim didn't respond, the doctor took a little step back, angling toward the door. "I'm going to go check on her. Want me to leave you in the room?"

"For a moment."

"We're going to do everything we can."

"I know. Thank you, Doctor."

Only a few concrete images emerged from the haze of the next few hours. Tim's colleagues popping by in shifts. Quiet voices, shy eyes. Tim nodding and nodding to the repeated pronouncement, uttered like a verdict, "It wasn't your fault." Guerrera and Zimmer in the back, discussing leads in whispered tones as if the topic weren't appropriate. Dray's four brothers harassing doctors and flashing badges until the oldest collapsed into a chair, ham-size fists pressing into his sweaty face. Mac pacing in the waiting room, stuck in a loop—"I just *saw* her at the doughnut joint. Happy's? I just *saw* her." Mac's and Fowler's sheriff's deputy uniforms recalling Dray's, cut to tatters beneath her gurney.

Finally the doctor came out and brought Tim up to the ICU, hand on his back, a priest leading the condemned. Tim sat in the bedside chair and stared dumbly at his wife. Beneath her gown her belly thrust up, round and firm. A tube ran from the hole in her chest into a bubbling machine that sounded like a bong. Vaseline-impregnated gauze

hid the sutures, but a few peeked out, shiny and black like the antennae
of some hidden insect. Her legs were sticky and smelled faintly of
urine. Her knees were pressed together and laid to the side in a way she
never would have held them. It seemed grotesque—someone else posi-
tioning her knees, her limbs. What *was* a person other than how she
held herself?

All of a sudden, steaming at the joints and burning through the
shock, it came. Rage.

*Rising, making his way past his colleagues, down the hall, into the bath-
room. Leaving his badge behind on a closed toilet tank, stepping onto the lid,
pulling himself up and through the window. Purpose quickening his step
through the parking lot, the night sharp at the back of his throat.*

*Dray leans against his car, arms crossed, a knowing smile touching her
lips. "I'm a sheriff's deputy, Timothy. It comes with the job. You don't get to be
stupid about this."*

Poleaxed, gun hand hanging limp at his side.

*She studies him, reading his answer in his eyes. Then she laughs. "You're
not gonna get those fuckers for me. No way. That's a prescription for incompe-
tence. You're gonna get them because they need to be got."*

Tim's eyes narrowed at the sound. Tannino's voice.

"—anonymous tip saved her life. Otherwise she would've lain there
for God knows how long." Tannino checked Dray's pulse as if he knew
what he was doing, his olive fingers nestled paternally alongside her
throat. Working his lower lip between his teeth, Bear crouched at Tim's
side.

Think, Tim. Where were they going?

"Moorpark's a long way from the Rock Store," Tim said. "They ran
the canyons and back roads, probably. Mulholland, Topanga, Box. Too
many holes to plug in those hills. You only need a few brief spurts on
freeways. You can pop out high on the 118, gets you on your way north
keeping you out of L.A. County."

"What's north?" Tannino asked.

Tim and Bear said in unison, "The mother chapter."

"You think they went there?"

"Nah, they wouldn't take heat to the club," Bear said. "Safe houses
up around there, most likely. We've put all local units on high alert."

Tim realized he'd been clenching his jaw; he released it, felt the
ache deep in his teeth. Tannino watched him, releasing a sigh that said

his insides hurt. "There's no way you could've known. I'm sure you're telling yourself otherwise, but you did the right thing on that stop." He ran a hand up his face, over his head, his gold wedding band glittering in his dense hair. "We need live heroes. Dead ones only work for public relations." He bit his lip, possibly regretful of his choice of maxim.

Tim felt the pull of sorrow, but again Dray's voice cut through it like a blade. *What's the next step?*

"Get the video," Tim said. "From Dray's car."

"Right," Tannino said. "We'll have a copy ASAP."

He and Bear withdrew, leaving Tim alone with his wife.

15

He woke up fully clothed on his and Dray's bed, the morning light angling through the blinds directly into his eyes. The clock showed 6:27 A.M.; he'd slept an hour and a half, having stayed with Dray until the night-shift nurse's kind invocations of the visitation rules grew stern. He lay motionless, a wrinkle of fabric pressed up against his mouth, as last night replayed in his head. His headlights illuminating Den's face. The five bikes peeling out in formation, kicking up dirt. The spray of Dray's hair across the gurney, as if she'd fallen there from some great height.

Despair overtook him, and for a moment he was certain he couldn't move.

Get up.

He raised his head.

Shower. Eat.

"I'm not hungry, Dray," he managed.

I don't care. We've done this before. You can do it now. I promise.

He pulled himself to a sitting position, placed his hands on his knees. After a few minutes, he rose and showered. He stood before the mirror afterward, steam swirling around him, and gazed at his reflection. He lacked the crisp good looks that had served his father well on so many cons; Tim's more generic brand of handsomeness was better suited to undercover work. Now his features were slack, expressionless. He told himself to towel off, and a moment later he obeyed.

Standing over the kitchen sink, he forced some cereal down his throat. The faucet dribbled, and he fussed with it as fruitlessly as usual; the leak abated only when the handle achieved a resting angle known to no one but Dray. Every time the phone rang, his heart pounded, anticipating the hospital telling him his wife had died. And every time it wasn't the hospital. The command post. *L.A. Times* telemarketer. Bear.

He looked in on the nursery. They'd dutifully sanded and repainted Ginny's crib until, aggravated by the symbolism, they'd returned it to the garage rafters and picked up a cheery new one at Babies "R" Us. He glanced from the empty crib across the hall to the master bedroom and thought, quite simply, This is where my family goes.

He returned to the bedroom to claim his Smith & Wesson from the safe. He housed it in his right hip holster, then strapped a Spec Ops–issue P226 nine mil to his ankle for Onion Field insurance. He taped a handcuff key under his watch for easy access in case he was taken hostage, a precaution he'd implemented since spending some quality time with cult leadership in a locked maintenance closet last April. He preferred to exclude the handcuff key from his key chain anyway; it was as much a giveaway to alert eyes as a magnetic plate on the dash for a Kojak light. Before leaving, he made the bed army style—boxed corners, quarter-bounce smooth.

His Marshals star lay on the kitchen table by the files where he'd dropped it on his stumble to the bedroom last night. After all the time he'd put in to reclaim it, now he found himself in the one position where he didn't want it. He regarded the silver-plated brass. A love-hate relationship, to say the least.

Pick it up. You carry that badge. To remind you.

He lifted the badge, slid it into his back pocket. It tugged uncomfortably.

He flipped open the top file, and Den Laurey stared up at him from his booking photo. Flat eyes like skipping stones. The broad, playful mouth of a rock singer. Dark hair wiry at the sideburns. Tim stood perfectly still as the sun inched up behind the Hartleys' pines and cast the kitchen in a faint gray light.

He spoke softly to the flat eyes, his voice little more than a murmur. "Pray she lives."

16

The command post hushed when Tim stepped through the door. Zimmer's hand went to the laptop keyboard, and the projected image vanished from the wall. A few deputies mumbled greetings; the others got busy in the field files. Malane was absent, a minor blessing, as Tim was in no mood to stomach FBI-Service friction. He spotted the empty jewel case beside the computer.

Tim sank into a chair between Bear and Guerrera and said, "Go on."

Zimmer reluctantly clicked a button. The CD rasped into motion inside the laptop, throwing the footage from Dray's patrol car back onto the opposing wall. The vehicle cam, mounted in the center rearview, activated automatically when the overheads turned on, providing a panoramic windshield shot.

A bumpy view as she pulled to the side of the desolate highway, Den riding trapped in the spotlight in front of her. Dray had been able to make the ID only because Tim had ordered Den to toss his helmet at the last stop—a stroke of luck soon to go bad.

Dray keyed a few bursts on the siren to make sure Den got the point, and then her voice came loud over the PA: "Pull over! Motor off! Hands up!"

Her nervous breathing was audible as she sat for a moment, gathering her adrenaline for the approach. A vicious barking exploded over the PA system. Dray kept a recording of a German shepherd in her car to deter arrest resistance when she patrolled alone. She pretended to soothe the dog, then the car rocked a bit, and they heard the sound of a door opening, Dray's boot setting down on gravel.

Dread sat like a medicine ball in Tim's gut.

Dray finally stepped into view in the spotlight's fringe, all muscle and belly, gripping her Beretta with both hands. As her pregnancy had advanced, Tim had objected to her working a squad car alone, but her arguments had already been sharpened against her reluctant captain. Her station was short on manpower and long on casework, and Dray was short on patience for special treatment and long on obduracy.

Her olive green baseball cap sported a molded bill and a Ventura County Sheriff's badge. Blond hair shot out in clean strokes behind her ears. She lumbered toward the bike. "That's it. Keep those hands up. Step *off* the bike."

The engines scarcely gave warning before four bikes materialized from the darkness, two from each direction, pulling tight around Den. The nomads' security travel formation, as Tim had learned last night, was geared for precisely this contingency. The bikers angled their mirrors away so the spotlight wouldn't blind them. Den alone squinted into his rearview, braving the glare to keep the bore of the handlebar shotgun sighted.

Dray stopped, caught halfway between Den and her vehicle. Tim registered her fear in the slight crouch of her posture. The knowledge of how she felt and what was coming made his breathing quicken to match hers. He'd been in precisely the same position an hour before she was. Bear raised a hand halfway to his eyes as if unsure whether he wanted to cover them.

The other bikers wore helmets, but Tim could tentatively identify Chief, Tom-Tom, and Goat from their builds and postures. The fourth, too slender to be Kaner, wrestled off his helmet, revealing a familiar sallow face framed by ragged hair. The elastic eye-patch strap indented his hair on either side. He shifted, and the armband came into view, as well as the gaudy pinkie ring. The striker. Either they'd picked him up en route to Moorpark or he'd hung back out of view during the nomads' encounter with Tim.

The striker's words barely reached the camera mike: "You'd better back off, bitch."

"Get back to the car, Andrea," Tim said sharply under his breath, drawing a few glances from around the table.

"Hands up. *All* of you. You, too." Dray eased back a few steps, her shoulders to the camera. Tim found himself, dumbly, hoping for her safe retreat.

The crackle of gravel was barely audible as an additional bike rolled up, out of the camera's view. Kaner?

Dray's head snapped back, offering a clean profile over her right shoulder. She tracked the phantom bike forward as it passed her car, then her present position. Judging from the angle of her head, the bike stopped on the shoulder to the right of the others, just out of the camera's scope. She kept her eyes on the phantom bike, her gun on the cluster of men in front of her.

Her tone was authoritative; probably Tim alone could tell it lacked her usual confidence. "Okay. Stay still. Relax." It seemed she was speaking as much to herself as to the Sinners.

Tim made a noise of frustration, rubbed his mouth, let his fist fall to the table. He silently urged her to turn tail, to seek cover in the car as he had. The guy with the armband shouted at her, "Get the fuck outta here!"

"I'm not going without—" Her words were drowned out by a refrigerator truck barreling obliviously by in the near lane, its aluminum side catching the spotlight and bleaching out the footage. She was facing away, making lipreading impossible.

She tightened her grip on the Beretta, steeling herself. Den's right foot dropped, bracing for the recoil. His face remained a tan smudge in his mirror, etched with the nearly invisible crosshairs.

A drawn-out moment as Dray made her decision. She studied the phantom biker, her cap casting her eyes in shadow. Her jaw firmed. Her mouth tensed.

She moved forward toward the unseen bike, her second step bringing her into Den's range. A flame leapt from his left grip. Dray was already airborne by the time the boom hit the camera mike. She left her hat and one boot behind. Her hair fanned up and out as if on an underwater descent. Her foot was bent at the ankle as if broken, but floating two feet off the ground.

A drift.

And then she struck asphalt. Her pants were stained at the crotch; her bladder had released on impact.

The others' eyes made Tim suddenly aware that he was cringing back in his chair, turned almost sideways, one arm raised off the table. He fought his shoulders square, forced his posture straight.

Den blew a kiss at the camera. The Sinners laughed and fired up their engines. Den jerked his head at Dray's body, then called something to the phantom biker, his words lost in the engines' roars. They motored off, debris from their wheels showering her body. Engine noise seemed to indicate that the unseen bike circled around the back of the car and took the dark left lane of the highway, still clear of the camera's field.

A sudden quiet, broken only by the static-filled inquiries of the watch commander. A trickle of blood from Dray's ribs formed a pool that grew to a certain width and stopped.

Someone coughed uncomfortably. Jim rose and left the semidark room. After a pause, Haines and Maybeck followed. Tim sat and watched his wife's sprawled form for the entire eight minutes until the paramedics arrived.

Finally he said, "I want a name for the prick with the eye patch."

Bear's voice cracked, and he cleared his throat and tried again. "Okay."

The paramedics carried Dray offscreen. Tim's throat thickened.

What's this give you, Timothy? Come on, moping's not gonna get you to me.

Tim pressed his fingertips to the beads of sweat that had sprung up at his hairline.

It's a case like any other, or nothing gets done. Where do you start?

Tim's voice was dry, brittle. "What do we got on the anonymous tip?"

"A male voice, muffled," Bear said. "The call went in to a private line at the sheriff's station. No recording, no tracing."

Suspect, to say the least.

"Babe's an accomplice now," Tim said. "Put a local unit on the apartment. Shake up the roommate."

"We're running low on manpower," Bear said.

"Use the guy who sat on the Cholo clubhouse. I'm sure he's free now."

Freed gave a double take when Tim's meaning dawned.

Bear said, "Why would the mystery biker give a shit to avoid the camera? They're all known-and-wanteds. Den vamped for us, for Christ's sake."

Guerrera: "It's gotta be Kaner, no?"

"Maybe the mystery biker's not a fugitive," Thomas said. "Maybe that's why he's ducking his airtime."

"As far as we know, the striker's not a fugitive, but you didn't see *him* going back to pry the footage out of the trunk lockbox," Bear said.

"Whatever the reason," Tim said, "the other guy doesn't want to be seen."

Watch it again.

Tim took a deep breath and held it before exhaling. "Play it over."

Zimmer took it from the top, Tim doing his best to detach, to observe. The spotlight bleached out Den's face. The glossy flames licking the front fork were pristine, scratchless. Freshly painted? Tim's eye caught on the distinctive design. "We get anything back on Danny the Wand?"

Freed shook his head. "I'll stay on it."

"That's his work on that bike. Might be recent. Have ESU blow it up and check if there's any dirt or roadwear on the paint. Burn me a copy while you're at it. The whole thing."

Bikes resolving from the night. Dray's initial crouch, so much like a scared dog's. The truck's racket swallowing her words. Pellets dimpling her nylon jacket. Her weightless drift across the tarmac. Gravel spray. Growing pool.

Tim's stomach roiled. "Back," he said. "Again."

The truck passed again with the stubborn inevitability of a recurring dream. Den's leg tensed beneath his black jeans. Flame leapt from his fist. In slow motion Dray's brief flight looked almost peaceful.

"Hang on." Tim stood, moving closer to the image. "Back it up. Slow forward. There. Again. Give me a little more volume."

Zimmer moved the recording backward and forward. Tim stood mere feet from Den's mouth, reading its shapes as Den called out to the phantom biker over Dray's body. A few of his consonants were barely audible over the revving engines. Tim watched the segment over and over until he stiffened. He took a step away and eased himself into his chair.

"What'd he say?" Freed finally asked.

" 'We should practice on this heifer.' "

Dray lay on the road, one arm flung up over her head. The perfect stillness was disrupted only by the wind riffling her hair and the thin, dark stream of blood making its way languidly from her exposed side to the highway.

Guerrera ducked his head, and when he looked up at Tim, his eyes were shiny. "The way I see it, those boys just made the worst enemy they'd ever want to make."

"*If* Tannino lets you stay on," Thomas said directly to Tim.

"They'll let him stay on," Guerrera said angrily. "They have to."

Thomas's mustache bristled with the hidden movement of his lips. "Okay, kid."

Line four rang through, and Bear answered it, grunted, and put the receiver to his shoulder. He bobbed his head, resigned; he'd been expecting the call as much as Tim had. "The old man wants to see you."

17

Tim shoved through into Tannino's office, face red from the crisp walk across the quad. "Don't pull me off this case. I can nail these motherfuckers."

Tannino, angled with half an ass on the edge of his desk like an insurance salesman, kept his hands laced across his knee. "Rackley, please come in and say hello to the mayor." He lifted his dense eyebrows and tilted his head to Tim's right.

Tim turned, face still flushed, to take in the mayor. "Sir."

Strauss's eyes smoldered through the puffy skin surrounding them. Tim guessed that his own exhaustion looked as obvious. "I'm very sorry about your wife," Strauss said.

"Dray's a fine woman. Strong as hell." Tannino bobbed his head, emphatically agreeing with himself. He almost continued but stopped short of making foolish assurances.

"Listen," Tim said, "I know what you're both thinking."

Strauss's eyebrows rose, almost imperceptibly. "Maybe so, but I prefer to speak for myself just the same." He exhaled mightily through his nose, his flushed jowls tugging low at his jawline. "A city has certain barometers of fear. A good mayor keeps an eye on them to stay attuned to his constituents. In the two days since the media started screaming 'gang war,' firearm sales are up thirty percent. Guard-dog companies have run out of canines. Locksmiths are booked days out. Den Laurey and Lance Kaner are racking up more sightings than Elvis. We're fielding nearly two hundred tips an hour on the hotline—everything from looted TVs to girls snatched off street corners. Make no mistake, I'm aware that the Sinners represent a clear and present danger in their own right, but this has plugged in to something primitive in the people of this city. It's Jaws at Amity." He popped out his bottom lip with his tongue as if checking for stray bits of tobacco. "Our job is to assuage the fears of our citizens and extinguish this threat. As you well know, that takes a lot of feet on the streets. The Service's resources, the sheriff's department resources, LAPD's resources—they're all overextended."

"That's exactly what I'm trying to say. I'm a resource here." Tim's tone was driving, adamant. "We'll lose time getting someone else up to speed to take over. Don't reward their shooting Dray by burning those man-hours."

"As far as I'm concerned," Strauss said, and Tim's spirits sank at the finality of his tone, "if we drop a deputy from duty when a family member gets attacked, it'd be like advertising how to disrupt an investigation. We don't want to dangle that carrot in front of crooks and terrorists."

"Den and Kaner killed two of our boys," Tannino said. "This manhunt *is* personal already. It doesn't matter who takes it."

Strauss said, "There's no case to taint. The case has already been made. These are wanted, convicted felons, lawfully tried and sentenced. I—and the public—don't give a shit if you bring 'em in in cuffs or feet-first. I just want them off the street."

It took a moment for Tim's brain to catch up to the words. "So what are we arguing about?"

"You're the only one arguing here." Strauss angled his head toward the door. "Like I said, you're our Troubleshooter. Go shoot some trouble."

18

Bear plucked another heart off the skewer with his teeth. The charred smell of chicken over fire moistened the air. A bedsheet of a sign flapped by the entrance, featuring a minimalist chicken and the paintbrush-rendered name of the restaurant: Yakitoriya. Tim leaned back from the stick of chicken throats dividing his plate and gazed out at Sawtelle Boulevard, a strip of Japantown transplanted to the West Side.

Bear nudged Tim's untouched dish, concerned. "C'mon, now."

Tim tapped a smoked quail egg on the dab of four-alarm mustard coloring his plate and popped it in his mouth. Forced himself to chew, to swallow, to refuel. Dray had once eaten fifteen quail eggs in a sitting—Cool Hand Luke gone exotic. On his hurried final phone call with her, chicken neck had been her last request. It suited her better than the mythical staples—a T-bone, cigarette, apple pie.

Having endured the unendurable two years ago, he knew better than to indulge his grief. He knew he needed food to continue functioning, and he knew he didn't want to go home, so he'd let Bear drag him here, figuring he'd try to eat Dray's favorite meal for her rather than gag down hospital gruel.

He managed a few cubes of thigh meat and drank half his glass of water, doing his best to ignore the weight of the cell phone in his pocket. At any moment, the phone could ring. And she could be conscious again. Or not.

It chirped as if on cue, and Tim tensed. But when he fought it out of his pocket, the screen remained unlit. Then he noticed Bear snapping open his Nextel and felt foolish. Bear uh-huhed a few times at Freed in the command post and hung up.

Bear picked at a chicken throat, a tiny tube crisped like a french fry. "Back when I started, New York days, we worked the mobsters sometimes. They knew we were watching them, we knew they knew, but we managed. We made it work. We wouldn't bust a guy's balls until we had a case built. They never took a shot at one of us. Not once. We'd leave them alone on family outings. There was a kind of code." He used his skewer to impale one of his remaining quail eggs, the only time in Tim's memory he'd left food on his plate. "Mutts are getting too good at their jobs. No honor, no remorse, nothing. It's hard not to think things are getting worse. Bikers were losers, but they stood for something—or at least pretended to. The Angels stood for something. But the Sinners? I don't buy the gross-out biker veneer. It's costume design. Underneath it they're stone cold." He poked at the egg, again piercing its rubbery brown skin. "People don't stand for anything anymore."

The waiter asked in broken English if they wanted beer. They declined and sat quietly, flushed with the sting of mustard and the heat of the open grill.

Tim replayed his last conversation with Dray on the phone: *The captain needs someone to pick up a few overtime parole hours. . . . I'll take 'em if it'll be a late one for you.*

It will, he'd replied, sealing her fate.

"If I hadn't slowed them down," Tim said quietly, not lifting his eyes from his plate, "Dray wouldn't have pulled them over. They would've been fifteen minutes farther up the road. Den would've had his helmet on."

"It's not your fault."

"I didn't say it was. I'm saying chance is fucked."

Bear's eyebrow rose at the anger in Tim's voice.

"It would be great if I felt guilty. But I don't. I'm pissed off at her. Everyone keeps telling me I did the right thing. I *know* I did the right thing. You don't take down five outlaw bikers on a deserted road without backup." His voice was wobbling, and Bear looked on, horrified and starting to mist up himself. "She fucked up."

"Maybe she thought—"

"There's no 'maybe,' Bear. You know it, and I know it. She should've gotten her ass back to the squad car. It was just Dray being stubborn. What'd she say? 'I'm not going without taking you in'? What kind of cowboy bullshit is that?" He took a moment to be unabashedly furious with Dray, a solo, pregnant deputy failing to retreat from a lethal biker gang. He swore quietly, used the napkin to dry his face.

"Okay," Bear conceded. "It looks like an error in judgment. A bad one. Maybe she was more emotional. She *is* pregnant."

You gonna cuff him upside the head, or should I?

Tim felt a faint grin tense his lips, catching him off guard.

Bear furrowed his forehead. "What?"

"Being pregnant wouldn't have affected her judgment. You know Dray."

"Which means she had a reason." Bear met Tim's eyes evenly. "Something we're missing."

"You're right," Tim finally said.

Bear rose and threw down a few bills. They exited through the split fabric of the sign amid a chorus of Japanese farewells. Tim found the CD in the glove box, twirled it between his thumbs. The shooting of his wife preserved on 700 megabytes.

Bear looked from the CD to Tim's thoughtful face. "You thinking of calling him?"

"Yep." Tim pulled out his phone, dialed a mobile number.

The familiar voice answered. Tim explained his predicament.

"Sure, I'll look at the footage, but that's it. I don't go operational. I know how things got last time you took something personal—people getting their heads blown apart and shit. So remember: I don't fight. I don't shoot."

"It's not like that," Tim said. "I'm doing this on Service time."

"So why are you calling me?"

"Because you're the best."

No argument there. A pause. "Meet you in two hours."

"Where?"

But Pete Krindon had already hung up.

19

Mac sat nervously in a vinyl-upholstered chair by the door, his tousled hair and two-day stubble roughing out his appealing features. He stood at Tim and Bear's approach, hefting his gear-heavy belt and throwing a sigh that smelled of Clorets. As Dray's partner he was sometimes territorial; that he nursed a long-standing and hopeless crush on her didn't help ease tensions between him and Tim. Tim took a moment to smooth down his annoyance at the sight of this man sitting sentry outside his wife's room.

"Any change?" Tim asked.

Mac shook his head. "Nurse is with her now. But they're only letting in family."

Tim pushed on the doorknob. When Mac went to follow, Bear laid a thick hand on his shoulder.

"Can't I come in with you, Rack?"

"I'd rather be alone with her."

"Look, can I just—?"

"Not right now."

Sleeplessness and grief had left Mac looking loose and a touch unpredictable. He appeared to be working up a retort, but Tim slid past him into the room.

A nurse leaned over Dray, her arms moving industriously. Thumb on one lid, then the other, *click-click* of a pen flashlight. Over her shoulder: "Hello, Mr. Rackley."

Tim sank into the bedside chair. "Hi. Have we met?"

She turned, showing off her name tag, her jet-black hair twirled around a pen. "The night Andrea came in. We spoke a few times."

Beige liquid coursed up a clear plastic tube through Dray's nose and into her body. Her finger swelled into a pulse-oximeter. The cardiac monitor blipped deadeningly.

The nurse made a fist out of Dray's pliant hand and slid two fingers in. "Now, squeeze my fingers, Andrea. Go on and squeeze."

"She's Dray," Tim said, "unless you're mad at her."

The nurse smiled and tried again, using her nickname. She looked up and gave Tim a little head shake before jotting on a clipboard. When she finished, she used a moistened washcloth to wipe an iodine stain from Dray's forehead.

He worked up the courage to ask the question. "How's it look?"

"The doctor will be in to talk to you in a second."

Tim's vision went a little glassy. "I see." As the nurse walked past, he took her arm gently. "Thank you. For cleaning her face."

The doctor entered a moment later and greeted Tim warmly.

"No surgery," Tim said.

"That's the good news. The pellet is wedged against her rib cage at the back of the chest in the serratus anterior. It's not bothering anyone back there, so we're gonna leave it in her."

"What's the bad news?"

"The longer she stays unconscious . . ."

"Yeah?"

"The odds diminish."

"Of what?"

"Of her coming back. Or coming back easily. But it's not even been twenty-four hours. It's early yet."

"The baby?"

"By all indications the baby's healthy. Of course, this is a fragile situation. Do you know the sex?"

Tim shook his head.

"Do you want to?"

"No. We wanted to wait."

"Okay." The doctor paused at the door. "I'm sorry for what I said when you came in. When I talked about myself. I made some assumptions, and, frankly, my timing sucked. Husbands losing wives is a tough one for me. I'm sorry I didn't use better judgment."

"Believe me, I've used worse." Tim offered his hand, and the doctor took it. "I'm glad she's in your hands."

"I'll take care of her."

"Please."

The door clicked, leaving him with the headache beep of the monitor and the white noise of unseen moving parts. Dray's hair remained dark at the tips from dried sweat. Tim rested a hand on the mound of her stomach. His thoughts took him to the waiting crib in their nursery, and he remembered his first three weeks home with Ginny when C-section complications had left Dray hospital-bound. He tried to envision those three weeks of solo parenting stretched into eighteen years, and then he pictured not even having that option.

The thrill of their honeymoon, a four-day weekend in Yosemite he'd squeezed between deployments, had been heightened by his impending departure. The orange glow of moonlight filtered through tent nylon. Dray's form emerging from the flannel sheath of a sleeping bag. The muscles in her tapered back, arranged like river stones beneath her smooth skin. Her face smudged up against her shoulder so her cheek grew chins. A fall of lank hair split over her left eye. Tim tended hot—the exertion had overheated him—and he was sitting Indian style at her side, fingertip-tracing the dip between her shoulder blades.

Her voice was muffled by her shoulder. "How 'bout if I lost a leg?"

"No."

"Both arms?"

"Nope."

"Hysterical blindness?"

"We'd get through it together."

"Chronic halitosis?"

"We'd figure something out. Buy stock in Listerine."

"Hmm." Her eyes were closed; she moved toward his touch like a contented cat. "Would you divorce me if I started collecting Hummels?"

"No."

"God, you really took those vows literally. Just so *you* know"—with

exaggerated exertion she shoved herself up so she could look at him—
"one false move, I'm outta here, pal. I'm talking allergies, facial tics,
whistling while you pee, disfiguring scars, referring to yourself as 'this
guy,' bringing home sport-themed couch pillows—"

"I'll watch my step."

She hugged him at the waist and curled into him, suddenly serious,
inundated with feeling. She spoke to his ribs in a hot whisper. "I want
you to *always* be happy. If anything ever happens to me, you can marry
someone else."

She was twenty-two and new to emotion. He was twenty-five, convinced of his greater maturity, and invincible.

"Nothing's going to happen to you," he'd said.

Now her milky arm protruded from the papery gown, exposed to the
armpit. He lifted her hand. It came limply, as if detached. He ran his
thumb across her short-cut fingernails, then over the recent wrinkles that
pond-rippled from her middle knuckles. He pressed his face to the skin
at her inner wrist—the smell of her, disguised by hospital soap and sweat.
He slid his finger into her fist to feel the soft press of her skin all around
him. "Squeeze, Dray. Go on, squeeze."

He waited for the faintest pulse. He lowered his head, closed his
eyes, choked on a breath.

What are you doing here?

"Visiting you."

*Leave the hound-dog-at-the-grave routine to Mac. He's got nothing bet-
ter to do.*

"I wanted to see you."

*Great. Wring your hands. Rend your hair. Fall asleep on the visitor chair,
too—that one always looks good on TV movies. This isn't me. Come on. You
spent thirteen years enlisted, eleven with Spec Ops. You know better than to
sentimentalize this.*

"What do you want me to do?"

*She laughs, crow's-feet bunching around her impossible green eyes. Get out
there and bag some crooks.*

20

mbulances lined the unlit berths like worn-out predators. Tim and Bear walked through the dark underground bay, heading up the slope to the open air. A GMC Safari van waited in the turnaround circle up top, bubble lettering announcing DRAIN-CLEAR PLUMBING. Tim rested the heel of his hand on the butt of his hip-holstered gun. As they passed, the door slid open. Tim halted but didn't draw—too much like a bad South American kidnapping to occasion hard-edged concern.

Pete Krindon's voice issued from the dark interior. "Get in."

Tim and Bear stepped up into the van. Rim seating, carpeted walls, embedded surveillance screens, wires protruding from the torn-apart dash. Pete veered around the block, easing behind a Dumpster in a supermarket parking lot. He cut the engine and pivoted, his thin arm fish-white against the navy vinyl of the headrest. "Turn off your cell phones. You don't have BlackBerries, do you? Good. Those wireless PDAs might as well be billboards advertising your location. I told you before, Rack, the Mark of the Beast'll be a bar code worn on the palm."

Krindon, a technical-security and surveillance specialist, could remote-monitor a man's every movement, or reconstruct a woman's life from the cards she kept in her wallet. Though he was too paranoid or too informed to work for the government, he sometimes contracted in, delivering sensitive intel while maintaining a freelancer's distance. Tim and Bear used him on occasion to acquire information that warrants couldn't flush out.

Bear nodded at the gaping hole in the dash. "You tore out your OnStar."

"You wouldn't believe the information embedded in those fuckers. If people knew the half of it." A world-weary head shake. "They're remote-operated—Big Brother can send a signal that turns off your engine. I tracked a mule from Matamoros once, remote-locked him into his Buick by satellite. *Federales* came, he was at the windows like a lizard in a jar, fifty bricks of coke locked in there with him." Krindon chuckled sadistically, scratching his vivid red hair as he scrambled into the backseat.

Tim withdrew the CD from his jacket pocket, and Krindon slid it into a unit beneath the passenger seat. Dray's approach played on a mounted screen. Krindon watched it through once, his face remaining impassive. He offered Tim no condolences, instead tugging on a catch that released a folding instrument panel from the wall. He stopped the recording when Dray's head jerked to the right to track the phantom bike's approach, and he set to work on the digital enhancer. After comparing each pixel to those surrounding it, the artificial-intelligence program either sharpened or flattened it, bringing the freeze-frame into greater resolution—it was like watching a cheap repro of a Monet transform into a photograph.

Something seemed to catch Krindon's eye, and then he zeroed in on Goat's rearview, angled to the side to deflect the squad car's spotlight glare. He advanced frame by frame until he picked up a darting movement—black on black, like a bat against the night sky. He captured the reflected blob, then enlarged the image and fussed with the contrast, bringing a partial silhouette into view. The mystery biker. An immense man astride a motorcycle. Kaner.

"What's that?" Bear squinting, leaning forward.

"Don't touch the screen." Krindon zoomed in farther, and then the screen rippled downward to pick up a protrusion from Kaner's boot. Krindon worked on it awhile, the screen rendering the image in waves of clarity.

"It's a shoe," Bear said.

"He's double-packing," Tim said. "Someone's on the bike behind him. We just can't see him because Kaner's so wide."

"Her." Krindon focused in on a fan of wrinkles at Kaner's side. Four fingers with cherry-painted nails, clutching Kaner's shirt.

Tim and Bear waited patiently, letting Krindon fuss over the segment, but the phantom bike never reappeared in the other bikes' mirrors, nor did the female passenger. Krindon sat back, frustrated, letting the footage roll in real time. Though Tim had seen it now many times, he couldn't tear his eyes from the screen.

Dray's profile, frontlit by the spotlight. "Okay. Stay still. Relax." The striker's snarl: "Get the fuck outta here." The refrigerator truck blasting past, on its way to another stop, another city, Andrea Rackley little more than a passing speck. Just another deputy harassing a few bikers. Nothing to turn a trucker's head.

Krindon slowly drew himself up until he sat erect, locked in the grip of an idea. Bear started to ask something, but Tim stayed him with a gesture. Krindon reversed the footage. The blood sucked back up into Dray's side. She drew herself together, bounced off the ground onto her feet, holstered her weapon and reverse-waddled a few steps. The truck flew by, also in reverse, winking back the spotlight. Krindon froze the bleached-out screen. He fiddled with knobs, darkening the truck's aluminum paneling. A reflected tableau resolved, like ghost characters emerging from a Polaroid fog. Kaner on his bike, a teenage girl clinging to his back.

"That's why Kaner made sure to keep out of the camera's range on his departure. He didn't give a shit if we saw *him.* He didn't want us to see *her.*" Bear studied the girl's terrified face. "What would the Sinners want a Mexican girl for anyway?"

Krindon made a sucking noise, his tongue against his front teeth. "Nothing good."

Tim recalled Strauss's words this afternoon: *We're fielding nearly two hundred tips an hour on the hotline—everything from looted TVs to girls snatched off street corners.* Bear met his eyes, nodding, already on the same page.

Krindon's reverse frame-by-frame quickly confirmed that the young woman was Kaner's captive. A hefty girl, she was sobbing, face streaked red. Her mouth opened at Dray's approach—a cry for help? When the girl struggled, Kaner threw an elbow to her temple.

"Okay. Stay still. Relax." Dray's voice sounded softer not because she was rattled but because she was speaking to the young woman.

Hey, Timmy. How 'bout you give me the benefit of the doubt next go-around?

Krindon said, "Let me bring up the audio." A twist of a fat dial warped the striker's voice into a retarded drawl. "Get the fuck outta here."

And then Dray, interrupted by the truck's roaring appearance: "I'm not going without—"

Pete detached the audio track, rewound and enhanced it. The last word rang out over a hiss of high-fidelity static. "—her."

Kaner's hidden reply. "Fine. Take her." A female cry, then a grunt as a body struck the ground.

Dray's cheek tensed—the grind of her teeth. She gathered her courage, stepped toward the fallen girl. Den's shot blew her off her feet.

21

Tim was relieved to have a lead to follow, an excuse to avoid going home, and a distraction that would keep him from calling the hospital to check in every twenty minutes. Bear leaned against the faux wall that partitioned off the phone banks from the command post, but the warning creak it emitted straightened him back up.

"The mayor told me about a call you guys fielded on a girl who got snatched?" Tim said.

The court security officer tugged at the textured bags under his eyes with a thumb and forefinger. He flipped through the call log—textbook thick and growing. "Yeah, I think Mattie P. took that one. Here it is. Some girl called, hysterical, said her friend got nabbed off a street corner by bikers."

"Where?"

"Owensmouth in Chatsworth." He smirked. "Prime real estate."

"What'd you do with it?"

"Since the alleged victim had family, I told the friend we'd need an immediate member to file a missing person's. That we usually wait forty-eight hours, but if she wanted to call Sheriff's, she could see if they could move on her report. She said she'd have the mother call back." He flipped a page. "Never did."

"That's all you did with it?" Tim's frustration, he realized, was directed at himself. He'd adopted the dismissiveness in Strauss's tone and disregarded the piece of information. Dray's admonishment came at him: *Everyone counts. And everyone counts the same. Getting personal is like putting on blinders. It blocks you from weighing deaths equally, which blocks you from weighing* clues *equally.*

"We got nearly a thousand calls in twenty-four hours." The CSO worked up an impressive scowl. "The Sinners had just shot a deputy. I assumed they'd be on to more important matters. Plus, the woman—*or* the mother—never called back. I figured it was a hoax or a mix-up or something."

"Do you have a trace number for the call?"

As the CSO grumbled and clicked away at his computer, Guerrera leaned around the corner. His face sharpened with concern when he saw Tim. "What are you doing back? I thought you were gonna get some sleep."

"Sleep's overrated."

The CSO jotted a phone number on a piece of paper, ripped it from the pad, and handed it to Tim. "Happy tracking."

Lydia Monteverde came out on the porch to speak to Tim, Bear, and Guerrera because her baby sister and five-year-old daughter were sleeping in the living room. Battle-scarred holiday decorations clung to the walls, survivors of Christmases past—Frosty with a torn abdomen, Santa sporting crayon scribbles, amputee Rudolph. From the scattered toys and TV trays, Tim guessed that at least three others lived in the tiny apartment. Lydia wore a T-shirt with the sleeves cuffed up above her shoulders and a polyester maid skirt, freshly washed but stained.

Bear thumped a cigarette out of a crumpled pack—he didn't smoke but kept Camels on hand for precisely this reason—and she gladly took it. After a shallow inhale, she blew a shaky stream of smoke and gestured with the two fingers clinching the cigarette. "Right over there. That's where Marisol and me was talking."

A chain-link view of broken-down playground equipment festooned with graffiti tags. Owensmouth Avenue—a stretch of North Valley depravity, a mainline through the crack-and-porn hub of the nation. Lydia gazed up the street as if seeing it with them for the first time, her eyes momentarily blank.

"By the park?" Tim asked.

A jerky nod. She crossed her bare arms, rubbing them. She'd refused Tim's jacket earlier.

"I was too scared to see good. They vroomed past me on both sides. I ran, hid over there." She pointed to a jungle gym in the far corner, glistening like a mass of steel wool. "They circled around her on their motorcycles, revving the engines." She was trembling with the cold and the memory. "So loud. Marisol was screaming, but no one heard. Not around here."

"How'd they grab her?"

"One guy—big guy—drove by and just yanked her like this, around her neck and arm, and dragged her up on his bike behind him. He kept going." She was crying now, her frail shoulders shaking. "They passed me first. They could've grabbed me. It should've been me. But then I ran, and so they circled around Marisol."

"Was Marisol involved with any biker gangs? Any friends or boyfriends who were Cholos?"

Lydia laughed, swiping at her tears. Her knees cracked when she sat on the front step. "No."

"Did she live around here?" Tim caught himself using past tense a second too late.

A mousy nod. "With her *abuela*."

"We'd like to talk with the grandmother. Can you tell us where she lives?"

Lydia's eyes darted away. "You're gonna find out anyhow?"

"Yes," Guerrera said. "But don't worry. That doesn't interest us."

Bear furrowed his brow inquisitively at Tim. It took a moment for Tim to catch up to Guerrera, but then he put together why the mother hadn't made a follow-up call to the hotline.

"I have the address inside."

"Did you notice anything about the bikes?" Tim asked. "Or the bikers? Any distinguishing marks?"

She closed her eyes, drifting back through the scene, then shuddered. "One of them had a tattoo."

A baby's sputtering cry from inside set her on alert. She rose, dusting the wrinkles from her stained skirt.

"What kind of tattoo?"

"A burning skull. Like a devil. Real mean-looking." She flicked her stub at the pavement, where it sent out a shower of sparks. "And it was laughing."

T he front door opened tentatively to reveal a rotund Mexican woman, pronounced black doughnuts ringing her puffy eyes. Her fearful expression—not surprising given the late-night ring at the door—yielded to panic. "No take me away. Please no take me. I no cause trouble."

Tim and Bear stood behind Guerrera on the front step. Bear prodded Guerrera with an elbow, and Guerrera said, *"No somos Inmigración. No se preocupe. Estamos aquí solamente para ayudar a su nieta."*

But the woman was hysterical, bending deep on her knees as if contemplating collapse. "I no cause trouble. I jus' want to be here for when *mija* come home. I no cause trouble. Here. *Mira, mira.*"

She grabbed Guerrera's arm and dragged him down a brief, dark hall, past a doily-draped side table with guttering Advent candles. A tortured Jesus hung from a porcelain cross; it seemed more a fixture than a holiday flourish. Kitchen humidity had spread through the apartment, tinged with the smell of cooked onions. Tim and Bear arrived at the bedroom door as the woman crumbled, weeping, one hand clutching Guerrera's pant leg. Neatly made bed, cutesy animal posters, costume jewelry laid with care on a pink towel covering the bureau. Marisol Juarez looked out from a picture frame, teased hair framing a plump, cherubic face. Eyeliner tailed beyond her eyes; russet lipstick widened the lines of her mouth. Generous smile, a dot of neon green bubble gum glowing at her molars.

"Por favor. She come home soon. I be here for her. You take me then."

Guerrera crouched beside her and spoke soothingly in Spanish. The woman finally calmed, overcome with relief. He helped her to her feet, and she reappraised them gratefully. She squeezed her eyes shut, muttered a prayer, then led them back to a small couch by the front door. She patted the cushions, then deferentially removed the plastic cover from the footrest. Tim's and Bear's soles were muddy; they kept them on the floor. Her insistence grew oppressive, so finally, to her apparent pleasure, they raised their boots to the spotless fabric.

Guerrera followed her into the kitchen, which flickered with candlelight. Tim clicked the lamp beside him, but no light cut the gloom. Evidently the funereal candles also served a pragmatic purpose. A few used tea bags punctuated the base of the lamp.

The old woman fussed over the sink as Guerrera murmured questions in Spanish. She emerged proudly bearing four steaming mugs on a tray. She plucked a desiccated tea bag from the side table and plopped it into one cup, which she reserved for herself. Reverently, she withdrew a box from the cupboard, removed the cellophane wrapper, and dropped fresh tea bags into the three remaining mugs. She handed them off, nodding encouragingly until they all sipped.

"You will help my Marisol? You will find her?"

"We'll do our best," Tim said.

She and Guerrera spoke for about twenty minutes, Tim and Bear straining to keep up with the Spanish, Guerrera pausing from time to time to fill in the blanks. They turned up no new information and no compelling reason her granddaughter might have been targeted. The woman must have read the disappointment in Tim's face, because she clutched his arm at the door and asked, "You bring her home to me?"

After the battering of the past twenty-four hours, the question hit him hard; his emotions had bled close to the surface. "We'll do everything we can."

She looked to Guerrera, who translated, and then her shoulders sank. Two skateboarders rolled past, their wheels snapping over cracks in the sidewalk.

Bear and Guerrera headed back to the rig. Tim paused on the walk and turned. Her squat, shadowy form remained at the door, candles mapping orange sheets on the walls behind her.

"Thank you." He gestured as if raising a cup to his lips. "For the tea."

Her face warmed, if only briefly, and the door swung shut.

22

Muffled feminine whimpers found resonance in the high corners of the deserted warehouse. A leaking pipe had corroded the far wall, leaving the air musty with the bittersweet stench of mold. The soggy drywall had buckled, dragging over the nails of the studs like sloughed clothing. Partitions and cubicle walls divided up the concrete expanse into a labyrinth—narrow runs, sharp turns, cul-de-sacs. Broken-down machinery accompanied the compartmentalized workspaces—crumpled conveyer belts, rusting metal desks, spills of bolts.

The industrial carpet lining the desk area of the office suite carved out of one corner gave over to a concrete floor slick with oil, worsened by the sweating engines of the four Harleys and the Indian. Den sat at a managerial desk, a hand rasping over his stubble-sharp jaw. Kaner, Chief, and Goat lounged in chairs opposite him; they might have been reviewing first-quarter estimates. Goat's scar cysts had flared up, the flesh on the right half of his face weeping a clear fluid. Kaner spun a finger in the links of his weighty drive-chain necklace.

Tom-Tom stood in the flimsy doorway, staring impatiently across the vast warehouse. "Thafuckizee?"

The closet door behind Den rattled. A stifled sob deteriorated into gagging sounds and moist snuffling.

The bowie knife pinned down a stack of papers to Den's left, glinting red stones lending the flame to the Sinners skull. Den picked the knife up, let it dangle between thumb and forefinger, then slowly lowered the tip to the desk blotter. He tilted the knife, letting its weight draw the point the length of the material. He leaned forward and blew, the blotter neatly halved along the blade's line. Pleased, he settled back in his chair.

A muffled screech, and again the closet door banged in the jamb.

Kaner's low growl of a voice came softly, his lips barely moving: "Let's shut her up already."

An entrance across the warehouse was announced by a bang, a column of thrown light, and the near idle of an engine. Diamond Dog rolled toward them, weaving through machinery. He drove right up into the office and killed the engine. He removed a saddlebag and tossed it onto the desk before Den, equipment rattling within.

Den flipped the reinforced-leather top, looked into it, and smiled. "Good." With a slide of his eyes, he indicated the closed closet door. "Let's get the show on the road."

Chief disappeared back into the warehouse, Tom-Tom hopping after and whooping with excitement. Kaner tugged open the closet door. Marisol Juarez lay pressed against the jamb, arms wrenched painfully behind her considerable back and bound at the wrists. A ribbon of duct tape indented her pudgy cheeks—the bordering flesh rubbed raw. Snot ran over her lips; sweat curled her dyed hair. She tried to retract into the shallow closet but had nowhere to go.

Diamond Dog considered her for a moment, then nodded. "She'll do."

Goat and Kaner lifted her effortlessly despite her weight. They propped her in a chair—she sat compliantly—and cut the tape from her wrists, ankles, and face.

She sucked deep breaths, smeared the sticky hair off her face. "Please don't rape me."

Goat laughed. "We don't do Mexi-*cans*."

"Why am I here?"

"To shut up," Kaner said.

He, Goat, and Diamond Dog returned to their chairs, and everyone sat quietly, almost sociably, around the desk. Marisol's eyes went to the jeweled bowie sitting on the slit blotter before her. Her chest jerked; she took in hiccups of breaths. Den looked from her to the blade, the set of his face suggesting amusement at the implicit dare.

From deep in the warehouse came a screech. Marisol stiffened as the sound grew steadily louder. Her thin beige top clung to her sweaty torso like a film.

Tom-Tom's humming carried to them—a histrionic rendition of "Here Comes the Bride" followed by a spray of laughter. Marisol watched the doorway, terrified; Den kept his focus on her, enjoying the entertainment.

The sound of metal scraping concrete reached an unbearably high-pitched wail, heralding the object's arrival.

Marisol cried out, "What did I do? Why do you want me?"

Den's mouth pulled to one side, a private grin. "We *don't* want you, bitch. You're just practice."

Chief backed into view, guiding a large object behind him, and then it, too, slid within the doorway's span. A stainless-steel embalming table. Tom-Tom brought up the rear, overcome with delight. "Ta-*da*!"

Marisol emitted a whimper from somewhere deep in her chest. "God, don't hurt me."

Den's hand moved in a blur. The blade was back on the table as if it hadn't moved. "You're already dead," he whispered.

Blood streamed from the slit, a window blind descending. Her uncomprehending eyes blinked. Her hand rose to her throat, came away red. She gurgled, and then her knees rattled against the desk and she flopped forward onto the sliced blotter. Kaner kicked out the chair, and her body shifted, then flipped back, landing on the floor.

Tom-Tom giggled, his white-blond curls swaying. Kaner and Goat each grabbed two limbs and hoisted her onto the embalming table. Blood pattered on the floor.

Den peered down at the body, fingering his blade. "Now, let's make this thing work."

23

The command post had the tired vibe of a bar ten minutes after last call when the lights come up. The deputies on shift browsed through files, repositioned the surveillance shots tacked to the walls, and pored over crime-scene photos, their skin tinted green from exhaustion and the unforgiving overheads. Malane alone looked alert and sharp, jotting notes and chewing the inside of his cheek. Jim was slurping from his coffee mug, holding it at an odd angle. Tim realized he was covering the words on the side—SUPPORT THE MENTALLY HANDICAPPED. TAKE AN FBI AGENT TO LUNCH.

"Why grab a girl when you're on the run from the law?" Bear was agitated, as if angry at the Sinners' lack of circumspection. "I mean, literally *on the run*. They'd just faced off with Rack, what, an hour earlier? They knew the heat was coming."

"Race killing?" Freed offered from the far end of the conference table.

"Hate crimes are too low-rent for these guys at this stage," Bear said.

"Maybe they wanted to turn out a cutie." Thomas finished his second cup of coffee in as many minutes and tossed the Styrofoam cup across the command post. It bricked the lip of the trash can and bounced across Malane's oxblood loafers.

"These guys are too smart for that," Guerrera said. "After planning a picture-perfect break and a mass execution, they're not gonna derail for a piece of ass."

"Then what the fuck they doing with her?" Bear's meaty finger tapped Marisol's photo, borrowed from her grandmother's house.

Tim was sitting back, his eyes closed. "They picked her."

One of Bear's eyebrows went on point. "What?"

"They chose her. Lydia said they could have grabbed her first. She's smaller, easier to control. Why would you take a bigger girl?"

"I don't know." Haines shrugged skeptically. "Fetish?"

Jim fussed with the wad of cotton in his ear. "Like serial killers?"

Tim remembered Den's parting words over Dray's body—*Let's practice on this heifer.* The recollection threw him back into his grief, a coldwater immersion. He waited for his disgust to wash clear. "Biker-gang serial killers sound more tabloid than plausible. These guys are strategists."

Murmured acclamation. The deputies at the table sat thoughtfully, listening to the pulsing rings at the phone bank.

Dray had said that everyone counts and everyone counts the same.

Tim knew this to be true. He also knew she counted more to *him* than anyone else. He was supposed to carry his badge through the gray zone between those facts.

"Marisol is the key," he said. "Not Frankie. Not Mancone. Not Dray. We figure out a motive for the snatch, we're on our way." He rubbed his temples, refocusing. He'd dozed off in Bear's rig on the ride over. "All right, where else are we? Anything on Danny the Wand?"

"Still looking," Freed said. "But we got a tentative address on the deposed Sinner—Lash. A CI got word from a mechanic, matched the nickname to a billing address for a radiator. Take it or leave it. We were gonna follow it up in the morning."

"Me, Bear, and Guerrera'll take it now. Stay on the motor shops and Danny the Wand. Haines—how'd the prison interview go?"

"Like shit. Word of the break's reached the inside, given the Sinners a fresh tank of defiance. No one's talking except to gloat."

A mounted dry-erase board at the front mapped out the mother chapter's hierarchy, only a few blank slots remaining. Deeds and slags filled out the split branches. It looked like a dating tree from one of the celeb rags Dray pretended not to read in doctors' waiting rooms.

Tim did a double take at a new Magic Marker–rendered name. "You got us an ID on the striker?"

"That's right," Zimmer said. "Rich Mandrell, aka Richie Rich."

Tim's voice, beaten flat by exhaustion, managed a modicum of animation. "His tag is *Richie Rich*?"

"Diamond pinkie ring. Doesn't take much." Thomas flashed a grin. "Troubleshooter."

"Rich Mandrell," Bear repeated slowly, trying to place the name.

"You get anything on his date to the funeral?" Tim asked.

"Tough broad, played chaperone?" Zimmer said. "No, still can't match her. She might not even be part of the club."

Guerrera tugged her eight-by-ten surveillance shot from the wall behind him, and Tim looked over his shoulder. Her cheeks were pitted from earlier bouts with acne, but her features were clean, even pretty.

"She wasn't wearing a property jacket," Guerrera said. "And she sure as hell didn't act like a slag."

Tim said, "So who is she?"

The thoughtful silence barely had time to establish itself when Bear said, "Wait a minute." He held up his hands, as if having to stave off throngs of rock groupies. "*Rich Mandrell?* He that guy who popped . . . ?"

"Raymond Smiles," Malane said. "One of ours."

Jim said, "It speaks."

His first joke—a classic Denley slam on a Feeb—caught everyone off guard. The deputies smiled, more with relief than amusement. Malane kept his eyes on Bear as if he hadn't heard or didn't get it. But then his anger seemed to get the better of him, and he turned to Jim. "Raymond Smiles was a good friend."

Jim studied Malane for a moment, then bobbed his head. "I'm sorry. That was an asshole comment. But I wasn't talking about Smiles."

Mercifully, Zimmer broke the silence. "We have the hit on a restaurant security cam." He spun his monitor around, and Tim and Bear watched the soundless MPEG video clip play. A black FBI agent sat at an elegantly set table, perfect posture emphasizing the sharp cut of his suit. He wore a red silk pocket square that blended into the blossoms of the too-high centerpiece of roses. His companion headed off, presumably for the bathroom. A moment later a man stepped into view, back to the camera. His shoulder jerked twice, and more red bloomed on Smiles's shirt, encompassing the handkerchief. Smiles fell forward into his plate. The assassin turned—same eye patch, same flash of pinkie ring, same clammy-looking flesh.

They watched it through a few more times, Tim growing unsettled. Maybe he'd just soured on reviewing footage of law-enforcement officers getting whacked.

"The hit took place October third," Zimmer said. "It seems to have gotten Richie Rich bumped from prospect to striker. Word is, he came out of the San Antonio chapter. A real bruiser. And he's another disappearing act—his last-knowns put us back to '03."

"Where are the case files?" Tim asked.

"We can't get them. We keep running into red flags, classified Feeb bullshit." Zimmer shot a sideways glare at Malane, picking up the thread of a not-so-buried disagreement. "And we're not getting much interdepartmental cooperation from our task-force liaison."

Bear directed a displeased scowl Malane's way. "Can't you play well with others?"

"Yes, but I can't break Bureau protocol. I've issued a request to try to expedite matters. That's the best I can do."

"Have we gotten the Uncle Pete files?" Tim asked. "The Continuing Criminal Enterprise stuff?"

"I've also put in a request to—"

"Stop requesting. Start *doing*. You're here for a reason."

"I know why I'm here, Rackley."

"Good. Then work with us. We could certainly use it."

Put a pin in the anger and use your head. Get results from this joker or get some answers.

"On second thought," Tim added, "what *are* you doing here?"

Malane matched Tim's calm stare. "To help. What else?"

Bear's brow was furrowed, deep ripples in shiny skin. Keeping his eyes on Malane, he said, "Freed, how 'bout that address?"

Tim rose, stretching through the pain in his lower back. He took the slip of paper from Freed and followed Bear and Guerrera out. The white face of the wall clock above the door looked down as he passed under.

Twenty-four hours since she was shot.

24

It was nearly 2:00 A.M. when they eased up to the two-story North Hills apartment building. Pink stucco and cheap concrete had fallen away in chunks, rebar twisting from the holes like spider legs. Around cars, stoops, and rickety ovoid barbecues, men gathered in tight, menacing clusters, all glittering eyes and hands in pockets. Bing Crosby crooned holiday tunes from an eight-track deck in an off-kilter eggshell blue Karmann Ghia, an anachronism of Russian-nesting-doll proportion.

Tim, Bear, and Guerrera rolled out of Bear's Dodge Ram, and the groups seemed to hunch together. Overpowering Bing's velvet ba-rum-ba-pum-pumming, brassy Wagnerian trills wafted from an open second-floor window. Tim picked off a slouched kid with a scruffy goatee and a cocked-back Stetson. "A biker named Lash live around here?"

"You mean the Great Mustaro?" A few of his cohorts snickered, and the kid lifted his eyes to the window screen upstairs. A curtain undulated between the mesh and a man's form in a bodybuilder flex. Thick shadow. Biceps like softballs.

Tim and Guerrera gladly let Bear lead the way. He knocked, but the classical music had reached a deafening pitch. The doorknob gave up 180 degrees. Bear leaned into the room, a hand riding his still-holstered gun.

A refrigerator of a man, naked, did deep-knee bends, exhaling prodigiously. The Sinners logo occupied his entire back, the flaming skull rippling with the movement of his muscles. SINNERS had been excised from the tattooed top rocker—a purple twist of scar tissue in its place—so his back read, ridiculously, LAUGHING . . . and then, beneath, FILLMORE.

On a flickering black-and-white, a hunting-cap-bedecked Elmer Fudd goosestepped through a forest to staticky *Walküre* accompaniment. Lash turned, revealing twinkling eyes, a nest of facial hair, and more, and grinned agreeably. He gave voice to the rising crescendo with a not-bad bass.

Tim flashed on Kaner's hulking figure facing him down on the Malibu road, the nomad's sheer size impressing itself on him anew. Huge as Lash was, Kaner still had a good four inches and hundred pounds on him.

"Mind if we turn down the TV?" Bear roared.

"What?"

"Mind if we turn down the TV?"

"What?"

This repeated a few more times until Bear resorted to sign language. The volume eased, and pleasant introductions commenced, the man shaking their hands vigorously, Tim's elbow aching with the snapping gesture. Lash seemed unsurprised by the appearance of three deputy marshals, even pleased to see them.

A circular scar stretched tight and shiny over his right biceps, pinched at the edges like a Reese's peanut butter cup. The twitch at his jaw and scurrying fingers showed off a meth high in overdrive; pockmarks said it wasn't a new habit. A silver-dollar-size patch of skin at his massive left pectoral fluttered to his heartbeat, an incongruous fragility. Scabs and bruising spotted the crooks of his elbows, his wrists, between his fingers. Continuing to stretch, Lash stepped on the end of each of Bear's sentences.

"We understand you used to ride with the S—"

"Seven years of full-color-flying mayhem."

"We had a few questions—"

"No problemo, podnuhs. You pay, right? For info? I'll leak you a few words for a price. Times are tough, my friends, times are tough."

Bear fed Lash a twenty to keep the wheels greased, letting the hundred show beneath his money clip. Lash snapped it up, the bill disappeared into a drawer, and then he was stepping into a seventies-appliance-yellow wrestling singlet, bouncing on one hairy leg as he strained into the Lycra.

Bear asked, "Why'd you get kicked out?"

"Little trouble with the needle." Lash fluttered the curtain a bit, letting the breeze pull through the screen. " 'Scuse the ripeness, lads, enchiladas been chasin' me around the room all night."

"The club gives a shit you used drugs?" Bear asked.

His fingers picked at the fabric, readjusting it to his contours. "Loyalty to the needle is greater than loyalty to the Sinners. We could sell but not partake. That's a lot of road time with the lady calling out from the saddlebag. I never liked the 'ow' in 'willpower.' And so it goes, my friends, and so it goes."

Guerrera indicated Lash's disrupted top-rocker tattoo. "The nomads take the 'Sinners' off your back?"

"Yup. With a wire brush. I'm appreciative, actually. They could've knifed the whole backpack—infection woulda killed me for sure." He gripped his biceps, displaying the circular scar as if offering it for purchase. "Burned over my one-percenter tat with a hot spoon. I miss that one the most, cuz I saw it every day."

"How long ago?"

"It was, shit, two years back. Before they went down for croaking those spics." A glance to Guerrera. "No offense." Lash hoisted one knee to his chest, then the other, grimacing at the hamstring tug. "They're not bad guys, Den and Kaner. They showed up, we was all like, 'Let's get this motherfucker done.' They let me have a few shots of whiskey before they held me down. Didn't use the electric drill or nothin'." He broke wind once, decisively, and headed for the door. "I'm late for an appointment. Walk with me. Your cash is still good across the street."

Lash took the steps two at a time, his stentorian humming picking up the Teutonic Warner Bros. melody. They scrambled to keep pace. He crossed the dark street, a few of the guys laughing at him and calling out. "Hey, Great Mustaro, good luck."

Lash offered a warm, crooked grin and a celebrity's departing wave. "Thanks, lads." They approached the double doors of a decrepit gymnasium, Lash still humming.

Bear said, "Listen, we really just need a few more minutes to—"

Lash hit the swing panels, and the roar of the waiting crowd inside was so shocking it put Tim back on his heels. The ropes of the elevated boxing ring had been restrung with barbed wire. The wall-folding bleachers were packed with chanting fans, men and women holding up fistfuls of cash like cartoon gamblers. A menacing form clad in orange tights and a flickering cape waited in the boxing ring. A banner overhead announced EXTREME FIGHTING SEMIFINALS.

A voice thundered, "And his opponent, at six-six, three hundred and five pounds . . ."

"I haven't seen three-oh-five since the eighties," Lash muttered to Bear, giving his fellow scale-tipper an elbow jostle.

". . . the Great Mustaro!"

The room erupted. Lash continued his Mike Tyson charge to the ring, with Bear, Tim, and Guerrera still pursuing, befuddled. "They say grapplers are tougher than strikers," Lash shouted to them above the clamor, "but I'll take on a grappler any day."

Lash waved off an anxious older man—the gym owner? "The badge boys are okay. They're with me."

The fighter in the ring who—unintentionally?—resembled one of the dreadlocked albinos from *The Matrix*, beckoned with both hands; the gesture was Bruce Lee by way of Chris Farley.

"All right, lads, gimme a sec." Lash fisted the barbed wire and hoisted himself into the ring, leaving the deputies standing in the front row.

The albino charged in a football tackle, and Lash caught him over the clutching arms and hurled him against the barbed-wire ropes. The guy hung for an instant, snagged, before hitting canvas. He staggered to his feet, and Lash caught him in a surprisingly fluid fireman's carry, flipping him. He slammed the canvas so hard Tim felt it through his boots. The albino rose, snapping his fingers, and his cornerman tossed him a wooden chair. He grabbed it by a leg, whipping it at Lash's head. Lash caught the chair, yanked it free, and set it down on all four legs. He head-butted his opponent, who staggered in a sloppy circle before collapsing into the chair. Lash straddled him stripper style, continuing to administer fore-head smashes like a deranged woodpecker. The chair disintegrated, but Lash kept banging away, sitting on the guy's stomach like a kid playing Chinese torture, his face splattered with his opponent's blood.

Before the deputies could intervene, the whistle blew and Lash rose. His opponent gasped and coughed blood. Tim scrambled into the ring and rolled the albino on his side; he drooled out a crimson mouthful. Lash grabbed Tim's hand and raised his arms in victory, the crowd going wild, referees and cut men pouring into the ring. Lash fisted the barbed wire and tugged it down for Tim to step over. He blazed through the boisterous crowd, Tim, Bear, and Guerrera following in his wake and ducking high fives.

They finally arrived back in a small office, the closed door providing an abrupt and disorienting silence. Lash settled into a chair, gauging the cuts in his hands with a scientist's detachment. "Sorry, lads. Where was we?"

Perspiring heavily from the near confrontation, Bear looked unamused. "The Sinners."

"Oh, yeah, right. You got more dead presidents in that pocket of yours, chief?"

Bear withdrew another Jackson but kept the Franklin buckled down. Lash added the twenty to his take from the fight—fifty-five bucks in crumpled tens, fives, and ones.

Bear said, "You know about the transport-van break. And the Cholos massacre. Something big is going down. What?"

"I dunno. I'm out of that game. But Den and Kaner, those boys don't fuck around. From the aftermath, looks like they got their mitts into something tasty."

"Like what?"

"Two years out, pal. Can't help you there."

"You know anything about a Rich Mandrell? Goes by Richie Rich?"

"Must be a new addition."

"How about a Danny the Wand?"

"Course. Best sprayer you'll ever meet. An artist."

"You have a real name?"

"Nope. Just Danny the Wand."

"This Danny, he rides his rep pretty hard."

Lash's hearty laugh was part roar, part grumble. "You'd better not tell Danny that, man."

"Why not?"

"You'll see."

"Where can we find him?" Tim asked.

"Beats the hell outta me. Used to have a shop over on . . ." Lash snapped his fingers a few times. "I think it was by the Harley dealer in Glendale. But Danny closed up shop. Have spray gun, will travel. I think freelance spraying pays better dough anyway. We lost track."

Bear removed his money clip, tapped it against his palm. Lash's eyes tracked its movement; he reflexively fingered the bruises on his arm.

"We want to find the nomads," Bear said.

"Good luck, man. The Sinners got safe houses all over the state, no papers on 'em, nothing. They roll 'em over every six months."

"Do you have any addresses? Relatives, girlfriends, ex-wives? That's what we need here, Lash, an address."

Lash chewed his lips for a while, his beard bunching like a fist. "Intel officer's who you want. He's the keeper of the plans. The one with the files, the hard facts."

"Chief?"

Lash looked surprised that Bear had produced a name. "Yeah, that's right."

"Where's he lay his head?"

"No one knows. Not Uncle Pete. Not even the other nomads. And that's God's truth. The intel officer runs separate from the pack, never goes to the clubhouse. Keeps his own safe house, even. That's where all the dirt is."

Bear slid his fat money clip back into his pocket and angled toward the door. Tim and Guerrera shadowed his body language.

Lash half rose out of the chair. "He's got a deed, Chief, but you won't get shit from her. Not a *damn* thing. Don't even bother. The Cholos one time got ahold of her, kept her for three days. She didn't squeal. Not a sentence. Den and Kaner caught up to the spics six months later, took care of them. Chief showed up for that party. Yes, sir, Chief loves that cunt something fierce."

"You got a name?"

Lash took a long time thinking about that one, pinching the mouths of his hand wounds and watching the blood flow. "Hell," he said at last, "not like it's a big secret. Even the Cholos know about her. It's just a name."

"That's right," Bear said. "Just a name. Like, say, Benjie Franklin."

"Terry Goodwin." Lash's eyes darted around the room. "There. I said it." He scratched a scab at the base of his biceps, drawing a red smear. "Now, where's that hundo?"

25

By 3:00 P.M. Tim's lower back ached every time he shifted, but he didn't complain, since Bear and Guerrera had been sitting the stakeout all the way through. At least Tim had been able to sneak away to drop fresh flowers off in Dray's room—irises to greet her awakening if he couldn't—and then spend the morning at the command post. Even so, he'd memorized every detail of the exterior of Terry Goodwin's house, a ranch style on a corner lot in Valencia.

Tannino had expedited their middle-of-the-night warrant request, personally waking up a federal judge. Tim, Bear, and Guerrera had stalked the property cautiously the night before, not wanting to blow the lead if Chief wasn't present. Tim had beheld Terry's sleeping form— solo in the California king—through the bottom seam of the bedroom blinds, a pair of night-vision goggles helping him fill in the picture.

The RV trailer they'd hooked from the Asset Seizure warehouse at least permitted them better viewing comfort. Sunflower seeds over-flowed two cups in the front holders. Tim leaned over, finger in one ear so he could hear Freed giving him a cell-phone breakdown on chop and spray shops that had closed in the past few years around the Glendale Harley store. He and Thomas hadn't stumbled across any paperwork with a "Danny," "Daniel," or "Dan" on it.

Guerrera was lying on the shag carpet in the back, staring up at the ceiling. "She still at the kitchen table?"

From his post at the tinted window, Bear said, "Yup."

"What's she doing now?"

"Reading the paper."

"Which section?"

"Front page."

Ten minutes later. "And now?"

"Sports."

"Finally. Who won the Citrus Bowl?"

Bear readjusted his binoculars. "Dunno . . . she's flipping back and forth. . . . Mia Hamm pulled a hamstring. . . . Turning the page . . . Miami."

"*Yes.*" Guerrera pumped his fist.

Tim finished with Freed and snapped the phone shut. The RV's smell—salsa and stale cigarettes—and his exhaustion, now verging on sleep deprivation, added to the burden of his frustration. "This is stupid."

"I said last night I didn't want to sit the house." Bear, hater of stakeouts, failed to keep the resentment from his voice. "We don't have time to wait and see if Chief's gonna swing by to play a little grab-ass."

"I agree," Guerrera weighed in. "Not the best use of our time, here, *socio.*"

"So what is? This is our strongest lead."

"*If* Lash's information is good," Bear said.

"He's a junkie. He needs money, and he knows if he does us right, we'll be back with more. Beats ping-ponging around barbed wire for a few bucks."

Guerrera said, "It'll catch up with him. You don't tell tales out of school about the Sinners. He'll be killed. Sooner or later."

They sat in silence, the only sound the autozoom on Bear's binocs. Though he hadn't remarked on it, Tim had taken a shine to Lash, and he'd gleaned that Bear and Guerrera had, too.

Finally Bear said, "Let's hope later."

"Why don't we knock-and-notice her, search the house?" Guerrera said.

"Because if nothing turns up, then we lose the angle," Tim said.

"You think she has Chief's number to alert him?"

"If she does, I'm not betting our one solid lead on the notion that she's dumb enough to write it down." Tim took the binoculars from Bear and trained them on Terry, who'd moved on to Entertainment. A healed knife scar glittered on her right cheek, maybe a parting gift from her three-day stint with the Cholos. "That phone number's in her skull. It's just a matter of getting it out."

"How?" Bear asked.

But Tim was already dialing Pete Krindon.

K rindon unloaded his bag of gear and glanced around the tight camper interior. "Nice digs. I particularly like the neon sign on top flashing 'Stakeout.'"

"You take care of the junction box?" Tim asked.

"Yes. But we're gonna need backup. If this chick is as street-savvy as you say, she'll use a cell phone." Krindon withdrew a parabola mike from his bag, the receiver surrounded with a cone collar. He slid open the window, hiding the mike behind a rust-orange curtain, then tossed a cell phone to Guerrera. "Lay on the Mexican accent something fierce."

"I'm Cuban."

"I don't think," Krindon said, "our girl will discern the difference."

As Guerrera dialed, Tim kept the binoculars trained on Terry's kitchen window. She rose, picked up the phone. Guerrera hissed, "We got your *hombre, puta*. We gon' kill heem." He hung up.

Terry slowly replaced the phone's receiver. She stared at it, as if expecting it to ring again. She was surprisingly calm, a weathered deed. Tim had been betting on her to maintain her composure, to think matters through. She sat down at the kitchen table, set her elbows in the puddle of newspaper. She thought long and hard. Krindon's mike picked up some of her whispering with remarkable clarity. ". . . a scam. Just a fucking crank call." Her agitation grew. She paced a few times, her bare feet squeaking on the cheap linoleum. With his own spouse comatose on a hospital bed, Tim couldn't help but feel a jolt of empathy.

Terry picked up the phone, then hung it up abruptly as if it had shocked her.

"Go on," Krindon purred. "Go on."

She disappeared down the hall, popping back into view in her bedroom window. She pulled a cell phone from the pocket of her jacket, which was slung over the doorknob. Three beeps as she started to punch in the number, and then she hung up. She sat on the bed, phone in her lap, whispering a mantra. "God, let him be okay. Let him be okay."

She dialed. Krindon made a fist at his side.

Terry let out a deep exhale. "You all right? . . . No, course I'm not on a landline. . . . Weird call. From a Cholo, sounded like. . . . Okay, baby. Me, too."

Terry clicked a button and flopped back on the bed, relieved.

Krindon pulled back from the window and replayed the eleven tones he'd captured as she'd dialed. He matched them slowly on his Nextel until he'd duplicated the tuneless melody. He jotted down the number, handed it to Tim, and vanished out the RV's narrow door.

26

They materialized from behind parked cars and the narrow alleys between broken-down houses, crouching in makeshift formation, MP5s pointing up like the tips of a wrought-iron fence. Indistinct forms in one-piece olive drab flight suits. U.S. MARSHAL patches on the left arms, subdued gray U.S. flags on the rights. Black Hi-Tecs with quiet neoprene soles. Marshals' stars machine-embroidered over their hearts like targets. Wearing a thigh holster at crotch level, each deputy sported a .40 Glock.

Except one.

Tim thumbed free the cylinder on his .357, gave it a spin to watch the six brass dots whirl. With a jerk of his wrist, he snapped the wheel into place, then reholstered the revolver, letting it sling off his thigh. Chief's safe house was barely visible down the street, a block of darker shadow against the moonless sky. Husks of leaves littered the gutter and car windshields, glowing green, then red in the flashing Christmas lights.

Guerrera arrived at the staging point last, pulling into the curb between a battered VW van and a dilapidated hearse that provided further ambience. He emerged in a low crouch, document flapping, Judge Andrews's signature a fountain-pen smudge at the bottom of the page.

"Ready to light up this *pendejo*?" Guerrera whispered.

Miller folded the warrant into a cargo pocket and nodded at the abandoned hearse. "His ride's waiting."

Guerrera squatted and got a jingle. He emptied a few coins from his pocket onto the asphalt, then removed his watch and set it on the tire of the hearse beside him—no on-the-hour beep or night-glow dials across the dark threshold. The deputies extinguished the volume on their Motorola portables and pulled into a tight-stack formation, drifting silently across asphalt.

Miller halted, the explosive-detection canine and the column behind him freezing on the sidewalk. The house had been split into a duplex, both sides staking claims on the address Pacific Bell had relinquished.

They studied the matching doors, the dark, still windows.

" ' 'Twas the night before Christmas . . .' " Jim intoned quietly.

A whispered conference. Tim drifted closer to the house. An Indian bike leaned against the side wall of the left duplex unit, unchained but secure behind a locked gate. Tim gestured Guerrera over for confirmation, and Guerrera nodded excitedly and whispered, "The kick starter's been cut in half and raised an inch or two. Only a little guy would need the extra leverage for leaning into the ignition."

They approached the row of tacked-up deputies, who'd pulled back to the neighboring house. "Left duplex," Tim said.

They hugged the wall to the front step, Maybeck pressing the top of his beloved battering ram up against his cheek. Miller directed Chomper to sniff along the door, and Chomper hesitated but didn't sit—no booby trap.

Tim lined up in the number one, Bear behind him toting his cut-down twelve-gauge Remington. Jim started his nearly inaudible pre-entry hum. For good luck or as a private show of respect, Jim tapped the black band at his biceps—Frankie Palton remembered. It struck Tim that the loss of his partner, only three days old, was still fresh to Jim. To Tim it felt distant, dulled by the fresher horror of seeing his wife shot off her feet time and time again. Even now as he muscled toward her maybe killers, her body wavered, indifferent to his desires or hers, making up its own damn mind.

The men lowered their night-vision goggles into place, Maybeck drew back the battering ram, and Tim rode its momentum into an unfurnished living room.

Before the hazy green world pulled into focus, a blaze of fire erupted from the couch, throwing Tim's view into violent brightness. Four slugs pinged the wall at his head, and one hit the stock of his MP5, shattering it and spinning him in a half turn. He slammed against the wall and struck carpet, flinging the NVGs off his head. Bear and Guerrera dove for cover as the others stacked at the door, the lead deputies trying to push back against the inward rush so as not to be driven into the line of fire. The familiar gunfire cadence continued, the song of the converted AR-15.

Though Tim's vision was still bleached out, the gun-muzzle starbursts from the couch gave him target acquisition. He slid the .357 from his thigh holster and fired sideways over his head. A cry of pain, masculine but surprisingly high-pitched. The automatic weapon clattered to the floor.

Tim's eyesight had recovered enough for him to make out a diminutive form scrambling across the room. Tim rose and charged after him, the other deputies just beginning to recover at the door. Chief ran in a furious limp and dove through the pass-through window into the kitchen. As Tim came around the jamb, a skillet took flight at his head. He ducked, and the aluminum dinged drywall, expelling a cloud of scrambled eggs. He dove and caught a leg, but Chief kicked free and bolted down the hall, Tim seconds after him as he slammed through a doorway. In a mad dash for his bed, Chief threw a rolling chair behind him; Tim got a foot on the bucket and leapt. He crashed down on top of Chief, pinning him to the mattress, his pistol to the back of his ear. Chief's hand froze half withdrawn from his nightstand drawer, gripping a Colt .45.

Tim's adrenaline had ignited an explosive fury. He heard the low, rageful growl of his own voice as if it were separate from him. "You choose."

Chief's defiant eyes strained to take in Tim. His biceps tensed, and then his gun hand whipped from the drawer, finger dug through the blank eye of the trigger guard.

Tim squeezed.

Breathing hard, he remained for a moment with his knee dug between the slack shoulder blades, listening to the moist descent of brain matter on the opposing wall. Then he drew himself up, checked the closet, and shouted "Clear!" down the hall. Spread on top of the nightstand were diagrams of explosives. He gathered them up, doing his best to make out the cramped scrawl in the dimness as he headed back toward the front of the unit. Pipe bombs. Scored tubes to create more shrapnel. He flipped to another diagram, squinted at the dark sketch.

BBs. Gunpowder filler. A filament wire.

The lines took shape as a light-socket bomb. He glanced up as Maybeck reached for the switch.

"Wait, *don't*—"

The floor jumped with the boom. The screech of rent metal. The whine of ricochets. When he heard only the tinny white noise of eardrum aftermath, Tim glanced up from the carpet. The five deputies in the entry stirred, finding their feet, dusting themselves off, picking shrapnel from their tactical vests. Maybeck's nylon raid jacket was sliced neatly down the front. With trembling fingers, Maybeck plucked a twisted metal shard from the Kevlar covering his stomach. His fingers went to the gash, came away bloodless. His sigh of relief was shaky, verging on tearful. He helped Bear up, and they all limped outside, patting themselves down for leaks and gashes.

Miller held a black Mag-Lite knuckles up, surveying the interior. He chewed his lip, his jaw tight, facing off with the darkness. Tim noted a tremor in the sun-beaten skin at the corner of his eye. His own nerves had not yet calmed. Malane showed up and poked around, nodding to himself as if dispensing approval.

Watching the FBI agent explore the front shrubs, Bear spoke in his version of a whisper. " 'Liaison' my ass. He's working a cross-agenda."

"Agreed," Tim said. "So let's figure out what it is."

Malane observed the empty American Spirit pack impaled on his pen.

"I feel more like he's playing spy guy. Lining up the case for his funny-handshake brethren to take over. Slowing us down where he needs to."

"Good luck there."

They broke apart from their mini huddle as backup arrived. It took the LAPD Bomb Squad nearly an hour to clear the building. As outlets and sockets were ruled safe, lights clicked on, illuminating the duplex a section at a time. The bomb technicians used their own dogs; Chomper watched alertly from the sidelines, licking his chops and whimpering wistfully. They found trip wires in closet thresholds and a scattering of shotgun-shell-loaded mousetraps in drawers.

Bear discovered a file cabinet hidden behind hanging clothes in the bedroom closet and went to work on the lock. The see-no-evil, hear-no-evil, speak-no-evil stickers—one monkey on each drawer—seemed not only a fine specimen of dry Sinner humor but an indication that the cabinet held confidential material.

Criminalists from LAPD's Scientific Investigation Division showed up to give the Sheriff's CSI guys, who'd already started processing the body, jurisdictional grief. Marshal Tannino was en route; Tim figured he'd let him untangle egos.

He took a moment before reapproaching the body. If a kill was within ROEs or Service regs, if it adhered to the laws of fair play im-perfectly defined in his own heart, he could sleep soundly at night. He'd killed often with the Army Rangers, though he'd never taken to it the way some of his platoonmates had. He'd inured himself to the guilt and horror over time, but he still felt enough to register his impassivity as a loss.

Staring at Chief's body now, he felt renewed rage about his wife's unresolved fate. The emotion unnerved him.

If you feel that much, you shouldn't be killing people.

"Not now, Dray."

Thomas glanced over. "What'd you say?"

"Nothing."

You feel good about wasting that guy?

No. Yes.

Can't tell us much now, can he?

I guess not. "I didn't have a choice."

Right. You had to put the gun to his head. You couldn't have shot him in his gun hand. You don't exactly have shitty aim, Troubleshooter.

The guy looked on while Den shot you off your feet. You left a boot behind on the asphalt.

Nice try, but you know damn well what I'd want. Leads. Answers. Not just bodies.

Tim stared at the spray across the pillow, the wall.

Don't get me wrong. I'm not crying over Chief's demise. I'm just saying, if you kill 'em, you can't much use 'em.

Bear stopped fussing with the lock and walked over, his brow furrowed with concern. "What are you doing?"

"Just talking to myself."

"Don't make it a habit. The church elders will gossip." He shot Tim a warning stare and withdrew to the file-cabinet lock. Bear was terrible with a pick set, but he wouldn't admit it. Tim had once waited a half hour for him to fumble his way into a school locker.

Snapping on latex gloves, Tim regarded the corpse with greater detachment. First step: confirm ID. No wallet in the back pocket made sense, given Chief's hours in the saddle. Tim tilted the already stiffening body and tugged a wallet from the front pocket, freeing a few coins and sundry bits of pocket trash. Looking at the license photo—the proud, meticulous lines of facial hair etching the beard; the erect, compensatory posture—Tim couldn't help but think of Terry Goodwin, Wünderdeed. Her relieved collapse back onto her bedspread after she heard Chief's voice on the phone. The memory, in combination with the ripe odor, made him faintly nauseous.

Nestled in the sheets beside two pennies and a generic book of matches was a torn paper crumpled around a wad of gum. Fuzzy with pocket lint, it yielded grudgingly when he unwrapped it. A ripped receipt, *Flying J Travel Plaza, Nov 8*. A partial credit-card number terminated at the tear: *4891 02—*. With a purchase date and location, they'd have no problem retrieving the full data.

"We've got a credit-card number," Tim called out. "And I assume this isn't the one Teflon Pete uses to buy clubhouse groceries." Freed was waiting with a plastic Baggie. Tim dropped the gum-laden receipt inside and said, "Get on the horn to Visa and figure out how to get those statements. And if it's linked to a bank account, I want ATM hits, too."

The smell was starting to get to him, so he stepped outside. Tungsten-halogen lights glowed over the roof; Tim could hear the field reporters starting their on-site pickups. He walked around to the side to get a peek at the news vans crowding the curb.

Guerrera crouched beside the motorcycle at the gate. He'd removed the seat and set it on the concrete at his feet. Dressed in bathrobes and sweats, neighbors milled around on the other side of the street. Tim waved at an elderly woman staring out from her porch, and she retreated inside as if caught doing something wrong.

Collapsing his telescoping mirror against his thigh, Guerrera rose. "*Coño.*" He gestured at a toggle switch on the handlebar. "That's the kill switch."

"For what?"

"For the pin-trigger mechanism laid in the frame tubing just below the seat. Someone tries to steal the bike, he gets a shotgun spray right up the *culo*. Penetrates the gut—not an easy way to go." Guerrera reached in gingerly with his pocketknife and withdrew a twelve-gauge shotgun shell from the center post. "A trip wire runs to the rear wheel. I saw a cruder version once in Miami. The discharge'll tear the spine right out of a person." He shook his head, admiring the engineering.

"Tom-Tom's work?"

"Likely. Which means it's probably standard feature on all nomad bikes. You don't watch your ass when we seize property, it'll get ripped right off you."

Bear shouted from inside, and they headed in. A few file-cabinet drawers stood triumphantly open. Shirts pulled up over their noses, hands turned magician-white in latex gloves, Thomas and Freed flipped through files, laying out documents on the carpet.

"Check this." Bear used a pinkie to open the bottom drawer. A bunched mass of cracked leather, the CHOLOS top rocker partially visible. Bear poked at the jacket with the end of a pen, bringing a fold-hidden patch into view. CHOOCH MILLAN.

"Okay," Tim said. "But we don't need evidence. We're not making a case. We need current red flags."

Thomas pointed at the diagrams and schemas spread on the floor. "We've got operation plans for the transport-van break *and* the Palmdale massacre."

"Any *future* plans?"

"Not so far."

"So what else is in there?"

"These two drawers are filled with intel on the Cholos," Freed said.

Thomas broke in. "More than you'd ever want to know about a bunch of dead guys."

"Hangouts, relatives' addresses, ex-wives. There's a list in there must have every woman El Viejo's put his dick in since the Wall fell."

Bear dropped a binder into Tim's hands. "This makes for the best reading."

Inside, Tim found mini dossiers on cops, prosecutors, and rival bikers. An eight-by-ten of Raymond Smiles was crossed out in red—Richie Rich's diploma. An attached report identified Smiles as a top federal enemy of the club, detailing his field experience, which ranged from anti-narcotics to counterterrorism. When Tim flipped the page, he found his own face staring back at him—a shot of him lying on his stomach taking pictures at Nigger Steve's funeral. Once the chill subsided, he realized that part of him was flattered he'd made the hit list. A thought caught him off guard: What if he got taken out and Dray awakened alone? Or worse—if she didn't and *they* were gone. No Rackley left. It would be as if their family, for ten years the self-important center of their own production, had never existed. Or yet another disturbing variation: Their child could be orphaned before birth, excised from an insentient body to be greeted by two pensions, a garage sale, and Bear.

Their jobs gave them a courtside view of the void, a comforting illusion of separateness and control, but never before had the costs been so evident. After Ginny's death Tim had rejected the law and his badge, weary from the essential uselessness of it in the face of universal mechanics. He'd wanted back in the Service so desperately, and now he was in, but with his wife shot and a crosshairs on his own head. The dullness Jim had carried behind the eyes the past few days suddenly clarified; Tim felt the sentiment it bespoke resonate in his bones, a low-register chuckle not unlike Uncle Pete's.

What were his options? Get a job selling mattresses? Urge Dray to take up quilting? The notion of retreating under fire would be as unappealing to her as it was to him.

At Bear's urging, Tim continued through the binder. The last section contained images of dead Cholos—crime-scene shots, news photos, and, most disturbing, moment-after Polaroids.

The deputies perused the files, their discouragement growing as little useful information was revealed. If nothing else, Tim had to admire Chief's spy skills; the intel he'd managed to acquire on the Cholos was staggering in its scope and specificity. The Sinners were wise to keep Chief—and the files—segregated from the rest of the club.

Lash had told them as much—*The intel officer runs separate from the pack, never goes to the clubhouse. Keeps his own safe house, even.*

Guerrera muttered, "This shit might be useful if we were going after the Cholos."

Tim's hands stopped their movement. His head snapped up. "Exactly." He shoved the binder at Bear and began digging through the hanging files in the two drawers dedicated to Cholo intel.

"Rack?" Bear said. "What's going on?"

"We're in the wrong house." Tim sensed the others reacting with puzzlement, but he continued blazing through the file tabs, racking his brain to match the names to those on the list of the dead from the Palmdale massacre. *El Viejo.* Dead. *Frito Terrazas.* Dead. *Gonzo Ernez.* Dead.

A name finally distinguished itself from the others; Tim didn't recognize it from the coroner's roll. He yanked the file free and flipped it open. Meat Marquez. Identifiers, bike information, and an address were typed neatly beneath a surveillance photo. Bear, Guerrera, Thomas, and Freed crowded around, realization dawning.

Tim nodded at Chief's stiff corpse on the bed. "We got the wrong intel officer."

"Huh?" Bear said with mild irritation. "Which intel officer do we want?"

"Not the Sinners'." Tim grabbed the page from the file, thumb creasing the Lancaster address. Guerrera and Bear barely kept pace down the hall.

They passed Tannino in the entry. Without a word he took Tim's .357 into evidence, handed him a fresh one, and continued back toward the body.

27

Needle-nose pliers protruded from the hole that had been Meat Marquez's nose. His head was wedged in the jaws of a vise, distorted by the pull of his body weight. Tim, Bear, and Guerrera stood in a loose triangle around the body, motionless on their feet as if the slightest movement might wake Marquez up. Bear's great, broad shoulders sagged, worn down by disappointment. Tim glanced at the sheet from Chief's file on Meat, the typed address matching the brass numbers hammered beneath the light outside, then crumpled it up and shoved it into his pocket.

Meat had been the last nomad of his kind—the hearts of the other three, Den and Kaner had left on the Cholo clubhouse doorstep, the bit of improvisational surgery that had won them matching convictions. After the past three days, Tim understood the strategic implications of the first rule of biker gang warfare—kill the nomads.

The deputies' preliminary walk through the garage conversion had turned up nothing in the way of files.

The complaint of the A/C explained the merciful chill in the air; the nomads had likely maxed the unit while they tossed the place so they wouldn't be assailed with the stench as Meat started living up to his name. A flipped cot soaked up engine grease. Tufts of mattress stuffing floated in oil puddles. Plate shards littered the kitchen. Smashed floorboards stuck up like stubborn weeds. A porcelain Virgin Mary lay shattered at the base of a shelf.

"At least we know how they intercepted the Cholos' funeral route," Bear finally said.

Guerrera broke their unspoken vow of stillness, toeing the remnants of the tchotchke Holy Mother. Tim figured Guerrera was being sentimental until he called them over and pointed at the interior of the statue base. A clear key outline showed against the sticky dust that had accrued inside.

The tip of a footprint—boot edge rendered in oil—pointed toward the bathroom. Guerrera picked up its next appearance after a six-foot interval, the long stride indicating Kaner.

Tim and Guerrera stood shoulder to shoulder in the tiny white square of the bathroom, Bear crowding them from behind. In the main room, the air conditioner groaned like a tired engine on a steep hill.

Guerrera ran a hand over the tiles that sheathed the lower half of the walls like wainscoting. An offset edge. He tugged gently, and the tiles swung as one piece, exposing a file cabinet set back in the space between wall studs. Tim felt a long-overdue flush of excitement.

The top drawer slid too easily under the tug of Guerrera's finger. The hanging file folders remained, each tab listing an individual Sinner, but the contents had been pulled. The next two drawers revealed the same. After killing Marquez, the nomads had wisely purged all the intel on their club. Tim stared at the empty Den Laurey file and cursed sharply. They withdrew to wait for CSI. Doubleheader Friday for the crime lab.

Standing over the rigor mortised body, Bear grimaced. "Whatever groundwork they're laying, it's thorough as hell."

"But for *what*?" Guerrera's rhetorical hung in the refrigerator-cool air.

Flashing blue lights cast a glare through the garage-door windows, mapping waves across the ceiling. A few more vehicles pulled up outside.

The A/C emitted a creaking groan. Tim walked over and examined the main vent. The rush of air felt uneven. He placed his hand in front of it. Cold air was seeping from the edges, but the center gave off nothing. He pried the panel free and removed the dusty filter. A folder slipped out from behind, slapping the floor. Tim snatched it up.

An assassination dossier, containing surveillance photos of Goat.

Astride his Harley. Weaving through traffic. A familiar, horrifying close-up of the marred flesh of his face. Emerging from a commercial building into an alley. The location of the last shot was nondescript— no address, no telling marks on the wall. But captured in the background was a sliver of the world's most recognizable image—the golden arches. One enormous yellow leg had been captured, and a segment of pantile roof. A Dumpster blocked part of the alley, its faded stencil showing a floral emblem.

Tim slid the photo back into the file and rolled up the garage door, revealing four black-and-whites and a CSI van cramming the brief driveway. A few more units turned onto the street, lights flashing soundlessly, a KCOM news van drifting ominously behind. Having been assailed by reporters outside Chief's duplex, Tim quickened his step.

The three deputies threaded through the growing mass of cops, climbed into Guerrera's G-ride, and disappeared into the night.

28

Tim lowered the photograph, but the scene remained, a midnight rendering of the identical angle. Same thin run of alley, same doorway, same yellow half arch, now filtered through Bear's bug-splattered windshield. Despite the ubiquity of McDonald's, the combination of identifiers—oversize freestanding arches, pantile roof, Renegade Rose's Rent-a-Dumpster—had enabled them to cross-reference surrounding areas and narrow the field fast. The doorway belonged to a seemingly disused warehouse in Simi.

"We're just looking around, right?" Guerrera asked as they climbed out.

Bear pulled his shotgun from the trunk. "Sure."

Tim emptied the new .357, checked the trigger tension again, then refed the six rounds. Guerrera nodded once, mouth pursed, and followed them silently toward the building. Securing the door, a shiny new padlock didn't match the rust of the hasp. Guerrera squatted and retrieved the severed pin of an older lock from a cluster of leaves.

Tim gestured, and they eased around the back of the warehouse. No cars or motorcycles in the parking lot or alongside the building. The sole window looked in on an office and beyond, the expanse of the warehouse proper. Parked inside the office was a Harley. Tim clicked on his Mag-Lite and drew the beam across the room. A russet pool glittered on the desktop. Smudges down the side. A wide stroke along the carpet, the signature of a dragged body.

Bear's exhale breezed over Tim's shoulder. "I'd say there's our probable cause."

Tim leaned on the window, which had been paint-welded to the sill. It gave with a creak. As Tim pried it open, Bear called for backup, requesting an ambulance and advising a stealth approach in case the suspects were still inside when the units rolled up. Guerrera took rear cover, his eyes darting nervously around the empty parking lot and neighboring buildings as Tim climbed over the sill.

Once he was in, Bear followed suit, then Guerrera. The air was dank, sweetened with the faint smell of mold. Tim tapped his knuckles to the Harley's craggy engine—faintly warm. He recognized the panhead engine and the checkerboard skull pattern on the stretched tank from the surveillance shots of Goat they'd found at Meat Marquez's.

Weapons drawn, they followed the blood trail. Tim led the way, his wrists crossed to keep the barrel of his .357 nearly parallel with the beam of the flashlight.

Outside the office an embalming table gleamed, a stainless-steel anomaly among the industrial equipment. Tim paused beside it, Bear and Guerrera halting behind him. What looked like oil rippled in the table's gutters. Tim didn't require a closer look to know, but Guerrera's flashlight beam proved the liquid crimson. A puddle on the far side, then a wider path snaked back into the warehouse interior.

He heard Guerrera take a gulp of a breath, his own stomach knotting with the certainty of more ugliness ahead. Few noncombat experiences were more hideous than the slow-motion unfolding of a crime scene.

They wound through heaps of dilapidated machinery. A faint glow up ahead. A rumble from the interior announced footsteps. The sound of cheery whistling.

They eased around a partition. In the sole stroke of light cutting through the warehouse gloom, Goat tugged a woman's partially disemboweled body. He shuffled backward, hands gaffed into the front of her so they disappeared in the folds of her armpits. Her head lolled, hidden beneath a mask of tangled hair.

A desktop lamp, set on the concrete floor, provided meager illumination and funhouse effects. It threw Goat's pitted face into fierce relief and stretched his shadow up the wall, bending it across the ceiling. Between blinks the etched skull stared out from his glass eye.

Tim gestured for Bear and Guerrera to spread out along the perimeter of the darkness, then stepped into view, light falling across him like a sheet. "Hands up! Hands up!"

Goat jumped a bit at the intruding voice. He released the woman, smiling almost sheepishly, and raised his arms. The body didn't flop back to the concrete; her shoulders and upper back remained banana-curved, rigor mortis defying the laws of physics and propriety.

Both hands steadying the .357, Tim walked forward. A rectangular flap had been laid open in the woman's gut. A loop of intestine waggled from the gap, hanging like an ankh between her legs. Her face remained invisible behind a scraggly wall of orange-tinted brown hair. A few feet beyond them, a floor hatch angled back on its hinges, revealing a black square of crawl space.

Tim stopped a couple of yards from Goat, sights aligned on his upper sternum. The smell of the corpse reached him—a battlefield stench, the odor of Ginny on the coroner's table—and he looked up into Goat's marred face, feeling the cool air tingle across the band of sweat dampening the back of his neck. He thought of Dray drifting a few feet above the shoulder of the highway, hair on end from the impact.

The crisp report of a gunshot jarred him back into the present.

For an instant Tim thought he himself had fired, but then Guerrera's boots pounded behind him, Tim hit the ground, and Goat flashed into the darkness. Tim twisted to look over a shoulder, picked up Guerrera at the edge of the shadows, gun now pointed down, standing over a sprawled form. Bear charged past Tim after Goat, and Tim leaped up and followed him into a maze of modular partitions.

The whine of a bullet past Tim's cheek broadcast that Goat had located a gun. Tim and Bear split the aisle, backs to the partitions, stalking forward. A gooseneck in the path dumped them in the corner of the warehouse. The muzzle flashes of Goat's gun—pistol, semiauto, poking blindly around the corner—revealed a backdrop of concrete wall.

The slide of Goat's gun locked to the rear. The gun disappeared, and Tim heard the click of the mag dropping. He crossed the open space, shoulder-slapping the far partition, now within feet of Goat's position. Bear held down the wall just before the turn. Tim heard Goat's mag click into place.

He snapped his fingers at Bear, holding up his hand. Bear tossed his Remington across the four-foot span, the walnut forearm slapping Tim's raised palm. Goat's pistol poked back around the corner as Tim raised the shotgun and fired at the wall a yard away. The double-aught buck tore at the concrete, ricocheting around the corner.

As the thirty-five pounds of recoil shuddered Tim's torso, he registered Goat's scream. Bear rolled around the turn first, disappearing into the haze of concrete powder. Goat groped at his head, shrieking. He'd taken most of the pellets in the face. His glass eye was missing, lost somewhere in the darkness; fluid streamed from the socket and from his good eye. Bear kicked the gun from its loose dangle in Goat's hand and put him down on his chest. A knee in the back, a quick frisk—Bear was unparalleled at escort control—then the flex-cuffs cinched tight. Bear tried to hoist Goat to his feet, but Goat kicked and thrashed violently. Bear deep-grabbed the hair at the base of Goat's skull and pulled back and down hard, forcing his chin up. He kept the leverage firm and steady, forcing Goat to ride his chin up to his feet. As Bear steered him back toward the light, Goat babbled and sputtered, streams of blood matting his face. He was a fearsome sight.

Shoulders slumped, gun drawn but at his side, Guerrera stood over a body.

Diamond Dog Phillips.

Approaching, Tim noticed Guerrera's boot pinning down a .45; he'd secured Diamond Dog's gun but not picked it up. Tim called out, "Did you clear the area?"

Guerrera snapped into motion. Bear cuffed Goat to a forklift and left him whimpering. Tim shined his Mag-Lite at the banks of overheads, checking that they weren't rigged, then found a switch panel. Section by section, the warehouse flickered into light.

After a quick search, the three met up again in the open area. Bear followed up with backup—two-minute ETA. Goat had mercifully passed out, cuffed arm dangling over his head. The deep rumble of his breathing and his pulse—when Tim checked—showed strong vitals.

It did not surprise him when Dray weighed in.

So I neglected to mention maiming.

I didn't kill him.

Maybe not, but this is a pretty close second. Doubt he'll be talking much with his face blown off. Next time don't take me so literally.

Don't second-guess me on this one, Dray. If I don't put him down, he shoots me or Bear or both of us. My options were limited.

I guess you're right. And believe me, we don't want you ending up where I am. It's really dull, and the food sucks.

Goat shifted onto his back, mumbling.

Can't say I'm torn up inside. I mean, the guy's biggest contribution to society is putting a tourniquet on his arm when he masturbates so it feels like someone else is yanking him off.

Really?

Check his case file. At least he gets points for originality.

Tim crouched over the woman next. Her hands had contracted into claws, the finger webs already opaque. Not wanting to compromise the crime scene, he used a pocketknife to lift her snarled hair away from her features. It took some maneuvering, but he finally did. Bear, at his back, heaved a sigh. Tim looked at the familiar face, feeling a dead weight tugging on his insides. "Damn it," he said softly. He wanted to cover her but knew he had to leave her there for CSI, bare on the concrete.

Guerrera looked down blankly at Diamond Dog, his gun still at his side. He made a fist around his bangs, his mouth pulsing. Tim gently grasped his elbow and wrist and guided his Glock back into his hip holster, Guerrera barely noting his presence.

Fine lacings of blood, erupted from the chest wound, had stained Diamond Dog's T-shirt.

"He was gonna pick you off from the shadows. Guerrera spotted him first." Bear frowned down at the centered bullet hole, nodding approval at the shot placement. His eyes lifted to the girl, and Tim saw a glimmer of sorrow cut through the toughness. "Why the hell would you kidnap a girl from Chatsworth and cut out her stomach?"

Torture? Satanic ritual? Diversion? Tim shook his head. "That's what we have to figure out."

Guerrera's face had gone gray. Bear returned Tim's glance, catching his drift and nodding—get the kid some air.

"Rey," Tim said. "Come with me and wait for backup."

Once outside, Guerrera took a few hard breaths and gestured at the step. "Okay if I take a seat?"

"Of course."

Guerrera squeezed one hand in the other, both trembling slightly. It took Tim a few beats to recognize what he was muttering in Spanish as the Lord's Prayer. When Tim's shadow blocked the light across his face, Guerrera quieted abruptly, as if catching himself.

Tim crouched beside him, inhaling the crisp air. "You don't kill that guy, he kills me."

"I know."

Tim took note of his sick expression. "Remember this feeling. Don't get used to it."

Guerrera tilted his head, looking up at Tim. The streetlamp lighting smoothed out his skin, making him look like a college kid. He shifted his gaze quickly, embarrassed. "*You* have."

Tim rose. "That's why I'm telling you."

The cavalcade made a grand entrance—black-and-whites, unmarked cars, CSI van, two ambulances, Tannino's white Bronco bringing up the rear. Guerrera was on his feet instantly, puffing himself back up.

Tannino hopped out, animated and mouthy. "The warehouse clear? Then get every swinging dick outta there until CSI finishes its sweep." He took Guerrera's gun into evidence, talking past him at Miller. "Let's get him to the hospital. Simmer him down, maybe a sedative. And someone call the Hug Squad, get a counselor on the hook."

"I don't need to go to the hospital. Rack put a hole through Chief and didn't—"

"Rackley," Tannino said with undisguised ambivalence, "has been through this drill a time or two."

In the alley a garbage truck closed in on the Dumpster, forks sliding beneath the unit with a screech. Why was the loudest street work always conducted at 4:00 A.M.?

Bear jogged out, breathing hard, as if he'd just finished a 5k. "I took a turn through the office in there with CSI, looks to be whistle clean. Nothing in the drawers, the closet, trash can—" He stopped short, keyed to a sudden idea, and then ran across the lot, waving his arms. The Dumpster halted midrise. The trash-truck driver rolled down his window, talked to Bear, then lowered the unit back onto the ground and backed off it. Bear flipped up the top and hoisted himself, the unit nearly tipping over as he peered inside, the very image of his nickname.

The others watched with puzzlement.

"He looking for a late-night snack?" Jim asked.

Bear straddled the lip, the flashlight a yellow spray from his fist, then disappeared into the Dumpster. Tannino and Tim exchanged vaguely comic glances, and then Bear's around-the-fingers whistle split the air. Tim headed over, Aaronson and another criminalist instinctively pulling behind him. The Dumpster was nearly empty, though it reeked and the walls had rusted in patches. Three white trash bags gathered in the far corner like fat geese, branches and leaves poking through the plastic. Bear crouched, almost sitting on his heels, peering into the sole black bag.

Aaronson stiffened and offered the criminalists' refrain: "Don't touch anything."

Bear kept his head toward Tim, his flashlight bobbing as he clicked it back on—a variation of the no-look pool shot. Light shone into the cinched, fist-size mouth of the stuffed bag.

Bloody rags.

"Okay. We got it from here. Climb out over there. No, *there*. Thank you." The criminalists took over, prowling the unit, exchanging abbreviations and acronyms in the murmuring voices of lovers.

Tim and Bear arrived back at the warehouse as two fire-department medics wheeled Goat out. He'd regained consciousness, moaning quietly. Miller smirked. "Two down, three to go."

Jim lunged for the gurney as it passed, and it took Maybeck and Thomas to restrain him. "You piece of shit!" Shouting, he was still hoarse. "How *you* like it, motherfucker?"

Tannino glowered at Jim. "Shut the hell up, Denley. Back it down." He strode over, inserting himself between Jim and the departing gurney. To the others: "Let him go." The deputies released Jim, but Tannino stood before him, five feet seven inches of tough; even at a head's advantage, Jim didn't dare make a move past him.

The medics loaded the gurney into the back of the ambulance. Scowling, the marshal looked from Guerrera and Miller to the cluster of deputies surrounding Jim—headaches all around. "Who wants to baby-sit Scarface?"

Malane appeared out of the tangle of personnel and vehicles. "Want me to take him for you? You guys have had a long day."

"Thank you, Jeff."

Bear shot Tim an irritated look behind Tannino's back. Malane climbed up into the rear of the vehicle, the doors slammed, and the ambulance pulled away.

Tannino signaled Tim with a finger, and they stepped outside the circle of men. Tannino put his back to the others. "What's your read on Jim?"

The others watched Tim, gleaning the conversation's content. Anger lingered in Jim's light blue eyes, enough to embolden him to stare.

Tim said, "He seems a little wobbly."

"Think I should pull him?"

"I would."

"Would you pull *you*?"

"Probably."

Tannino let out a sigh meant to illustrate executive stress. "What about in there? Was it a good shooting?"

"Yeah. Guerrera saved my ass. Talk to Bear—he saw it."

"The kid can shoot. Who'da thunk it?"

"Not you?"

"I thought he might be all talk. You never know until you know."

Tim was distracted, scanning the empty parking lot.

"What?" Tannino said.

"We got two dead bikers and one bike."

"Maybe they rode in together?"

"Sure, right after their commitment ceremony."

Tannino whistled Freed over. "Give a drive around the surrounding blocks. We're missing a chopper. Check alleys, too."

"Diamond Dog's bike," Tim said. "Call someone at the post, get it tagged from our funeral surveillance shots. Goat's hog is inside."

Freed nodded and withdrew. Tannino spit on the asphalt as if clearing a hair from his mouth.

Tim said, "Don't release Diamond Dog's name to the press. Give up Goat, but I want until at least tomorrow on Diamond Dog."

"Fine. I'll give you till noon. Move your ass and make the play. We gotta build Rome in a day here, Rackley." Tannino shot his cuffs like an old-school gangster and squared his shoulders. He entered the warehouse. Emerged a minute later. "What the fuck is *that*?"

"That seems to be the prevailing question."

"Sinner business or entertainment?"

"Don't know."

"Was she pregnant?"

"Don't think so. Just a big girl."

Tannino took a deep breath and walked back to the cluster of deputies. He pointed at Jim. "You. Go home. You can do light duty at the command post, but you're done going out of pocket for this case."

Jim's glare went from the marshal to Tim. He spun and headed back to his wife's Saturn; he'd been roused from bed.

Tannino turned his attention to Guerrera. "To the hospital. That's not a suggestion." Another quarter rotation brought him face-to-face with Tim. "You and Bear handle the advise-next-of-kin. Take Guerrera's ride for a respectful showing. We don't need you rattling up to the curb in Bear's heap. What, Rackley? Why the face?"

"Guerrera handled her before, the grandmother, and her English isn't so hot. I thought maybe it might be easier for her to hear it from—"

"I'll tell you what," Tannino said, already heading back to his Bronco, "we'll do ethnic outreach on the next one."

29

Guerrera's duty car was an Impala that Bear hated because of the creepy autonavigation voice—a spacewoman on ludes calling out each turn. *"Left in two hundred yards."*

Bear looked ridiculous stuffed in the driver's seat; he didn't do well in cars.

Tim hadn't done an advise-next-of-kin call since he'd received one himself from Bear the night of Ginny's death. He thought about asking Bear to handle tonight's, but he felt he owed Marisol's grandmother both their presences in the face of the news.

"The old man asked me if I thought he should yank Jim."

"I figured."

"Right turn in forty-five feet."

Tim looked at the camera mount on the center rearview mirror, the same model that had captured the assault on Dray. "Do I come off so coldhearted that my wife gets shot and the marshal asks me if *another* guy's taking the case too personal?"

"I think—"

"Oops. Make a U-turn."

"Shadd*up*, lady. Jesus Christ, I want to get nagged like that, I'll get hitched." Bear turned the car around and got them back on course.

"I think since you fucked up on that front so profoundly, the marshal bets you won't go that route again. And more important . . ."

"What?"

"Well, you do go stone cold, Rack. When you're mad. You don't get stupid, and you don't get sloppy. Stupid and sloppy are what Tannino— and the mayor, for that matter—is worried about. And frankly, if you handle business and the rest of the Sinners wind up ten toes up like Chief, I don't think anyone's gonna lose any sleep. But it's gotta be clean work." They drove a few minutes in silence, but eventually whatever thought Bear was working on got the better of him, and he said, "Jim's an easy call to pull off the case right now. He's not the one who the marshal—and you—should be worried about."

"What does *that* mean?"

"I dunno. Young deputy. A comer. Could go this way or that way or some other way. And—as everyone but you has noticed—idolizes you. For all the wrong reasons, I might add."

"Guerrera?"

"You *think*?" Bear shot Tim a you'd-better-think-about-it glare and feigned a sudden absorption in the cookie-cutter triplexes flying by on his left.

A few minutes later, they eased up to the house. Bear let the car idle, ignoring the solicitous autogal—*"Next location, please."*

Bear stared at the house, his face shifting. "Fuck. I hate this. I fucking *hate* this." He bounced his forehead off the top of the steering wheel a few times. "Okay, let's go."

At the door Bear's and Tim's painful Spanglish only made the encounter more demeaning to everyone and prolonged the agony of the revelation. Immediately the woman took in their dread by osmosis, but they had to run through "We're *siento*, Marisol is *muerto*" three or four times until the denial-fueled hopefulness dwindled from her eyes and her composure crumbled. One of her arms flared to help her keep her balance and Tim caught it and walked her to the couch, but she refused to sit. The footrest, now re-covered in plastic, bore a few stains from their last visit.

Tim focused hard on her hysterical Spanish and figured out she was asking variations on what he and Bear had termed the Impossible Rhetorical—*"¿Cómo pudo pasar?"* How could this happen? He was having a difficult time keeping his emotions in check; they came at him from hidden angles, each trailing a memory: Bear's mud-caked boots the night he came to tell him and Dray that Ginny had been killed. The sheriff's dispatcher's static-laced voice announcing that a pregnant deputy had been shot point-blank. Tim's exhaustion caught up to him in a rush, and the room seemed to close in on him—the oppressive kitchen humidity, the sticky-sweet smell of the Advent candles, the woman's anguished sobbing.

Everyone murdered is a son or a daughter. Cops and deputies start burning out once they acknowledge this simple fact. The awareness— the *true* awareness—leads to a kind of insanity, a blurred vision. So they fight it tooth and nail. They fight it with the bottle. They fight it by pushing away what *is* theirs with what is not. The smart ones fight it with a cynical eye and gallows humor. And some of them—sometimes the toughest of them—just decide to give up one day and eat their guns or ride motorcycles into brick walls. To acknowledge the essential humanity of each bludgeoned face, each sprawled corpse, each Dumpster baby, is to run the gauntlet with every nerve exposed. But *not* to acknowledge it is a kind of denial, a kind of death in itself.

The shotgun blast that had entered Dray had also knocked Tim's careful system of balance and countermeasure out of whack. His compartments bled into one another; his boundaries slid; his lines blurred. In the haze he sensed a barely conscious choice at hand: He could take either nothing personally or everything. He could either connect the dots between his comatose wife and the other victims or deny them all a place in his heart.

Somewhere the woman's halting English returned. "She will be home. She have to come home to me."

And Bear's soothing murmur: "I'm so sorry, ma'am. We're so sorry."

She looked impossibly frail in Bear's embrace. Tim cleared his throat and blinked away the wetness in his eyes.

"I just make her bed again. Her bed is ready for her." The woman tore at her shirt, her knuckles knobby from years of hard work. She collapsed on the couch, face pressed to the cushion.

Bear did a double take at Tim. "You all right?" he mouthed.

Tim wiped his nose, nodded.

"Why don't you go to the car?"

"I'm fine."

"You'll be finer in the car."

The woman's hoarse sobbing was audible all the way down the walk.

Bear climbed into the car twenty minutes later. Tim's eyes and nose were rimmed red, the contrast severe against the pallid skin of his face. His breathing had settled, the calm after the storm. Bear looked more than a touch unsettled. Tim wouldn't turn to meet his gaze, so Bear faced forward, hands on the wheel, elbows dangling. His head was ducked; he was at a loss.

They were pointed east, and morning leaked at the horizon, a slow, orange bleed.

Tim's voice was cracked and quiet. "Take me to Dray."

30

The waiting-room TV, suspended from a bracket in the corner, offered a virtual face blast of information. Shots within shots, subheadlines with bullet points, an Energizer Bunny crawl across the bottom: *Laughing Sinner killed in Fillmore shoot-out. . . . Pregnant deputy shot by fugitive Den Laurey still in critical condition. . . . Another Cholo found dead. Authorities believe killing related to biker gang war. . . . AP: Mutilated female corpse discovered in former IronClad Parts warehouse. . . .*

Tim caught a few stares from the waiting wounded, who—as a corralled TV viewership on a bureaucratic timetable—had no doubt watched grainy, zoom-lensed Deputy Rackley poking through one of the three high-profile crime scenes that had emerged last night and this morning.

Dray was alone in her room, arrayed peacefully under the covers, her head tilted just so on the pillow. He spoke her name, half expecting her to rise and greet him. Her skin felt hard and waxy and gave off the scent of antiseptic. He missed the smell of her, and it struck him that there was no way to recapture it unless Dray reentered her life, unless she showered, sweated, ate her vast yet specific array of foods, rubbed jasmine lotion into her hands in her elaborate manner that made her look like a cartoon villain scheming. Her smell captured the combination of countless variables that were her life, that were her alive.

A middle-aged woman—a physical therapist by her ID card—entered and introduced herself. She was heavyset and to the point. "The nurses in the CWA told me you're the guy. In charge of catching those bikers? I have a daughter who lives out in Simi. . . ." Her thought trailed off into a dark corner. "You catch those guys."

She pulled the sheets off Dray and rearranged her body with practiced, no-nonsense movements. Dray's arms looked thin, dwarfed by her belly.

"How's she doing?" Tim asked.

"Still not arousable to stimuli. No purposeful movements. The doc says the baby's going strong, so that's good."

She grasped Dray's calf and foot and rocked the leg, as if shaking off dust, then bent it back. She repeated the motion a few times before switching legs. He watched her work. Seeing Dray animated, even falsely, gave him a stab of irrational hopefulness.

Tim cleared his throat. "What can I expect here?"

"There are significant variations based on the nature of the injury—"

"No bullshit," he said softly. "Please."

She paused and regarded him, Dray's foot in hand, before returning to her task. For a moment Tim thought she wasn't going to answer. Then, without looking up, she said, "I can't speak to brain damage. My area of expertise is muscle atrophy. She has a week or two before there's appreciable deterioration. Rehabilitation gets harder after that. And, you know, the likelihood that . . ."

"That she won't be able to."

The physical therapist contemplated Dray's leg bends with renewed focus. Tim watched the knee rise, fall, rise.

Think this is the best use of your time?

"Shut up, Dray."

The therapist caught his murmur, raised an eyebrow in his direction.

I miss you, too, babe, but you have more important things to do than watch me play cadaver Twister.

Tim watched the physical therapist rotate Dray's foot in precise circles.

So you won't leave?

Not right now.

Make yourself useful, then.

The therapist placed Dray's heel on her own shoulder and elevated the leg to stretch the hamstring, her fingers laced to brace the knee straight. She finished and jotted a few notes on her clipboard.

"Can I?"

She looked up at Tim, surprised. Her eyes twinkled with a sad grin that never made it to the rest of her face. "Of course, hon."

Tim set his holstered gun on the neighboring chair and rose. The therapist paused at the door, monitoring him before withdrawing.

Tim started at the beginning of the routine. Dray's bare sole fit perfectly, as always, in the curve of his hand. He'd stretched her enough, before their early-morning runs, to note that her muscles were now tight and cranky. He rotated her arms, compressed her shoulders, kneaded her neck.

He kissed her cool lips before slipping on his holster and heading back to work.

31

Wristwatch Annie shoulder-slumped against the chain-link outside the Sinners' clubhouse, twisting a high heel into the curb and negotiating with a guy in a gray Pinto who was leaning across his passenger seat, john style. Despite the weather she wore a miniskirt, her leather jacket huffing around her shoulders.

When Tim slammed the door of the Explorer and headed across the street, the guy sped off. Despite having grabbed no more than a few hours' sleep, Tim felt surprisingly lucid.

Annie dropped a Baggie to the curb and slid it back with her heel until it slipped through the sewer grates. She smiled sweetly at Tim, showing off matching shelves of creative dentition.

Tim nodded at the grate through which the drugs had made their getaway. "Crank or heroin?"

Her eyes had the infinity stare, pupils dilated wider than the morning sun allowed. "Just sugar, sugar."

"You'd better be careful. I'll write you up for littering."

She returned his smile. "You're a naughty boy. Go to my room."

"How'd you get the name Wristwatch Annie?"

"You *really* wanna know?"

He'd fallen into his and Dray's bed last night grateful for his exhaustion; he'd been unable to muster the energy to be mournful. The light had never made it on, so he'd barely distinguished the house as his home—he'd entered a dark box, slept, and left while the air was still slate at the windows. Knowing he was on the Sinners' hit list, he'd gone as he'd come, over the back fence, a fugitive on his own property.

A Christmas morning very different from the one he would have chosen to wake up to. Annie's game attitude lightened it up, for a moment.

It required three separate parties to escort Tim through the yard and clubhouse upstairs to Uncle Pete's room. Hound Dog, looking displeased beneath his fluffy topknot, balanced atop a card table. Sitting on what looked like a reinforced piano bench, Uncle Pete revved up an electric razor and sculpted the poodle's tail pom-pom. Curls of white hair clung to Uncle Pete's forearms and lay like shorn wool at his feet. The dog's lip wrinkled into a soundless growl at Tim's appearance.

Ash-laden cigarette dangling aesthetically from the corner of his mouth, Uncle Pete flicked the razor at the dog's underbelly. His arm jiggled; stretch marks interrupted his biceps tattoo like vertical blinds. He wore a black shirt with white block letters across the chest: DEEP THINKER. Aphoristic T-shirts seemed a bikerwear staple.

"This here"—Pete leaned back, admiring his work—"this here's the English-saddle clip. Standard poodles are like Harleys—well-designed machines. Waterfowl retrievers. Truffle hunters. Vaudeville performers. They're the smartest dogs, you know that? Clean, too. They don't shed. You leave that to us, don't you, Hound Dog?"

In response the poodle made a sound like a whinny.

Uncle Pete's eyes finally pulled north, taking in Tim. "Where's your backup? The spic and the muscle? Ain't you worried we gonna carve you up?"

"Not a bit."

Pete pinched his cigarette like a joint, sucking a final inhale. The ash fell across his chest, and he brushed it to the carpet with a few delicate flicks of his hand.

"Diamond Dog showed up dead," Tim said. "Wouldn't you know it, he was running with Goat."

A flicker of alarm showed in Uncle Pete's face before receding beneath his usual calm. It was only an instant, but it was precisely what Tim was looking for.

"No matter how I try to keep those boys away from trouble . . ." Pete shook his head. "Ain't it the damnedest thing?"

"The damnedest."

Uncle Pete lifted Hound Dog off the card table, the dog licking his face until he set him down.

"Diamond Dog's one of yours," Tim said. "Not a nomad. This case is at your doorstep now. Thought I'd give you a knock-and-notice."

"Characteristically thoughtful."

"Just another service we provide to taxpaying citizens."

Uncle Pete puffed out his cheeks with a troubled sigh. "Shucks, that *is* bad news about Dog. A lot of my mother-club boys are discipline problems. Impervious to reform, no matter how we try. Now and then they run with the wrong crowd, choose a lifestyle that's socially irresponsible. You let me know if there's any way I or the Laughing Sinners can be of assistance. *Deputy*." His head was pulled back contemptuously, the stick of braided beard pointing at Tim like a gun barrel. "In the meantime I'd recommend you watch yourself. These are some deep, dark rabbit holes you're scurrying down. Keep up the pace, some of the boys might be inclined to start shooting back."

"We got you in our sights now."

"Yeah, Trouble?"

The doorknob twisted behind Tim, and he turned as Dana Lake entered. A Christmas Day house call spoke to the size of the retainer checks she was depositing. She tossed her sleek briefcase onto the recently vacated card table and shoved her seventies-porn-star tinted glasses up onto her perm. "Conversation over."

"Yeah," Tim said, "it is."

"I thought I made myself clear earlier, Deputy Rackley. This afternoon I'll file a complaint with the IA division of the Marshals Service and start a record with the federal prosecutor." Dana produced a sheaf of filled-out complaint forms. "If you bully my client *one more time*, you'll find yourself facing a civil action for the violation of my client's constitutional rights, a restraining order, and harassment charges."

Tim kept his eyes on Uncle Pete. "You feeling harassed?"

Pete held up his hand, thumb and forefinger calibrating about a half inch of air.

"My client's feelings aren't your concern. Nor is he one of the disenfranchised slobs you're used to intimidating, and I'm not some low-rent public defender who just limped through Boalt. You push us, we push back harder. This is a different league, Deputy. Watch that the rarefied air doesn't make you light-headed." The forms disappeared back into the fine-grain leather. "In the meantime I'll be handling the substantial casework from the series of raids you and your death squad carried out last night. You keep killing Sinners, you'll pay off my mortgage."

"I'm surprised it's not already paid off."

"I meant on the house in Vail." Dana snapped her briefcase closed. "Say good-bye, Mr. Rackley. You want to see my client again, you'd better bring a warrant and formal charges."

"That," Tim said, "seems like a fair arrangement."

"Don't let the bikers hit you on your way out."

Uncle Pete grinned. "You heard the woman. Believe me, you don't want to cross swords with this bitch." He moved to smack her on the ass, but she caught his hand at the wrist and threw it away, her eyes never leaving Tim's.

Another pinkie-free mistress led Tim back downstairs. Outside, the two Sinners standing guard over Dana's platinum Jag convertible threw Tim matching glares.

He offered a grin. *"Feliz Navidad."*

32

A rush of deputies hit Tim at the command post's door.

"We got the time of death back on Meat Marquez," Thomas said. "Seventy-two hours, give or take. That puts us back to the early morning after Den and Kaner's breakout—"

"The bomb diagrams you found at Chief's?" Zimmer was animated, his voice higher than usual. "We matched the handwriting to Tom-Tom. Pulled a sample from his booking sheet in an old police report. The specs on the design for the saddlebag special that killed Frankie was in his hand, too."

"—can't link anything from Chief's to the mother chapter," Freed was saying.

"Or from the warehouse," Thomas chimed in. "Aside from Diamond Dog's dead ass, of course."

Tim waded forward into the room. Someone had hung Chief's originals on the wall, like a scalp. Four empty nails beside it awaited the other jackets.

Exemplary professionalism. You gonna let that stand, Task Force Leader?

Tim sighed and pulled Chief's jacket down, then used the hammer to pop the nails from the drywall—game over. There was no need for a speech; the others could take his implication. He turned, dusting his hands and picking up where he'd left off. "Blood match from the embalming table?"

Thomas again: "Still waiting on the lab. But they came back on the body. Surgical incisions in the stomach. Very clean, incised wounds, like from a box cutter or scalpel. Her throat laceration had some abraded edges and bridging of the connective tissue—it was cut with something bigger, a hunting knife maybe. Sounds like Den Laurey to me."

"Any organs removed?"

"Yes, but all accounted for. Stomach was sliced up pretty good."

Tim sought Freed in the cluster of men. "You locate Diamond Dog's bike last night?"

"Nope. I blanketed the area. Not a single chopper."

"Where are we with Chief's credit card?"

"Getting a warrant."

"Lean on that judge. Or find another. How's Guerrera?"

Maybeck: "Shook up and making it worse by pretending not to be."

Bear alone was sitting, a still presence in the swirls of movement. Tim dropped into the chair beside him. "Well?"

"CSI finished sorting the Dumpster trash. The bag I found was the only hit. It was stuffed with bloody rags." Bear inhaled and held his breath for a count, troubled. "They also found *these* loose among the other crap."

He tilted a manila envelope and a crime-scene Baggie slapped the table. It held three rolls of film. Black and white. ISO 1600. Each was numbered with a red pen.

"No latents, but CSI matched the red ink to a pen in the warehouse office. Given that the warehouse is deserted and the Dumpster gets emptied weekly, there's low odds that someone else besides Diamond Dog, Goat, and Co. tossed these in there." Bear held up his hand. "But before you get excited . . ."

"What?"

"They're blank. Unexposed."

Tim rocked back in his chair, disappointed. "What kind of film is it?"

"Used mostly by professionals. It's super high-speed, which yields lower resolution. Best for low-light conditions, motion, grainy arthouse shit."

"I doubt Cindy Crawford's limo was en route."

"So what, then? Snuff shots of Marisol?"

"What stopped them?"

"Maybe they used rolls four through six."

"Get it developed."

"There's nothing to see. I told you, it hasn't been shot yet."

"Just have it processed. Maybe there's a hidden image or something. Anything." Tim pivoted in his chair. "What gives on Goat?"

Malane, sitting calmly, said, "He's under hospitalization."

"Let's press him. Where is he?"

"Unconscious."

"That's not a location."

"For him it is." Malane returned Tim's gaze, stonewalling him.

"I'm getting tired of fucking around with you." At Tim's tone the room quieted. "Where's the fugitive *we* took into custody?"

"I can't disclose that at this time."

Bear stood and walked over to Malane so the agent had to lean back in his chair to look up at him. "I've about hit my limit. I'll ask you once: What are you up to?"

Bear's quiet voice drew Tim to his feet; the only time he worried about Bear was when he got unreasonably calm. Though Malane met Bear's eyes, he made no move to rise. Tim was unsure whether he was contemplating an answer or merely staring back, but either way Bear's patience didn't seem likely to hold.

The door banged open, and Tannino stormed in. "Get *this* bullshit." He grabbed the remote from the tabletop and raised the volume on the TV in the corner.

Melissa Yueh, more shoulder-padded than usual, was wrapping her report. "—confirming, at the abandoned warehouse FBI forces stormed late last night here in Simi." Footage rolled of an FBI task force— agency initials rendered in camera-friendly yellow block letters on raid jackets—storming the empty cinder-block facility. Tim took note of the sky's coloring—dawn, probably an hour or two after the Service had cleared out. No one could question the FBI's proficiency at PR.

"You did a fucking raid *simulation* for the cameras?" Tannino tugged at his collar, his affect blown Archie Bunker broad. "After my guys risked their asses in there?"

Melissa Yueh egged him with her curt, newsroom delivery. "A Bureau spokesman confirmed for KCOM that this is the first arrest in the escalating turf war between the Laughing Sinners and the Cholos."

Tannino unleashed a stream of invective at Malane, some of it in English. The deputies watched, arms folded, wearing told-you-so expressions. Even Jim, who'd been sulking in the corner, perked up a bit at the dramatics. Malane stood and leaned forward into the tirade, fists on the tabletop, repeating quietly, "Take it up with my supervisor."

A court security officer yelled over the commotion. "CSI line four."

Tim pointed and mouthed, "Other room." He pulled Bear—who was relishing the confrontation—toward the door. On his way past the marshal, Tim leaned over and said, "He also took Goat to an undisclosed location. We have no access to our prisoner. Take that up with his supervisor, too, please."

They could hear Tannino's shouts all the way down the hall. They ducked into an empty conference room, and Bear knuckled the blinking light, then the speakerphone button.

Aaronson's voice came through. As usual he was distracted, speaking slowly. "I was processing the embalming table, right? And I picked up this hair tangled in the gutter drain. It was black, not dyed orange like the others, so I ran the follicle—short tandem repeats to check the DNA. We got these new kits from Cofiler, they're much faster—"

"Aaronson," Bear said. "The DNA."

"Well, it doesn't belong to Marisol Juarez. It belongs to another woman who recently died. Jennifer Villarosa."

"Why's Villarosa's DNA on record?" Bear asked. "She a felon?"

"A soldier. They got her DNA in the system before Iraq, the optimists."

"How'd she die? And when?"

"Accidental, two months ago. But the really weird thing is . . ."

"Yeah?" Tim and Bear asked together.

"She died in Mexico."

Guerrera was sitting cross-legged in the unlit basement, little more than a round shadow against the dark workout mats. He was hunched over, as if in prayer, his fingertips rimming his forehead at the hairline.

His eyes were focused on the rubber; he hadn't raised his head at Tim and Bear's entrance.

"We need you to take point upstairs. Let's go—we'll ride up with you, fill you in." Guerrera stayed motionless, so Tim repeated, "Let's go."

Guerrera's voice came low. "Maybe I could've just wounded him. Maybe I didn't have to kill him."

"I was there," Bear said. "You had to kill him."

"No one *has* to do anything."

Bear raised his eyebrows in exasperation and looked to Tim—too philosophical for his blood.

"You're right," Tim said, "You wanted this, Rey. And you got it. And it doesn't feel like you thought it would."

Guerrera kept staring off into the dark corners, his eyes distant.

"But we're in the thick of it right now," Tim said. "I'm sorry, but you don't come, this case leaves without you."

A long pause. Tim looked at Bear. Bear grimaced, then ambled over, pausing above Guerrera. He offered his hand. It hung in the air for a while.

Guerrera took it, pulled himself to his feet, and followed them out.

33

"She survives thirteen months in Iraq, dies snorkeling in Cabo." Mr. Villarosa, a distinguished man with graying sideburns and erect posture, smoothed his sleek mustache with his thumb and forefinger. "We dropped her off at LAX smiling, beautiful. She came back three days later in a casket."

His wife's delicate blue eyes leaked at the corners; she'd had tissue in hand even when she answered the door. Mr. Villarosa was more stoic—he had a profile cut from stone—but the pain still showed in the creases in his upper cheeks, the rigidity of his carriage. The suffering couldn't penetrate his façade, so it had worked on him from the inside. Tim wondered if his own erosion was as evident to a practiced eye.

Focus on them, *Timothy. You owe them that.*

Both parents, speaking nearly perfect, unaccented English, had been gracious when Tim and Bear had apologized for interrupting their Christmas afternoon. Cinnamon candles enlivened the air, and a bird was roasting deliciously in the oven, but the holiday embellishments seemed added by rote. The house was still suffused with grief. Jennifer had died October 29, less than two months ago.

Wicker-and-glass cabinets displayed gold-rimmed china and a few pieces of dubious crystal. The carpet was plush—too plush—and bore vacuum-cleaner stripes. Porcelain sylvan figurines were arranged on doilies with great pride. When Mr. Villarosa offered that he'd run a household-appliance repair business for twenty-five years, his hand pulled toward his pocket, an instinctive move for his business card. Tim watched the impulse extinguished, brutally, the moment Villarosa recalled the meeting's purpose.

A glass-framed photo of Jennifer and a carefully constructed wreath decorated the lid of an off-white upright piano. A tough-looking, hefty woman with a bull neck, muscular shoulders, and shorn hair, she wore a stern face, peering out from beneath her ROTC cadet dress hat.

"Why was she in Mexico?"

"She won a trip there," Mrs. Villarosa said softly. "She went with her . . . *friend.*"

Mr. Villarosa handed them some papers with GOOD MORNING VACA-TIONS cheerily lettered across the top in predictable yellow. *Congratulations, Ms. Villarosa, you've won an all-expenses-paid trip to Cabo San Lucas!!*

"Where's her friend now?" Bear asked.

"Back in Iraq."

"Were you apprised of the circumstances of her death?"

"Yes, the army aided us in looking into it. They poked around with the hotel and the detectives down there. We were spared the details, but we were told there wasn't anything to find out. A—what did they call it?"

His wife answered quietly, "Shallow-water blackout."

Tim folded the papers into his pocket. "This is an awkward question, Mr. and Mrs. Villarosa, and I apologize, but we need to know if Jennifer ever rode with or had any relationships with bikers."

The man's laugh took Tim by surprise. "No way. She was a school nerd—very straitlaced. A good, good kid." He looked down, studying his thumbnail. Mrs. Villarosa pulled a tissue from her shirtsleeve and dabbed her eyes. "The travel company was very honorable, thank God. They got us our Jennifer delivered right to the funeral home up here. We gave her a good Catholic burial."

"I wish there was something better I could say," Tim said, "but I'd like to offer my condolences. Jennifer seems like she was a lovely person."

Mrs. Villarosa turned her face and wept silently into her tissue. Her husband nodded. "Thank you for using her name."

Tim and Bear rose to leave, standing awkwardly to see if Mrs. Villarosa was going to look up so they could say good-bye.

"Can I ask what this is about?" Mr. Villarosa asked. "It was an accidental death, that's all."

Bear said gently, "I'm afraid we can't—"

"A girl was killed last night," Tim said.

"And you think it's somehow related?"

"We don't know at this point. We really don't."

Mr. Villarosa's face stiffened, anguish pulling his skin taut. "If there's *anything* we can do, please give us the opportunity."

His handshake was desperate, as if he couldn't make himself let go.

"We will," Tim said.

34

The Impala's steering wheel looked tiny in Bear's grip. The marshal had been beating the drum on agency image, and after the FBI's maneuver this morning, Bear wasn't about to inherit his excess wrath for taking his beat-to-hell Dodge Ram to question a bereaved family. He and Tim had their windows down, letting the cool air clear their thoughts.

Tim watched Guerrera's St. Michael medallion sway from the rearview. "They'd just accepted it was a freak accident. Then we come in . . ."

"There's no connection." Bear forged ahead. *"None."* For a reason Tim had yet to grasp, Bear liked to get angry when he thought through a case. "We have a broke girl from Chatsworth and a first lieutenant from Sylmar. One was murdered in Simi, one was an accidental death in Mexico."

"So how do you explain them sharing trace evidence on the embalming table?"

"Could be anything. I know you have an undying respect for the men and women who wear our proud uniform, but who knows what the girl did when she was home on leave? Maybe she doesn't live up to her dad's image. The Sinners run those clubhouses as fuckshacks. Maybe she takes a walk on the wild side, leaves a stray hair in Goat's underwear that hitchhikes around town, winds up in the wrong place."

"Because Sinners love Mexican girls."

"Right, right, stupid theory." Bear chewed his lip. "Plus, the girl looked like she caught every tour of the Indigo Girls, you catch my drift. Too bad the 'friend' is in Iraq—not that she saw shit, judging from her statement." He adjusted the seat for the fifteenth time—still no space-enlarging technology. "It *is* just a hair. I mean, it's not like they found her blood. A hair you can get anywhere. Maybe it got tracked in on someone's shoe."

"Big coincidence. The hair of another dead Mexican girl?"

"Okay," Bear said. "Maybe the embalming table was taken from the funeral home that processed Villarosa's body. Let's have Thomas look into it." He hit speed dial, but his elbow knocked the passenger chair and he dropped the phone.

Tim scooped it up as Bear swerved and cursed. On the phone, Thomas was hurried. "Yeah, okay. I'll try to source the embalming table. Might open up some angles."

Tim asked, "Where are we with the credit card?"

"We got the subpoenas over to Visa. Chief's statements should arrive in our fax momentarily."

"Okay. I also want you to check out other Mexican and Mexican-American females in and from L.A. County and Ventura County who've died in the past couple months."

"Died or been killed?"

"Pull murders and deaths under questionable circumstances. Villarosa was a supposed accident. There's something going on, we're not sure what."

"You want me to check all dead Mexicans?"

"Let's say fifteen to thirty years old. And overweight."

"Overweight? Fatter's harder. To kidnap, control, *and* dispose. Are they killing to type? If there's some serial-killer bullshit going on, we'd better get ready to mend fences with our buddies at the Fucking Bunch of Idiots."

"Mr. Hoover's organization hasn't risen in popularity since we left?"

"Tannino pulled his Pacino routine on Malane for a good half hour, booted him off the task force."

"Any chance he coughed up where he stowed Goat before he left?"

"Nope. And I never got the Uncle Pete files from him. The Feebs definitely haven't shared their toys on this one." Someone shouted something in the background, and Thomas said, "Oh, yeah, we got your film back from the lab. The prints from the Dumpster? They're all black. Surprise, surprise. But the good news is, we might have gotten a line on Danny the Wand. A business used to sublease some shop space over in Glendale, went by Danny's Bike 'n' Boat Designs. Closed up in May '03. Records are a mess, but we found a year-old forward-mail request to an address in North Hollywood. Danny Pater."

"That's over our way. Give us the address. We'll check it out on the way back."

Tim punched the address into the navigation system and waited a moment until the woman's frosty automated voice set them on course.

He called Aaronson, who'd promised to follow up with the Cabo San Lucas morgue and peruse the coroner's report.

"Standard diving death, far as I can tell," the criminalist said. "Drownings are tough to unwind, but I didn't see any red flags. I think we chalk this one up to fate's sense of humor."

Tim thanked him and hung up. When traffic inevitably thickened at the 118 exchange, Bear set the magnetic light on the roof, letting the siren burp a few times as they navigated the lanes. They exited, passing through a residential area. A few of the houses had clothes displayed on lawns and across bushes, leftovers from holiday *mercado*-style yard sales.

A local shock jock, in a fit of decency, had taken up Dray's cause, fielding phone calls from sympathetic listeners. The tearful words of support from strangers made Tim at first uncomfortable, then emotional, so he changed the station. A midstream commercial promising listeners they could say good-bye to unwanted hair . . . for*ever* . . . made the whole episode seem mildly ridiculous. Bear thankfully withheld comment.

They found the address, a strip-mall installment nestled between a pager-and-cell-phone shop and a check-cashing operation. Bear eased past the entrance—DTW PAINT DESIGNS vividly airbrushed on the blacked-out windows—parked at a bent parking meter, and shoved the keys in his pocket. The navigation system feigned immense pleasure: *You have arrived!*

Bear regarded the field file in his lap. "So we're thinking this guy might—"

The Impala's back window shattered. The headrests blocked most of the flying glass, but jagged bits tore at Tim's neck and ear. He and Bear tried to duck into the footwells as more bullets hollowed out the dash.

The car's interior was turning to shrapnel all around them as the chuffing of unseen weapons continued—the unremitting percussion of the full-auto, the sporadic pop of a handgun. Bear was hunched forward, steering wheel jammed into his cheek; they were completely pinned down. Tim saw a flash of inspiration touch Bear's face, and then Bear reached over and tugged the trunk release. The metal lid flew up, shielding them from the onslaught and giving them momentary cover to bail out of the car.

Bear threw his weight against his door. The Kojak light, still magnetized to the roof, whipped around the top frame, clocking Bear in the forehead and knocking him across Tim's just-vacated seat. Set in a high-kneel shooting position on the sidewalk, Tim returned fire at the starburst holes in the blacked-out windows. Only in the following silence could he hear how loudly his ears were ringing.

Casting a glance at Bear's dazed body sprawled across the front seats, Tim rose and sprinted to a position of cover beside the front door. He inched the door open with the barrel of his .357. A gunman lay between the tall counter and throw of chairs that constituted the reception area. His biker-long hair had fallen like a sheet over his face, his gasps making it pulse over his mouth. Blood from a chest wound continued to spread through an airbrushed jungle-design T-shirt, the widening splotch devouring pythons and panthers. Tim couldn't recognize the downed man from his build and bearing. Still, the biker clutched a handgun—a little .32 Centennial from the looks of it. Clearly he'd been backed by meaner firepower.

A wall behind the counter segregated the workshop proper—though, judging by the eye-watering intensity of the paint fumes, not well. Tim ran in a ducked position, kicking away the handgun and squatting over the biker as he secured his wrists with cuffs. Tim kept his eyes on the beaded curtain behind the counter. "Danny Pater?"

The biker's head jerked, clearing the hair to reveal eye shadow and a delicate nose. Blood colored the lips, flecked the chin. The woman on Richie Rich's arm at the funeral.

Tim's eyes pulled to the framed business license on the wall: Danielle Pater.

She coughed, her shirt fluttering above the chest wound, and died with her mouth open against the worn carpet.

A scurry of footsteps in the back. Something toppled and made a clamor on the floor. Smith & Wesson straight-armed in front of him, Tim headed behind the counter. He paused to the side of the curtain, pulse quickening at the prospect of being in the same building as Den Laurey. The gaps between the still-rippling beads showed darkness. He reached through, groping for a light switch but having no luck.

He gathered his courage and sprang through, landing flat-bellied against the inside wall to control the silhouette threat. He blinked hard to stimulate his night vision. Proning out made him vulnerable to ricochets, but he didn't want to get on his feet until he had his bearings.

A wall of paint cans protected him. A few had been knocked over, Lion's Tongue Red puddling across the slick concrete.

He found his feet and shouldered against a ceiling-high metal rack that held elaborately painted gas tanks. Natural light leaked around a closed door in the rear, maybe a bathroom with a window. Tim caught a giggle, and then a wide form topped with a familiar mop of hair flashed across the faint glow—Tom-Tom having fun. Tim's aim was an instant late. He didn't fire, not wanting to broadcast position, but his barrel must have given up a glint, because a spray of yellow erupted from the far corner, and the tanks behind him jumped and spun. He rolled maybe ten feet, winding up with a back wet with paint and his face pressed to the wheel of a Harley. The barrage of gunfire quieted, and then Tom-Tom made kissing noises at the darkness, as if calling a cat.

Something metal clattered across the concrete, and an explosion blew the rack off its moorings. Empty tanks rained down, making an impressive racket. The brief blaze wisped off in blue curls, picking up extra mileage from the paint fumes.

Tim watched the darkness through the spokes of the wheel. His soldier's ear told him that two men were circling the space separately.

A sliver of red footprint stood out between a couple of half-sprayed Harleys. Moving silently, Tim followed the trail, weaving through bikes, the drip of grease into oil pans penetrating the silence with maddening regularity. The tread impressions grew fainter. Tim reached the north wall, easing around a workman's bench.

A form up ahead, a pair of hands holding a Glock upright next to a cheek.

The head turned, the faint light giving Tim an eclipse profile of the right side—choppy hair, eye patch, armband. Then Tim made out the upside-down FBI patch stitched to the jacket, a trophy for burying two bullets in Raymond Smiles's chest as the agent had eaten dinner. Tim took aim at the block of critical mass. He pictured his target reclined on his bike, sneering at Dray, *You'd better back off, bitch.*

Dray's voice cut through Tim's rage: *He's no good to us dead.*

Richie Rich's pinkie ring blinked a star of light, removing all doubt, and Tim stepped forward and swung the butt of his gun into his temple. Rich grunted and collapsed, and Tim darted for cover before Tom-Tom could track his movement by Rich's thud to the concrete. Too late he heard the pipe bomb scuttling across the floor after him like an angry rodent. He opened his mouth, exhaling hard so his lungs wouldn't rupture with the overpressure, an instinct pounded into him in Ranger training.

The blast slammed him against the far wall. A bank of blacked-out windows blew, permitting a sudden insurge of light, and Tim came to in a heap against the Sheetrock, covered with a film of dust.

Breath jerking, ribs aching, torso slick with red paint or blood or both, he heard a shuffling and looked up. Still half blinded from the explosion and the sudden sun, he barely discerned the movement before him, but the tip of the auto pressing against his throat was all too clear.

Tom-Tom dimly resolved into view, a pale, stocky outline against Tim's still-bleached field of vision. Platinum curls, a boulder of a head set directly on broad shoulders, the amused, irrepressible grin of a misbehaving child. Stubble dusted his cheeks like white sand. Another pipe bomb protruded from his pocket like a rolled-up comic book. He looked down at Tim over the sights, one-arming the AR-15 so the stock rested against his meaty biceps.

"Couldn'ta been worth it," he said.

Tim felt no fear, just the slow-motion grimness of reality setting in, and he thought, So this is where it ends.

The sharp report of a bullet. Tom-Tom fell stiffly, as one rigid piece, revealing not Bear but Rich Mandrell. The right side of the biker's face was swollen so badly from Tim's blow it looked as though the skin might split.

Rich said, "God*damn*it," as if he'd dinged his Porsche with a shopping cart. He thrust the barrel of his Glock into Tim's hands and said, "Cuff me. Get them on *now*. Handle me rough and get me the fuck outta here."

35

W ho the hell are you?" Bear asked.

Richie Rich reclined on the wall-mounted bench, his shoulders and head propped against the bars. They'd put him in Cell Block's keep-away zone, behind the holding pens for the standard fare—gangbangers and second-tier mafiosos awaiting court appearances. Additional steel doors covered the mesh gates back here, protecting the identities of the detainees. Witnesses offering testimony against high-profile defendants were stored here, as well as HIV-positive prisoners, hard cases, and juveniles. The single-occupant cells were metal wonderlands—aluminum toilets, steel-reinforced security cams, sturdy sink columns. Everything was bolted or welded down.

The paint on Tim's shirt had hardened, staining the fabric Lion's Tongue Red. A trickle of a less virile tint had dried behind his ear; he'd spent the ride back to Roybal picking bits of windshield glass from his matted hair. Tannino had swapped out his .357 at the command post, wearing a droll expression—"And to think you objected to the nickname." The marshal was back in his office now, lighting up the phone board.

Tim and Bear had pulled in Guerrera, who leaned quietly against the bars, preoccupied. Bear had presented him his St. Michael medallion from the Impala's rearview mirror, and he'd taken it reluctantly, like a war widow accepting Old Glory. The bullet-riddled vehicle had required a flatbed tow.

"We have you on tape shooting Raymond Smiles." Bear grimaced and rubbed the red indentation on his forehead. His headache and the ribbing he'd gotten in the command post—Thomas and Freed had wrapped bandages around their heads like turbans, and Jim had adhered a battery-operated police light to his crown with heavy-duty rubber bands—didn't seem to be helping his mood. "FBI agent you capped in a restaurant in October. You left him facedown in his tiramisu. You remember?"

Rich tore off a dirty thumbnail with his teeth and spit it on the floor. "He was still on the entrée."

"Did you switch teams, Richie Rich?" Bear pressed. "You go on someone's payroll?"

Rich gingerly touched the nasty bruise by his temple.

Tim watched him closely. "You're undercover," he said. "Customs or DEA?"

Rich's lips barely moved. "FBI." His first unsnide utterance.

"FBI?" Bear said. "Great. Spectacular. So *now* you wanna tell us why we can't scrape you guys off our boots?"

Finally Rich raised his head. A blood vessel had burst in his eye, a red flare across his unhealthy-looking, yellow-tinted sclera. "It's worse than you think."

A double knock on the door—the detention enforcement officer's warning—and the steel swung back with a creak. Dressed impeccably in an olive suit, Raymond Smiles walked into the cell. The black agent paused and raised his hands ever so slightly, a magician's flourish to underscore his resurrection.

In a Spanish murmur, Guerrera invoked saints' names and swear words. Rich held up his wrists, and Smiles unlocked the cuffs.

Bear stared at the FBI agent, risen from the dead. "What the hell," he said, "is going on here?"

Tannino was at the cell door, Jeff Malane beside him. "Why don't you two come back to my office, and we'll get this goatfuck untangled as best we can."

Tannino had one foot up on his desk, providing the others in the couches and chairs an inadvertently vulgar vantage. He'd cracked a window before sitting, but still the office air was stale and warm.

"We've had our task force on the ground in Los Angeles for three months," Smiles said.

"It's called Operation Cleansweep," Rich said.

"We have an operation going on, too," Bear volunteered from his arms-crossed lean against the wall. "It's called Operation Take a Fucking Shower."

"You got a lotta mouth for a guy knocked himself unconscious with a police light." Rich's black eye had gone from purple to an unlikely shade of brown; he'd had to score it with a razor blade to take the swelling down.

"You were firing an AR-15 at us."

"I told you, that was Tom-Tom. I was in the back when the caps started flying."

"The roses," Tim said abruptly.

His non sequitur drew looks from all quarters.

"We saw the video clip of your fake hit on Smiles at the restaurant," Tim continued. "Nice clean angle for the eight o'clock news. But the table you were sitting at"—a nod to Smiles—"had a tall centerpiece. Roses. Live rounds would've knocked over the flowers on the way to your chest. Blanks wouldn't."

Rich nodded, impressed. "I'm glad Chief didn't have your eye."

"You knew Smiles was already in Chief's hit binder, so when given the choice of targets, you picked him."

"Only way to make striker and ride with the crew," Rich said. "Cap a copper."

"You did *nothing* while a pregnant sheriff's deputy was shot point-blank in the chest." The intensity of the anger in Tim's voice brought Tannino upright in his chair.

Rich spread his hands, palms to heaven. "What the fuck was I supposed to do?"

The vehicle-cam footage remained vivid in Tim's mind. The twitch of Rich's scowl. *You'd better back off, bitch.* Tim registered the words now as a hidden caution. Rich's cry the moment before Dray stepped into range had not been an angry shout but a panicked warning—*Get the fuck outta here!* And after the shotgun blast, Rich's taut face and bared teeth were, Tim realized, an expression of horror, not atavistic release.

"Look, my hands were tied at the scene." Rich's cheek twitched; the guilt had been working on him. "I took a risk right after and made the anonymous call to the station that probably saved her life."

"Let me dust off a medal of valor for you," Tim said.

"My hands were *tied*. There were five of them."

Six if you count Marisol Juarez.

Tim picked up Dray's rebuke. "Six if you count Marisol Juarez."

"Who's that?"

"She was the Mexican girl on the back of Kaner's bike who we found disemboweled last night in a warehouse. You met her at the same time you let Den Laurey shoot Andrea Rackley right above her highly visible pregnancy. Guess your hands were tied there, too."

Contrition flashed on Rich's ragged face, a surprisingly soft expression beneath the scars and stubble. He shored himself back up, adjusting his eye patch with a snap that had to sting. "Some Mexican girl they killed doesn't make their top ten. These boys'd put a hole in someone's head just to have a place to rest their beer. A girl who got cut up is—sadly—the fuckin' least of it. I've got bigger responsibilities, a task force living on what I can feed them. I don't have the luxury of breaking cover just to get myself *and* their intended victim killed. There are bigger stakes here. I can't tell you the shit I've seen."

"You'd better start," Tannino said. "Right now."

The three FBI agents offered one another an array of eye contact that suggested staging, and then Smiles, the head suit at supervisory special agent, cleared his throat and said, "Allah's Tears."

Tannino said, "Huh?" with great annoyance.

"A new form of extremely fine heroin. The purest to hit our radar. It's a liquid concentration, translucent like water. AT's potency, compared to regular heroin, is off the charts. It takes an enormous amount of raw product—the output of hundreds of acres of poppy field—to yield a liter of this stuff. The chem jockeys worked out the production technology so that even saline-diluted to twentieth strength, a milliliter'll put you on the nod for six hours. It's highly addictive, makes black-tar withdrawal look like giving up ice cream for Lent. Easier to smuggle, too—requires minimal storage space. You mule in a fist-size shipment, dilute it, dole out drops in vials, and it'll go like wildfire."

Rich took up his hair in a fist, forming a makeshift ponytail. "Think the crack epidemic Supersized."

"But this product's even easier to move. Crack's appeal is that it's cheap to the consumer. This is economical for the distributor. And now AT's ready for a test run. L.A.'s the target market." Smiles traced his glistening, well-manicured mustache with a thumb and forefinger. "That's the good news."

"The bad news," Rich picked up without missing a beat, "is that this shit is straight from labs in southern Afghanistan. Affiliated with guess what loosely structured global Islamic terror organization? This particular Hydra head is a Sunni extremist group splintered out of As-bat al-Ansar, call themselves 'al-Fath.' Their guy on the ground in L.A. is Dhul Faqar Al-Malik, a Pakistani, alias is 'the Prophet's Sword.'"

Tannino's grimace said he knew the name. Al-Malik had probably achieved topic-of-discussion status at Head Feds briefings.

"He's the point man, tasked with establishing financial and opera-tional footing so they can help generate sleeper cells and bankroll fu-ture operations in the city." Smiles paused, his dark eyes showing the depth of his concern. "We strongly believe that the Prophet has forged an alliance with the Laughing Sinners."

"Don't fundamentalist terrorists have greater concerns at this mo-ment than dicking around with bikers and junkies?" Tannino said.

"A lot of their assets—particularly those in the U.S.—have been frozen since the post-9/11 crackdown. And since we put the screws to the banks, moving money across borders is harder. We've seized more money coming in than I'm at liberty to disclose. AT is the newest wrin-kle. It eliminates the need for al-Fath to smuggle large quantities of heroin into the country, or money, and it also cuts the need to set up a false-flag operation." A hint of admiration found its way onto Smiles's face. "The money's made in L.A., and it stays in L.A."

"Until it funds God knows what," Rich said. "L.A.'s been the brass ring for the ragheads since the Towers fell. You saw the contingency plans they squeezed out of Khalid Shaikh Mohammed."

Malane offered a now-you-see-what-I've-been-dealing-with dip of the head. "The Sinners' drug-distribution network's already up and running—al-Fath's just tapping in to it. No start-up costs. No added exposure. In turn the Sinners get a cut of the action and an opportunity to corner the market on AT—everyone wins."

"As you well know," Smiles said, "no one on the West Coast can touch the Sinners when it comes to distribution."

Tannino lifted a crime-scene photo from his leather blotter—Cholo corpses baking in the Palmdale heat. "Especially now."

A little nod. "Especially now."

Rich said, "Since the U.S. invasion, opium production in Afghanistan is up two *thousand* percent."

Guerrera alone looked shocked. "What? Why?"

"Because the big producers are the warlords *we* backed to oust the Taliban," Tim said. "If we cracked down on poppy production, we'd suffer a backlash from our supposed friends."

Rich looked at him, as if puzzled by how a mere federal deputy could grasp international intricacies. Then another expression rippled across his face—something approximating respect—and he said, "You were there."

"Early days. Through the fall of Kabul."

"Army?"

"Rangers."

Smiles said, "The warlords control the areas where the poppies are grown, but they can't make it into heroin. They used to ship it to Pakistan and other neighboring countries for the refining process. But now it gets trucked to al-Fath-run labs in the nearby countryside, and the warlords get to keep more of the profits."

Guerrera again: "So the warlords helped us out until the terrorists made them a better offer."

Noting the frustration on Guerrera's face, Tim thought back to when he, too, had believed that there were clear sides in wartime, that allies aligned based on ideologies, that loyalty and consistency could be factored as part of a strategic equation. It was before he ever saw combat. Where he'd been deployed, the old rules hadn't held. And so now he found the Sinners no more surprising an addition than the Afghan warlords; the bikers were a terrorist-affiliated group as dangerous as any other. Just because they didn't cleave to a particular ideology hardly made them less menacing. Or easier to fight.

"For obvious reasons," Smiles added, "the shift to domestic heroin refining in Afghanistan has increased pressure for more efficient means of exportation. Thus Allah's Tears."

Night was at the windows and the fluorescents were headache-inducing. Tim's thoughts wandered to his wife, and he fought them back to the case. "Do you have a bead on the Prophet?" He read the disappointment on all three agents' faces; it was a case they'd been taking personally for a long time.

"No," Smiles said. "With the Sinners running the drug operation, Al-Malik gets to remain in the background. If we roll someone up, odds are he's wearing originals and long hair. As you've seen."

"How about bank records? I doubt he's trusting the finances to Uncle Pete."

"The terrorists have wised up. They used to funnel money through Middle Eastern Studies professors or Islamic charities, but they've gone another step removed. They put no records under Arab names anymore. No bank accounts, cell-phone bills, nothing. They deal in unattached launderers, pay and play, no zealotry required. All that's required is a rudimentary understanding of banking, a clean record, and an Anglo-Saxon name."

"What's the size of shipment?"

"Our intel suggests the package is two liters."

"What's our timeline?"

"Right fuckin' now," Rich said.

"How do you know the shipment's not already in the U.S.?"

"We don't," Rich said.

Smiles intervened calmingly. "We're taking the prison break as an indication that the Sinners are ready to go live with the next phase. Den and Kaner will likely oversee enforcement for AT's introduction to the market. And they wasted no time cleaning up the competition, as the marshal indicated earlier."

"How's the product coming in?" Tannino asked. "Obviously it's not riding the Kabul Concorde to LAX."

"From the south," Smiles said. "Mexico's easy. Penetrating the U.S. is the challenge."

Guerrera piped up for the first time. "How do you know it's Mexico?"

Smiles took a deep breath, and he and Malane shared a solemn glance. "A red flag sailed across the desk of our attaché in Manzanillo last Monday."

"Day before Den and Kaner's break," Bear said.

Smiles again: "An Afghan shipping company slipped something through a few days prior on a license with a pre-2005 code. Only problem is, the license was ostensibly issued six months ago. Great fake, just two numerals reversed. Our attaché started pulling documents, put together that the company—under ten layers of bullshit—is an al-Fath front. The shipment presumably held lapis lazuli jewelry, but he discovered that an airport security worker was bribed to keep the narcotics dogs clear. Trace elements on the shipping label tested positive for AT."

"And the shipment itself?"

"Lost track of it once it left the premises."

Rich said, "The Sinners are taking over the product in Mexico, and it's on them to mule it into the U.S. My money says the product's with them already. Or their proxies. Waiting to ship."

Malane offered a dry grin. "Ready for the veins of America."

"Air, sea, or land?" Tannino asked.

"We're not sure, but we're ready," Smiles said. "We're running high alert at the borders. Customs and DEA are ramped up. Plus, AT's got a few drawbacks that work to our advantage. It gives off a strong olfactory signature that makes it susceptible to narc dogs and electronic noses. And al-Fath can't afford to lose the product. Way too much raw opium at stake, and way too much of the Prophet's credibility. Making AT is basically betting the whole crop on a few liters. Not to mention the refining process, which is time-consuming and expensive as hell. A single bust wipes out the season for them."

"And it wipes out al-Fath's burgeoning reputation in the international terrorism industry," Rich added.

"Seems like they're setting up a pipeline that's full of risks," Guerrera said.

"That's the beauty of it," Smiles said. "They don't need a continuous pipeline, just a one-off—a single risk with a huge payday. Two liters smuggled in and diluted out will give them a nine-month supply to market."

"A lifetime in the drug trade," Tim said.

"And about fifty million dollars."

"That's a lotta box cutters." Ignoring the others' grimaces, Rich picked something out of a molar with a fingernail. "It's high stakes all the way around. The Sinners'll want to track it in—this ain't no see-if-it-flies coke shipment in the back of a coyote's pickup."

"So the Sinners'll be hands-on with it," Tim said.

Rich nodded. "We think Diamond Dog set up the operation down there with two other guys from the mother chapter, Toe-Tag and Whelp. They made three Mexico runs before you ventilated Diamond Dog's chest."

The memory of the shooting creased Guerrera's forehead.

"Why would Uncle Pete send mother-chapter members instead of nomads?" Tim asked.

"Fugitives can't risk border crossings. Uncle Pete had to loan out some of the clean-cut mother-chapter boys."

"Regular Cub Scouts," Bear said.

"You alerted Border Patrol to log them coming and going?" Tim asked.

"Of course," Smiles said. "Those three were frisked head to toe coming back across each time. Nothing on them, nothing on the bikes. Every time."

"Which border station?" Tim asked.

"San Ysidro–Tijuana," Rich said.

"How long do they stay in Mexico?"

Malane handed Tim an interagency memorandum. "About five days. Once in the end of October, once in early November, once at the end of November."

Tim studied the dates. "They were down there when Jennifer Villarosa died. October twenty-ninth."

"Who's that?" Smiles asked.

"We found a hair of hers on the embalming table. Best we can tell, she died snorkeling in Cabo."

"Cabo's a ways down the coast from Tijuana," Bear said.

"The mother-chapter boys had five days," Tim said. "It's only, what? Nine hundred miles?"

"Fifteen hours in the saddle?" Guerrera said. "That's nothing for guys used to cross-country biker runs. They love it."

"Villarosa's death was an accidental," Bear said.

"Maybe she saw something she wasn't supposed to," Tim said.

The FBI agents bristled impatiently. The theory sounded thin even to Tim's own ears.

Malane produced a new border report. "Toe-Tag and Whelp crossed over again yesterday morning."

"You hold them?" Tannino asked.

"What charges?"

"You follow them?"

An embarrassed silence. Finally Rich said, "They played musical vehicles in a parking garage. Mexican agents lost 'em outside San Antonio del Mar."

"Didn't you have Border Patrol put transmitters on them?" Tim asked.

"Sure." Smiles's lips got tight. "On the bikes they ditched."

"So they're receiving the package in Tijuana as we speak?"

"Unless they're decoys," Rich said. "All we know, they just swung through for a donkey show and some 'tang."

"So what *do* you have on the smuggling operation?" Tim asked. "I mean actually *have*. How much of this is hypothetical?"

"I've been able to pick up some low-res intel without getting a lot of specifics."

"That's really helpful," Bear said. "While you're at it, why don't you raise the threat level to fuchsia and urge citizens to exercise caution?"

"They were bringing me inside. All the way." Rich stood up, angry, and Bear came off the wall a step to match him. "I was right on the verge—days away, maybe hours. I already had the distribution center nailed down—Danny the Wand's shop. She draws Sinners from all over the county. Oh, I'm sorry. She *drew* Sinners from all over the county. Because that lead is *gone*."

His anger seemed undercut by something softer, maybe sadness. Tim wondered—as he had when Rich had paused over Danielle's body on their way out of the shop—if Rich had gone beyond role-playing in his undercover relationship with her.

"And guess what happened there?" Rich continued. "You guys came storming in during the preshow, guns ablaze, fucking up the game plan."

Tannino rose and set his fists flat-knuckled on the desktop. "You trip through our sanctioned investigation and have the audacity to blame us for stepping on your dick? *You* should have alerted *us* that the shop was a hot spot. And your liaison"—Tannino's head snapped over to Malane—"did nothing in our meetings besides sneer and play hide-the-files. How many resources were we supposed to burn chasing these pricks with half the facts and you letting air out of our tires?"

"We spent *months* getting our guy inside and couldn't risk his cover being blown," Malane said.

"There wouldn't have *been* a risk if you'd told us Danny the Wand's shop was a no-fly zone. But you couldn't even chance us talking to Goat Purdue. Our own prisoner?"

"We couldn't have you prying around with Rich sunk undercover in the middle of it. You know how it goes."

"Where'd you stash Goat?"

"He's no longer useful." Malane nodded at Tim. "You put a pretty good charge into his face."

"We busted our asses to nail him," Bear said, "and you snaked him."

"Nail someone else."

Tim looked at Rich. "We will."

"You want to know why everybody hates the FBI?" Tannino's voice was calm, conversational. "No forest. All trees. If *ever* there was a time for interagency cooperation—"

"Look," Malane said, "we're trying to work with you on this now."

"And the only reason you're not still working *against* us is because your fucking agent wound up in my cell block."

"It shouldn't be news to you, Marshal, that federal agencies sometimes cross agendas. You hardly would've back-burnered a Top Fifteen fugitive chase that had already claimed two of your men."

Tim spoke slowly to keep his rage tamped down. "It's claimed two of our men"—here his voice wavered—"maybe a sheriff's deputy, two civilians, *thirty-eight* rival bikers, and counting."

Malane met Tim's stare evenly. "Modest stakes compared with what we're up against. We cannot—will not—allow al-Fath to fill its coffers for future operations."

"And your agency's got to learn that that can't be a justification for *everything*."

"Look," Smiles said, "I know this is an emotional case for you. I'm sorry your marshal buddies died. But we couldn't move on the nomads early without losing the big fish. We've got a shot at rolling up al-Fath's top West Coast affiliate and dealing a death blow to an incipient drug operation. Al-Malik *has* to surface when the shipment arrives from Mexico. He's got to confirm to the powers that be that it penetrated our borders. He'll want to eyeball the product, put his hands on it before it gets carved up and shipped out in vials."

"We need to get beyond the bullshit," Tannino said. "So where do you suggest we go from here?"

Malane moistened his lips, then rested a hand on Rich's shoulder, the little gesture revealing a friendship between the two. "Sit him in jail until tomorrow, then let Dana Lake come to bail him out. We ask that you leave the investigation in our hands."

"We can't do that."

"Why not?"

"You need us, and *even now* you're too arrogant and stupid to know it. We have an inside line on this case that you need. And we'll give it to you. For what *we* need."

"You're playing with fire here," Smiles said. "With all due respect to the Marshals Service, you're a bit out of your depth."

Tannino started to retort, but Tim cut in with a question. "How's Marisol Juarez figure in? Why'd they cut her up?"

"I don't know." Malane shrugged. "Hobby."

"They're not gonna take a Ted Bundy time-out with everything going on."

"These guys are psychopaths," Rich said. "They need to take five minutes to pressure-valve Den Laurey's bloodlust, they'll fucking take it."

"You buy that explanation, you're even dumber than your getup. You might not want to overlook the—what did you call them?—'modest stakes'? Maybe if we pay attention to the dead little people, we might find some answers."

Rich stood up and shook out his long hair with a jerk of his neck. He addressed Tannino. "The bottom line is, I can't get my terrorist with your renegade deputy stirring up the heat. We were on course, and your guy fucked it up. You need to have your deputies stand down on the small fish. I want the Prophet. And I'm gonna get him."

Tim said, "If you think I'm gonna let Den Laurey ride if I get him in my sights, you're out of your head."

Rich's hand rasped across the stubble of his face. They'd taken his leathers and his armband, but his undershirt reeked of smoke. He took a step over and glowered down at Tim. "Next time you interfere, don't expect me to save your life."

Cocked back in his chair, Tannino looked from Smiles to Malane to Rich, and then his eyes glinted darkly, and he nodded at Tim. "Your prisoner, Rackley."

Tim rose, spun Rich around, and cinched the cuffs back on, Rich wincing at the bite of the metal. Bear and Guerrera fell into step as Tim led Rich back to his cell.

36

They sat in the command post awaiting word back from Tannino. He was in with the mayor right now, conference-calling the higher-ups and pretending to have some say if their task force would be subsumed by the FBI's or vice versa. Despite the Hanukkah jingles audible from the criminal clerk's screensaver down the hall, the mood was less than jolly. It was only 9:00 P.M., but it felt to Tim like the middle of the night. A check-in call to the hospital—no news means what?—only added to his sharply felt frustration. He flipped listlessly through photos of Den and Kaner, chewing on a brown swizzle stick until his molars ached.

Mounds of files overflowed the table, the floor, the empty chairs. Paperwork drooped from pushpins. The chief's assistant had dropped off crullers with red and green sprinkles, the few stale survivors collecting off-season flies in their pink box. The marshal's wife's fruitcake sat untouched on the tabletop, its pristine two-tone cellophane intact; Mrs. Tannino's baking, even when it didn't involve candied fruit and dark corn syrup, was eat-at-your-own-risk.

Scrupulously balanced human-interest holiday reports compensated for the paper-thin local news—a *dulcería*'s Jesus cookies cried cinnamon tears; a Tarzana housewife made a giant menorah evoking the Hollywood sign; a crippled kid got his operation thanks to an Islamic charity. Even the CNN crawl had gone syrupy, bringing news of marshmallow-eating contests and a Star of David on the White House tree.

Most of the task-force members were home with their families. Slumped over the intersection of his forearms, Jim caught some shut-eye at a corner desk; light duty or not, he was in for the haul. Freed, divorced, had stayed back so Thomas could sneak dinner at home. Even if he'd wanted to leave, Bear had nowhere to go. He had his feet on the conference table, and he stared at the ceiling, his cocked-back chair doing its best to stand up to his weight. Tim checked in with the ICU doctor for the third time that day—no Christmas miracles there. He felt a stab of guilt for not going in, but Dray cut him off. *The Sinners don't take a night off. You're sure as shit not going to just so you can stare at your comatose wife.*

Haven't heard from you in a while, he thought.

That's because you haven't killed anyone in a while. Been, what, four hours?

I miss you.

But he heard no response.

Maybeck and Haines finally made for the door, wearing guilty expressions, though no one faulted them.

Jim raised his head at their departure. "Merry Kwanzaa."

Maybeck, white boy personified, smiled and flashed him a thumbs-up. "See you in the morning."

"If we still have the case," Tim said.

A roomful of dour faces looked back at him. From his recline, Bear grunted, and they went back to waiting for Tannino.

Guerrera finished arguing the latest girlfriend off the phone with a suddenly overplayed accent, casting embarrassed glances at the others. "I *tole* you not to use the work line, baby." He hung up.

Still gazing at the ceiling, Bear said, "Jean Ann?"

"Alicia."

Bear didn't quite smile, but his face shifted. He rolled his head over to face Tim. "Our boy is back."

Everyone stood when Mayor Strauss entered with Tannino. His face was hard and red, a mallard green tie loose at the collar. His breath smelled of red wine. "After extensive discussion with the East Coast, we've determined to let you and the FBI keep your respective bailiwicks.

I've been pleased with your progress, and I—and Director Reyna—are disinclined to halt your progress. The FBI will, of course, continue with Operation Cleansweep simultaneously, and you are to liaise and share information. If you let your egos get in the way of the well-being of this city, you will answer to me personally. Understood?"

Nods and assorted affirmative mumbles. Tannino added, looking to City Hall for confirmation, "And the Bureau's agents are under the same orders."

"Now"—the mayor reverted to politician—"has anyone fed you boys some turkey?"

"We're fine, thank you, Mr. Mayor," Miller said.

Strauss nodded and exited, as Bear stared at Miller resentfully.

Tannino paused behind him at the door. "Someone eat a slice of the fucking fruitcake before the wife comes in." No one moved, and he sighed a tired marital sigh. "Bear, dispose of the thing, would you?"

The door slammed behind him.

Tim exhaled, relieved, and a few of the guys exchanged solemn high fives.

"Next move?" Freed asked.

"Jim, you've got a hook at Border Patrol, right?" Tim asked. "Get him on the horn. I want to know all the border-crossing data they logged on our boys at San Ysidro–Tijuana. What they were riding, plate numbers, the whole nine yards."

Bear thunked his chair back to an upright position. "What if those shitheads are decoys, like Rich said? I mean, the AT could already be here. It might be hitting the streets as we speak."

For the first time since the shooting, Guerrera spoke decisively. "I know how we can find out."

37

Bear looked right at home behind the wheel of his Dodge Ram, though Guerrera had to squeeze between him and Tim on the bench seat. The Sinners' clubhouse sat up the street, a sprawling monstrosity behind barbed wire. From inside came women's cackling, speaker bursts of heavy metal, and the occasional tinkle of shattering bottles.

Bear dug in the plastic gas-station bag at his feet and came out with a quart of eggnog and some Styrofoam cups. He poured, and the deputies toasted.

"Merry and happy," Bear said, the same three words he offered each year at Tim and Dray's kitchen table before wordlessly ingesting half their Christmas ham.

Guerrera added, *"Y rezos para la salud de su esposa."*

They drank.

A Sinner stumbled outside and hopped onto his bike, his deed mounting up behind him. They motored off. Bear raised an inquisitive eyebrow at Guerrera, but Guerrera shook his head.

"He's double-packing."

"So what?"

"If a guy's on club business, he leaves his deed behind to call lawyers and bail bondsmen in case he winds up in the clink."

A moment later a solo Sinner exited the clubhouse and drove off. Bear followed the bike at a good distance, picking up the plate and radioing Freed at the command post to have him ID the biker from the database. He came back as Fritz, a mother-chapter member of no special distinction.

"Wait till we get to that stretch of flat road up ahead." Guerrera's directives were crisp; having recovered from the post-shooting haze, he seemed emboldened. "Not yet . . . not yet. . . . Now hit the siren."

Bear gave the siren a few bursts, and Fritz gradually pulled over. Tim and Guerrera waited in the Dodge while Bear searched the bike and the disaffected Sinner. Fritz offered Bear a few choice words about police intimidation and sped off. The charade over, Bear returned to the Dodge. Tim and Guerrera climbed out as he neared, each with a flashlight. Bear pulled the truck around, rolling slowly behind them and shining the headlights on the tufts of roadside chaparral to aid their search. Finally Guerrera came up with a packet of white flake. "Still looks like good old-fashioned meth to me."

Bear stuck his head out the window over the V of his elbow. "Crystal?"

"Nah. Shit chalk. We'll have to lab it, but looks like a battery-acid and cough-medicine special."

Tim pulled another few packets from where they'd landed in a tangle of elephant grass. Guerrera held the Ziploc up to the headlight's glare. "Doubt they'd be selling this shit if they had the real deal in-country. They'd get the AT on the streets ASAP."

"They can't sell both?" Bear said.

Guerrera colored, then matched the edge in Bear's tone—something Tim had not known him to do before. "Just thinking out loud."

"All we know is that they're still running meth," Tim said. "Let's get our ears to the ground, see if we can pick up if a hot new shipment's crossed the border. Right now we can't be sure."

Guerrera had already climbed in; the truck sat idling, waiting. Bear cracked a grin. "Why don't we ask the Great Mustaro?"

They pulled up to the pink-stucco apartment building and climbed out. Christmas had thinned the clusters of men around the neighboring stoops, but a few holdouts remained. Backward baseball caps and brown-bagged bottles. One of the guys flipped them off, and Bear nodded and tapped him a salute.

They climbed the stairs, reaching Lash's place at the end of the hall. Take-out menus had accumulated on the doorknob, the fallen surplus covering the mat like leaves. When Tim glanced up, Bear's face was tight. He pointed to the closed casement window. About fifteen black flies crawled along the seams, eager to get in. The breeze shifted, and Guerrera's face wrinkled.

The three deputies stood silently before the chipped door, bathed in a throw of rusty light from the flickering overhead. Eminem's fricatives were barely audible from a street boom box. They took a quiet moment. It wasn't much, but it was the most Lash was going to get.

Bear removed his pick set from his back pocket and jogged the rake and the tension wrench up from the vinyl case like cigarettes from a pack. Tim took them and went to work on the lock. The door clicked, and the three stepped in to greet the body.

38

They stood back out on the street, breathing the dark air. Tim couldn't recall being more relieved to turn over a crime scene to CSI. The humidity had gotten to him. And the smell. They were indistinguishable, a paste on the skin. Bear and Guerrera flapped the bottom hems of their T-shirts, airing them out. Guerrera still looked a touch queasy, but he managed a stoic façade. The local would-be hoods had come out to watch the body bag load as if the scene were a sporting-event finale. They clutched cans of beer and pointed, and in not one of their faces did Tim note fear or consternation.

Den and Kaner had taken their time with Lash, twenty-five puncture wounds in all. Judging from the seepage on the kitchen linoleum, he'd been alive for most of it; they'd wanted him to talk. Den's knife work was surgeon precise, as touted, dodging arteries and bones until the decisive nick of the femoral artery. Tim tried to take a positive from it—the torture's escalation could be read as a sign of Den and Kaner's frustration after losing Chief, Goat, and Tom-Tom. But still he felt the gnawing of a quiet, determined guilt. He, Bear, and Guerrera had found Lash, and they'd pressed him. He'd been willing—happy, even—to inform, but that almost made it worse.

Freed emerged from the building, his thin face covered with a sheen of sweat. He nodded once. "All right, then. I'll take over here. Miller's holding down the post, Thomas is wrapping up at home."

"Did Jim get us the info from Border Patrol?" Tim asked.

Freed held out his notepad. A list of vehicle descriptions and license-plate numbers. Toe-Tag, Whelp, and Diamond Dog had crossed the border on their Harleys, except on December 7 at 2:13 P.M., when Diamond Dog had gone through solo in a burgundy Toyota Camry, plate number 7CRP497.

Tim tapped the car description.

Freed's eyes widened, an amusingly green response from a veteran. "Diamond Dog's missing bike at the warehouse was a car."

"Might be. We'll take a look. Who's it registered to?"

"It's a dummy reg. Valid but under a false name."

"Our girl Babe Donovan's work at the DMV?"

"I'm guessing."

"Such a giving soul," Bear said.

Freed's pager hummed on his belt, and he tilted it out so he could read the Blue Curaçao screen. "Chief's credit-card statements just hit the fax. I'll rescue Thomas from the in-laws, and we'll get on it." He hustled back to his Porsche, a seal gray Carrera GT underwritten by his family's twenty-seven-state furniture chain. "Have Sheriff's take over here, see if you can find the car, and I'll meet you back at the office."

B ent into Diamond Dog's Camry, Aaronson contorted at an angle generally reserved for Playmates. Tim heard his breathy whisper— "Gotcha"—and then he eased himself out, grasping a 7-Eleven cup by the rim with a pair of tweezers.

Bear rolled his eyes and stepped back toward the curb; they'd been observing the slow-motion processing for the better part of a half hour. He and Guerrera had already voiced their preference for hot-assing it back to the command post to dig into the credit-card records. Tim, familiar with Aaronson's predilection for a deputy on-scene, had promised the criminalist some on-site time. Besides, Thomas and Freed were the best financial investigators they had, and he wasn't about to rush back to the post to stare at Visa statements over their shoulders.

They'd found Diamond Dog's car in minutes, parked less than a block from the warehouse where the biker had taken Guerrera's bullet in the chest. It was road-trip sloppy, which Tim had hoped for, but so far Aaronson had excavated little more than fast-food wrappers, a few issues of *Easyriders,* and a crumpled poncho that looked more like a movie prop than an article of clothing.

At Tim's request, Aaronson had left Lash's apartment early to process the car. He was an unhurried but meticulous worker, a finder of hidden gems. He'd once pulled a DNA sample from a piece of dental floss he'd found in the tread of a boot in the back of a crash-pad closet. Tim was looking for him to strike fertile soil again.

Bear tapped his watch. It was eleven forty-five. Christmas was still hanging on by its fingernails. Tim couldn't believe it was the same day he'd started with a visit to Uncle Pete at the clubhouse.

Aaronson peered into the 7-Eleven cup, nose wrinkled curiously.

"What do you see?"

He moved the cup under Tim's face, and Tim leaned back from the smell.

"What is that?" Guerrera asked, his interest piqued.

"Tobacco spit." Aaronson swirled the murky brown liquid. "Dip. Skoal Wintergreen from the smell of it. But look here." He tilted the cup, revealing a soaked piece of paper at the bottom. Through the sludge Tim could make out some faint lines, but the paper was too crumpled and stained for him to discern a pattern.

"Why would he put paper in the bottom?" Guerrera asked.

Tim, reformed stakeout dipper, said, "So it won't splash out of the cup when you drive." He peered over Aaronson's shoulder. "Can you dry it out to get a read on the markings?"

Aaronson was on his knees on the sidewalk, draining the liquid into a specimen jar. He used the tweezers to tease the paper flat without tearing it, and then he hooked a flexible-rod flashlight behind his ear and bent over the evidence with a magnifying glass. He looked like a Halloween costume come to life.

Flattened, the marks were clearer, if abbreviated by the torn edge. A few squiggles locked within a circular perimeter, almost like a yin and yang. They appeared to be part of a logo. An alphanumeric was left, apparently in its entirety: *TR425.*

Aaronson folded the soggy slip over and rubbed the back with a thin, blunt probe. "See that? It's gummy."

"Sticker?" Tim asked, jotting the number in his notepad.

"I'd say part of a shipping label. The number would be the confirmation or tracking code." Aaronson pulled over a pad and meticulously sketched the visible lines of the logo. He ripped the sheet off and handed it back over his shoulder to Tim, his eyes never leaving the sample. "This should do until I get it under the sterozoom."

homas leaned against the wall at the head of the conference table, exasperated. The room was lit, but a left-on projected photo of Den Laurey faintly colored half his face. "Look, we ran through all the ground-ballers on the credit-card statements, but it's gonna take some time. We have nine months to cover—a lot of charges to run down. Visa's got limited info, and we have to wait for businesses to call back." He glanced at the clock. Half past midnight. "Which ain't gonna happen until the A.M."

"How about the bank trail?" Bear asked. "Past cards? Visa must've run a credit report."

"Card was issued under Fred Kozlanski. Chief paid the bills from a checking account registered to the same name. Guy died a year back, Chief borrowed his identity."

"Who could do a thing like that?" Bear offered Tim, occasional ID thief, a sardonic smirk.

"No ATM withdrawals?" Tim asked.

Thomas said, "Credit card only."

"Any secondary cards linked to the account?"

Freed shook his head. Miller exhaled and leaned back in his chair, lacing his hands behind his neck. About six more deputies had trickled back to the post, but the majority would return in the morning. Malane, technically still the FBI liaison to the task force, was conspicuously absent, probably plugged in to the Operation Cleansweep command center. Now that the undercover agent was out of the bag, he was no longer required in Roybal to regulate and impair. Smiles, dead man walking, had to disappear again to protect Rich's cover.

The days-old fruit rotting within the trash overflowing the can added a sickly undercurrent to the smell of coffee and glazed sugar. Tim glanced at the papers covering the surface before him like a tablecloth. The team had broken down the gas charges from Chief's credit card, using the prices on the respective days to calculate the gallons purchased, and marked the location of each station on an L.A. County map with accountants' "sign here" arrows. Chief had charged gasoline only at five stations near his crash pad. Tim studied the Post-its beside each arrow—3.25 gallons, 2 gallons, 24.92 gallons, 3.17 gallons.

His gaze caught on the anomalous amount. Chief's Indian sported a Fat Boy 3.5-gallon tank. The range of Sinners' tanks, based on Guerrera's appraisal of the surveillance photos of Nigger Steve's funeral, only ran north to six gallons.

"What's with the twenty-five-gallon charge?" Tim asked.

"It's the one standout," Thomas said. "We don't know what to make of it."

"Maybe he bought beer, put it on the card," Guerrera said.

"That Shell doesn't have a convenience store."

"How about cigarettes, oil?"

"It was an autocharge at the pump. Comes in under a different code."

"Twenty-five gallons. Must be an SUV," Bear said.

"A *big* SUV," Guerrera said. "Like a Hummer, maybe. Or a U-Haul truck or something."

"That's the thing." Freed held up a sheaf of DMV printouts. "The Sinners and deeds all have bikes or little Jags and Beemers. Not an SUV among them."

"Too coppish," Guerrera said. "They want the opposite of big."

"So who's filling up an SUV?" Bear's hypothetical hung in the air.

Tim thumbed through the photograph prints from the rolls of film Bear had found in the warehouse Dumpster. Solid black. All three sets. Every last one. Just as Thomas had reported.

Tim tossed them on the table, frustrated. He rubbed his eyes so hard he knew he'd leave them bloodshot, but it felt so good he didn't care. "Let's run through the murder list again."

Miller raised his head. "Mexican girls between fifteen and thirty?"

"We told you," Freed said, "no red flags."

"Humor me."

Thomas shot a sigh and exchanged one hefty set of files for another. "Maria Alvarez. Twenty-two years old. Hit-and-run at Temple and Alameda. Alma Benito. Sixteen. Shot in a drive-by outside Crenshaw High." The names kept coming, alphabetized, jurisdiction after jurisdiction, a roll call of the young and dead.

Los Angeles, city of dreams.

In the past three months, forty-seven deaths fit their search demographic. Thomas paused to catch his breath, and Bear said, "You forgot Venice."

"No questionable deaths in Venice fit our target demographic."

"Really? Happy day."

"Torrance," Tim said.

"I thought I read Torrance. Nothing there anyway. Just that chick who died on vacation."

"Vacation where?"

"Cabo San Lucas."

"You crossed files. Jennifer Villarosa was from Sylmar."

"Not Villarosa. Sanchez, I think it was." Thomas wrinkled his forehead. "Villarosa died in Cabo?"

Tim thumbed through a line of file tabs, then whisked out the folder and flipped it open. An Immigration-application photo of Lupe Sanchez, plump face smiling beneath a heap of curly hair, was stapled above the report. Date of death: November 30.

A jolt of adrenaline made Tim's skin crawl, the tingle of still-dawning epiphany. The buried thread of the answer started to rise through the sand.

Bear was on his feet. "How'd she die?"

Thomas said, "Hiking accident."

"Jesus." Guerrera was already dialing. The room quieted as everyone became aware of the sudden shift in energy.

Tim grabbed the three packs of film, spilling some of the black rectangles as he pulled out the negatives. The first set of strips were foggy, as were the second. The third roll's negatives were clear bluish gray.

He looked back at the Post-it—24.92 gallons.

Den's sneering comment over Dray's bleeding body echoed in his head—*We should practice on this heifer.* In her ninth month, Dray was big. Big like Marisol Juarez. Like Jennifer Villarosa. Like Lupe Sanchez. Tim had read Den's lips on the vehicle cam's recording, missing the intonation shift on the second-to-last word. *We should practice on* this *heifer.*

He felt a meshing of gears, then the drop of cog into slot as the facts aligned and the solution pulled up into awareness.

He knew how the Sinners were muling the drugs in even before Guerrera racked the phone and said, with bright, excited eyes, "Sanchez won a free Mexico trip through Good Morning Vacations."

40

Drops of sweat cutting through the dust powdering his dark face, Gustavo Alonso readjusted the obese cadaver onto its left side, struggling with its weight until he found a better resting position. He paused to catch his breath, then tipped the chin to the chest to keep the esophagus open. A thin placement catheter ran down the girl's throat, attached to an intragastric balloon that he'd already positioned in the ample stomach cavity. The endoscope dangled from the monitor cart like a black snake. He inserted the scope through the mouth, following the catheter down. His trembling hands made it difficult to steer past the hump of the lower esophageal sphincter, but he managed, and the weight-loss balloon loomed on the viscera-flecked monitor.

Now he had eyes on the inside.

He paused, exhaling and wiping his brow. His frayed scrubs were damp, with dark splotches extending down the sides. The task at hand was not making him perspire—he'd operated as a mortician on a forged license for the better part of twenty years, and between floaters, decomps, and barbecues, little could turn his stomach. He was sweating because of the scabs on his arms. They were hungry.

Funeraria Sueño del Ángel was located up Highway 1 from Cabo San Lucas, on the inland outskirts of San José del Cabo. The run-down funeral home hid off a dirt road in a throw of local houses left unwatered by the tourist corridor. The noises of the bikers, carried on a dry breeze from the sagging porch, reached Gustavo in the mortuary. A loud punch line, slapstick shuffling, smokers' laughter. Earlier, one of them had accidentally put a boot through the rotting wood.

Checking on Gustavo, Toe-Tag pressed his face to the screen door. Always within gunshot range. He and Whelp had arrived last night and taken over possession of Allah's Tears from the well-dressed Middle Eastern gentleman who'd shown up around midnight.

Gustavo refocused on the body; his arms would not get fed until he completed his work. He removed the guide wire from the fill tube protruding from the cadaver's gaping mouth. A bag of Allah's Tears lay on the surgical tray to his side, labeled as saline but holding instead a liter of fluid euphoria. He primed the fill tube, then spiked the bag. Using a 50-cc syringe, he withdrew the liquid heroin, then shot it down the filling tube. On the monitor the intragastric balloon swelled, the pulse of a synthetic fetus.

Taking great care to ensure that the fill tube stayed slack, he repeated the process, each plunger push street-valued at over a million dollars.

It was painstaking work.

The embalming table had not been well maintained; flakes of rust stuck up, lodging in the doughy white flesh of the eighteen-year-old body. Because the corpse had to look presentable at the end of its travails—with Catholics you could count on an open casket—he'd taken all the appropriate steps. He'd removed the clothes, then massaged the mounds of blue-veined flesh, manipulating the extremities to break up the incipient rigor mortis. He'd cleansed the body with antibacterial soap, working up a good lather, then sprayed it down with disinfectant. He'd swabbed the orifices with cavity fluid and packed them, except for the mouth, which he left accessible. Because of the facial cyanosis, he'd applied massage cream with a light touch to avoid further bloodstaining. He'd rinsed the eyeballs with a mild solution before inserting eye cups to hold the lids in place. The big toes he'd tied together to keep the legs in line, and he'd sutured the pillowy breasts together near the nipples so they'd be held in position. He'd inserted the trocar above and to the left of the belly button and used the long, pointed instrument to suck out the contents of the organs. He'd lifted arteries at the embalmer's six points—the right and left carotids, axillaries, and femorals.

The right carotid protruded just above the breastbone, the tongue depressor underneath still holding it above skin level though he'd long disconnected the pump. He'd already drained the blood, replacing it with embalming fluid and a solution to keep the skin bile pigment from turning the flesh green.

It was a well-cared-for corpse.

The shadows at the screen were steady now as the bikers watched from the safety of twenty feet and an outdoor breeze. The first intragastric balloon reached its liter limit. After the syringe's final stroke, Gustavo pushed the residual through the line, then pulled back on the plunger, creating a vacuum in the valve and sealing the balloon. Gently, he withdrew the tubing, leaving the freestanding balloon inside the stomach. Though obese corpses were difficult to work with, larger stomach capacity was required for the procedure, and abdominal fat would help disguise the distention.

He laid the corpse flat on its back. He embedded a hooked barb in the upper and lower gum line, then used a wire to cinch the mouth neatly closed. The chubby hands he positioned left over right, leaving the fingers slightly cupped.

Relieved and exhausted, he leaned over and kissed the girl's pale forehead.

Shirt up over his nose, Whelp entered and retrieved the final fill bag from the crate of tribal trinkets. For all their rough-and-tumble posturing, the bikers were feeble around cadavers. They were skilled at *making* corpses; they just couldn't stomach the extended aftermath. After all Gustavo's meticulous preparations, they'd mucked up the first three corpses on the other end, unable to cleanly incise the stomachs. He sincerely hoped that the new guy, with his much-ballyhooed blade skills, would prove a more effective craftsman.

Drops of sweat hung from the ends of Gustavo's hair. He rubbed his nose, and his fingers came away greasy. He scratched his arms—the imaginary bugs were back, just beneath the skin. "A taste?" he said in strong-accented English. "Just a taste?"

"Not yet." Toe-Tag stood behind Whelp, arms crossed.

Gustavo followed his gaze to the far side of the mortuary, taking in the enormous corpse lying humped and naked on the second embalming table.

The twin sister.

Gustavo's shoulders settled a few inches lower. He wiped his face on the inside collar of his scrub top and nodded a few times, sadly.

Taking the bag of Allah's Tears, he shuffled over to the second station and resumed his work.

41

The school-bus yellow backhoe lurched, the boom lowering the bucket into the plot. A clank as the teeth struck casket. Tim turned away from the spotlights illuminating the dark cemetery, pressing the cell phone tightly to his ear.

What he heard was the unamused 2:00 A.M. voice of Jan Turaski, the LAX Customs resident-agent-in-charge who oversaw a joint task force that included Customs and Border Patrol inspectors. Tim had met her during his four months at the Federal Law Enforcement Training Center; she'd been a field agent back then, on a cross-training stint.

"You'd better give me a damn good reason, Rack. Or tell me you're joking. I can smell the undue-hardship lawsuits already." She laughed, a single dead note. "I can't start popping coffin lids without some serious PC."

"I'm getting probable cause as we speak."

"If I'm gonna put my name out, I need it on my desk already."

"Then just *hold* all incoming caskets from Mexico. Cabo San Lucas in particular. Give me an hour."

"Without any hard evidence? *Or* a warrant? Not an easy PR move to slide past grieving families. Let alone my SAC."

A three-month maternity leave earlier in the year hadn't landed Jan in the graces of the special agent in charge running the field office downtown.

Behind Tim, Bear waved off the backhoe like an airplane marshaller gone mad. Four deputies with shovels descended into the plot. Clods of dirt flew.

"How about with a personal call from the marshal?" Tim offered.

"From the marshal? What are you into here?"

"More than a drug operation."

Jan made an exasperated noise, something like a growl. In the background Tim could hear the annoying Christmas Muzak piped through the airport terminal.

"One hour, Jan. Please."

A heavy sigh, then the sounds of Jan typing.

Zimmer walked by, and Tim covered the phone and said, "Has Haines reached the Cabo police yet?"

Zimmer said, "Last I checked in, he couldn't get anyone, but he'd left a few messages. Cabo, ya know? They're probably out arresting girls gone wild."

Jan came back on. "In the next hour, we've only got one inbound from Mexicali. So fine, I'll give you till three."

"And if a coffin comes in on that flight?" Tim asked.

"I'll call in the duty agents, persuade them to run behind schedule. The way they work, shouldn't be tough. But Mexico flights start rolling in early, and I'm not gonna have coffins piling up on the tarmac."

"Thank you. I'll see you in an hour."

"Bring me something concrete or don't bother," Jan said, and hung up.

Tim snapped his phone shut and inhaled deeply as the deputies hauled out the casket. Four grasped the swing bars, reverse pallbearers, and two tugged on a nylon strap looped under the fine wood. Maybeck's boot slipped, and he stumbled, a streak of mud across his thigh. The casket hit turf with a thud.

"Good thing we're doing the Feebs' job for them," Guerrera said.

"This is for our case," Tim said. "We follow the drugs to Den Laurey."

Aaronson, dressed ridiculously in pajama bottoms, a sweatshirt, and a corduroy blazer, tapped the casket's seam excitedly with a fingernail. "Lead lining is required for international transport aboard a common carrier. Lucky."

"Why?" Maybeck asked.

"Keeps the maggots out." Aaronson's face gleamed in the harsh spotlight. "Know what else is required for importing a body?"

"Uh, no."

"Embalming. That's more good news for the home team." Aaronson held up his palm, and Maybeck reluctantly gave him five before handing him a chisel and hammer.

Jennifer Villarosa's father had been exceedingly helpful. Despite being woken up Christmas night by Tim's knock on the door, he'd signed the documents for his daughter's body to be exhumed. Tim was relieved to proceed with the family's consent, glad to let the backup court order expire in Bear's glove box. Jennifer was their sole shot to corroborate Tim's theory; Lupe Sanchez had been cremated shortly after her return to the United States. No family members had showed up to claim her body—not a big surprise, given their illegal-alien status. Her occasional work as a cleaning lady hadn't left enough money to provide her with a burial. She'd been interred in a common plot with the ashes of the destitute and itinerant, a wretched homecoming from a free vacation that must have seemed to her heaven sent.

The task force had moved like a tornado since the revelation at the command post. Screeching tires, faxed pages, wake-up calls. Freed had pulled a rabbit out of the hat, backtracking the online promotion code Good Morning Vacations had used to book Villarosa's plane ticket, and hitting upon another girl killed on a Cabo trip. Maribel Andovar had suffered a fatal heart attack while sleeping in her beachside hotel. The cause of death was plausible because she was nearly 150 pounds overweight. She, too, had been shipped home through LAX and cremated. She hadn't shown up among the names Thomas had pulled for review because she'd lived in Kern County, north of their designated search area.

Tim glanced at his notepad, the pattern evident.

Jennifer Villarosa. Died October 29, Cabo San Lucas.
Body cleared LAX Customs November 1 on Mexicana Flight 237.
Diamond Dog, Toe-Tag, Whelp in Mexico October 28–November 2.

Maribel Andovar. Died November 8, Cabo San Lucas.
Body cleared LAX Customs November 9 on AeroMéxico Flight 13.
Diamond Dog, Toe-Tag, Whelp in Mexico November 6–November 10.

Lupe Sanchez. Died November 30, Cabo San Lucas.
Body cleared LAX Customs December 1 on American Airlines Flight
2453.
Diamond Dog, Toe-Tag, Whelp in Mexico November 28–December 1.

The women had been lured to Cabo and then murdered, Tim believed, so that their corpses could serve as dry runs to assess the shipping route and test the airlines' security systems. The Sinners had to ensure that the bodies were processed smoothly before the actual drugs were risked. The bikers were zealous in their disregard for life; these women had been killed merely to determine how incoming caskets were screened at baggage claim.

In Cabo each victim had been put up in a different hotel on a different beach to delay local authorities from discerning the pattern. Not surprisingly, no corporate, tax, or International Air Transport Association records had turned up for Good Morning Vacations, all imaginable variants on goodmorningvacations.com turned up no Web site, and Google drew a blank. The contact e-mail on the letter to Jennifer Villarosa—the sole means of communication employed—had been discontinued. Guerrera had been the one to spot the clause hidden in the Terms & Conditions' small print: *In the event of the death of the award recipient during the period of the vacation, Good Morning Vacations shall assume sole responsibility for the body's preparation for international transport, conveyance to the country of origin, and delivery to the family of the deceased.* Neither Villarosa's nor Andovar's stateside funeral director could offer any helpful information on the delivering vehicle.

The gas charge of 24.92 gallons had tripped Tim's memory of the beat-to-shit hearse outside Chief's safe house, the one on which Guerrera had rested his watch just before the ART entry. Larger vehicle, larger tank capacity. Miller had redlined over to see whether it was still languishing at the curb. Given the sophistication of the Sinners' plans, Tim doubted it would be there.

To avoid arousing suspicion, the Sinners had wisely targeted women from jurisdictions covered by different law-enforcement agencies. After the army had gotten involved after Villarosa's death—however minimally—the Sinners had dropped further down the socioeconomic ladder, selecting victims they thought no one was going to miss. Choosing women with family members illegally in the United States ensured that no one would raise a fuss.

Since the new victim—and first actual drug carrier—would be dead, she certainly couldn't pass the drugs through her system like a body packer; the AT packages would have to be cut out of her. The task force was desperate to get a lock on her but had no way of identifying her. If the Sinners had sent her to Cabo on the free-vacation ruse, as Tim suspected, they'd wised up, dispensing with the traceable promotion code when booking her ticket. Tim knew only that the woman the Sinners would single out for this ultimate task would be overweight, to accommodate and disguise the drugs stored in her dead belly.

Aaronson had offered the best explanation for why the dry-run victims were also obese, despite having no drugs to conceal in their bodies. Their corpses would provide practice for the Sinners on the receiving end to learn how to navigate through excessive abdomen fat. Because the heroin was liquid, there'd be little room for error on the extraction—a misjudged incision would pop the package, spilling Allah's Tears throughout the corpse's innards. After being used as dissection fodder, the women would be stitched back up and turned over to their grateful families for burial or cremation, thereby preserving the Cabo scheme for another round.

Marisol Juarez, whom the Nomad Sinners had picked up in Chatsworth on December 22, seemed to shore up Aaronson's theory. Den had implied that she was the practice "heifer." The body hadn't been disemboweled, but the intestines had been exposed and the stomach sliced open. Den, the new cutter, had been rehearsing for when the stakes were higher, for when he'd be unable to afford a stray slip of the knife.

Tannino was working up a press statement now, warning the public and soliciting information about Good Morning Vacations. He was weighing whether to put it out in the upcoming news cycle or sit on it a few days. Obviously a media statement would alert the Sinners, probably causing them to abort the mission. The task force had nailed down quite a few of the variables, and the marshal was understandably reluctant to blow an opportunity to trap Den and Kaner and seize the drugs. Still, there were lives at stake.

The next victim, the carrier for Allah's Tears, was probably vacationing in Cabo right now, under the watchful eyes of Toe-Tag and Whelp.

Time to liaise with the Feebs.

"Jesus Christ, Dray, they've been nothing but detrimental," Tim muttered.

Guerrera paused, his back to Tim. He turned. "What?"

Tim waved him off.

Forgive and forget. And fast. You can't afford to play Lone Ranger. Not with what's riding on this one. You need to pool intel.

We have the intel.

Then maybe they need it. Or maybe they've got the missing jigsaw pieces. So you've got info on their case—you think they don't have their own dirt on the Sinners? Quit pissing in the corners and work together.

Bear stripped the rubber gasket from the casket seal, Aaronson gave the chisel a final whack, and the lock caved through the softened wood. The lid hopped an inch or two, the odor sending Bear, Guerrera, and Maybeck back a few steps. Tim moved forward as Aaronson threw the coffin open.

The face had rotted first, as faces do, but the combination of the sturdy casket, the cool ground, and the embalming had left the body surprisingly intact. Guerrera and Maybeck coughed, but Aaronson leaned in, unperturbed, and went at the soiled clothes with paramedic shears. Though Tim's eyes were watering, he stepped forward as the criminalist beckoned him closer.

"Now, with a drowning there should be minimal marks on the body," Aaronson said. "The corpse wasn't autopsied, so we shouldn't find any Y-pluck incisions." He peeled back the two sliced halves of Jennifer Villarosa's service jacket, revealing a dress shirt. "The trocar and cannula used during the embalming process to puncture the body cavities for fluid aspiration leave only a small circular scar in the upper . . ."

The shears ran up the length of the shirt, revealing a tight-fitting plastic undergarmet, like a toddler's onesie, no doubt superglued into place before her body was turned over to the Sylmar funeral home to be dressed in her uniform. Another slide of the shears, and all at once Jennifer Villarosa's considerable stomach came into view, incisions and sutures traversing the loose gray flesh like railroad tracks. Aaronson crouched to take in the scene up close and personal. The abdomen had been punctured several times with sloppy slashes. Even the stitches had been hastily tied. No wonder Den's knifework was now required.

Still bent over the corpse, Aaronson muttered, "I'd say you've got your probable cause."

42

"eady to answer some questions, scumsuck?" Bear grabbed Rich
by the hair and the union of his cuffs and slammed him against
the cell block's wall. The detention enforcement officer buzzed the door,
and Guerrera held it open. Bear shoved Rich out into the hall and
walked him into an empty conference room. Tim unlocked the cuffs,
and Rich stared at the three of them, rubbing his wrists, his face red.

"Christ, I know you're covering my ass, but go easy on the method
acting."

"I'm not acting," Bear said.

"We've got information," Tim said.

Bear said, "You want to work together or you want to play your
Feeb games?"

Rich's eye darted around. "You talk to Malane?"

"He's a paper-pushing prick."

"We've been ordered to liaise with the FBI," Tim said. "We're running down some leads. If someone's gotta ride along with us, we'd prefer to deal with a field operator. You can coordinate with your team
from there and nail the Prophet. What *we* want is your intel on the bikers." He crossed his arms. "You get your guy, I get mine."

Rich cocked his head, a fall of hair blocking his good eye. "Why
you so hot for Den Laurey? Want a Top Fifteen on your résumé?"

Bear said, "He has three."

Rich started to respond, but Tim cut him off. "What's it gonna be?"

Rich held up his hands, a gesture of surrender. "Okay."

"Where's Goat?"

"We're holding him in the Federal Building in Westwood. He's drugged up, under heavy medical supervision. We haven't been able to get shit out of him—he's too scrambled. What's your information?"

"Not yet," Tim said. "I know you've been working Uncle Pete."

Rich bounced his head from side to side as if debating whether to give up the goods. "We intercepted some of Uncle Pete's cell-phone transmissions, but I'm not at liberty to disclose—"

"Then we're not at liberty to take you along." Bear snatched the cuffs from Tim and descended on Rich.

"Whoa, whoa, whoa. We know he's in on the drugs. But we need to let it play out."

"So you can get the Prophet?" Tim asked.

"And because we need material evidence to make a case against Uncle Pete. We need the drugs, or else all we've got are recorded conversations about shit that we can't prove happened."

"You got enough for a warrant?" Guerrera asked.

"Again, not without material evidence to support the recordings."

Bear said, "Maybe we get a warrant. We're tighter with the bench."

Rich laughed. Even in the brighter light, his skin looked yellow. "Dana Lake'll put her pump so far up your ass you'll taste the Gucci logo. And besides, the evidence isn't with Uncle Pete. Or at the clubhouse. He's too smart for that. That's the whole reason he *has* the nomads. This ain't about warrants and kicking down doors."

Bear made an aggravated noise. Guerrera raised his hands when Tim glanced at him—your call. Down the corridor two prisoners were having a mouth-off in opposing cells, yo' mamas flying like shrapnel.

Rich grew uneasy from the pause—he wanted back in. "Help us get the drugs, and we'll sink Uncle Pete." He eyed Tim. "And you can get Den in the process."

Tim chewed his lip, still deciding. Finally he turned for the door. "Let's take a ride."

43

Wisps of steam curled up from Jan's styrocup of McDonald's coffee. She inhaled it, as if trying to snort the caffeine. The skin under her eyes was pouched and gray, and her rumpled blouse sported stains at the right shoulder. New mom and resident agent in charge. Not an easy schedule. She kept walking purposefully through the late-night travelers straggling between the gates of Terminal 1, with Tim, Bear, Guerrera, and Rich moving swiftly to keep up. For the brief public walk, Rich kept between the deputies, his head lowered. Though he had left behind his armband and originals, he still had his shaggy rock-star hair, eye patch, and jail-cell odor. Upon meeting him, Jan had regarded him with a cocked brow, then turned her eyes to Tim with an unvoiced question, waiting for Tim's nod before cutting him in to the conversation.

"Inbound caskets rank right up there with diplomatic pouches," Jan continued. "In other words, they aren't checked."

"What's the real story?" Rich asked.

She gave a quick glance around. "Under the right circumstances, even a diplomatic pouch might require a furtive scan." She pointed to the sheaf of documents in Guerrera's hands. "But now we're in the clear. This is sufficient probable cause to buy us X-rays on all inbound caskets. If we get a hit on body packing, we'll need a warrant to cut open the corpses, but we can cross that bridge then."

"What if they're lead-lined?" Tim asked. "The caskets?"

"They will be, by federal regulation. We'll have to pop the lids and remove the bodies to do the scans. It's invasive. That's why I needed strong probable cause in my back pocket."

"Do we need to worry about private planes?" Rich asked.

"Good luck getting a corpse through here in a private plane. It's against regs—security *and* health—and we screen all large incoming cargo. But I'll put out a whistle, just to be safe."

She ducked through a doorway, and they followed her down a staircase to an open space on the lower level that had been transformed into a temporary workstation. A few irritable-looking duty agents reviewed paperwork at school-size desks. The desks were oddly arranged, leaving a square of central floor space unoccupied. A tarp draped across the ceiling provided the only separation between them and the restricted-access section of the luggage carousel overhead.

Jan had to raise her voice to be heard over the rumble. "This way."

She led into a separate office and closed the door behind them. The noise reduction was a welcome relief. Through the wide window, Tim watched a duty agent shoving a phone to his cheek, one finger plugging his other ear.

"I see your funding isn't keeping pace with your responsibilities," Tim said.

"They want us doing twice the work with the same resources," Jan said. "We make do." She looked from Tim to Rich. "Like we've all had to."

A sapphire blue Swiss Army suitcase tumbled through the ceiling tarp and crashed onto the empty floor space between the carefully arranged desks. The agents kept working, unperturbed.

"They should file for hazardous-duty pay," Bear said.

Jan directed them to chairs and sat behind a metal desk. "It's a brilliant plan they hit on—especially given the lead lining of tranport caskets. The only way to detect a drug packet in a corpse's stomach is to *open* the casket, pull the body, and X-ray it. Which, as I said, we aren't technically supposed to do."

"But you have," Tim said.

"Hell, yes. We spot-check. Now and again."

"Cargo from certain airlines and flights stands a higher likelihood of getting X-rayed?"

Jan's mouth arranged itself into a smirk. "Now, why would you say that?"

"Are foreign carriers more thoroughly checked than American carriers?"

"No, but yes." Jan paused, hesitant. "You didn't hear it here, but we might be more inclined to take extra precautions when it comes to foreign carriers. Suffice it to say, if a body's coming in from Jakarta, it's gonna get zapped."

"Racial airline profiling," Guerrera said. "How quaint."

"Wait a minute," Rich said. "Terrorists kamikaze four of *our* airplanes, and now you're screening Aer Lingus. What's that logic?"

"Our airlines screen our own planes when they take off at any point in the world. For other planes that we can't screen, we're less concerned that people will blow them up than that they'll smuggle something in. So we screen them on our end—for drugs *and* weapons."

Tim removed the sets of blank film from his pocket and dropped them on her desk. "That explains these."

She pulled out the black photographs and thumbed through them. "What's with the Rothkos?"

"My guess is they sent the film through with the bodies. High-speed film, more sensitive to—"

"Ionizing radiation." Jan thumbed out the negatives and found the first two sets cloudy from the X-ray exposure. "These were foreign airlines?"

"Yes. Mexicana and AeroMéxico. Villarosa and Andovar were X-rayed."

"But Sanchez?"

"Flew the friendly skies with American," Bear said.

"That's United," Jan said.

"What?"

"The slogan. 'Fly the friendly skies.' That was United."

"Oh," Bear said.

Tim cut in: "They found their carrier route on their third try. American Airlines Flight 2453 into LAX—no X-ray."

Jan checked her monitor. "That flight's slated for a nine A.M. arrival. From today on, we'll be crawling all over it. And any other inbounds from the area." She blew her bangs off her forehead. "There's no way we catch this without your intel. When the dogs give their once-over, a decaying body loaded with formaldehyde would cover the scent pretty good. No way they'd hit on heroin inside a corpse."

"AT gives off a strong scent," Rich said. "They had to come up with something strong to overlay it."

Jan said, "Nearest international airport down there is . . . what? San José del Cabo? You alert Mexican Customs?"

"Yes," Rich said. "President Fox made a round of bullshit reforms, but there's still so much goddamn corruption at the ports it's hard to tighten up down there. You know what they say—*Con dinero, baila el perro.*"

"I didn't know they said that. Live and learn." Jan said it without looking at him. "How are they getting the drugs into the stomachs?"

"We haven't figured that out yet," Tim said. "But we're assuming in some way that gives no overt indication that the bodies have been altered."

"Right, so even if a dog gets a soft hit and we take a closer look, run a hand along the coffin lining, peek under a blouse, everything's copasetic. No Y-pluck, no stitching. Lowers the odds that we'll yank the body out of there for an X-ray, especially if it's riding a domestic carrier."

"Maybe they force the victims to swallow a drug packet before they're killed," Guerrera offered.

"Either way," Bear said, "*someone's* getting paid to prep the bodies on that end."

"What do you have in the way of a paper trail?" Tim asked. "What's required to ship in a body?"

As Jan dug in her file drawer, Tim's eyes pulled to the photo of her newborn on the empty bookshelf behind her. She followed his gaze when she came up for air.

"Congratulations, Jan," he said. "I don't think we've talked since . . ."

"Thank you." Her face softened. "I'm sorry about Dray. I didn't bring it up because . . . you know. You holding up?"

Tim sensed Rich's stare and felt his face get hot. "Holding up."

Jan plunged into the paperwork. "Lead-lined coffin, proof of grounds of burial or place for cremation, passport, two certified copies of the death certificate, a letter on funeral-home stationery describing the preparation and treatment of the remains signed by the embalmer and notarized, a letter from the local health department verifying the absence of any contagion."

"And where are the caskets received on this end?"

"A standard holding area. Nothing unusual there. If it's going straight to a service, the mortuary usually sends a hearse or van for the pickup."

"Can we get copies of all the paperwork from our three victims?"

"Absolutely. We're a bit of a mess here, but I should be able to pull it together in a few hours. What?"

"We might not have a few hours."

"Then I'll do it quicker."

"Thank you, Jan. We're gonna get you a joint Service-FBI team in here."

Jan drew her head back, wrinkling her chin. "Jesus. Really? You want to give me the full story now, Rack?"

Because the al-Fath angle was under FBI jurisdiction, Tim deferred to Rich, who scrunched up his face in an expression that was almost endearing and shook his head.

"Sorry, Jan," Tim said. "I'll tell you in a few weeks over a drink."

"The sound of this," Jan said, "we might not be around in a few weeks."

44

Tim's Explorer followed Bear's Ram, Rich fiddling with the radio like a teenager. AC/DC's "Dirty Deeds Done Dirt Cheap" seemed to please him. He rocked for a while, scratching the slope of skin that formed his weak chin.

They twisted up Century Boulevard, leaving the rumble of LAX behind. At the Sepulveda intersection, fifteen glowing pylons built of steel and frosted glass sculpted a gateway to the airport. Each piece of the installation, illuminated internally by color-changing fixtures, rose a hundred feet out of the landscaping. The pylons strode down the lawned median of Century, descending to mimic an aircraft's landing or, from the other direction, ascending in symbolic takeoff. Tim watched the monoliths morph from lavender to emerald. Because of its chameleon effect, the mile-long lightwork had been dubbed "Psychedelic Stone-henge" by locals. Mayor Riordan had flipped the ceremonial switch in 2000, and ever since, the $112 million piece of marketing had greeted arrivals to L.A. The pylons had a quality that was quixotic, lavish, and seductive, much like the city itself.

Dray had once likened them to glowing tampons.

Tim's lips pursed at the memory. Dray had been in the ICU for three days now. And every day she remained under, the doctor had warned, the odds diminished for a viable return. The last three days had been nearly unbearable without her. He couldn't imagine another fifty years.

The lights transformed to a vivid orange—the same shade the sun turned the smog at dusk, making the lung-cancer risk seem worth it. Tim felt the glow on his face. The pylons had watched a lot of life go by. They'd welcomed movie stars and tourists and immigrants. They'd seen off heads of state and diplomats and extraditable war criminals. They'd looked on as girls drove past in cars and returned in hearses. They were unyielding and unmoved, like cops, like doctors, like soldiers, like any bystanders on a thoroughfare. And if Tim failed, if the task force failed, if Rich and Malane and Smiles failed, the pylons would welcome Allah's Tears to the city with the same mute indifference.

Bon Scott finished his muttering, and Rich clicked off the radio. "Who's Dray?"

A car veered into their lane, and Tim swerved and honked. By the time Rich finished yelling out the window and settled back in his seat, he seemed more pensive.

"That was some really fine investigative work," he said.

"Yeah?" Tim said. "Maybe you could've cut us in earlier, and we'd be farther along."

Rich made an irritated noise and looked out the window.

They drove a few minutes, wheels rattling over asphalt.

Then Tim said, "Thank you."

"Don't thank me. You're the one who tracked the shit down."

"I meant for Tom-Tom. You risked your cover to save my ass."

Rich watched the cars fly by on the far side of the road, his tongue poking a mound in his cheek. "Yeah," he said with the faintest grin. "I did."

45

By the time they returned, the command post had kicked back into high gear. About ten minutes prior, Haines had finally synced up with the graveyard shift's watch commander at the Cabo San Lucas police department. The force had been busy that morning investigating a murder and the disappearance of an American girl, Lettie Guillermo. She'd been staying at the Costa Royal as part of a complimentary trip issued by Good Morning Vacations. A witness, who charitably described her as *gordita*, reported seeing her book a snorkeling trip from a street vendor. The boat had been found in a nearby cove, the diver killed gruesomely with a gaff. No sign of Lettie Guillermo.

"You track down her parents?" Tim asked.

"They're coming in," Haines said. "Merry fucking Christmas."

Tim checked his watch: 4:30 A.M., December 26. Three days since the paramedics had carried Dray off the asphalt.

"We can use them." Rich glanced around at the morose faces. "Hey, we were all thinking it, I just said it."

"That's why I'm bringing them in," Haines said. "But I'm not sure they'll be useful. The dead diver, you know?"

"What?" Tim asked.

"Well, the Sinners no longer care about keeping things clean in

Cabo by staging an accidental death. That means this isn't another dry run. It's *the* run."

"Unless things went bad. I mean, *unplanned* bad. But point taken."

"So I doubt they're gonna bother having Good Morning Vacations inform the parents. They have the body they need. They can forge documents—we know they're good at it—ship the girl in under a false name, and dump it when they're done. Why do the extra work of coordinating with a family and risking the extra exposure?"

"But killing her instead of posing it as an accident sends up a flare," Tim said. "Why would they risk *that*?"

"First, another *accidental* death of a Hispanic SoCal girl in Cabo would almost be more conspicuous. This breaks the pattern. And second, the Sinners have no idea we're onto the body-packing scheme. An American girl goes missing in Mexico, everyone assumes she's been kidnapped or killed locally. The last place anyone's gonna look for her body is at the American Airlines baggage claim getting smuggled back into the U.S. in a coffin." Haines held up his hands. "Look, of course we'll monitor the parents, see if they're contacted, I'm just saying let's not pop any bottles of Cristal."

"Has this opened up any more inroads into Good Morning Vacations?"

"No, nothing's tracking." Thomas threw down his pen on the conference table, leaned back in his chair, and rubbed his face. It emerged from his hands red, the hairs of his mustache tweaked up. "The hotel's a spring-break college shithole. We could barely get the basics."

"How about the paperwork from Jan Turaski?" Tim asked.

With the help of Malane and additional FBI support, Jan had managed to produce the CBP records with alacrity. Malane had, surprisingly, rushed copies of all documents over to the command post. Rich's hushed call from the phone banks might have had something to do with that.

"Everything looks airtight," Freed said. "Fraudulent top to bottom, but they got real seals and forms from the health department down there. The funeral home on the letterhead—surprise, surprise—doesn't exist, nor does the embalmer who signed off on the body."

"How about shipment payments?" Tim asked.

"Just like the passenger tickets, casket fees were paid by check from a dead-end account. We're still on it, but the forecast is cloudy, chance of rain."

"Don't be so dreary," Maybeck said. "All we have to do is wait till the package lands, then nab 'em coming in to pick it up."

"Right," Rich said. "Because Den Laurey and Lance Kaner are gonna ride their Harleys into LAX for a pickup. Hell, maybe the Prophet'll show, too, with a T-shirt says 'Kiss Me, I'm an Islamic Fundamentalist.'"

Jim chuckled, and then a few of the others joined in, Maybeck offering each a good view of his middle finger.

"Jim, you talk to Aaronson about the embalming biz?" Bear asked.

Jim put a knee on the tabletop and tapped the pad against it. "You got your embalming fluid, preservatives, cavity fluid, preinjection solution. There's this trocar, really cool, sucks out the—"

"Stay on message."

"Sorry. Bottom line: nothing in the way of traceables. Aaronson said the bodies were prepped with customary materials. We might as well look up every mortuary in Mexico."

"Good idea," Tim said. "Let's put together a list, starting in Cabo and radiating out. Coordinate with the local police down there."

"Because they've been so helpful."

"I can help you there, you need it," Rich said.

"We do," Tim said. The Service's field office in Mexico City, consisting of two deputies, wasn't staffed to handle a major work request.

"We been working closely with the attorney general's office down there, and AFI," Rich said. The Mexican Agency of Federal Investigation had broad-ranging authority and was centrally organized, making its agents less susceptible to local corruption. "I'll ask my hook to start checking out mortuaries and funeral homes in the area. But I'd guess this is a mortician—or a doctor—working freelance." He tapped a cigarette from a pack of American Spirits, tossed it toward his lips, and caught it perfectly in the corner of his mouth. He lit a match off his thumbnail, held his first inhale, then shot a stream of smoke at the ceiling. "What happened with the hearse? The one you said was by the curb at Chief's house?"

"Gone," Miller said.

"Anything with an outdoor security cam on the block? Gas station? ATM? We review those tapes, maybe we spot it driving by. We pick up a plate, we could put it out on the street."

Tim's right thumb and forefinger went to his wedding band. His voice came fast, excited. "We don't need to."

Bear offered him a what-the-fuck eyebrow raise.

"Guerrera, you took the Impala that night, right?" Tim asked. "You parked right behind the hearse."

Guerrera smiled, realization dawning. "Our old friend, the vehicle cam."

Glad I'm good for something.

"I'll pull the tapes," Haines said, "get you a plate number."

A flicker of concern crossed Guerrera's face. "But the Impala's on an evidence hold in the impound lot off Aliso. It was shot to shit. The footage probably got Swiss-cheesed in the trunk."

Haines stood, grabbing his notepad. "Worth a check anyways."

He was almost at the door when a married couple who looked to be in their fifties entered the command post tentatively. They appeared lost, and the woman seemed deeply concerned. They were both over-weight.

"I'm sorry, this is a restricted area," Haines said.

"We were told to come in," the man said with a pronounced accent. "Something about the vacation company."

"I'm sorry. Reception should've directed you to the conference room. Please come with me."

"Our daughters are okay, *sí*?" The woman's voice took on a note of pleading. "Please tell us they okay."

"Daughters?"

"*Sí, Lettie* y *Monica Guillermo*. They won a trip to Cabo San Lucas. They're down there now." The man took note of the sudden silence in the command post. His face registered dread, as if he knew before be-ing told. "Why? *Por favor,* tell us what's wrong."

The wife took in the crime-scene photos pushpinned to the wall and let out a little gasp. Haines moved a step over to try to block her view. He extended his arm, steering them out into the hallway.

The command post filled with a sheepish silence. Rich put out his cigarette on the bottom of his boot. An anguished cry from the hall broke the quiet. A conference room door opened and closed, and there was silence again.

Thomas rubbed his bloodshot eyes. "Morning on the East Coast. I'll see if I can track down any of Chief's credit-card charges originating there."

"Sunday, day after Christmas," Rich said. "Good luck."

Tim grabbed the credit-card statements and passed them around, everyone taking one. He perused Chief's September charges. "He ship a lot from back east?"

"Chaps, clutch plates, chain drives. All under the fake name to the safe house."

"What's this one? In Florida?"

Thomas leaned over, squinting at the statement. His eyes were getting old, but he refused to buy reading glasses. "Orange mark. That means it's on my follow-up list."

"Lite Companion Inc."

"I figured it for a bike-part joint. Taillights, headlights, something."

"Spelled wrong."

"They call that," Jim said grandly, "rationalized orthography."

"They like their gear light," Thomas said. "Lite lights, ya know?"

Tim swung a monitor around and slid over a keyboard. He did a search on the company, found a Web site. He clicked the link and waited for the page to come up.

The blank screen loaded, rendering the HTML block by block.

Lite Companion® Intragastric Balloon System. Help your patients lose weight easily, painlessly, and without hunger pangs!

Tim felt the rush of blood at his ears, in the heat of his face. Reading his reaction, Bear hopped to his feet and came around the table to his shoulder. The others gathered behind him.

Figure 1 showed a sketch of a balloon nestled inside a stomach. The corporate logo was an abstract take on the same image, circles floating within circles. Tim pulled Aaronson's half sketch from his pocket, taken from the ripped shipping label crumpled in the bottom of Diamond Dog's cup of tobacco spit. He folded the piece of paper over where the sketch terminated and held it to the screen. The logo completed the image, filling out the circles. A perfect match.

A few excited murmurs. Someone grabbed Tim's shoulder and

shook it. He clicked the "Track Your Shipment" tab. Glancing at his notepad, he typed in the code he'd copied from the shipping label: "*TR425.*"

A clock icon spun and spun. Finally a new screen flashed up.

Your package shipped on September 3 to Funeraria Sueño del Ángel, 3328 San Juan Delamonga, San José del Cabo, Baja California Sur, 23400, Mexico.

46

Navy SEALs with catchy monikers closed in on a compound, spraying fire from automatic weapons. A hostage taker took a head shot, sending out a simulated burst of PlayStation blood. Whelp hooted and raised the cordless control triumphantly in the air, almost spilling the liter of tequila between his legs. Whelp and Toe-Tag wore UBS headsets so they could communicate like soldiers over the action theme blaring from the TV speakers. They sat on the floor, shirtless, backs to the couch, guns within reach. They had on a bizarre smattering of Afghan jewelry—tribal necklaces, coin chokers, sterling cuff bracelets, Gypsy nose rings. After eating their first round of tequila worms, they'd gotten into the shipping crate that had stored Allah's Tears. Whelp sported a beaded veil, looking like Disney's idea of an unsavory belly dancer. Toe-Tag had forsaken his trademark adornment, a lapis teardrop dangling from the pierced nipple.

Behind them on the cushions, Gustavo slept a blissed-out sleep.

Just beyond the darkened windows, an AFI Spec Ops group crept forward in olive drab fatigues. They arranged themselves tactically along the funeral home's wall, M16A1s angled low-ready across their chests. Up ahead a gust rattled the screen door's hook in its eyelet.

The video-game SEALs died gruesomely, and Whelp started up a new game. He and Toe-Tag leaned as they fired, spilling tequila across their thighs.

Outside, the commander inched to one side of the screen door. The column of tightly stacked men behind him halted, boots shoved into the mud. The commander raised his gloved hand for the countdown.

One by one, his fingers descended back into his fist.

47

All eyes were on the black octopus of the speaker unit dominating the conference table. A mound of Rich's cigarettes grew from a Styrofoam doughnut plate like an ashen artichoke. Early-morning light filtered through the shades, pale and weak, losing itself in the fluorescents.

At last a clicking issued through the unit as Roberto García returned to the phone on the other end. A liaison from the Mexican attorney general's office, he spoke clear English, unaccented and formal. "Ricardo, are you still there?"

Fingers drumming on his knee, Rich leaned forward over the speaker unit. "Still here, bud."

"The raid was a success. The Special Operations Group killed two Laughing Sinners in a shoot-out. We took the mortician alive."

Whoops and cheers and a smattering of applause.

García said proudly, "My girl is sending the faxes through now."

As if on cue, the machine behind them whirred to life.

"Next time you come, my friend, bring some of that single-malt."

Rich smirked. "That stuff ain't free, *compadre*."

"I will supply the Cubans. Our customary arrangement."

Guerrera held the fax paper impatiently as it printed, then held up the crime-scene photos of the late Toe-Tag and Whelp to the others. Excited nods and high fives.

Tim slid the speaker unit to his side of the table. "Did you find the bodies?"

"Bodies? No bodies. The funeral home is disused for many months now. But we did find two cadaver tables with fresh fluids."

The celebratory mood dissipated immediately. Bear's shoulders sagged as if he were deflating. Jim swore sharply, his legal pad landing on the table with a slap.

Rich made a ticking noise with his tongue against his teeth. "I need another favor, Roberto. There are two corpses we gotta track down. Is the funeral director talking?"

"Not a word. He's loaded on heroin. He knows enough only to be terrified of the biker network. He will not talk."

In the background Maybeck said, "Even if the bodies shipped, we've got eyes at LAX. We're covered."

"We have to be sure," Rich said, at the same time Tim said, "We've got to question him."

"Can we get him extradited?" Guerrera asked.

"He's a Mexican citizen," García said.

Tim's tone was bitter, discouraged. "They can't deport him, and a Mexican court won't extradite."

"So let's get country clearance from OIA and go interview him," Guerrera said.

The D.C. Office of International Affairs was notoriously bureaucratic. Tim spoke what everyone was thinking: "Won't happen within our time frame. That takes weeks, not hours."

Guerrera pressed on. "Maybe we can reclassify him as an international fugitive."

García's voice came through clearly: "Gringo? Relax."

Wearing a sour face, Guerrera mouthed, "Gringo?"

García said, "We have our own ways of dealing with matters such as this."

Rich's smile came fast, the gleam of his teeth standing out from his scruff. He reached across the table and pulled the speaker unit back in front of him.

"Our usual spot?" he asked.

48

They rattled along the desert in Tim's Explorer, Bear riding shot-gun, Rich and Guerrera in the back. Yet another Border Patrol jeep drove past, slowing until the flash of Tim's badge hanging from the rearview came visible. The patrol officer lowered his assault rifle and waved.

The sun bleached the ground to a near white and made the border fence gleam. They were east of Tijuana, so the expensive fence had given way to a rougher design—runway metal used in Kuwait during the first Gulf War, stripped and rammed into desert sand. Each post went deep into the ground to discourage burrowing. They were in a desolate stretch—no houses, no bushes, just a floodlight every hundred feet, countless jeeps, and the endless barrier.

Twenty-six times as many CBP inspectors occupied this fence line as the one at the U.S.-Canada border. Since NAFTA and 9/11, the Mexican border had tightened up, the initiative propelled, as always, by a set of nifty designations. Operation Gatekeeper firmed up matters in California; Arizona needed its own Operation Safeguard, whereas Texas required Operation Hold the Line.

It was a few years since Tim had spent time along the southern seam, and the rise of militarism took him by surprise. He studied the dead, cracked land on which so many Mexicans died trying to get to paradise. Looking around, it was difficult to see the appeal of the side north of the fence.

They passed a tanker truck spraying water to keep down the dust along the sandy road. The hum of the power lines remained audible. A few miles back, when a corralled mustang had passed under the swaying lines, the static bleed-off had raised the hair of his mane.

"Right . . . *here,*" Rich said.

The Explorer skidded off the road, angling for the fence. Rich got out and headed for a three-armed cactus. The deputies followed suit, Tim looking around at the miles and miles of sand.

Though they'd just exited the air-conditioning, Bear was already sweating through his shirt. "You want to tell us what the hell we're doing out here in the middle of nowhere?"

"Are you getting us across to interview the guy or what?" Guerrera chimed in.

"No," Rich said. He counted off a few steps along the fence line from the cactus, stopped, and let out a whistle.

A figure sailed over the barbed wire, dark against the sun, screaming. He landed hard, sand sticking to his cheek and neck. The man was hogtied, arms and legs bound behind him with cloth. His gag had come loose.

Tim put his face to the fence, making out the AFI insignia on the transportation-unit van on the other side. The agents on the roof offered Tim casual, two-finger salutes and went back to their game of cards.

Rich cut the prisoner's restraints and hauled him to his feet. "Gustavo Alonso?"

The man remained bent over, sucking wind, fighting to catch his breath. He managed a nod. "Y-yes."

Bear frowned and nodded, impressed. Guerrera's eyes were like coasters.

A Border Patrol jeep slowed, and they all waved except for Gustavo. The driver waved back and kept on.

Gustavo trembled, going at the scabs on his arms with his fingernails. From his urgency it was obvious he'd been waiting a long time to scratch. He looked terrified.

"Now, listen," Rich said. "*Closely.* I know you don't want to roll on the Sinners. Hell, if I was only up against some shaky aiding-and-abetting bullshit, I wouldn't want to either. But things are different now. You see this?" He toed the sand. "This is American soil. Congratulations. You just reached the promised land. So the problem is . . . the *problem* is, you were dicking around in an operation that threatens—as the song goes—this land that I love. Big time. Not just Laughing Sinners on their tricycles but terrorists. Muji motherfuckers, straight off the hijacked plane from Buttfuckistan. *Comprende?*"

Sweat streaking his face, Gustavo nodded. But he looked baffled.

"Now, on *that* side of the fence, you're all a bunch of big-family-having, God-fearing Catholics. You know what that means?"

"No."

Guerrera launched into a Spanish clarification, but Rich cut him off.

"It means no death penalty. But on *this* side of the fence, we're a bunch of pissed-off-cuz-we-got-caught-with-our-pants-down, vengeance-wreaking infidels. Guess what *that* means."

"Death penalty." Gustavo sounded sure, but he was looking at Guerrera, who nodded gravely.

"Very good, Gustavo. Now, you can play tough guy and prolong your visit to America for, say, the rest of your will-be-shortened life. Or you can talk and go back over the fence. Choice is yours."

Gustavo's eyes darted about. The tip of his tongue inched out and poked at his dehydration-cracked lower lip. "What we talk about. You won't give to them?" He jerked his head at the fence and the AFI agents beyond.

"We can consider this an unofficial powwow." Off Gustavo's blank look, Rich added, "No, we won't."

"What you want?"

"You prepared the bodies?"

Gustavo nodded.

"Stomach balloons full of Allah's Tears?"

Rich's question seemed to catch him completely off guard.

"But only I know my end. I am skilled, prepare well. The bikers mess up the bodies, wreck the *estómagos* before. They need to learn."

Made of silicone, the intragastric balloons were durable, designed to remain inside patients for months at a time and, by extension, able to withstand embalming chemicals for a few days. Under ordinary circumstances they were filled with saline to make overweight people feel full and promote weight loss. When their utility was exhausted, the balloons were simply popped, the saline was digested, and the balloon passed. There was no proper way to extract a balloon's contents. The Sinners probably weren't going to risk the exposure of getting involved with physicians and endoscopes to finesse out the AT. Trying to improvise was not only difficult but it required skill and a coroner's stomach. Thus Diamond Dog's botched work on the dry-run corpses. And Den's neater job on Marisol Juarez.

"They talk about new guy, better with scalpel," Gustavo said. "I am done with all this. I want no more."

"So the bodies already shipped?" Rich asked impatiently.

"I don't know. They leave in morning for two hour. They talk about airport. I hear phone call when they talk."

Tim's shoulders lowered with his exhalation. At least the AT would be picked up by Jan on the other end.

"American Airlines?" Rich asked.

"I don't know."

"For LAX? Los Angeles International Airport?"

"No LAX," Gustavo said, and Tim felt the sweat on the back of his neck go clammy. "They decide not to risk."

Tim screeched up into the gas station, hopping from the Explorer before the vehicle stopped rocking. The others were at his heels as he ran to the occupied pay phone. His badge tapped the glass enclosure, but the woman inside turned her back. He took her by the elbow, gently steering her out as she screamed at him and even went so scripted as to hit him with her purse. Of course, they'd been out of cell-phone and radio range when Gustavo had blindsided them with the change of plans. There had been an uncharacteristic dearth of Border Patrol jeeps after they'd sent Gustavo flying back over the barbed wire, so Tim had floored it to the nearest gas station.

Bear and Guerrera talked the woman down while Rich crammed into the phone booth with Tim. Jan picked up her cell phone on the second ring.

"Hold all bodies coming into Burbank, Ontario, Long Beach, and San Diego." Tim said. "Right now."

"Okay." No questions asked, Jan put him on hold. He waited, baking in the refracted sun and getting an earful of "The Girl from Ipanema."

He worked a hangnail with his teeth. About five minutes later, she came back on.

"You're not gonna like this."

"What?"

"Two caskets came into Burbank Airport on an American Airlines flight from San José del Cabo this morning. They were picked up less than an hour ago."

"Damn it." Tim hit the phone booth's siding with the heel of his hand, the plastic cracking. The woman, still arguing with Bear, got quiet and hurried to her car. "Caskets aren't spot-X-rayed at Burbank?"

"No."

"Why not?"

"Burbank's not on bin Laden's short list."

"And we all know terrorists strive for predictability."

"Our resources barely cover the high-profile airports."

Rich shoved out of the booth, his palms to his forehead. Tim heard Bear ask him what was wrong.

"Sorry," Tim said.

In a quiet voice, Jan replied, "I'll track down the paperwork, get it over to the command post."

"Thank you, Jan."

Tim racked the phone gently and stared at it a moment before stepping back into the hot desert wind.

49

Tim asked Bear to drive; he had to sleep. His body ignored his intention. Every time he drifted off, lulled by the hum of the Explorer's wheels over asphalt, he jerked awake and ran through the string of tasks they had to begin when they returned. They were all weak suggestions; the others at least did their desperate musing silently. Rich sat in the back, watching the freeway roll past. He hadn't spoken since his cell-phone update to Malane.

They arrived in the city shortly after noon. Bear parked in an alley so Tim could get the cuffs on Rich before they cruised into Roybal. No telling where the Sinners had eyes. Though Rich said nothing, Tim kept the cuffs loose so as not to grind his raw wrists. Tim took back the wheel. He pulled into the underground lot.

"You coming back to the post?" Bear asked.

"Nah," Rich said, "can't keep me out much longer. We gotta get me behind bars again, keep things looking normal."

The men all sat as if there were something left to say. Finally Bear headed out. At Tim's nod Guerrera reluctantly followed, leaving Tim and Rich in the Explorer. Tim looked in the rearview. Rich was doing the perpetrator hunch in the backseat, leaning forward to accommodate his cuffed wrists.

Rich checked out the dashboard clock. "Dana Lake's supposed to come by in the next few hours, get me processed out."

"Need anything in the meantime?"

"Nah," Rich said.

"What are you gonna do?"

"Catch up to the boys again. Christ, we need me in there now more than ever. I'll start with some of the hangs, see if Den and Kaner send word. A lot of dirty work to be done yet. They'll need an extra set of hands."

"Be safe."

"I will." Rich jerked the hair off his face, blowing at a stubborn bang that clung to the band of his eye patch. "Listen, that fake door kick at the warehouse the boys set up for the news? After you guys got Goat? That was chickenshit. I'm sorry about that."

"It's not your fault. We can't regulate the games the desk jockeys play for funding."

"Yeah," Rich said. "Guess not."

Across the lot a few Secret Service agents left a Bronco and headed upstairs. Business as usual. Cheap suits and bad coffee. Trying to think five moves ahead to stop the drugs, the murder, the terrorist action. The chess match continued, one big game except for the live ammo. How many of L.A. County's 10 million lives were at stake if the Prophet got his revenue stream up and running? How many lives in the state? Beyond? Once the drugs and cash dispersed, it would be nearly impossible to stem the flow. The agents and deputies could add their efforts to the great ash heap of unsuccessful wars: The War on Poverty. The War on Drugs. The War in Iraq. It would persist, the slow-motion planning, the subterranean simmer. And one day they'd awaken to find that the forces had erupted once again and all they were good for was cleaning up the mess. Jim's rambling eulogy had been embarrassing, but it wasn't entirely off the mark.

Rich cleared his throat, and Tim's focus sharpened. The band of Rich's face in the rearview mirror looked pallid, drained of blood.

"I never answered your question," Tim said. "Dray is the pregnant deputy who got shot in Moorpark. She's also my wife."

In the mirror Tim watched Rich's face alter. His eyes widened; his forehead smoothed. For a moment he looked shocked and maybe even sorrowful. Then, slowly, his face gathered itself back up into its customary squint.

"Jesus," he said.

Reaching with cuffed hands, he opened the door and climbed out.

50

Tim. Tim. *Tim*."

"Dray?"

Bear said, "No."

Tim awakened in the empty cell, clutching his pager in one hand, his phone in the other. Bear stood over him, blotting out the bright Cell Block lights. After returning Rich to his cage, Tim had gone into one of the other keep-away cells, relishing the quiet. He'd touched base with Thomas and Freed, who'd been following up at Burbank Airport for the past few hours. When he'd lain down on the plastic bench to think through his next step, he'd ended up dozing off.

"Tell me it's good news."

"It's good news," Guerrera said. He was holding Tim's tactical vest.

Tim swung his feet over the edge of the molded bench and ground the heels of his hands into his puffy eyes. He checked the cell-phone clock—he'd been out seven minutes.

"Haines pulled the vehicle-cam footage from my Impala," Guerrera said, helping Tim into his vest. "It was intact—that shit is secured in a black box in the trunk. He found the hearse—a 1998 Cadillac Miller Meteor, license plate clear as day, lit up by my headlights. We put out a BOLO to all agencies. But guess what?"

Tim's voice was cracked from sleep. "Registered to a false name."

"And a fake address." Bear pulled Tim to his feet, and they all exited the cell. "Thank you, Babe Donovan."

"So we checked where the registration crap shipped to," Guerrera continued. "A P.O. box. Bear got a telephonic warrant, called your postal inspector from the cult case—"

"Owen B. Rutherford," Bear chimed in.

"—found out the P.O. box is still active."

Bear turned and waved at the black bulb of the security camera at the far end of the corridor. A moment later the door buzzed, and they stepped out of Cell Block.

"Even if we—or Sheriff's—could spare the men for a stakeout, the Sinners aren't gonna send anyone important to the P.O. box to pick up the mail," Tim said. "We'll wind up with Wristwatch Annie."

Bear hit the elevator button, and the doors dinged open. "We don't need a stakeout. Rutherford found us a gas bill for service to a Fillmore address."

Tim's pulse quickened when they drove by the two-story clapboard house. Flaking white paint revealed patches of rotting wood. Blown-off composite roof shingles peppered the lawn. Blankets draped the windows. Located in a formerly middle-class part of Fillmore across the 126 from the Laughing Sinners clubhouse, it was an ideal safe house. Other residents would not notice comings and goings or motorcycles; the houses on the block were decently spaced for privacy, some distinguished by pit bull runs along the sides, others by aboveground pools. A few ambitious souls had already tugged their Christmas trees to the curb.

The deputies did a slow approach, Guerrera sliding around back while Tim and Bear peeked through the front and side windows. The blankets had been tacked to the frames and sills, but in places they'd pulled free, enabling Tim to make out the interior.

The house appeared deserted, no furniture in evidence. Knee-high mounds of kitty litter sloped from the corners. No cat shit. No scratching posts. No claw marks at the doorjambs. Rust-colored stains climbed the walls. Unplugged fans and coils of plastic tubing had been left by the windows, rolled-up towels near the doorways. Wires protruded from holes in the ceiling where the smoke alarms had been. After using the house for a while, the Sinners had cleared out. Like all smart dealer/distributors, they kept their meth labs mobile, moving them every few weeks to stay one step ahead of the DEA and the competition. Once the heat blew over, they might hermit-crab their operation back into a house they'd used months before, or the nomads could use it as a place to hole up.

Tim reconvened with Bear and Guerrera on the old-fashioned porch, all three keeping to the side of the door. Bear had gone out to his Ram and retrieved some of his gear. A mound of *L.A. Times*, some yellowed already, buried the mat.

Bear pointed to the newspapers and whispered, "Nice ruse."

"Really looks like it's vacant," Tim said.

Bear gave a skeptical frown. They drew their guns, Guerrera's hand jiggling in a nervous tic. The doorknob lock yielded in seconds under the pick, but Tim took a bit more time with the dead bolt. He raised his gun and stepped back, letting the door swing inward to reveal the still-empty entry.

Bear stuck his side-handle baton lengthwise along the seam inside the hinges to prop the door ajar. A second door opened to the kitchen. Bear placed a wooden wedge with a nail driven through it, guiding it with a boot. It stuck in place, stopping the door on its backswing. They waded through a heap of kitty litter, globbed up from the toxic gases absorbed in the meth-cooking process, and pushed forward into the living room. Though they were close to the center of the ground floor, wind whistled past them from the open front door—no barriers along their escape route in case they needed to beat a hasty retreat.

The room-to-room went quickly, given the lack of furniture. They triangulated, only one deputy moving at a time. They made silent progress, their backs toward the walls, careful not to let their shoulders whisper against doorframes. Accustomed to full-bore ART kick-ins requiring heavy firepower, Guerrera didn't handle his Beretta with the same facility he did an MP5. Tim caught him holding the handgun up by his head and gestured for him to straight-arm it or keep it in a belt tuck. The *Starsky & Hutch* position was good solely for catching a close-up of an actor's face in the same frame as the gun; in real life a startle reaction to a sudden threat would leave an officer momentarily deaf and blind, or with half his face blown off.

Every so often they'd pause and listen. An upstairs floorboard creaked, and they waited. A few seconds later, a slight rasp put them back on alert. Neither sound was quite pronounced enough for them to determine whether someone was moving up on the second floor or if the house was merely groaning.

Tim and Bear ascended the stairs, back to back, then waved Guerrera up. The second floor comprised a wide master and a bathroom. Guerrera kept his gun on the bathroom door, waiting for Tim and Bear to clear the bedroom. Beside a bare mattress, cigarette butts stuffed a shoe-box lid, making it look like a nicotine planter. Bear waved a hand over it and shook his head—no heat. Tim opened the closet door, gripping the knob with his fist, thumb up, prepared to shove if he felt sudden pressure. Two wire hangers dangled inside.

Guerrera waited for them to get into position before pulling open the bathroom door. He remained flat against the wall, allowing Bear and Tim to enter first. An empty square of chipped tile. Tim swept back the shower curtain with his arm and checked out the empty tub.

Bear let out his breath in a rush—disappointment or relief. "It was worth a shot."

Tim's eye caught on the flexible showerhead. It had been shoved nearly to the ceiling to accommodate a man larger even than Bear.

Guerrera followed Tim's stare and mouthed, "Kaner?"

Bear raised the toilet lid with his boot. A half-smoked cigarette bobbed in the gray water.

Tim ran his thumb along the sink drain. Shaving whiskers.

When he looked up, Guerrera had his Beretta pointed at the ceiling. An attic hatch, nearly seamless. Bear was already telescoping his mirror. He was too big and the space too tight, so he handed off the mirror to Tim and stepped out of the bathroom.

Tim took down the shower-curtain rod and set the rubber plug against the hatch. Guerrera returned his nod, gun still trained overhead, and Tim pushed. The hatch popped up easily. As Guerrera aimed into the dark slit, Tim eased the mirror up into the attic. The stripe of light provided minimal visibility. He made out tufts of pink insulation, crossbeams, swirling motes. The gable window was blacked out. Tim rotated the mirror another quarter turn.

Two dark eyes, illuminated sharply in the reflected band of light, consumed the small rectangle of mirror. Tim dropped the shower-curtain rod, the hatch falling back into place with a thud an instant before the ceiling exploded.

51

Bullets spit up chips of tile. Tim kicked Guerrera in the hip, and Guerrera flew back through the open bathroom door, rolling into the master. Tim charged behind him as chunks of drywall fell and the light fixture showered sparks.

They returned fire, but their handguns were no match for the invisible firepower. Bullet holes chewed up the bedroom ceiling as Kaner mirrored their movement overhead.

Bear grabbed Tim and Guerrera and practically threw them down the stairs. They tumbled over each other, Bear miraculously there before they landed, yanking them to their feet again. They reached the front door, Bear going a mile a minute into his radio.

Breathing hard, Guerrera reloaded and started back inside, shooting Tim an inquisitive look. Tim shook his head, so Guerrera ran outside to keep an eye on the upstairs windows until backup arrived.

Tim and Bear waited in the entry, sweating, weapons drawn, eyes on the stairs. Though the automatic weapon had silenced, dust rode the air down from the second floor, depositing sediment on the top steps. Tim pressed his ear to the doorframe and listened to the house, picking up the thump of boots two floors up and the chink of a new mag in the well. A creak as Kaner sat and then, most unsettling, the silence of the patient hunter.

Eighteen units responded within five minutes. Tim directed them into position while Bear continued to coordinate with the comm center. Even before the street was cordoned off, four major news-channel helicopters circled overhead, one painted KCOM's trademark banana yellow. The front door remained open, Bear's baton still wedged in the hinges, leaving a clear view through to the staircase. Sheriff's quickly determined that there were no live telephone lines going into the house; if they wanted to talk to Kaner, a deputy would have to risk his ass running up to deliver a phone. Malane was there with three suits from Operation Cleansweep. They kept a respectful distance, huddling behind the sawhorses, recognizing that the Service took lead—for now—on the biker front. As soon as the operation dovetailed back with the AT investigation, they'd roll up their sleeves and plunge in.

Sheriff's SWAT was up on the neighboring roofs, scopes glinting in the sun. Sniper-qualified with the Army Rangers and SWAT-certified as a deputy, Tim was eager to get his eye on a scope, too, though he knew that his job today was on the ground. He'd done his retraining at the Sheriff's Academy before adopting the more media- and law-enforcement-friendly title of *counter*sniper, though he had to confess that his precision-marksman instinct was still to play offense, not defense. The military had permitted him ample opportunity to hone his proficiencies; law enforcement had taught him restraint.

The ART squad gathered in the street behind the Beast, a retrofitted ambulance they used for deployment. Tannino jogged over, bent at the waist until he had the oversize vehicle between him and the house. Tim grabbed a ballistic helmet from the Beast and tossed it to him.

Tannino screwed it down over his poufy Erik Estrada do. "How much ammo you think he has in there?"

As if in answer, a burst of automatic fire blazed from the gable window, drilling holes in a Sheriff's Department car. A few of the younger ART members crouched, despite the Beast's protection. The tip of the AR-15 withdrew into the darkness of the attic.

"Not sure," Tim said.

"What's the play?"

Miller spit through his front teeth. "Burn it down."

"We want him alive," Tim said, as if Miller had been serious.

"Let's go in there and get him," Guerrera said.

"He's got position on us," Bear said. "We march up those stairs, we're gonna get our asses shot off."

"We've got numbers."

"Great—we can *share* the body bags."

Miller said, "From the roof?"

Tim said, "We're not going in at all."

A few puzzled glances made the rounds.

Thomas said, "What's left, Troubleshooter?"

"We'll make him come to us."

Maybeck braced himself against the Beast and fired the short, big-barreled breach projectile launcher. An OC canister flew from the 37-mm, punching a fresh hole in the top of the blacked-out gable window. Within seconds, white-gray smoke wisped up into view. Tim lowered his binocs and nodded at Maybeck, who popped the breach open, ejecting the spent casing, and loaded the next round.

A persuasive blend of three hundred varieties of pepper plants, OC was ART's preferred weapon for area denial. OC not only redlined pain receptors in the mouth, nose, stomach, and mucus membrane, but it could incapacitate the esophagus, trachea, respiratory tract, and eye muscles.

Maybeck, as the resident breacher, managed the less lethal weaponry under Miller's supervision. His first day in the district office after his transfer from St. Louis, Maybeck had won a steak dinner at Lawry's, spelling oleoresin capsicum on a chalkboard in the old squad room when Jim snidely bet him he couldn't unwind the abbreviation.

Tim tipped his head, and Maybeck let another perfect shot fly.

"He's fighting it right now," Maybeck said. "Got his shirt up over his head, probably. Give it a minute."

They waited as the plume of gas escaping the shattered window rose and spread. Then a violent hacking came audible, and the sound of Kaner stumbling around in the attic.

"Wait till Bear and I get in position, then fire in another," Tim said. "Hit the rear of the ground floor heavy—I want that back door fogged off. Lose the shotgun and throw grenades if you have to for better aim."

"Make sure you cook the grenades for three or four seconds after you pull the pin so he doesn't have time to send 'em back our way." Miller shot a glare at Thomas. "Sound familiar, jackass?"

Tim and Bear broke from the cover of the Beast, sprinting across the front yard. They shouldered up on either side of the doorjamb. Tim reached across and yanked Bear's baton from the hinges. The door banged closed.

Tim watched another canister disappear into the house. A loud thump as Kaner deserted the attic, jumping down into the bathroom. Tim signaled at Maybeck, holding up two fingers, and Maybeck fired three more canisters through the second-floor window.

Wheezing and gagging. Shoes scrabbling across the upstairs floor.

"Come on, big boy," Bear muttered. "Come to the fresh air."

The house shook as Kaner stumbled down the stairs to the first floor. Through the door they could hear him gasping and grunting, less than ten yards away. Tim signaled again, and Thomas and Freed ran along the sides of the house, heaving grenades through the windows. The bark of Kaner's cough grew louder.

Kaner's raspy voice rose into a warrior's roar, rage tinged with pain. Tim white-knuckled the side handle of the baton. Bear settled down on one knee a few feet back from the hinge side of the door, the stock of his Remington braced against one shoulder, the barrel aimed gut level.

Kaner's footsteps quickened as he thundered toward the front door. Tim tensed his knees, his shoulders, watching the doorknob six inches from his hand. Heart hammering, he drew back the baton, starting his windup. Still bellowing, Kaner hit the door like a 'roid-raging linebacker, knocking it clear off the bottom hinge and splintering the wood. His momentum carried him onto the porch, the AR-15 rising in his right arm. Tim pivoted off the wall, meeting Kaner's skull with the baton and dropping him flat on his back.

52

Holding a five-foot Plexiglas shield before them, three officers wearing gloves and helmets advanced on Kaner in the holding cell. Though his hands were cuffed, he swung his elbows, backing up and bristling like a bull. His cheeks were cherry red and still glistened with tears from the pepper; his eyes looked like something out of an R. Crumb comic. The shield was see-through and concave, designed so the curve could trap a prisoner against a wall like a bug. Tim, Bear, and Guerrera watched the cell extraction from the safety of the corridor.

They'd stripped Kaner of his originals, his jeans, and his drive-chain collar, putting him in an orange jumpsuit. They'd given up on fighting him into new clothes in Booking, and so the top half of the jumpsuit remained unbuttoned, hanging at his waist, his T-shirt proclaiming STOP LOOKING AT MY COCK. He paused to glare at Tim, then put a shoulder down into the Plexiglas and lunged, knocking the lead man over. The two others jumped in, taking up the broad shield, but not before Kaner managed to stomp the fallen officer's knee, which gave with a crack.

As the injured officer howled and crawled away from the scuffle, the other two hammered Kaner against the wall, struggling to hold him in place. One dropped to all fours, reaching under the shield and pulling Kaner's feet out from under him. Kaner hit the concrete hard, banging his head. While he was dazed, they got him in a restraint hold and moved him out of the cell, four detention enforcement officers leaping in to help.

"Put him in the interview room next to Booking," Tim said. "Cuff wrists and ankles to the chair."

Kaner lunged at Tim as he was dragged past, cursing, spittle flying from his lips with the effort.

Bear's breath passed through his teeth as a whistle. They followed at a distance. A one-way mirror occupied a wall of the spacious interview room, a cardboard box below it. In the far corner, a metal chair was bolted to the floor. The officers double-cuffed each of Kaner's limbs to the chair and left him with Tim, Bear, and Guerrera. Kaner strained against the cuffs, throwing his weight violently from side to side, trying to budge the chair. Bear stepped forward, but Tim held up his hand. Kaner thrashed and swore for about ten minutes, finally settling back in exhausted defeat.

He was massive, overflowing the chair. A shadow cut his face in half. Same shock of black hair from the photos, same fleshy ears, like cuts of meat, laid flat to the skull. His forearms were like bars, barely tapering at the wrists. The cuffs rustled against the chair when he stirred, detention wind chimes. The windowless room smelled of his sweat, strong and musky.

Tim took a step closer. Finally at close quarters with a Sinner nomad. Tim's first chance to address one of the outlaws present when Dray had been shot. He forgot about Tannino and Malane behind the mirror; he forgot about everything but himself and Kaner and the brief stretch of concrete separating them. His anger made him numb; it altered his depth perception so he saw Kaner's features as juts and recesses.

He drew his gun, aiming at Kaner's head. Kaner regarded him with curiosity.

Tim tossed the keys to Guerrera. "Uncuff him."

Guerrera looked at Tim with concern and maybe a little excitement.

"Temper tantrum's over," Tim said. "We're all grown-ups here. We can share the sandbox. Can't we?"

Disheveled from his struggling, Kaner settled back in his chair and smirked. "Sure thing." His larynx sounded one step short of cancerous.

Guerrera freed his wrists from behind but left his ankles cuffed to the chair legs. Tim kept his .357 raised until Guerrera had moved out of Kaner's reach, then lowered it. Kaner rubbed his left wrist, where the handcuff had drawn blood during the in-cell takedown. Dangerous eyes gleamed through the wisps of hair.

"You might have noticed we were looking for you," Tim said. "Where you been?"

Kaner offered a docile grin. "Oh, here and there."

"Is that right."

It was odd to have hostility and civility juxtaposed so quickly.

"Where's Den Laurey?"

"Haven't the foggiest."

"I know you're coordinating plans. Where is he?"

"Hey, man, we do our own thing. I don't know where he holes up, he don't know where I do. That way one of us gets popped, the other's in the clear." He ran a strangely wide, flat tongue across his teeth.

"I don't believe you. I think you know where Den Laurey is. I think you know where he sleeps."

"Why you so fixated on the Man?"

"I want to send him flowers."

"You can't catch the Man. The Man's an apparition. Only reason you got him last time is he didn't know you were looking. But now, hell, you can't do nothin' but ride his wake."

Bear tried a new tack, probably because Tim wasn't making headway. "That T-shirt supposed to keep the boys off your back in the pen? Maybe we put you in general pop at MDC, let you play catch-up with a few Cholo Rovers."

"You dumb fuck. There's no rival clubs in prison. On the inside we're all brothers."

"Even the spics?" Guerrera asked. "I'm not sure they'd agree after the Palmdale massacre."

"'The Palmdale massacre.'" Kaner sucked his teeth. "Got a ring, don't it?"

Bear poked around in the cardboard box. "Hey, guess what we got in here?"

"Michael Jackson's nose."

Bear withdrew Kaner's drive chain. He whipped the concrete floor with it. Kaner regarded him, a hint of nervousness creasing his features.

But Bear turned away, looping the drive chain around his neck and admiring himself in the one-way. "What do you think?"

Kaner's face rearranged itself into a sneer.

"I think it's a great look," Bear continued, still preening in the mirror. "But how do you get around your grease problems? Ajax? Bleach? Or do you order direct from the Village People?"

Kaner smirked at some private thought. "You hate me because I'm different. I hate you because you're all the same."

"No," Tim said, "we hate you because you kill people."

Kaner shrugged. "Trample the weak, hurdle the dead."

"You should start a bumper-sticker factory," Bear said. "All these aphorisms. How do you guys come up with them? Do you sit around the clubhouse, going, 'Stomp on the weak, leap over the dead. No, that's not right. It just doesn't sing.'"

"Let's get something straight. I'm not gonna tell you shit. No matter what. So all this business"—Kaner waved a hand around— "you ain't gonna get a rise outta me."

"Hey, wait," Bear said, still doing his shtick. "Something's missing." He dug through Kaner's personals in the cardboard box, then halted, snapping his fingers. "Hey, I know."

He strolled out into the hall and returned with an article of clothing encased in dry-cleaning wrap. He hung it on the door and stripped away the cellophane to reveal Kaner's originals. The collar had been starched, and the leather was now pristine; even the patches seemed to shine.

Kaner made a noise like a gurgle deep in his throat and charged off the chair. The ankle cuffs held firm, and he slapped against the floor, where he seemed to remember his predicament. Calmly, though without grace, he restored himself to the chair, his eyes eerily calm.

He gestured with a flick of his chin. "That's a declaration of war."

"Haven't you heard?" Bear said. "We're *already* at war, motherfucker."

Tim pushed forward, hard, trying to keep Kaner off balance. "We know about Allah's Tears. About Good Morning Vacations. About the girls. About the corpses. We know about everything."

Kaner couldn't keep the surprise from his face, but he covered quickly, a scowl tightening his features. "Not everything," he said. "Or you wouldn't be talking to me."

"That's a helluva scheme Uncle Pete dreamed up," Tim said.

"Who's saying Uncle Pete knows shit?"

"I am. It took us a while to figure out what you guys were up to, but we did."

"No shit it took a while. No one misses a spic bitch. Not even spics. They don't got no respect for their property, not like we do. No one fucks with my deed. No one."

"Not like you can fuck with Mexican girls." Tim moved closer, getting in Kaner's space, cutting off his view of Bear and Guerrera. A mano a mano confrontation. Whether Kaner talked or not, he was going away for life. His ass was already nailed on the escape offense and resultant murders. He had nothing to lose. If Tim pushed him hard enough, he hoped he could get him to flaunt his superiority.

"Damn straight."

"But you dumb fucks picked them at random. No plan."

"At random," Kaner repeated with disdain. "At random? Then why'd it take you so long to catch on? I'll tell you why: We dodged all the triggers."

"What triggers?"

"The triggers that make people notice. We needed chunky ones, but we knew to steer clear of pregnant broads. Brings too much static. Look what happened with Laci Peterson. Who needs that mess? You don't give people a reason to give a shit in this country, they won't. That knocked-up deputy's on every channel. Kill a pregnant bitch, you got a news story. Kill a fat Mexican broad, hell, you got a statistic."

After all the death and destruction Tim had witnessed from Croatia to South Central, he still found the Sinners' regard for human life uniquely sickening. There was no cause, not even brainwashed zealotry, behind the violence. Just greed and malice, pure and simple. Cops and rivals were obstacles to be annihilated; drug profits would be reaped even if it meant lining the pockets of dealers of mass destruction; women were reduced to test-run luggage. Dray's words returned to Tim: *Everyone counts.* The Sinners had banked on apathy when selecting their victims, and they'd gotten far doing it.

"So you chose Jennifer Villarosa."

Kaner made a gun with his hand and clicked off a shot in Tim's direction.

"But the army brought the heat on her," Tim continued. "Caught you off guard."

"Barely a wrinkle. They don't care much 'bout dead dykes. Poked around a bit, didn't find a thing. And we took care of that, went after fat, *broke* Mex bitches next. No employers who give a shit. Their families ain't got no money to fly down, ask questions, ain't got no pull on this end neither. They can't talk to a cop or they'd get their brown asses deported. Let's be honest, who gives a shit about chubby chicanas from Chatsworth?"

"I do," Tim said.

Kaner met his stare with blazing eyes. "Bravo, brother. You and no one else, 'cept maybe your friend back there." His eyes pulled to Guerrera, who was trying to look impervious despite a clenched jaw. "You know the other thing about pickin' fat broads? They're sluggish, not so frisky. Gut slows 'em down. Kinda like that bellied-out cunt cop we shot."

Tim felt his face grow hot. His mouth cottoned. "Oh, she's pretty frisky."

Kaner's face shifted. "You know her?"

Tim stared at him.

Kaner's delight showed in the gleam in his eyes. "I woulda liked to have split her like a banana, too. Filled her with cream."

Tim heard Bear coming. He turned in time to get an arm around his waist, slowing his charge, but Bear dragged him another three feet toward Kaner, and Tim had to get his other arm up to stop his roundhouse. He heard himself shouting, and then Bear threw him off and stormed away to regroup, his mighty chest heaving while Kaner laughed his ten-grit laugh.

"Oh, that's rich," Kaner said quietly, studying Tim. "You're the deputy husband." He laughed again, shaking his head with delight. "Now and then, when things ain't lookin' so hot, fate comes to the rescue."

Tim licked his dry lips. "A philosopher."

"My new hobby."

"You'll have plenty of time for it."

"Maybe so, but you lost the war. Allah's Tears is in-country, and it's here to stay. While I'm tanning in the yard at Lompoc between sets on the bench, you can philosophize about *that*."

Bear was muttering in the shadowed back corner—giving Kaner the idea he was getting to them was the right strategy. Still, Tim fought to regain his focus. To keep Kaner gloating, he had to continue dangling bait. "How do you know it's here?"

"I know."

"How do you know we didn't seize it at Burbank?"

Kaner leaned forward, face twisted with vindictiveness, and Tim felt a stab of excitement at what he'd reveal in his anger.

"Because—"

The door banged open, and Dana Lake stormed in, a court security officer at her heels. "What the fuck is going on here? What have you answered? What have you told them?"

"Not a thing they didn't already know." Kaner offered a fat grin. "Who gives a shit anyways? I'm just adding up life sentences."

"Listen, dipshit, if you don't want to rot away with no possibility of *ever* getting parole, keep your fucking trap shut."

Amazingly, Kaner heeded the advice of counsel.

Bear found a surrogate target for his anger, blasting the CSO. "Why the hell is she in here?"

The CSO offered an apologetic shrug. "We had to, man. You know how that goes."

"Get her out. He's a captured fugitive. He doesn't have the right to an—"

"You bet your ass he does," Dana said. "I'd assume you're charging him with new criminal offenses, at the very least an escape offense. He has the right to remain silent. He has the right to an attorney—"

Bear scowled and stormed out of the room. Guerrera grabbed the cardboard box and followed. Dana glared at Tim, arms crossed, one foot turned out, showing the sharp curve of her calf beneath the hem of her skirt.

Tim said quietly to the CSO, "Call in six detention enforcement officers. Have the prisoner moved to an attorney room. If he resists *at all*, he goes to a keep-away cell, and Ms. Lake can try her luck again later."

Passing Dana, he caught a whiff of high-end perfume. She smiled sweetly. "Thank you, Deputy Rackley. I knew we'd see eye to eye on this one."

53

oddamnit. We were right fucking there. He was just about to talk." Bear grabbed the prisoner-effects box from Guerrera and threw it against the wall in Booking. Loose change and keys clattered on the floor.

Two detention enforcement officers hustled a Mexican Mafia hitman out of the room, leaving them alone. They stood still for a minute, brewing in their frustration.

Tim thumbed open his phone and got Dray's captain on the line. "The Sinners know now. I don't want to rely on hospital security anymore. Can you keep someone on her room at the hospital?" He grimaced. "I'm sure he would be."

He hung up.

Bear's eyebrow pulled up, as if attached to a string. "Mac?"

Tim nodded.

Bear blew a sigh. He crouched, his knees cracking, and began picking up Kaner's belongings and returning them to the box. He sat on the aluminum table, putting his feet on the bench seat. After a moment he smiled. "Bet you threw a scare into Malane when you pulled the .357 in there."

"Where's Malane now?" Tim asked.

"Arguing with Dana Lake," Guerrera said.

"I wonder who wins that battle."

Bear said, "I'm putting my money on Lawzilla. You couldn't get a dime up her ass with a sledgehammer."

"Be worth a try, though," Guerrera noted from the table where he watched Tim divvying up Kaner's possessions.

Bear smirked at Guerrera's newfound bravado and slid down across from them. "Did someone track down records on the safe house?"

"Thomas and Freed." Tim tossed Bear a wallet, and he turned it inside out, checking the lining. "We've got water and gas, but no phone bills. House hasn't had an active line in over two years."

A metal ring held the key to Kaner's Harley and a house key that they'd already matched to the safe house's dead bolt. Guerrera ran his fingers along the cuffs of Kaner's jeans. They reeked of dirt and pepper spray. Strands of pink insulation stood out against the denim.

"What's this?" Tim reached across and tugged the waistband of the jeans, revealing markings in the front right pocket, where an object had worn the fabric. A small rectangle, clearly not a tin of Skoal. It was well defined—time on the bike had meant a lot of friction. "Which pocket was the wallet in?"

"Don't know."

Bear slid the wallet into the pocket, but it was too big to fit the frayed outline. "What's this from?" He stuck his finger through a small hole that had eroded in the pocket's top corner.

Tim bit his lip, examining the outline. He heard an echo of the words he'd just spoken—*We've got water and gas, but no phone bills. House hasn't had an active line in over two years.*

He gestured at the worn spot in the denim. "Antenna."

Guerrera and Bear looked at each other. Guerrera nosed through the remaining items in the box. "It's not in here."

"Of course not," Bear said.

Tim grabbed Kaner's keys, Bear and Guerrera trailing him out of the room.

They ducked the crime-scene tape, flashing badge at the sheriff's deputy working the sawhorses. He gave a nod reading Tim's creds, then looked up with a surprisingly soft expression. "I'm sorry about Andrea. I went through the academy with her."

"Thank you."

"How's she doing?"

"It's been four days."

"What's that mean?"

Tim studied a shattered bottle in the gutter, feeling the familiar dread twist his gut. "I don't know."

The deputy nodded severely, lips pursed, and Tim, Bear, and Guerrera headed for the house. Tim used Kaner's key to unlock the dead bolt, and they made their way upstairs. Though several of the windows had been left open, pepper aftermath spiced the air. Tim pulled his shirt up over his nose and mouth, and Bear and Guerrera followed suit. The second floor was a mess, the ceiling eroded from the bullets, plaster hanging down from the punctures like the fringes of flesh wounds. The spent canisters lay among the wreckage. As they headed to the bathroom, white dust clung to their boots and the cuffs of their jeans.

The criminalists had left a ladder beneath the attic hatch in the bathroom; they probably wanted to let the attic air out more before crawling around the closed space. Looking up at the dark square, Tim shook off a shiver recalling the mirrored glimpse he'd caught of Kaner's eyes. He climbed up, clicking on his flashlight. Because of the .223-caliber ventilation and the shattered window, the space wasn't as dark as before, but the air was thick and oppressive. Bent at the waist, Tim shuffled forward, rods of light playing across him like a disco effect. Mindful of his weight and the aerated footing, Bear was careful to balance on the joists. Brass casings shimmered in the insulation, nestled like eggs.

They searched for about twenty minutes, until Tim's eyes were watering and Guerrera developed a repetitive one-note cough. Tim's breath had moistened the collar of his shirt, still pulled up over his nose. The humidity and dust were making his head throb, and the flickering fingers of light were playing tricks with his eyes.

Guerrera finally said, "I need to go grab a gas mask." He headed for the hatch, stumbling over a raised corner of insulation.

Bear pulled back the pink strip. Lying against the plywood was a smashed cell phone.

The service rep, Bryant by his name tag, regarded the shattered cell phone skeptically. The top of the fold-down had been ripped off, the LED screen shattered. The battery was bent out of shape and the casing twisted.

Having progressed through a salesman and a store manager, they were finally backstage at the downtown Sprint PCS store on South Flower Street, blocks from the command post.

"Dude, we got some great deals on new phones."

"We need the information off *this* phone," Tim said. "We don't need it to work—"

"Well, that's good."

"—we just need to get what's on it."

"Looks like someone didn't *want* you to get what's on it." Off Bear's look, Bryant said, "Right. Right. Okay." He scratched the tuft of hair protruding from the top of his visor. "Lemme get Larry. He does some next-level shit."

He disappeared out a side door and returned accompanied by a thin East Asian kid with orange hair. The smell of cigarettes lingered in Larry's jacket. His eyes were hidden beneath mirrored Oakley Blades. Larry held out his hand like a surgeon requesting an instrument, and Tim laid the crippled phone in his palm. Larry took it to his workbench, Tim following and looking over his shoulder as he worked. After casting an annoyed glance at Tim, he screwed earphones into his head and turned the volume up so loud that Tim could make out the tinny lyrics—something about blood devils and suicide pacts.

Tim glanced back at Bryant. "You explain to him what we need?"

"Oh, yeah. Lar's on it, dude."

Lar swapped the battery, then dissected the casing, threading a series of wires over to a brand-new cell phone of the same model. He turned on the new phone, made some minute adjustments with what looked like an eyeglass-repair screwdriver, and tugged the earphones down around his neck.

Tim's Nextel chirped—the radio signature—and he keyed the "talk" button. "Go for Rackley."

Freed's voice filled the small service room: "The twins' bodies turned up, dumped naked in the wash by the Tujunga Bridge. Predictable incisions. Aaronson's handling the workups. What do you want him to do next?"

Tim pursed his lips, studied the tip of his boot. Bear and Guerrera exchanged a weary look—they'd all known it was coming, but that didn't make the reality any more pleasant.

"Clean up the bodies as best he can and give the parents a burial."

When Tim signed out, Bryant looked a touch queasy.

Tim raised his eyebrows at Lar—let's get back to business. Larry's face was softer than before, his tone agreeable. "Okay. You got the brains of the old phone on the display of the new phone." He handed the linked phones to Tim. "Be careful."

Bear and Guerrera crowded around as Tim trial-and-errored his way through the elaborate phone menu. He arrived at the address book, his hands sweating with anticipation, and clicked the icon. It was empty—no saved numbers.

His disappointment was sharp, but he couldn't say unexpected. If Kaner knew enough about investigative technology to want to destroy and hide his cell phone before being killed or taken captive, he probably wasn't dumb enough to input Den Laurey's numbers. Bear made various sounds of irritation, and Guerrera took a step back and sank his hands into his pockets.

But Tim kept his focus on the cell phone, using the arrow buttons to reach the submenus. All outgoing calls had been deleted. He thumbed around some more, and the missed-calls menu popped up, also empty. He backed out, highlighted "incoming calls"—the final play—and punched "OK."

Amid seven "blocked callers," the same phone number came up three times.

54

From the street nothing was visible, just a dark room off an unlit third-floor balcony, parted polyester drapes billowing in the breeze like languid belly dancers. The three-hundred-dollar-a-week, four-story apartment-hotel, ambitiously named Elite Towers, overlooked a quiet throw of street. Crowded along the far side were a parking lot, a biker bar named Suicide Clutch, complete with neon martini and padded door, and most critically, a wall-mounted pay phone.

Standing ten feet back in the hotel room behind a tripod-mounted, high-powered rifle, Tim observed the pay phone through the Leopold variable-power scope at 5x. If he zoomed in to 10x, the faded phone number above the pay phone's black receiver—the same number listed three times in Kaner's incoming-call log—would fill his field of vision. A KN250 attachment provided him night vision, more essential every minute. The drapes flickered, never intruding on the two-foot gap that provided Tim a clear line of sight. The only interruptions in his field of vision were the uprights of the balcony railing through which he aimed and a crisscross of suspended electric cable too high to matter.

After tracing the number to the location, Tim had organized the takedown, then headed home to retrieve his sniper rifle. He'd oiled and run a patch through his bolt-action Remington M700, which held four in the well, one in the chamber, then gone back to the master to shower.

After staring at the unmade bed and Dray's Gap sweats kicked off in the corner, he'd upgraded to his match-grade M14. It was semiauto, accommodating twenty magazine-fed rounds, and, if the necessity arose, it could turn Den Laurey into pink mist.

Based on his knowledge of the Sinners' chain of command, Guerrera surmised that Kaner took his marching orders from Den Laurey alone. The deputies assumed that Den Laurey was using the pay phone to place sensitive calls that he didn't want traced or logged. There was little question that Den still needed to be in contact with the higher-ups—Uncle Pete, the Prophet, the money launderer, or whoever was coordinating the drug-money exchange.

The breeze, unchecked even by a screen door, pressed against Tim's face. The tail end of dusk turned the street shades of gray. The air was grainy, dreary, heavy, like war footage. Tim remained frozen in a supported standing position, rifle butt to his shoulder, fiberglass stock pushing up his cheek, his face 3.25 inches back from the scope for proper eye relief. The end of the stock was slotted in the padded U atop the tripod. The rifle was balanced; if he let go, it would remain in position.

As dark overtook dusk, Tim turned up the illuminated mil-dot reticle so the crosshairs glowed red. He'd been standing motionless more than three hours, and he'd seen little more than a few off-the-assembly-line full-dressers come and go, and the occasional biker stumbling out of the cocktail dive. It was still too early for anyone but the dregs and the die-hard lushes. A parking attendant sat on the curb in front of the lot smoking a cigarette, ignoring the well-fed homeless guy crushing cans in the alley. A refrigerator van idled in front of the bar, a phallically tilted Miller Genuine Draft bottle rendered on its side.

Statue-still in the dark room, Tim watched and waited.

The soldiers in sniper training had square jaws and calves like softballs, and they all smelled of tobacco and Right Guard. They were funny in the darkest manner, a mordant kind of funny that kept moving so despair wouldn't overtake it.

Like Ma Bell told you. Reach out and touch someone.

Gonna give motherfucker a case of instant lead poisoning.

The Good Lord said it's better to give than receive.

Tim had never joked much. He'd stayed quiet and hit his targets, and somehow the others had found that all the more heartless. In joking they released their discomfort, but he'd taken his and swallowed it live, held it in the vise of his body as it banged against his insides, held it until it disintegrated. Dray had taught him, slowly, painstakingly, how to open himself up to the world instead of trying to contain the world inside himself. She'd taught him to be alive, and having Ginny had *forced* him to be alive, and then he'd paid the price, felt the searing pain at his tender core. Dray could manage pain and intimacy. Dray could balance private cause with public duty. Dray was the best part of him. If she died as Ginny had died, and if he continued as he would have to, he was not sure who he would be.

He heard the chopper before it came into view. His jaw tightened at the angry crackle of the engine, and then a helmeted biker eased to the curb near the pay phone and dismounted. The bike had none of Danny the Wand's telltale markings. It had been spray-painted black, and the license plate was illegible, caked with mud. The engine appeared to be a knucklehead, but Tim couldn't determine whether it was Den's. The street was quiet, almost desolate, the only noise the distant whine of traffic, the muffled thump of Whitesnake from the Suicide Clutch juke, and dead leaves scraping the empty sidewalk.

Tim's earpiece activated with a hiss of static, and then Bear said, "Got him?"

Tim spoke softly so as not to vibrate the rifle, the receiver on his Adam's apple picking up his voice. "Yeah. It's a chopper, but I don't recognize it. Can't make a positive ID."

Bear shifted in his homeless garb, sending a few crushed cans scattering. "Want us to hammer him?"

"Not until we make the positive ID." Tim shifted the scope to the parking attendant at the curb. The rifle stock felt like a part of his face. "Guerrera, you got an angle?"

Guerrera held the cigarette to his lips so they wouldn't be seen moving. "Nope. Eye visor's still down."

Tim tilted the rifle, following the biker to the pay phone. The biker paused, pulling off his helmet.

Den Laurey, magnified five times over, loomed before Tim's right eye.

Tim's voice came high with his excitement. "We got him."

"I'm within range for the takedown," Bear said.

The hum of the refrigerator van accompanied Thomas's voice. "Let's move."

Malane cut in on the primary channel. He was in one of five FBI sedans positioned up the street. "Not until he makes the call. That was the deal."

"You have one minute," Tim said. "And if he so much as breathes wrong, we're swarming him."

"Not until we get a line on the drug swap."

"The deal goes through with or without Den Laurey."

"Yeah, but without this call we don't know *where*."

"I'm not losing this guy."

"Just take it easy, Rackley. He's not going anywhere. We've got plenty of boots on the ground."

Casting a wary gaze over his shoulder, Den stepped in close to the pay phone. Tim kept the rifle steady, his trigger finger alongside it. With his left thumb and forefinger, he adjusted the dial, pulling back to 4x, which allowed him to fit Den's entire body in the scope picture and watch the surrounding area for civilians.

Bear's build suited him to playing homeless. Rags shifting about him, he dug in his shopping cart while red-vested Guerrera lit a new cigarette off the butt of his last. Den crossed his arms and leaned against the wall beside the pay phone. His sharp eyes picked over the scene, coming to rest on Guerrera. Guerrera played it cool, no eye contact, no rush, no angling for the Glock tucked into his belt.

From his post in the MGD van amid Thomas and six other ART members decked out in Kevlar and toting MP5s, Miller said, "Screw this. We don't move, he's gonna eyefuck Guerrera."

"He's not making a call," Tim said.

Malane said firmly, "Then he's waiting for one."

"We don't have the luxury of waiting with him. He's gonna make Guerrera. We gotta move."

"Give it a second," Malane hissed.

The phone rang. Tim exhaled through his teeth. "Hold. Hold your positions."

Malane said, "We're sending the phone splice through."

Keeping his eyes on the street, Den picked up the phone.

A quiet, accented voice on the other end: "I have an obligation to see that it arrived safely."

Den's lips barely moved. "So you can turn it back over to us?"

"I shall see with my own two eyes. Tomorrow, as we discussed."

"Noon."

"There had better not be a drop missing."

"There won't be. You can weigh it yourself."

Dhul Faqar Al-Malik said, "I intend to do more than that," and hung up.

"Let's move," Tim said.

"*Wait!*" Malane's voice was hard, driving. "We couldn't get a trace. He rerouted the call through UCLA's switchboard."

Den hung up the phone and started for his bike.

Tim said, "Sorry. You missed your shot."

"Are you kidding? Laurey's going to the stash house *tomorrow*. He'll lead us right in. We have ten agents here—we can tail him until tomorrow."

"No way," Tim said. "You know how easy it is to lose a bike."

"We won't let him out of our sight. Not for a minute."

"That wasn't the deal."

"The deal just *changed*. We couldn't trace the call."

"We can take him," Miller said. "This *instant*."

Den passed the mouth of the alley, crossing before Bear. Behind him, Bear offered Tim a frustrated glare.

"On three," Tim said.

"Goddamnit," Malane said, "we have Rich undercover right now, risking his life every minute to tie this thing up. Don't cut us short."

"*One . . .*" Tim said.

Malane was shouting, "We've got *no drugs. No money. No terrorist.* You play cowboy now, we lose the trail to the biggest threat on the West Coast."

Den paused beside his bike, securing the helmet over his head.

The handle on the beer truck's loading door rotated slowly until it pointed at the asphalt.

"*Two . . .*"

"You take down Laurey, the next 9/11 is on your head."

Miller's voice was high and angry. "We gotta move here. *Now.*"

Tim lined up the crosshairs on Den's chest and hooked his finger inside the trigger guard, ready to give the final order. The FTW tattoo stood out through a sheen of sweat on Den's collarbone. Tim pictured the burst of flame erupting from Den's fist. Dray's boot, empty and upright on the asphalt. The stain at the crotch of her olive sheriff's pants.

His head swam with desire; for an instant he forgot that he was here to provide overwatch for the ART team, not to execute a kill.

"We can do this," Malane urged. "We can tie the whole fucking thing up tomorrow."

Bear growled, "He's gonna walk outta here, Rack."

Tim listened for Dray's voice but for the first time couldn't hear it. She was done playing conscience. Everyone else was hidden, lost in disguise, holed up in trucks and sedans, phantom voices in his ear. Wind whistled through the balcony rails, cutting into the silence.

Bear again: "What's it gonna be, Rack?"

It was just him, the Troubleshooter, with the crosshairs on the man who'd shot his wife.

Den threw a leg over the bike and kick-started the engine.

"What's it gonna be?" Bear said.

Tim said, "Let him go."

Den carved a sharp turn, passing within feet of Guerrera. Scope to his eye, Tim watched him float unopposed up the street. The frosty MGD bottle flew by in the background. Den passed Haines's and Zimmer's Broncos, facing out of opposing driveways, ready to rev forward to form an instant barricade. Up the street a dark FBI sedan—probably Malane's—eased out from the curb behind the bike.

Moving through headlight splashes, Den drove evenly up the street, abiding the speed limit, signaling at the turn. Tim watched the black bulb of his helmet until it disappeared from sight.

55

Squeeze, Dray. C'mon. Give a squeeze."

Tim finally slid his index finger from his wife's limp fist. Her hand fell open to the sheet. He walked around the bed and tried her other hand, but to no avail. Someone shouted from a nearby room, and he heard the tapping of running feet in the hospital hall, the clatter of gurney wheels. He sat for a few minutes in perfect silence.

Then he retrieved Dray's brush from the bag he'd brought and ran it through her hair, working out the tangles. He wet one of her washcloths in the sink and cleaned her face. He traced her hairline, circled her eyes, rode the bridge of her nose. Then he stopped to feel the warmth of her curved belly. Gently, he pulled up her eyelid so he could see her iris. Her eyes were emerald—true emerald—an arresting shade that had depth and layers like the infinite refractions of the gem itself.

But now they seemed flat and vacant, devoid of inner light. No longer did he hear her voice in his head. He wondered if that meant he'd lost her already, if she'd drifted beyond the pale of recovery.

"I could've killed Den Laurey," he said. "And I didn't."

But if he was looking for approval or absolution, he'd have to look elsewhere. He let go, and the eyelid pulled back into place.

Night crowded the hospital window. From his place by the bed, Tim could see neither stars nor streetlights, just the black square of glass, the opaque end of a corridor of darkness. The hospital might have been the last outpost of civilization; it might have been perched on the edge of a cliff or drifting through outer space.

He rose wearily and stretched Dray's legs, her arms. Her face, slack now for four days, no longer retained the lines and shapes that made her unique, that made her Dray. In another few days, the muscle tone would start to weaken. And her chances of recovery would weaken with it.

He was massaging her jasmine lotion into her hands when a noise at the door made him look up.

Malane came in an awkward half step, one arm still clutching the doorframe as if to indicate his willingness to extract himself from the intimate scene should Tim desire it. Tim nodded, and Malane entered and sat in the opposing chair, facing Tim across Dray's body.

"I'm sorry to bust in on you. . . . Bear told me you were here."

Tim continued rubbing Dray's hands.

Malane flared a few fingers at Dray, a small, awkward gesture. "I, uh, I hadn't realized . . ."

"That's the job. For better or worse, it's part of the job." Tim blinked a few times, then said, "But that's not why you're here."

Malane took a deep breath, blew it out, and said, "The good news is, Den Laurey stopped again up the road, used a different pay phone to place a call to Babe Donovan."

"He addressed her by name?"

"Yeah. He calls her Dunny. We got him on the parabola mike. He told her to drop the car tomorrow in the Taco Bell parking lot at Pico and Bundy."

Tim rotated Dray's foot, the cranky ankle tendons putting up resistance. "And the bad news?"

"We lost him."

Malane watched him closely, but Tim merely continued with Dray's hands, lost in the smell of jasmine.

"We were closing in, and he dropped into a ravine and disappeared. Trails. The cars couldn't . . ." Malane's hands flew up, clapped to his knees. "We have a line on the drugs, Rackley. That's most important. We'll pick Den up again tomorrow."

Tim looked at him, expressionless.

Malane's eyes jogged back and forth, and then his voice softened.

"I'm sorry. I promised something to you, and I didn't deliver. I, uh, I at least wanted to tell you myself."

Tim said, "I appreciate that."

"You cut us in on your operation, now I'd like to cut you in on ours. You want to work with us on this thing tomorrow morning?"

Tim set Dray's hand by her side, smoothed her fingers flat. He rose and pulled on his jacket. "Yes."

Malane nodded. "Let's have us a takedown."

56

The morning sun blazed off the windshields of the parked cars. A few gardeners sat in the back of a dinged pickup, eating breakfast burritos and slurping soda from big plastic cups. One of them stood and belched, a splash of Fire Border sauce embellishing his dated FREE KOBE T-shirt. Gordita wrappers rolled across the asphalt, urban tumbleweed. Though it was past 11:00 A.M.—beyond the sticky reach of morning rush hour—still the intersection was clogged with runoff from the 10.

Tim sat in the passenger's seat beside Malane, the Crown Vic's air-conditioned leather a considerable upgrade from the dog-chewed bench seat of Bear's Ram. Bear had parked strategically across the street. Malane offered Tim the bag of sunflower seeds, and he took another handful and continued spitting shells into an empty plastic Coke bottle.

Bear came through the radio for the fifth time in as many minutes, and Malane stifled a smile. He'd given Bear and Guerrera FBI-coded Nextels for the operation, and Tim was getting the sense that the agents tended more conservative in their radio banter.

"Now, this fucking guy," Bear started, Guerrera the ongoing person in question, "this fucking guy, now, he says he thinks A-Rod's got it on Bonds in batting. *Batting*. Not in the field."

They'd been sitting on the Taco Bell since 8:00 A.M., and, as on most stakeouts, conversation was running thin. Aside from the Harley parked in the farthest parking-lot space that, at this point, they were presuming belonged to a TB employee, nothing had yet demanded their attention.

A background murmur came through, to which Bear responded, "I don't give a shit if A-Rod's younger. There's Barry Bonds, and there's everyone else. Don't give me your ethnic bias." Then, more clearly, "What's the vote?"

Malane said, "A-Rod," at the same moment Tim replied, "Bonds."

"All right," Bear said. "Then we go to Car Four for the tiebreaker."

An FBI agent cut in on the primary channel. "*Eyes up, eyes up*. Babe Donovan approaching in a . . . looks like a Pinto."

"A Pinto?" Bear said.

The car drifted into view. The orange coat had given way to rust, the subtle contrast lending it a strangely camouflaged appearance.

Babe Donovan parked the car in the tiny parking lot and hopped out. The gardeners let out a volley of whistles and catcalls that silenced immediately as soon as her Sinners property jacket came into view. One of the guys tugged off his Dodgers cap as she passed, offering her a deferential little bow. She ignored them, hopping onto the Harley and pulling out, heading opposite the direction she'd come.

"We'll take it." Bear's rig, parked facing east, eased out and drifted behind her.

Tim eyed the run-down Pinto. The AT, no doubt, was secured in the trunk. They only had to follow it home.

"Just shadow her," Malane said. "Don't take her into custody until we get to the stash house. We don't want to alert—"

Wristwatch Annie turned the corner on foot, sliding along the fence line behind the restaurant. She fumbled with a set of keys, then climbed into the Pinto and sped off.

Ten vehicles in the surrounding four blocks went on alert.

They followed her in shifts, each pair of cars turning off after a few blocks to be replaced by another. Malane and Tim carried her into the finish, a well-kept single-story house in a middle-class section of Mar Vista. She pulled into an open garage, which closed immediately behind her. They drifted past, turned around, and parked up the block, waiting for SWAT to move in.

Tim sat, working sunflower seeds between his teeth, occasionally shaking the Coke bottle so the soggy shells inside gave off a wet rattle. His focus, like Malane's, remained on the platinum Jag convertible parked across the street from the house, though neither had commented on the obvious.

Malane keyed his radio. "Sully? You on the rear fence line?"

"Yup. Got the parabolic on the rear window. Want me to cut you in?"

"Please."

A faint transmission played through Malane's radio.

The sharp feminine voice said, ". . . we all eyeballed it now, so we start with a clean accounting sheet. I don't want one of you whining that ten cc's dropped out of the deal."

The Prophet's velvet voice: "We are agreed."

"Same goes for the cash. Count the down payment again now if you have to."

"It is all here."

"Seventy/thirty to the producer this round."

"I am aware of the deal."

"Then you won't mind touching all the bases so there's no misunderstandings. The deal's on consignment—the money down gets laid off against profit. We hold up our end, next one goes sixty/forty. Then an even split between producer and distributor. I handle the money coming and going. That's what you signed off on. Agreed?"

"That is correct. I look forward to a long collaboration."

Rustling.

"*Wait.* I have not tested the product."

There was a faint rumble of tires, and then, from all directions, black trucks poured onto the street. SWAT members hung off the vehicles, riding the running boards, their vest pouches bulging with flash bangs. The trucks stopped, sealing off the street and giving the target house a half-block buffer. SWAT pulled into entry formation, at least forty agents closing the divide on foot, an organized swarm of black flight suits. A Sheriff's bomb dog led the charge, positioned to check the front door for booby traps. Only now did Tim spot a rippling of bushes at the back fence line.

He clicked on the radio. "Bear? Take her. We're going in."

The no-knock entry would've made the ART squad proud. The battering ram left the door flat on the entrance floor for the agents to trample. Tim and Malane crossed the street at a jog. Inside, there were shouted commands and a few yells, but no gunshots. Smith & Wesson aimed at the floor, Tim rode in on the aftermath, the safest lineup position he'd ever taken on a kick-in. His heart was pounding nonetheless. He moved room to room in search of Den Laurey.

The Prophet, Dhul Faqar Al-Malik, lay facedown on the shag carpet of the living room, a streak of dust coloring his dark hair like a skunk's stripe. A still-packaged extraction needle lay on the carpet where he'd dropped it, beside a portable lab kit. The FBI agents had uncovered a modest weapons cache in the front closet.

A shrill voice said, "Get your fucking hands off me."

Tim stepped around the corner, where two agents were securing Dana Lake. She glared at Tim, her milky cheeks flushed a sunset shade of magenta. The money launderer—nice WASP name, clean record, just as Smiles had predicted.

"What was your cut, Dana?"

"This is ridiculous. I'm here to broker a surrender for my client."

Behind her, Wristwatch Annie was being frisked. She laughed into the carpet and said to the SWAT member, "Easy, tiger. Any more and it'll cost ya."

Two translucent balloons filled with clear liquid sat on an electronic scale. The digital readout glowed red: 2.015 KG. A few agents regarded the spheres with awe. The bomb dog sat beside the table, eyeing a pizza box on the kitchen counter with interest. Next to the scale, an open computer carrying case displayed packets of hundred-dollar bills. Agents stomped through the house, industrious as insects.

Tim asked the SWAT commander, "Where's Laurey? Is the house safed?"

"House is safed. No one else here."

"Are you sure? Are you *positive*? You checked the attic?"

"Yes, we checked the attic." He turned to one of his agents, forearm resting atop his MP5. "Who is this fucking guy?"

Malane interceded, grabbing the commander's arm and talking to him in a whispered rush as Tim stepped back and holstered his .357. He checked the other rooms, moving desperately now, tearing aside shower curtains and dust ruffles. The FBI agents watched him with curiosity. Defeated, he returned to the living room.

Al-Malik's dark blazer had split along one of the arm seams, tufts of white thread sticking up at the shoulder. Seeing him now, Tim felt as he had when watching the televised army medic pick nits out of Saddam's beard: how disappointingly undersize monsters were in ordinary light.

Dana machine-gunned questions at the arresting agents: "What are you charging me with? Where's my phone call? Do you have a history of brutality, or are you starting fresh with this arrest?"

Malane stood beside her as she argued and jerked against the cuffs, calmly imploring her to sign an Advice of Rights form. Watching his levelheaded recitation, Tim felt a newfound respect for him. Maybe he'd misread some of Malane's earlier coolness.

Dana addressed Tim over Malane's shoulder. "Don't look at me, Rackley. You haven't won anything here."

He worked his lip between his teeth, his mind on Den Laurey cruising free as Peter Fonda, but without the fruity helmet.

"You've got some client list, Ms. Lake," Malane said. "Bikers and terrorists—hell, you've got a full roster. It's all about putting people together, isn't it? Putting them together while hiding behind attorney-client privilege. How many money launderers have you represented in the past five years?"

"Plenty. I'm a defense attorney."

"And a quick study, I'd imagine."

"These are baseless charges. They'll be dropped within twenty-four hours."

"Nice legalese on the Good Morning Vacations small print. Clever stuff."

"You have zero evidence to tie me to anything."

"Wrong answer," Malane said. "The correct answer is 'What's Good Morning Vacations?'"

Tim walked outside, sitting on a rickety porch swing. The neighbors were at their front doors and windows; a few kids circled behind the FBI trucks on their bikes, calling questions to the agents.

The SWAT commander hustled Al-Malik along the walk as a helicopter swooped over the rooftops and touched down on the street. Maybe the arrest would be announced on the evening news, maybe not. The Prophet would disappear into an unofficial holding cell somewhere, hidden in Homeland Security's long shadow, or he'd be shipped off to Guantanamo Bay, where international law—and the Constitution—couldn't get through the barbed wire and humidity. Watching Al-Malik being guided into the helo, Tim thought it likely that this was the last time he'd hear of him.

Tim reached Bear by Nextel; he and Guerrera had scooped up Babe Donovan and were headed back to Cell Block to book her.

Bear issued a grunt when Tim told him Den wasn't in custody. "I'll tell her her boyfriend won't be joining her."

"Just yet," Tim said.

He hung up and watched the ascending helicopter ruffle the picture-perfect lawn in liquid patterns. Dana Lake made her cuffed exit in time to have her sleek hairdo blown lopsided before she was helped into a black van. The copter banked and faded. The van cruised past the partition and disappeared.

After maybe fifteen minutes, Malane came outside and stood over Tim, thumbing his belt loop, hip cocked. His eyes, set deep in their sockets, sloped down at the outer edges. He looked hound-dog thoughtful. For the first time, Tim noticed the gold band on his left hand, dulled from years of wear.

"No Den Laurey," Malane said.

"No Den Laurey."

"How long you been married?"

"Ten years last month."

"Five myself. January. Second time through." Malane looked up the street where the media vans were gathering at the blockade. They seemed to transform, unfolding into studio-lit dioramas. Well-groomed women gabbed against the backdrop, camera lenses pointed at them like interested faces. Malane seemed to want to say something but couldn't land on the words. Finally he looked down at Tim, his eyes sad, or maybe it was just the shape of them. "I'll help you find him any way I can."

Some of the agents on the front lawn circled up, voices high, reliving the capture. ". . . when he was going for the closet, you put him *down*."

A passing agent paused on the porch to thump Malane's back. "Congrats, Jeff."

"Thanks." Malane's tone didn't match the triumphant mood of the others. He scratched his cheek, calm and detached as always, getting back to outstanding business. "Rich told you about the cell-phone transmissions we picked up on Uncle Pete?"

"He did."

"We have the evidence in hand now. That's enough to firm the case against him. You want to tell Bear and Guerrera to meet us there when we roll him up?"

Before Tim could answer, Malane's cell phone trilled.

He snapped it open. "Malane." He listened a moment, and then his face changed. "Ah, shit," he said softly.

He hung up and stood, running the tip of his shoe over a patch of splinters on the porch. His eyes were moist. A few of the agents on the lawn answered their phones and glanced at their pagers, celebratory smiles dissipating instantly.

When Malane glanced up at Tim, his face was taut, the skin blotched red on his pale throat. "I'm gonna need you."

57

El Matador isn't accessible by car or bike. The desolate beach is reachable only by a treacherous hike down a steep hill. Rock formations close in the beach, and a few large boulders thrust up from the surf, fighting the waves and sending sheets of mist across the thin strip of Malibu sand.

The oil drum lay half buried at the high-tide mark, draped in piss-yellow seaweed. Sandpipers hopped around on stick-skinny legs. An agent shooed a coat of seagulls off the drum, the FBI lettering glittering in the moisture on the back of his windbreaker. Another avian wave washed in almost instantly, hungry heads bobbing and picking at the metal.

One side of the drum seemed to pulse with life; it wasn't until Tim and Malane neared that Tim realized it was crawling with crabs. A few surfers bobbed offshore beyond the break, mellow rubberneckers.

Tim and Malane reached the cluster of agents around the drum. Some algae had collected on it, but the metal had mostly remained shiny. A blowtorch swung at the side of one of the agents. The drum's lid, now propped back in place to keep out the critters, had previously been welded on. An Evidence Response Team agent, nineteenth-hole casual in his Royal Robbins cargo khakis and an ERT polo, held the lid shut so the struggling crabs couldn't shove their way inside. When Malane stepped close, he let it fall.

Malane leaned over, hands on his knees, and looked inside. He let out a deep breath, then turned to the fresh ocean breeze.

Tim moved forward and crouched. Despite some bloating and the work the little fish had done around the mouth and eyes, Rich Mandrell's face was still recognizable. His eye patch's band had slid down around his neck, and his pinkie ring was dulled from the seawater immersion. A few pencils of light poked through the metal where holes had been drilled; the oil drum had probably floated for a while before sinking, prolonging his terror. One of the crabs had gotten a claw stuck through a hole; it bobbed obscenely, inches from Rich's sea-slick hair.

Safety-pinned to his jeans at the back of his thigh, beyond the reach of his trapped arms, was a Polaroid, faded from the salt water. But not too faded for Tim to make out the image—Raymond Smiles at the wheel of his sedan on the freeway, his face barely visible behind the tinted window and a pair of dark glasses.

Tim found his throat gummy, so he cleared it. "Time of death?"

The ERT agent said, "Twelve to fifteen hours ago. I'll know more once we get the body processed. Takes some time getting equipment down here."

"Morning high tide brought it up?"

He nodded, then pointed up the coast. "A bluff about a quarter mile north overlooks the water. I'm thinking that's where the dump was made last night."

"Any incisions made? Maybe with a hunting knife?"

The ERT agent paused, surprised. "Yeah, looks to be some of that on the popliteal spaces behind the knees. Someone knew their basic anatomy, severed the tendons so the victim couldn't kick against the lid going down."

The breeze whipped flecks of water at Tim's face. Salt stung the back of his throat.

"So he was still conscious," Malane said. "When he was welded in."

"Yeah, most of his fingernails are broken off." The ERT agent studied Malane. "He a friend?"

Malane stood watching the brilliant sun send gold divots off the water. The surfers bobbed on their boards as the ocean breathed. He nodded, not trusting his voice, then turned and started the walk back to his car.

58

alane was silent on the way to Uncle Pete's, and he didn't
speed. He drove slowly and deliberately, hands at ten and two,
staring ahead with a blank expression that on anyone else might have
looked cadaverous. Behind them, a scattering of agents in duty cars followed, as well as several extended-cab Suburbans stuffed with SWAT
members.

They reached the clubhouse, and Malane hit the brakes, idling on
the dirty street, taking in the chain-link, the row of bikes at the curb,
Uncle Pete's Lexus glittering in the driveway. The Dodge Ram was
parked up the street, Bear and Guerrera leaning against it, arms crossed,
awaiting the caravan's arrival.

The other vehicles remained frozen behind Malane's Crown Vic.
Tim waited for Malane to pull over and park, but he kept his hands on
the wheel, head forward. He revved the engine a few times and then
peeled out. The car bore down on the row of motorcycles at the curb.
Tim barely had time to brace against the dash before they smashed into
them. The bikes went down like proverbial dominoes. The Crown Vic
wound up tilted atop a stack of crushed metal. Tim rubbed the seat-belt
burn at his shoulder, grateful that the G-ride, like most, had its airbags
removed, saving him a nylon nose punch.

"Whoops," Malane said flatly. "Looks like she got away from me."

He shoved open his door and navigated down the mound of bike parts.

Sinners and slags gathered behind the chain-link, cursing and shouting. The SWAT team filed into the front yard, subduing them. One of the clubhouse dogs got a face-blast of Mace, after which she and the other succumbed to the come-along leash.

Malane placed his hands on his hips, regarding the heap of broken motorcycles. "You know, I'll probably end up paying for that," he said, his voice barely audible over the background shouting. "But it'll be worth it."

Bear said, "We'll all chip in."

Malane and Tim moved through the commotion, Bear and Guerrera at their backs. They breached the front door, heading up the stairs, handguns drawn but pointed at the floor. A few of Pete's deeds, marked by missing pinkies, slithered past them in the narrow upstairs halls, running to safety. The sounds of energetic sex issued from Uncle Pete's room, interrupted at intervals by a whirring noise.

Tim pushed open the door with his foot, keeping both hands on his .357. Uncle Pete sat in the darkness, an immense shadow, the light of the TV turning his face watery blue. Hound Dog sat at his side, and he stroked the poodle's topknot absentmindedly, eyes glued to the screen session. His other hand commanded the remote control resting on the arm of his padded lounge chair. His fat fingers twitched, and the porn tape fast-forwarded, played, fast-forwarded. Wearing boxers and a wife-beater undershirt, he filled every crevice of the chair. Hound Dog's black-marble eyes pulled over to Tim, his upper lip wrinkling in a silent growl. As they approached, he rose to all fours, snarling. Bear snapped his fingers, and the poodle sat back down and lowered his head to his paws.

Keeping his eyes on the screen, Uncle Pete said, "Howdy, Trouble. I heard yer grand entrance down there."

"You told me to come back with formal charges and a warrant," Tim said. "Here I am."

From downstairs came the boot vibrations of agents taking over the house.

Emitting a groan of exertion, Pete reached for his cell phone on the floor. "I gotta call my lawyer."

"We'll save you your daytime minutes," Tim said. "Hell, we'll put you in the same cell as her."

To his credit, Uncle Pete didn't give up much. His eyes widened a touch, the lines smoothing from his forehead, and his hair seemed to shift back slightly on his skull. But he didn't so much as turn.

He bobbed his massive head, settling back into his chair. "Let me wait for the money shot."

He fast forwarded a few more seconds, then let the tape play. Sounds of explosive release. He nodded at the screen. "Atta boy, Peter North."

With great effort he pulled himself to his feet and offered Tim his wrists.

59

The detention enforcement officer waited respectfully, key in hand. Tim pressed his knuckles on the cool steel door, gathering his focus. The command post was humming with activity; he'd slipped out unnoticed. By comparison Cell Block was peaceful, the quiet broken only by the squeak of boots on tile and the incessant hacking of a prisoner a few cells over.

The search of the clubhouse had turned up all order of incriminating evidence to shore up the case against Uncle Pete. Dana Lake's files would likely prove a treasure trove, but first the FBI would have to navigate through a minefield of legalities regarding confidentiality—the U.S. Attorney's office was on it full bore and feeling more confident than Tim had seen them regarding a major case. On his way into the command post, he'd caught Winston Smith, the AUSA, whistling in the hall in an uncharacteristic show of buoyancy.

Bear and Guerrera had followed Babe Donovan back to an apartment in West L.A., where they'd made the arrest. In the laundry room, they'd discovered a laminating machine around which were scattered the raw materials from a number of forged IDs, including an access card for a Burbank Airport maintenance worker. They'd also found a drawerful of badges from different law-enforcement agencies, awards for successful assassinations. The Cadillac Miller Meteor hearse had been hiding in the covered garage. An elderly neighbor reported that Babe used to park a yellow Volvo in her second space, the same make and model of the car left behind on the 10 freeway to clog traffic minutes before Den and Kaner's break. The building's garage security camera confirmed the plates; the Volvo tied Babe to the murder of two federal officers and a civilian.

Six hours after the clubhouse raid, the deputies continued to sift through seized papers. From the first wave of analysis, Smith was preparing to indict eleven other Sinners. Tannino had stopped by the post to declare that they had enough to sink the organization.

But, not surprisingly, nothing had turned up on Den Laurey.

Tim had put out alerts at the borders and airports and BOLOs to all agencies in the surrounding states. He'd contacted law enforcement in each city where the Sinners had a chapter, urging increased surveillance. The Service's public-information officer had released a selection of Den's photos to the news stations and was negotiating with the *Times* for tomorrow's front page. The more time passed, the greater likelihood that Den would slip away. And after a while Dray's assailant would recede into the Top 15, his face becoming one of many in the lineup of flyers posted in the admin corridor at the rear of the courthouse. Unsolved cases. Open investigations. Dangerous individuals whose pictures the deputies walked past every day on their way to new business.

Tim nodded, and the officer pulled back the steel door. Through the mesh gate, Tim could see Babe sitting on the molded plastic bench, her legs spread in a slightly masculine manner. He entered and stood opposite her.

Her feathered hair, seventies sexy, stood up in the back from her leaning against the wall. She had a big—perhaps enhanced—chest but a petite frame, so the orange jumpsuit bagged around her like a clown costume. A band of sunburn saddled her pug nose. Her surprising cobalt eyes remained impenetrable, but her face had loosened with fear or dread, her jaw held slightly forward as if to control her breathing. For the first time, Tim saw her as a kid, not far removed from college girls or the daughters of his older colleagues. Her file showed she was from a middle-class family. She'd taken a wrong turn and wound up on the back of a Harley and now here. It was almost hard to believe the role she'd willingly played in Den Laurey's assault on Greater Los Angeles.

"Hello, Ms. Donovan. I'm Tim Rackley."

She pulled her head back, regarding him over her nose. "You got a smoke?"

"Not on me, no." He crouched, bringing himself eye level. "There's no way around you doing some time, but I can help you."

"If I sell out my man? You gotta be joking."

"You're looking at a lot of time, Babe. Maybe life."

"So what? You can live on the inside. You can have a life on the inside."

"Who told you that? Den?"

"No, it wasn't him. We've had plenty of family go down."

"Being inside is hell, Babe. A year feels like a lifetime. After a few you won't remember who you are now. It's not a life."

"Neither's being a traitor. You citizens don't understand that."

"You don't think taking marching orders from bin Laden is being a traitor?"

"Sinners don't take orders from no one. Least of all a bunch of ragheads."

"So think for yourself now, Babe. This is the end of the road for you. It's the end of the road for Den, too. Help us close this thing out without anyone else getting killed."

She made a derisive noise deep in her throat. "Man, you're clueless. Even if I didn't love the Man—which I fucking do more than *anything*—selling out a Sinner is the lowest thing a member of the family can do. The *lowest*. There's a code, and you don't break it. No matter what."

"But you're not a Sinner." He watched the rage flare in her shiny eyes; his remark had cut her deep. He continued, more placatingly, "If you help us find him, we'll have a better shot at taking him alive. We can plan the takedown better. Control the situation. Make sure he doesn't end up coming in in a body bag."

"Why? So he can get the lethal injection or the chair or whatever you fuckers use nowadays? No way. We both know why you're here. You don't know where he is. And when the Man doesn't want to be found, he doesn't get found. You don't stand a chance."

"You gotta admit, we've done pretty well so far."

She broke eye contact, slumping back on the bench and blowing her bangs out of her eyes. The stretched collar of the jumpsuit dwarfed her delicate neck. "Sure, you got your news headlines. But a month from now, he'll just be another bad guy on another list. You'll forget all about him. He can live how he wants, even." Her eyes held a hope that was at once naïve and affecting.

"He shot my wife," Tim said. "I'm not gonna forget about him."

She jerked her head back. Her voice came high with her surprise. "Who's your wife?"

"The sheriff's deputy."

"Right." She bit her lips. "Right. So, like, I'd believe you that you'd try to take him alive."

"You're the only one who can help us arrange a lower-risk take-down."

"And if I don't?"

"I don't want to kill him. But if I have to . . ."

"You will." She read his face. Her eyes teared up, and she lifted them to the ceiling. For the first time, her voice trembled. "He'll never come in alive. *Never.*"

"You don't know that. I've seen things play out in ways I never would've predicted. You help us, we can work something out with the prosecutor. You don't want to be in a penitentiary for the rest of your life."

"You don't get it, asshole." Her sudden anger caught him off guard. She shoved back into the corner of the bench, hugging her knees to her chest. "I'm fucking *done*. That's the deal. And I honor my deals."

"What do you mean, you're done?"

"You think the Man's gonna talk to me now? Pop by for conjugal visits? You think he hasn't already changed all his numbers, ditched all his hideouts? *Our* hideouts. I'm in here—that means he's closed the book on me." Tears clung to her dark lashes. "If he walked by me on the street now, he'd keep walking. And I'm glad. Because that's what he needs to do to keep alive." She let the tears run, not bothering to wipe her cheeks. They slid down her neck and darkened the seam of her jump-suit. "Even if I *wanted* to help myself, I couldn't. He's too smart to trust me anymore."

Her face twisted, and she lowered her head into her arms and wept. Her cries were resonant and mournful, seeming to rise from deep within her. He could hear them even after he closed the steel door behind him, even after he reached the end of the cell-block corridor.

Already the other prisoners were screaming for her to shut the fuck up.

60

Thomas was cocked back in his chair, hands laced behind his head. Jim and Maybeck cleared the conference table, tossing crumpled papers at the corner trash can and mostly missing. Miller hauled out chairs, returning them to the surrounding offices. Bear and Guerrera pulled down the pictures from the wall, taking with them Scotch-tape patches of paint or leaving tacks behind. Bear had brought in his dogs, Boston, a Rhodesian Ridgeback, and Precious, the medically discharged star of the Explosive Detection Canine Team, named for Jame Gumb's companion in *The Silence of the Lambs*. Precious, whose nose had saved the life of virtually every deputy in the room, was greeted like the prodigal daughter, pulled from colleague to colleague to be scratched.

Tannino had dissolved the command post, which Tim grudgingly recognized was the right thing to do. It didn't take a command post to track a single fugitive. With the other nomads dead or in custody, the mother chapter crippled, the AT seized, and the distribution network disabled, the threat Den Laurey posed had been diminished, if not eliminated. The Escape Team could pursue him from the squad room, a priority among others, under Tim and Bear's direction. But Tim knew that the imperative dulled once the deputies went back to business and spread out among desks rather than gathering around a single table with a single objective.

He watched quietly from his chair as the post continued to be dismantled, trying to construct a strategy for the next phase and failing miserably. At this point Den was a cutout operative. The last series of arrests had severed all connective tissue; there were no links to trace back to girlfriends, fellow Sinners, or the mother chapter. Even the incipient drug operation had been rolled up. Den was accustomed to living in the shadows—it would take either a huge break or dumb luck to flush him out.

The others, heady from the series of busts, didn't seem to share Tim's despondency. Miller gestured at him apologetically, and Tim rose reluctantly so he could carry away his chair.

"Hey, girl," Jim said, guiding Precious to the end of the table. "Go on and eat a piece of Mrs. Tannino's fruitcake for us."

Precious sniffed the hardened crust, then backed up and sneezed violently.

The room erupted in laughter.

The scene triggered Tim's memory of the kitchen during Dana Lake's and the Prophet's arrests. A sudden uneasiness made itself known, a splinter working its way to the surface.

He thought of Babe lying in her cell. Aside from exercise breaks, that was about the most space she'd be permitted for the rest of her life. Her defiance had been undulled. *Sinners don't take orders from no one. Least of all a bunch of ragheads.*

He remembered his own words about the Sinners to Tannino and the mayor: *Don't expect honor among thieves—they're famous for double crosses, drug burns, cop killings.*

What had Smiles said about Allah's Tears? *That's the beauty of it. They don't need a continuous pipeline, just a one-off—a single risk with a huge payday.*

A chill washed through Tim. The German shepherd. At the Prophet's house. It had been sitting in front of the table holding Allah's Tears. The drug's powerful olfactory signature, even sealed inside the belly bags, should have drawn the dog's attention, not let it fix on a few stale pizza crusts across the room. Tim flashed on the extraction needle lying in the carpet near Al-Malik's head. Unused.

Tim gestured to Bear and Guerrera. They must have noted his intensity, for they came immediately, both dogs at their heels. Jim was gnawing his way through a slice of Mrs. Tannino's own, Miller making odds on his finishing it.

Tim, Bear, and Guerrera headed out of the evaporating command post, laughter trailing behind them.

61

Uncle Pete stared out through the bars of his holding cell at the three deputy marshals and the score of FBI agents. The cell was dimly lit, devouring his wide form, but his eyes floated in a band of light. Tim couldn't see his mouth but could tell from the crinkles at his temples that he was smiling.

A closer look at the down-payment bills—which totaled $7.5 million—had revealed them to be fake. Sweat beaded at Bear's hairline; he fanned himself with a packet of counterfeit hundreds. Malane was holding a test tube of the seized substance; minutes earlier, to emphasize his findings, the ERT agent had downed a shot of it. The Allah's Tears and Den Laurey were at large and, Tim was sure, enjoying each other's company.

Malane shook the test tube. "Sambuca."

Uncle Pete's voice emerged from the dark cell. "Is that so."

"You burned the Prophet. And al-Fath."

"I never heard of no prophet, friends, but I'll tell you this: We sure as shit ain't scared of a bunch of Allah-lovin' sweat monkeys hiding in caves halfway around the world." His eyes bunched with another smile. "In fact, it warms my heart to think you're fixin' a cot in Gitmo for another *A*-rab. We Sinners may be badass motherfuckers, but we ain't anti-Am*u*rican. So if you think we burned al-Fath, then hell, you can hang a medal around my fat neck. I assume that's what you're all here for? To honor my supposed intelligence work?"

He enjoyed a good genuine laugh, his bulky shadow rippling like a cape.

The Operation Cleansweep task-force headquarters overlooked the VA cemetery. The government-issue headstones formed razor-straight lines on the lush green turf. A few durable Christmas wreaths provided splotches of color, but not enough to detract from the smog and granite.

The similarities between this room and the Service's command post were striking. Same tacked photos, same day-old food, same weary air of expired adrenaline. Bear was speaking in hushed tones over the phone to Tannino, his posture indicating that the conversation was going about as expected. Tim and Guerrera waited patiently for him to finish so they could head back and regroup in the squad room.

Smiles sat on the table, folders resting across his thigh, one loafer tip dipped to the carpet as if stirring waters. Malane had pulled Tim aside and asked him not to make reference to the Polaroid found pinned to Rich's jeans. Tim had agreed reluctantly; he generally objected to office secrets, no matter the motive behind them, but it wasn't his command post and he couldn't see what would be gained by Smiles's knowing. Especially right now. Tim assumed he'd make a different call if he found himself in possession of like information about Bear or another colleague, but he'd learned that his preconceived assumptions weren't particularly useful to him or anyone else.

"So from Uncle Pete's perspective, how was the double cross supposed to play out?" Smiles asked. "I mean, once the Prophet does the test and figures out the Sinners ran the switch on him . . ."

"He kills Dana Lake, and then Pete doesn't have to pay her cut," Tim said.

"And Wristwatch Annie?"

"She's a slag, not a Sinner," Guerrera said. "Expendable."

"Why burn the producers? Kill the golden goose?"

"Two liters is enough to feed the street for nine months. I mean, *socio*, fifty *million* dollars in hand? Weighed against what? The stability of terrorists and the drug trade?"

Malane sat with both hands run into his thin hair; it protruded in tufts from between his fingers. "I can't fucking believe I missed it," he said, for not the first time. "We're dead-ended. All fronts." He lifted his head, a movement that seemed to require great effort. "We'll have to dismantle the Sinners's drug-distribution network, hope to seize the AT in batches as we go. It's not much of a plan, but it's all we have."

"At least we've got Uncle Pete nailed," another agent said.

Smiles continued to review Uncle Pete's seized financials. "These figures are *ridiculous*. Uncle Pete reported nineteen grand last year, but he drives a"—he turned aside the tax return and pulled out a yellow vehicle-purchase order—"seventy-nine-*thousand* dollar Lexus LS 430."

A youthful agent said, "No shit? That ride cost seventy-nine grand?"

"Oh, yeah," Smiles said. "Our boy needed chrome wheels, air purifier, headlamp washers, voice-command nav system, headrest massager—"

Tim bolted forward, snatching the document from Smiles.

Smiles held up his hands, feigning offense. "Is that any way to—"

Tim slapped the piece of paper with the back of his hand and looked up at the staring faces around the central table. Bear lowered the phone to his broad chest, his head cocked like a dog deciphering a bird call.

Tim said, "We need Pete Krindon."

62

Tim, Bear, and Guerrera waited in a pool of streetlight yellow outside the police impound lot. Bear heaved a sigh, and Guerrera rubbed his eyes. It was 9:45 P.M., and they'd been waiting on Pete Krindon since eight.

Bear clicked his teeth bitterly and said, "Here's where I wish I smoked."

A low-rider thumped by, the sunglasses-adorned driver bouncing his head to the beat, going for tough but looking more like a displeased chicken. He turned and stared at them, not breaking eye contact until his face drifted from view.

"Reminds me of home." Guerrera's smirk flashed, tensing his soft features, and then he stared out at the dark street, his eyes troubled.

Bear jerked his head to indicate the young deputy. When Tim responded with a shrug, Bear widened his own eyes imploringly. Tim returned the glare, exasperated.

"Rey," Tim finally said. "How you doing? About the shooting?"

"Fine. No big deal." Guerrera scraped his teeth with his tongue, then spit on the curb and stepped away. Discussion over.

Bear waved off Tim's palms-up hand gesture.

A van parked at a meter up the block, elegant lettering proclaiming

RUDOLPHO PAGATINI CATERING. The driver hopped out, straightened his waiter's apron over his tuxedo, and headed toward them in a stiff, formal gait.

"You gotta be shittin' me," Bear said.

Because of his coiffed hair, sleek mustache, and wire-rim glasses, Pete Krindon wasn't recognizable until he was within feet of them.

Bear said, "I'll have a ham on rye."

"How about you try the South Beach Diet instead." Krindon nodded toward the garage. "Let's get this done. I'm on a job."

"What? Serving meatballs to Lady and the Tramp?"

"Very funny, Rack. Move it."

Krindon trailed behind them as they headed to the security station. The guard looked up from a roast beef sandwich, a line of mayo fringing his mustache. As Tim explained their purpose, the guard's eyes took in the three displayed badges, then came to rest on Krindon's waiter's apron. His forehead wrinkled. "The fuck is this?"

"He's with us."

The guard tossed a clipboard down on the brief counter. "He's gotta sign in. You *all* gotta sign in."

"He's a freelance consultant," Tim said. "He doesn't sign."

From the warped radio on the counter, an AM deejay, revved up on caffeine and zealotry, ranted about Syria's weapons of mass destruction. The guard folded his arms and leaned back on his stool. "Can't let him in if he doesn't sign."

Krindon leaned forward and scribbled on the form. As he drew back, Tim read the cursive scrawl: *Herbert Hoover.*

"All set?"

The guard's glance lifted from the signature to Tim's face. Then he broke eye contact with an it's-not-worth-it expression of disgust and waved them through.

They found Uncle Pete's Lexus in a dark back corner. Locked.

Tim, Bear, and Guerrera debated who would have to go back to retrieve the keys from the irritable guard, but then they heard the door click open, and Krindon returned a decoding transmitter to his pocket and slid into the driver's seat. The car had been towed, the front seat still way back to accommodate Uncle Pete's girth, so Krindon had plenty of room to maneuver. He tugged up the leg of his formalwear, revealing a slim jim tucked into a garter. He angled the thin metal bar beneath the box of the navigation system, then pulled a corkscrew from his apron and used it for leverage.

The unit was well ensconced. After some directed jiggling, Krindon paused to wipe his brow. "I can usually get you down within a two-block radius. These nav systems are on satellite networks, so they trip sites like mobile phones or wireless modems. Same Orwellian shit."

Guerrera said, "So anyone can find out where a car's been?"

"No, not *anyone*." Krindon made an angry noise and turned back to the navigation system. "Nothing's ever truly deleted in a computer system. Only the pointers to the data get wiped out. But that data's in there. You just have to know how to find it. And to know how to find it . . . well, you have to be *me*." He jiggled the unit, and it finally gave, sliding into his lap. "So you want to trace Uncle Pete's footsteps. What are you looking for? A crash pad?"

"Or a safe house, a hangout, a business front, a meth lab," Tim said. "Anywhere Den Laurey could be laying his head in a back room. He's a little too recognizable right now to check in to a Best Western."

"How far back you want me to go?"

"Give us the last six months."

"Den Laurey's prison break was only six days ago."

"But this is Uncle Pete's car. I doubt he's visited Den since the prison break—I'm just hoping we can put together a list of Sinner-friendly locations and go from there."

Krindon tucked the nav unit under his arm and closed the car door behind him.

Guerrera said, "We'd better lock the door agai—"

Krindon's hand tensed in his pocket, and the Lexus's locks clicked. He turned and walked away, his shadow stretched long in the dim light. Over his shoulder he said, "I'll be in touch."

63

Though he doubted that Den would be dumb enough to play Hollywood stalker, Tim entered his house cautiously and safed each room, then double-locked the doors and closed the blinds. He kept the lights off.

He called Smiles and Malane and filled them in, coordinating activities for the morning. He hoped they'd be able to come up with enough leads to construct a new game plan.

The answering machine was maxed out. After the seventh media call, Tim pressed the "erase" button and held it down. When the case settled, he'd change the number. Again.

He opened the refrigerator door, grimacing against the waft of spoiled food. He cleaned it out, throwing away the perishables, and returned to see what he was left with. An onion, a jar of jalapeño mustard, a bottle of Newman's Own, two strawberry Crushes, and one turkey Lunchable.

He arranged the Crush and the turkey crackers on the silver tray as he had for Dray the night before her encounter with Den Laurey, then stood in the dark kitchen, unsure where to take himself. The TV's light would broadcast that he was home, so he ate at the kitchen table in the dark. Though he was accustomed to eating alone when Dray worked P.M. shifts, the new reality of his home life made even this simple activity a

painful one. His mood grew heavy; it became evident why he'd spent virtually no time at home since Dray was shot. If he kept moving, he didn't
feel as keenly. But now, with the trails gone cold and Pete Krindon working the sole lead on a freelancer's schedule, he had no choice but to be
still. A childish longing struck him, but he knew that sleeping beside her
at the hospital would be nothing more than an addictive falsehood.

At least half of Tim's child-size meal wound up in the trash. On his
walk down the hall, he paused outside the nursery and, without looking
over, pulled the door closed. In the bedroom he picked up Dray's sweats,
folded them neatly, and set them on a shelf on her side of their shared
closet. Each of her outfits, filled out by a hanger and gravity, matched an
evening out, a mood, a mental snapshot. Navy blue button-up with a
ketchup stain on the right sleeve—Dray pouty after consecutive gutter
balls, drinking Bud from a bottle shaped like a bowling pin. Morro Bay
sweatshirt—a pre-stirrups grimace before her last OB checkup two
weeks ago. Yellow dress with tiny blue flowers—the first night they'd
met, at a fireman's charity. She'd worn it again the morning she'd come
to meet him at the courthouse to take him home.

An empty house and a full closet were only part of what Den Laurey
had left in his wake, but Tim felt it as an utter and profound devastation.
Marisol Juarez's grandmother, knocking around her tiny apartment by
the dim light of her Advent candles, felt her granddaughter's absence the
same way. *We'll do our best*, Tim had promised her, and Marisol had
wound up split open on a warehouse floor. Her death had been a matter
of timing and chance, just as countless variables had aligned to land the
pellet at the back of Dray's rib cage. He wondered how, if he had to, he'd
wrap his mind around the loss of his wife. If he'd learned one thing from
Ginny's death, it was that—despite all certainty to the contrary—he'd
persist. Like the Northern Alliance fighter he'd seen through the blaze
of the midday Kandahar sun, stumbling along a treeless ridge with blood
streaming from both ears, carrying his own severed arm. He'd be separated from himself, diminished, but he'd stagger on.

He slid into bed, occupying only his half. His exhaustion was overpowering. He had only a moment to be thankful for that petty mercy
before slipping into sleep.

When he woke up six hours later, a stack of computer printouts was
waiting on the foot of his bed.

64

im had entered the squad room carrying the pages triumphantly. His energy proved contagious, and virtually all the other deputies had pulled chairs around his desk to dig back into the case. In the printouts Krindon had broken down the Lexus's headings into five-minute snapshots, yielding a profusion of numbers, but still it took maps, a military GPS computer program, and trial-and-error strategy to evaluate the data. In some places Krindon had pegged the area to within a hundred feet, in others within a few blocks. Not until lunch did they start connecting the dots to figure out travel routes, which they then harmonized with the street maps and traced with red pens. Tim Sharpie-marked as potential destinations anywhere that no movement was recorded between snapshots, but this assumption didn't account for traffic and was further complicated by the fact that satellite towers were not closely spaced in rural areas.

At 2:15, Jim looked up at the wall clock and said, "It's been a week. Since Den Laurey's escape. Since Frankie."

They returned to the data with newfound vigor. Routes overlapped, but Uncle Pete proved to be surprisingly mobile. It quickly became plain that they had more leads than they could parse in a feasible time frame. Even once they carved up the routes between deputy teams and pulled in the FBI, they looked to be weeks away from completing the follow-up, and if Tim knew one thing, it was that they didn't have weeks. Den Laurey would likely lie low until his face was off the front page and the news teasers; then he'd slip away to an ironically named desert town where cash was king and anonymity the rule.

Tim was just resigning himself to the new set of frustrations when Bear floated out of Miller's office holding a sheaf of faxes aloft like a waiter bearing a steaming entrée. "Do you know what I have here?"

Jim, gamely matching his tone: "Why, no, Bear. What have you there?"

"Here, my little friends, I have a set of billing records, sent to us by our dear friend at the Federal Bureau of Investigation, Mr. Jeffrey Malane."

Tim felt his heart quicken.

"And to whom, Mr. Jowalski," Jim asked, "do those billing records belong?"

"To one Dana Lake, Esq. And do you know what lawyers bill for?"

Miller, thrice divorced, said, *"Everything."*

"Including phone calls." Bear threw the sheaf on Tim's desk, and Tim grabbed the top page eagerly. It was in spreadsheet format, the auto-spit-out of a computer billing program attached to Dana's phone system.

DL Telephone Conferences 11/4
Laughing Sinners, Inc.

Time	*Number*	*Description*	*Hrs.*
10–10:14 A.M.	*(661) 975-2332*	*Scheduling*	*.25*
1–1:28 P.M.	*(818) 996-0007*	*Doc review*	*.5*
5:37–7:02 P.M.	*(805) 437-3178*	*Confidential*	*1.5*

The pages, maybe a hundred in all, were filled with type and red-stamped LAWYER-CLIENT MATERIALS. Between providing legal counsel and coordinating the drug-exchange and money-laundering operation, Dana was in constant touch with her number-one clients. And, Tim hoped, with Den Laurey.

"If there's one thing you can count on," Miller said, "it's that a lawyer will bill. Precisely and relentlessly."

Tim hit the speaker button on his phone and dialed the first number from the top page, letting it ring and ring. Finally a puzzled voice answered, "Hello?"

"This a pay phone?" Tim asked.

"Yeah?"

"Where?"

"I dunno." Confused pause. "Valencia."

"Look around. You see a sign?"

"Tipper's Liquors."

"Thanks."

As the deputies set about scrutinizing the records, they discovered that though plenty of the calls went into the mother chapter and Sinner-owned businesses, many were to pay phones. The pay-phone calls were most commonly made precisely at the hour or half hour, consistent with prearrangement. It was not uncommon for those numbers to repeat throughout, probably corresponding to pay phones convenient to Sinner haunts, operations, or safe houses. Dana had logged a lot of hours talking to Sinners who didn't want their locations known.

Nomads.

It took the entire Escape Team and half of the Probation/Parole Team nearly three hours to attach an address to each phone number and to cross-reference the locations on the maps bearing the data from Uncle Pete's sat-nav box. A profusion of purple dots now spread across the master street map, laid on a spaghetti bed of red-pen routes. They wound up with just over a hundred strong leads. Prioritizing the locations proved less time-consuming. Guerrera ranked them in rough order based on his feel for biker routes and habits, and the hottest overlaps—places where the black dots of Uncle Pete's destinations appeared to be within blocks of a Dana Lake–called pay phone. Tim put in a quick call to Malane, who promised three two-man teams for the first shift.

When he hung up, all the deputies were looking at him. "Okay, everyone takes eight leads. Me, Bear, and Guerrera'll take sixteen since we're a three-man team."

Jim cleared his throat uncomfortably, met Tim's eyes, then looked away. Light duty had been killing him; he seemed eager to hit the streets. The abrasions on his face from the shattered windshield glass had mostly healed, leaving slivers of scabs. His right ear had recovered nominal hearing.

"Gimme a sec, guys." Tim beckoned Guerrera out into the hall.

"What's up, *socio*?"

"You and Jim can give us another team. We need the numbers."

Guerrera's lower jaw slid out level with his top. A few days' worth of stubble darkened his face.

"You have a problem with that?"

"I'd rather stay with you and Bear."

"Why?"

"I don't need to baby-sit Jim."

"Maybe you do. Maybe not. But I need you to."

"Okay." Guerrera's eyes stayed on the floor tile. "Okay."

"You gonna be cool?"

"I'm gonna be cool."

"Unless you have to be not cool."

"Thass ride." The accent amped up with his defensiveness.

Tim headed back in and said to Jim, "We need you in the field, too."

Jim's face shifted. He nodded at Tim, took a deep breath, and rose. A few of the guys tugged on Kevlar vests beneath their shirts. The others rustled, checking their clips, their boot laces, the batteries in their flashlights.

Tim pulled Guerrera aside again. "We have to split our top sixteen. Me and Bear should take one through eight. I'm thinking the locations closest to the Sinner clubhouse." He indicated the scattering of numbers corresponding to pay phones on the outskirts of Fillmore and Simi. "That leaves you and Jim with the grouping around Kaner's safe house."

"How come Guerrera gets nine through sixteen?" Thomas asked sharply from across the room.

"Because Guerrera's been running the case with us from the gates," Tim said.

Guerrera touched Tim's elbow. "Listen, Rack, if you want the highest-odds locations, *you* should take the ones near Kaner's safe house. Den would want to hole up near another nomad."

"More than he'd want proximity to the mother chapter?"

"That's right."

Tim studied Guerrera closely, for the first time unable to read his dark eyes. "You're the expert."

The other deputies paired off and took their leads, and then everyone was silent for a moment beneath the quiet rasp of the heater.

Tannino, who'd appeared sometime in the past hour to lean crossarmed against the doorframe and watch with a sort of paternal pride, said, "You know who you're dealing with here. Watch your partner's back and use your judgment. I don't want to preside over another funeral."

The clock showed 9:14, but it might as well have been midnight for the silence in the rest of the building. No footsteps overhead, no doors shutting down the hall, no lit windows across the way.

"All right, guys," Tim said. "Let's fetch."

His mouth tight and his eyes on the carpet, Tannino kept his post in the doorway as they brushed past in groups of two.

Tim was one leg into the Explorer when Guerrera called his name. He paused, Bear grumbling impatiently from the passenger seat as Guerrera jogged across the underground parking lot.

The sheet containing the leads fluttered at Guerrera's side. Sweat from his hand had bled a half-moon into it. "Rack. I lied."

"About what?"

"The higher-probability locations. You were right. Nearer the mother chapter. Not Kaner's place." He offered the paper, looking uncomfortable under Tim's gaze. "Hey, they're just leads. Who knows. Maybe Thomas and Freed make the collar. Maybe none of us do. I just want to keep my backyard clean."

After a pause Tim swapped Guerrera's sheet for the one in his back pocket. "Why the change of heart?"

"I figure maybe Jim isn't the best guy to go through that door right now."

Tim arched an eyebrow. "Just Jim?"

A half grin. "Don't push your luck, white boy."

65

Tim and Bear checked three bars, a strip club, and a pay phone outside a motorcycle-parts store. Boston and Precious rode along, tongues lolling; after his schedule over the past week, Bear insisted on playing guilty weekend dad. Out in the field, he and Tim fell back into the interrogation rhythm they'd perfected over the past years. They spoke to a bald bartender wearing a dog collar, a woman walking her calico on a leash, two gas-station convenience-store clerks, and an exotic dancer who insisted on replacing her nipple tassels—to Bear's evident discomfort—while describing her on-the-side clientele. The only hit they got in the first four hours came from a homeless woman living behind an adult bookstore, whose eyes lit up at Den Laurey's photo; she ID'd him as the guy from *Gladiator*.

The blue panels of the sixth pay phone gleamed in the glare of Tim's headlights. Scarred by restroom wit and cigarette burns, the unit was bolted into a sawdusty wall off the front porch of a freestanding country bar. Despite saloon doors and Loretta Lynn's jukebox lament about pappy a-hoein' corn, the bar suffered from a confused identity. A punk sporting an algae-green Mohawk tossed darts with a lip-pierced person of ambiguous gender, while four unaffiliated bikers nursed drafts at the bar. ESPN recapped Pittsburgh's trouncing in the Continental Tire Bowl, as if anyone cared. A girls' night out had somehow wound up in a corner booth, grating laughter radiating from a trio whose feathered hair seemed more vintage than retro. Wine coolers and buffalo wings dotted their table, and the saccharine scent of drugstore perfume was evident from the doorway. Only the bartender, an old guy wearing a Stetson Cattleman and a belt buckle the size of a Christmas platter, looked at home in the decor. Then again, they were north of the fish hatchery, out where the Fillmore citrus groves faded into God knows what, so a watering hole earned its nickname here. They'd passed a gas station a quarter mile back, but before that it had been a long run of dusty road, with scattered lights twinkling out from the dark hillsides like Ewok eyes.

One of the corner-booth gals offered Bear a giggly wave as he and Tim headed for the bar. Loretta gave way to "London Calling"—three guesses who'd dropped that quarter—and a kid in grease-stained Dickies shuffled out of the men's room, trailing the smell of weed and a streamer of toilet paper. The bartender worked his way down to them, polishing nothing much off the bar with a rag that looked as if it had stuffed a hole in a flue for about a decade.

"What'll it be?"

Bear tilted his hand, showing off the photo of Den cupped inside. To try to lessen the false positives, they'd chosen a different picture from the one that had been running on the news. "Seen this guy?"

"Nah."

The kid from the bathroom leaned over, concerned. "You guys cops?"

"Yeah, but no worries, Cheech. We're after bigger game."

"Like who?"

Bear flashed him the picture, and the kid's eyes widened about a millimeter, the closest approximation of surprise he could currently muster. "Yeah, I seen that guy."

Bear looked skeptical. "Yeah?"

"Yeah. He came into the station." He twisted on his barstool, pointing back up the road. "Needed a spark plug."

"What was he driving?" Tim asked.

The kid blinked a few times. He pulled something off his tongue and flicked it, then blinked some more. "Uh, nothing. He needed a spark plug."

"So he walked?"

"Cars don't work so hot without spark plugs." He laughed a slow laugh, then took a pull from his Coors. His eyes went longingly to the bags of chips clipped up behind the bar.

Tim snapped his fingers in front of the kid's eyes, and the dilated pupils pulled back into semifocus. "He *walked*? No one dropped him?"

"Yeah."

"When?"

"Yesterday. Maybe the day before."

"How many houses are within walking distance of there?"

"Not many." The bartender returned, trailing his rag along the counter. "There's a pocket community up a half mile north where the pass drops, but aside from that you gotta good run of ranch 'n' farmland either direction."

"How many houses in the community?"

"I'd say thirty."

"You forgot the new mods they put up on Grant," the kid said.

"Yeah, so thirty-five."

"Did this guy walk in from the north?" Tim asked.

The kid squinted up his face thoughtfully and nodded. "Went back that way, too."

66

As the Explorer flew down the dark road, Bear tried to ease Tim's expectations. "We're working off the memory of a stoned kid. No one else in the bar recognized the photo."

"We got the location from both angles, Bear. It's a good, strong hit."

Uncle Pete had driven through the area only once, five and a half months ago. Tim hoped he'd done so to conduct some business at a Laughing Sinners safe house in the pocket community, a house where Den could now be lying low. They had Dana Lake placing a call to the bar's pay phone three days ago. The cross-ref had popped the location to the top of the list.

A reinforced-concrete barrier protected the patch of prefab-looking tract houses from the two-lane thoroughfare. Tim turned off into the small grid of streets, which terminated at the base of a forbidding hill. There were maybe five square blocks in all, and Tim moved through them systematically.

"Not a bad spot," Bear conceded. "You got no dead ends, and all roads dump out on the main road. Plenty of turnoffs within a mile either direction."

"Some open flats, too," Tim said. "If he got creative on a bike, it would be tough keeping up."

He circled the final block and pulled to the curb. Boston muscled in on Precious's space in the back, and Precious let him hear about it with a low growl. Bear turned around in his seat like an angry vacation dad, and they silenced.

Bear settled back into his seat. "I'd bet the safe house is gonna be forward on the first two streets. If the shit goes down, they don't want to get trapped at the base of the hill."

Tim killed the lights and cruised the first two streets again. One house amid all the others, virtually identical, caught Bear's eye. He pivoted, then indicated a side window barely in view above an empty, fenced-in dog run. A blanket, tacked from the inside, covered the glass.

Tim pulled past a few more houses, flipped around, and parked.

They sat for a minute, taking in the view. A dark house at the end of a dark block. A blanket blocking a window, providing some economical privacy. Just like at the abandoned meth lab where they'd run down Kaner.

Tim and Bear removed their watches, dumped their keys, and switched their Nextels to silent. Tim thumbed out the wheel on his .357 and spun it, watching the casings twirl. He snapped it shut and climbed out. Bear tugged Precious from the back in case they decided on a kick-in and needed her to check the doors for explosives. Boston, the bigger dog, wasn't tactically trained; he whimpered at being left behind, but Bear gave him the stink-eye, and he lapsed back into carefree panting.

Wide alleys, designed to accommodate boat trailers and still leave room for the garbage truck, sliced between the rows of houses. Sidearms drawn, Tim and Bear eased their way along the dirt trail, dodging puddles and tarp-covered mounds of firewood. TVs lit the back windows of nearly every house. A woman's laughter, reduced to bronchial wheezing, drifted out a screen door. Wheelbarrows. Refrigerator planters. A single-horse trailer hitched to a souped-up Camaro.

Precious, glad to make use of her training, stalked silently at their sides. They reached the corner of the house in question and stopped behind a shed.

Their eyes traced the two-story house. The roof overhung a vine-covered veranda that was jumping distance to the neighboring dormer, a carport, and the shed behind which they squatted. Two men couldn't cover all the ways out.

The gate latch gave with a click, and they crept through the backyard.

A thickening odor came from the dark crust of leaves turning to chlorinated mulch on top of the pool cover.

The TV blared, as in the other houses they'd passed. Melissa Yueh chattered on about pharmacist errors and pending lawsuits. The lights were off, the interior illuminated only by flickering blue light that mapped patterns on the ceiling and bare walls.

Tim and Bear eased up on the back veranda, half shadowed by a lattice of moonlight strained through the cheap pergola. Lozenges of light played over them, accentuating their movement, but when they stood still, they disappeared in the camo spatterings. Precious's claws scraped the warped deck ever so slightly. Gnats plinked against the porch lamp. A spill of kitty litter, probably dumped through the nearby kitchen window, textured the veranda's edge. Someone moved swiftly from room to room, wearing boots or heavy-soled shoes. A mosquito-eater fluttered along the rafters, beating itself against the wood. Intertwined with the overhead trellis, the long-dead carpet of nasturtiums scratched and rattled in the breeze.

Tim and Bear leaned over to peer through the windows on either side of the back door, but they looked in on an empty living room. Melissa Yueh continued to chirp, the TV on a wicker stand to the side of the carpeted staircase. The smoke detectors had been removed, and mounds of kitty litter occupied the room's corners. A yellow-and-rust couch with herniated cushions blocked much of the floor from view. An open door to the garage revealed a pristine Harley, faintly illuminated by a bare, dangling bulb. Danny the Wand–detailed with flame yellow and orange, the motorcycle aimed at the closed garage door.

Ready for takeoff.

A polished metal top case was mounted to a cargo rack behind the bike's seat. Bear pointed and mouthed, "Allah's Tears?"

Bear gestured for Precious to safe the back door. She nosed along the jamb, then rose to her hind legs, retracting her paws so as not to scratch against the wood panels. She dropped down to all fours but didn't sit—no booby trap.

A dark figure came in from a front room, holding two fistfuls of clothes. He passed right before the windows and sat on his knees on the water-stained floorboards of the living room, facing away, stuffing the clothes into a backpack. He was shirtless, his skin oily with sweat, and though he was shadowed, Tim could discern the tattoos swarming across his shoulder blades. Den strapped a snub-nosed .38 to his ankle and tucked a Colt .45 into his belt.

Tim and Bear pulled behind the pool, keeping an eye on the shadow in the living room. Bear radioed in for backup, speaking in a murmur.

Tim got Guerrera on the line and gave him a whispered summary.

"So you think the AT's in the case on the bike?" Guerrera asked.

Tim could hear the squeal of tires as Jim banked sharply—they were hauling ass. "I'm guessing. Why?"

"I don't see him making a getaway on a theme bike. Kind of dumb-ass for Laurey, no?"

"You think it's a decoy?"

"He wouldn't leave without *his bike*. Was it his bike?"

"I don't know. The new paint job."

"What was the engine? Panhead or knucklehead?"

"I couldn't see clearly."

"Were there aluminum heads on the engine?"

"Yes."

"That's a panhead. Not his bike. Remember, Den rides a knuckle-head."

Tim flashed on the unlikely trailer he and Bear had passed in the alley. "I gotta go check something out. Get here soon."

"Twenty minutes and closing."

Bear came back and crouched beside Tim.

"Comm center said twenty minutes for backup," he whispered.

"That's what Guerrera gave me. Could mean thirty."

"True."

"Guerrera thinks the garage bike's a decoy."

"So where's the real bike?"

"I'm thinking back there. With the AT."

Bear followed him only as far as the rear gate so he could keep an eye on Den's form moving in the living room. Tim climbed up the already lowered ramp to the lonesome horse trailer—an inconspicuous getaway vehicle if ever there was one. He picked the lock swiftly and swung the gate open. Pointing out at the ramp, a chopper. Spray-painted black. Knucklehead engine.

The bike looked the same as when Den had ridden up to the Suicide Clutch bar, except that a thick-lidded metal container the size of a shoe box had been bolted, then arc-welded, to the frame behind the seat. Tim took one look at the dense Medeco double-cylinder lock and knew he couldn't get through it with a pick. Or, from the look of it, with a blowtorch. He tapped it with a fist, and it gave off a hollow ring. Quarter-inch steel or thicker. A hefty safe for the product.

Ten yards down the alley, Bear was on his tiptoes, keeping the living room in view. Tim snapped Precious over and directed her nose to the box. She was explosive-detection trained, not a drug dog, so she hit on the booby trap under the seat first. It took some direction to get her refocused on the box, but when she was, she reacted strongly, licking the seam of the lid. Tim ordered her to seek, and she sat immediately; she'd registered a strong scent. It was hard to believe the small metal box could contain nearly $50 million of product.

At his post, Bear looked from Precious to the motorcycle. "This bike cannot leave here," he said. "No matter what."

Tim reached into a pocket and came out with his knife. He leaned over the bike for a moment, cut a wire in the frame tubing, and straightened up. "It won't," he said.

He and Bear made their way back to the veranda. They crept to the windows.

Den was where they'd left him, on his knees in the living room before the TV. He zipped up his bag and gave it a pat. His hand tapped what looked like an empty sheath, hung over his arm shoulder-holster style, and he cursed and headed back into the house's interior.

Bear gestured to where his watch would have been and whispered, "He's splitting. We gotta make a move."

"We should cover the trailer and let him come to us."

"What if he catches wind?" Bear pointed at the vivid Harley in the garage. "Just because it's a decoy doesn't mean it don't run."

"True. But we've got more doors and windows than we can stay on top of. We go in after him, he could get around us, and the AT's wide open." Tim ground his teeth, hoping Dray would contribute to the debate. It occurred to him that she'd been off the air for a time now, and he dreaded what that could mean. He'd never thought of himself as superstitious, but his inability to find her voice in himself—her vanishing—seemed a bad omen.

A deep breath fluttered Bear's nostrils. "You took care of the bike already."

"Not the Camaro. He can just pull the trailer pin and take off."

"If he's willing to leave his bike. And the drugs."

Tim stepped away from the glass. "Why take the gamble? I'll run back, disable the Camaro."

Approaching footsteps creaked the floorboards. Tim froze—too late.

He and Bear regarded each other on the back porch, Precious waiting silently behind them, pressed to their calves. Despite the cold, big drops of sweat stood out on Bear's forehead. They hung at the hairline, defying gravity. Tim felt his own heart pounding, making his face flush, his ears throb. His hands tightened around the grip of his Smith & Wesson.

He nodded.

He freed his Mag-Lite from his cargo pocket and pointed it at the ground. He would have preferred night-vision goggles to breach the dark house, but the heavy flashlight would have to do.

Den returned from the far room, now wearing a black tank top. The bowie knife gleamed, showing off its sinister curve until he jammed it into its sheath. He sank to his knees again, partially disappearing behind the couch, and dumped a few more items into the backpack.

". . . authorities believe that Den Laurey, considered armed and *extremely* dangerous, remains at large in the Greater Los Angeles area. . . ."

Den's head snapped up, the TV framing it almost perfectly. Then he reached for something on the floor. His shoulders rippled with an unseen motion of his hands, and then he rose, street-ready in his originals, the flame-ensconced laughing skull ascending into view from behind the couch.

Melissa Yueh continued, ". . . locates *this* man, Den Laurey, they are urged to contact . . ."

For once the local news star's irritating habit of hogging live screen time was a blessing. Den hovered in front of the TV, waiting to hit the "power" button until his coverage was done.

Tim and Bear exploded through the back door. "Freeze! U.S. Marshals!"

"Hands up! Get 'em up!"

The circle of Tim's light captured Den's face, frozen in surprise. His hands were raised, the FTW tattoo peeking out from the collar of his tank top. The leather jacket hid his knife and at least one gun.

Backing slowly to the wall, he squinted into the light. His stubbled cheeks tensed, then relaxed as his lips pursed in an intimation of a grin, his expression a perfect match for the mug-shot smirk filling the TV screen. "Troubleshooter." He might have been greeting an old friend.

"Freeze," Bear said. "*Now.*"

Den took another half step back, his shoulder brushing the blank wall by the staircase. An upside-down sheriff's deputy patch had been added to the filthy leather, right over the heart, a fresh addition.

Tim's anger flared, then burned down to a cool blue flame. He lined the sights just below Den's collarbone tattoo, right on the clean badge. His hands were steady, as steady as they'd ever been. At fifteen feet Den didn't have a prayer.

"This is your last chance to live," Tim said. "You run, you die."

His hands still held high, Den rubbed against the wall, like a grizzly scratching his back on a tree trunk. At the last instant, it hit Tim what he was doing, and he shouted and lunged forward as the light switch clicked on and the light-socket bomb exploded. A brilliant flash lit the room with instant, eye-scorching clarity, and BBs shot past his head. A hunk of shrapnel blew out the TV. Tim got the Mag-Lite back up while BBs were still rattling on the floor, but Den was gone.

Bear rolled to his side, coughing. "Yawright?"

Tim leapt to his feet. Den could've taken off through the garage on the Harley by now, but the door remained open, the painted bike in place. Footsteps pounded across the ceiling, and then came the smash of the second-floor window, the tinkle of falling glass, the creak of a drainpipe. Precious was barking as Tim ran out onto the veranda and Den's shadow thundered overhead, firing down in yellow starbursts, the whole structure creaking with his weight. Tim dove behind a post, skidding on the distressed wood.

More pounding footsteps, the latticed roof cracking as Den took flight, then the thump of his landing on the shed. Two more shots drove Tim back behind the post and Bear around the jamb.

A rasp across shingles, a thud of boots striking dirt, the creak of the trailer gate swinging open.

Tim sprinted around the fetid pool. Motorcycle wheels thrummed down the ramp. The cough of an engine, a gunshot, then a high, warbling howl.

Tim's ruthless backup plan come to fruition.

Tim pulled to a halt in the alley. The Harley tottered a moment longer at the base of the ramp, then fell. The shotgun blast had blown off the seat, taking Den with it. He must have been half on his bike when his booby trap had blown; judging from the bloodstains, the spray of pellets had entered him to the right of his bladder on the rise.

Somehow Den had landed on his feet. His eyes locked for an instant on the kill switch on his handlebar; he'd remembered to throw the toggle, but Tim had cut the connecting wire. Den had received the treatment intended for bike thieves—a Chief-designed shotgun blast up the frame tubing. The explosion had blown the metal box open. Two balloons filled with Allah's Tears had rolled onto the ground, where they sat quivering.

Den staggered to the side and sat down, his head lolling forward, a string of drool connecting his lower lip to the cracked dirt of the alley. He withdrew his hand from his jacket, and it came away artery red. He peeled back his jacket. His undershirt was soiled with blood, the fabric rippled like silt. It took him two tries to free the bowie from the sheath. The ivory handle winked in the darkness. He tried a feeble swing in Tim's direction but collapsed onto his back, a gurgle blowing a crimson bubble at his lips.

Tim walked over and looked down at him. Den's limbs shook; he couldn't muster the strength to lift his celebrated knife. The tiny rubies embedded in the butt glittered. Tim stepped on Den's wrist, pinning his hand to the dirt. He crouched and pried the knife free.

Den's head lay cocked back, his eyes straining in the sockets. Tim leaned over him with the blade. He cut Dray's new patch off the leather jacket and held it up before Den's dying face.

"Andrea Rackley," he said.

He pocketed the patch and stood. Den's eyes glassed over, and the bubble at his lips popped. Tim stripped the guns from his body and tossed them in the dirt. He turned around, and Bear was behind him, leaning on the shack, Nextel at his side.

The breeze shifted, bringing with it the rising cry of sirens.

67

Out on the street, news crews clamored at the barricades. Producers pleaded into cell phones; tungsten-halogen lights blared; sound guys hopped about, arms raised to support dangling boom mikes. Melissa Yueh herself showed up in a KCOM van that resembled a movie trailer. For high-profile stories, she'd forgo the anchor desk and roll up her sleeves. She paced outside, delicate yet ruthless, like a great cat. The public information officer had hauled a podium to the front walk and draped it in royal blue cloth in preparation for Tannino's news conference. A Marshals' arrest meant podium rights, which in turn guaranteed that the wooden Service seal would be front and center on all broadcasts.

Tim stayed in the house; a new Rackley scoop had been the holy grail for reporters—especially Yueh—ever since his highly publicized release from jail. He, Bear, Guerrera, Smiles, and Malane huddled in the corner, notepads out, checking off everything that needed checking. Deputies and agents mingled, Aaronson and the other criminalists chasing them off the carpets and out of bathrooms so they could process the scene. For once the celebratory mood was unalloyed—no missing nomad, no drug bait-and-switch, no dots left to connect.

Tannino made his triumphant entrance around 4:00 A.M. He paused in the doorway, surveying the scene until his eyes came to rest on Tim. He winked, then tilted his head in a deferential nod. He crossed and paused before Tim, looking up, his jaw set, his eyes dark and twinkling.

Tim unholstered his .357 and offered it, butt first.

"Any shots fired?"

Tim shook his head.

"Keep it."

The FBI brass rolled up, and the assistant chief deputy appeared at Tannino's elbow, pulling him away. Tannino played nice with the SAC, but it was clear that once cameras rolled, the marshal would be front and center, the special agent in charge floating behind his left shoulder, Ed McMahon to Johnny, waiting to field follow-up after the bombshells flared out.

Tim waited until Guerrera got his moment with Tannino. Then he passed by, patted Rey on the back, and said, "Good call on the decoy bike."

Guerrera didn't say anything, but his eyes crinkled with a smile he didn't let get to his mouth. Tim headed out through the splintered back door onto the veranda. Tannino shouted after him, "Mayor Strauss will be here any minute. He'd like to congratulate you, shake your hand in front of the cameras. Why don't you stick around?"

The assistant chief, weary from playing baby-sitter, materialized to steer Tannino back to more pressing business inside. Tim stood on the veranda for a moment, smelling the sewer smell of rotting leaves. Bear had retrieved Boston and put both dogs on a sit-stay by the rear fence. The white top of a CSI van protruded over the shed.

Tim headed around the pool. He shot Bear an inquisitive look, and Bear nodded—he'd hang back and play primary deputy.

Tim stepped through the rear gate. Jim stood about five feet away from the sprawled body, staring down at the man who'd helped kill his partner. Tim knew from experience that Jim was not feeling what he'd have wanted to feel. Revenge is a cheap high; it pulls up lame on the finish. Before the brutal lessons the past few years had handed him, Tim had expected to wear a he-got-his smirk through the aftermath. But it never worked out that way. There was just death, and then more death.

The criminalists zipped Den into a body bag and lifted him onto a stretcher. Standing old-man stooped, his shoulders curved, Jim watched the body load. Passing him, Tim saw that his cheeks were wet. Jim looked up at Tim, but his eyes didn't seem to register Tim's presence.

Tim walked down the dirt alley, passing behind the houses. Some of the TVs had gone to sleep. He came out the far end and stepped onto the street. The mayor's town car had just pulled up, setting off a fireworks show of flashing bulbs and providing Tim cover for a quiet escape. Strauss emerged, holding up his hands to settle the reporters, George Clooney hitting the red carpet. As he strolled up the front walk, Tannino exited the house to meet him at the podium. A fine orchestration.

Melissa Yueh, with the senses of a bird-dog, somehow spotted Tim from down the block. She all but hurdled her cameraman, sprinting toward Tim, adjusting the mike on her violet lapel.

She shouted from twenty yards away, and Tim saw the other reporters' heads pivot. "Deputy Rackley? Can you confirm that you killed Den Laurey?"

He quickened his step to the Explorer and climbed in. Yueh tapped the window with a cordless mike she'd produced from thin air, her breath fogging the glass. Behind her, her exhausted cameraman shrugged at Tim apologetically.

"Was it in retaliation for the shooting of your wife?"

He eased out, not wanting to run over her pumps. A few other news crews had closed in, reporters calling out questions. Tim nosed the Explorer through the crowd, finally pushing clear of the cables and makeup-laden faces.

He sped along the quiet rural road, window down, letting the chill breeze clear his head. One of his field files flipped over, and crime-alert flyers danced along the backseat—the nomads' final taste of the open road.

At the eastern seam of the horizon, the sky lightened, almost imperceptibly, from midnight black to charcoal. He thought he was heading for home, but he wound up in a bad part of the North Valley, the Explorer navigating itself as if on autopilot.

He parked outside the decaying apartment complex. Despite the hour, hip-hop thumped from an upstairs window. A guy sitting on his window ledge smoked a blunt, straight-brimmed Dodgers cap pulled low over his eyes. Tim got out and gathered a set of flyers from the backseat.

He headed up the narrow walk. Weeds sprouted from cracks in the concrete. He knocked softly on the wooden door. The sound of approaching footsteps. A curtain fluttered, and a dark face peered out through glass and security bars.

A moment later, the deadbolts clicked and the door opened. Marisol Juarez's grandmother stepped back, gesturing for Tim to enter. Clearly, he'd woken her. Her eyes and cheeks were dark and puffy, wisps of graying hair twisting out from her temples. She'd pulled on a loose dress, but it was twisted over her squat form. Thin ropes of fabric had been threaded through beads at the hem and knotted. A band of durable bra showed at the armhole. The dress clattered musically as she lit a few more Advent candles—a handful had been left burning—and then shuffled to the tiny couch. The plastic cover came off the footrest, the fabric of which still bore the mud from Tim's and Bear's boots. The smell of melting paraffin was oddly comforting.

She tugged over a rickety chair from the kitchen and sat opposite him. Wrinkles ridged her cheeks and textured her lips. The framed photo of Marisol had been moved to the front table by the candles. Marisol had been the most overlooked victim. A female civilian. Poor. Obese. She'd had no rifle salute, no *E! True Hollywood Story*, not even a two-line obit in the *L.A. Times*. And yet she'd cracked a case that ranged from the poppy fields of Afghanistan to the beaches of Cabo San Lucas. Tim recalled Kaner's sneering remark—*Let's be honest, who gives a shit about chubby chicanas from Chatsworth?*—and then Dray's gentle reminder: *Everyone counts. And everyone counts the same.* A new thought sailed into the mix: You don't follow up on a dead broke girl from Chatsworth, al-Fath fills its coffers and we all hear the hoofbeats of the apocalypse.

His hands were sweating, dampening the flyers. He spoke softly to try to keep the emotion from his voice. "These are the men who killed your granddaughter."

She shook her head, not understanding his English. He repeated himself, slower, as if that would help. With gestures and a few terribly pronounced Spanish words, he haltingly conveyed his meaning. "*Aquí* are *los hombres* who killed Marisol."

Then he set the first flyer on the footrest between them, facing the woman—Chief glaring at the camera. "*Muerto,*" he said.

He laid the next flyer over Chief's, as if dealing cards. Goat's scarred face and etched glass eye elicited a faint cry from Marisol's grandmother. "*Preso,*" he said.

Tom-Tom appeared surprisingly good-natured in his mug shot. *"Muerto."*

Kaner's features seemed to gather menace. *"Preso."*

And, finally, the Man himself, Den Laurey. *"Muerto."*

Tim wished he could have given her something more, but that was all he had for her. She closed her eyes and crossed herself, and when she opened them again, they were shiny with tears. She reached across the footrest and placed a warm, soft hand on his forearm. *"Que Dios te bendiga."*

Tim gathered the flyers and stood. She stayed in her chair, breathing deeply, wiping her eyes with a fold of her dress.

He showed himself out.

68

The sight of Dray's empty bed struck him like a gut punch. He stopped in the doorway, his flesh gone cold and clammy, his face tingling. The unplugged monitors and equipment, without their lights and bleeps, seemed not just lifeless but obsolete. The bed had been re-made, the starched sheet creased at the top to overhang the blanket.

Morning sun bled through the closed blinds, lighting the room in bands. The hospital halls were cold and empty and conveyed noise mightily; he heard a nurse at the station way down by the elevators complaining about Starbucks.

The first emotion to penetrate his shock was rage. The cell phone in his pocket had been turned to silent since before Den's takedown; he'd forgotten to change the ring setting. He pulled out the Nextel, saw he'd missed three calls from the hospital in the past few hours. His anger decayed swiftly, and he took a wobbly step to the side and lowered himself into the visitor's chair.

His hands trembled. He lifted them to his forehead, covered his eyes. *I'll be okay. Trust me. I'll be okay.*

Her voice moved straight through him. He could practically taste her. *Come on, you don't learn anything unless you're on your own. Let me go.*

Tears ran through the gaps in his fingers. He heard the plinks against the tile, one after another.

I'm okay. I'm okay now.

His breath caught in his throat. He stood, venturing cautiously out into the hall. Voices echoed up and down the corridor, confusing him. He moved rapidly now, almost panicked with hope, peering through doorways.

He reached the end room on the right, and there she was, the muscular line of her back visible through the gap of her patient gown. Standing weakly between the parallel support rails, she faced away, her short blond hair streaked with sweat. She clung to the rails, her bare arms tensed. The physical therapist was at her side, grasping Dray's arm and ignoring her complaints.

"I'm *fine*. I want to do this. I'm okay. I promise."

Tim tried to say her name, but it tangled up before it reached his mouth. He cleared his throat, but still he sounded feeble with disbelief. "Andrea Rackley."

She turned her head, regarding him across the ball of her shoulder.

The physical therapist said, "We've been calling you."

Dray couldn't quite pivot her legs, so she left them behind, twisting so she could see him more clearly. The low bulge of her belly drifted into view. Her dry lips pursed, opened. "I missed you, Timothy."

He tried to smile, but it came out a half laugh. Biting her lip against the pain, she stepped around so she could face him squarely.

Tim wiped his cheeks, still unable to move.

Dray's incomparable smile broke across her face, and for the first time he trusted the reality of what he was seeing. He reached to steady her through the next step.

"Come on," Dray said. "Let's get me home."

Acknowledgments

I'd like to express my gratitude to:

Ben Ahern, who taught me to ride a Harley (even, brave soul, with his credit card holding down the rental deposit).

Bret Nelson, M.D., and Missy Hurwitz, M.D., who made house calls for Dray.

Mike Goldsmith, former senior customs agent, who regaled me with tales of destruction and mayhem, and taught me how better to smuggle, maim, and kill.

Jimell Griffin, deputy U.S. marshal, ARTist, and public information officer for the central district of California, who always had Tim's back.

Maureen Sugden, my overly competent copy editor, for never permitting me to unnecessarily split an infinitive.

The men and women of the Morrows:

Michael "Maddog" Morrison—national president
Meaghan "The Machine" Dowling—chapter president
Lisa "Hellcat" Gallagher—road captain
George "Jacket Stainer" Bick—enforcer
Debbie "Red Knuckles" Stier—sergeant at arms

Libby "The Hammer" Jordan—intel officer

Kristin Bowers, Carla Clifford, Brian Grogan, Diane Jackson, Nina Olmsted, Carla Parker, Dale Schmidt, Mike Spradlin, David Youngstrom, and Jeannette Zwart—nomads

My other biker brethren:

The Guma, Pine-Man, and Andiman—club treasurers

Marc H. Glick, Stephen L. Breimer, Rich Green—the Crash Truck posse

Jess "Garbage Wagon" Taylor—wing collector

Rome Quezada, Diana Tynan, Julia Bannon, Sean Abbott, Al Alverson, Luis Millan, Carol Topping, and Thomas Sendlenski—1%ers through and through

And my number one club mama, Delinah.